# Chains of Freedom

**(The first book of the Chains Trilogy)**

by

# Selina Rosen

Meisha Merlin Publishing, Inc
Atlanta, GA

CHAINS OF FREEDOM

An MM Publishing Book
Published by Meisha Merlin Publishing, Inc.
PO Box 7
Decatur, GA 30031

Editing & interior layout by Stephen Pagel
Copyediting & proofreading by Josh Mitchell
Cover art by Charles Keegan
Cover design by Neil Seltzer

ISBN: 1-892065-42-8

http://www.MeishaMerlin.com

First MM Publishing edition: June 2001

Printed in the United States of America
0 9 8 7 6 5 4 3 2 1

## Selina A. Rosen, the author of
## *Queen of Denial* and *Chains of Freedom*.
## By C. J. Cherryh

This crazy book business...readers want the books, but the writers and the publishers have to swim upstream against a marketing system designed chiefly to sell tomato soup. It's a very, very difficult task for a writer to get a book into your hands...or to have it available when word of mouth finally lets you know it exists.

Rosen has a very good, very funny book with Meisha Merlin Publishing. *Queen of Denial* is available for order and should be on the shelves at bookstores. Just write to her and tell her you want to order *Denial*. You'll be met with open arms. Personalize it? You bet.

Rosen also, with Lynn Stranathan, her co-editor, runs Yard Dog Press, a small press that specializes in chapbooks, and sells, among other things, via Amazon.Com. You can buy the Yard Dog books from her, too.

Let me tell you the short details about Selina Rosen. She's a creative soul, a builder in wood and stone and words...knows farm life, knows how to build a room, or a plot...can cope with goats and chickens, or neophyte writers. Out of this absolute wealth of diverse experience come truly outrageous ideas and a way of looking at the universe with [in some books] humor and [in other books] attitude with a capital A.

You want a friend who'll show up with help and a truck when others are "busy that weekend", you've got Selina Rosen. That honesty shows up in the characters she writes. She's one in a million.

Does this honesty and the fact she writes really good, wise, funny and serious books mean immediate, widely reputed success in the writing business? No. It's easier to sell something "just like" the last thing, and Rosen's just-like nothing else.

Does it mean the books get distributed with grand advertising fanfare?

No.

So here we are.

*I'm* putting out the word, because I believe in her.

Buy this woman's books!

C. J. Cherryh
2001

# Chains
## of
## Freedom

# Chapter One

Bullets spat up dust all around him. Cobal's disembodied hand slapped the ground where it flopped at the end of the chain which had, till a few moments before, bound the two prisoners to one another.

What the hell had he been thinking? You couldn't escape from the Reliance. His own history should have told him that. Still, anything was better than dying with the rest of those spineless zombies. Death was all that waited back at the prison work camp. Better to die out here; better to die fighting for freedom than to give the Reliance the satisfaction of working him to death. Better to cause them some trouble, even if only for a few moments.

Poor Cobal, all he had wanted to do was his time.

He was an idiot! Just like all the rest of them. Like the people from David's village who had worked blindly for the Reliance. They didn't understand that there should be more to life than the few meager crumbs the Reliance tossed them. No one had listened to his father, and he had been a fool to think they would listen to him.

He looked at the sword in his hand. He had stolen it from the guard, and used it to sever Cobal's hand from his body when Cobal died. The blade dripped with a mixture of Cobal's and the guard's blood. He wouldn't think about it; he would just run. He would escape for all of those who wouldn't. He would escape for his father who hadn't, or he would die trying.

David continued to run long after he had lost them. He ran till he couldn't feel his legs anymore. He ran till he could hardly breathe. He ran till the stitch in his side was unbearable. He ran until he ran into something, and then he fell on his ass.

Stunned, he stared at the pair of boots straddling his calves. He knew the style all too well. The black leather boots with the big brass buckles that went up almost to the knee. It was the style worn by those Reliance soldiers lucky enough to be in the Elite Forces. But the tattered black jeans which were tucked into the boots didn't look anything like what an Elite would wear. There was a low-slung holster, and in it was the biggest, ugliest plasma blaster he had ever seen. A weapon which, like the boots, wouldn't be issued to anyone but an Elite. Where the thick black weapons belt should have been, a thick chain was wrapped around and around her waist and torso. Underneath the chain she wore what was left of a black T-shirt.

Her skin was very tan, her hair was white, and she had possibly the bluest eyes he had ever seen.

Her hair was cut in a Reliance Elite style. A little ragged, but still medium length, still well within regulation standard. She was tall, well over six feet, yet hardly the mountain she had appeared at first.

David couldn't decide whether she was an Elite or someone who had rolled one. Then she smiled an all-too-familiar smile: the "cat-that-caught-the-canary" smile that Reliance officers were famous for.

He raised his sword hand, only to realize it was now empty. He hadn't even realized he'd dropped his weapon. *Damn it. All this for nothing.* His muscles bunched to spring away, even as his brain acknowledged the futility of the gesture.

Her right hand moved towards her holster, and he froze. No phony baloney trial this time; she was just going to blow him away. David closed his eyes tight and waited. When nothing happened, he opened one eye carefully and saw an outstretched hand, no gun. He darted a quick look at her face. She was smiling broadly at him

"I have a camp not far from here. Food, clothing, shelter." Clearly she was not a person who wasted words.

He didn't take her offered hand, so she withdrew it, along with her smile.

"Fine, be that way. But while I don't need you, you most certainly need me."

David got shakily to his feet wishing he had taken her help when she had offered it. He dusted himself off, delaying the moment when he would have to meet those blue, blue eyes.

"What makes you think I need your help?"

She laughed. "We are sixty miles from the nearest town. You are wearing nothing but a prison tattoo on your head and what's left of your prison uniform. Like I said, I have food, clothing, and shelter. Not to mention that my camp is next to a stream where you could wash off that foul stench." She smiled again. "But, if you'd rather spend the night hungry and dirty in the cold forest with the bears, that's up to you." She turned and started to walk away.

"How do I know that you're not Reliance?" he asked, still suspicious.

She didn't justify his question with an answer.

"At this point, does it really matter?" she asked looking over her shoulder briefly at him.

David laughed shakily, and shook his head.

"I suppose not. Lead the way," he said, waving his hand in as flamboyant a gesture as his condition allowed.

She obliged, confidently striding away as if on her way to a fire. He had difficulty keeping up. David got the impression that she only had just the one speed. By the time he reached the mouth of the cave where he assumed her camp was, she was just stepping out with a bar of soap and a towel. Without a word, David took them and stumbled to the stream that ran in front of the cave.

By the time he returned, skin raw with scrubbing and blue with cold, the fire just inside the cave mouth was all he could see. When his brain thawed out enough to think again, he was huddled over the fire, towel wrapped around his waist, clutching his grumbling stomach with his arms.

As his eyes adjusted to the light, he stared stupidly at the crates stacked all around and inside the cave. Like a child excited about his birthday gifts, David greedily opened and looked into box after box. The woman walked over to him and pressed a bowl of soup into his hands without saying a word about him rummaging through her things. She motioned to a folding stool sitting close to the fire, and he sat down. His hunger took over immediately, and he ate three bowls of the soup before he even tried to talk.

"Thank you."

She shrugged and nodded.

"Where did you get all this,"—he motioned around with his hand—"stuff?"

She looked at him with all the tolerance of the wise for the very stupid, and replied broadly. "Why, the Reliance gave it to me, of course. They always give supplies to subversives who want to overthrow their power base." She slapped her forehead in obvious disgust, then asked, "Where do you think I got it?"

David shrugged.

"I stole it, dumbass!"

"Well, that's obvious, but how?" David was feeling defensive. In his town, being one of the few people who read, he was considered quite smart. He wasn't used to being talked to like he was an idiot. Except of course by Reliance personnel.

"I hijack shipments. I used to be Elite, so I know how they operate their shipping routes. It's really not very hard to do. Here on Earth they don't expect it. They aren't ready for it, and well...it's easy, that's all." She was obviously trying to be patient, just wasn't very good at it.

"My name's David. David Grant," he said, holding out his hand.

After a moment she took it, and they shook.

"RJ," she announced calmly.

David's jaw dropped. After a moment, he closed his mouth, and looked around. Well, that certainly explained the supplies.

"You're RJ? Where are your followers? How many of you are there?" he asked eagerly.

She laughed, and held out her hands as if to ward off his excitement. "Hold on a minute, farm boy. There are no followers. There's just me. A lone ex-Elite, doing my best to confound the system."

"But you're only one person!" He seemed to have a positive knack for stating the obvious.

"Yes, well, I was the last time I looked," RJ said dryly. She got up from her campstool and went to one of the crates. She came back with clothes for him, a first-class soldier's uniform.

He made a face, and she smiled.

"Beggars can't be choosers," she reminded him.

He turned his back to her and dressed. There were a million questions he wanted to ask, but right now his body was the enemy. Struggling with his fly, he turned, "Is there somewhere I can sleep? I'm exhausted."

"I'll get you a cot." She dug around till she found one and a blanket, too.

It was the warmest, the cleanest, and the fullest he had been in weeks. David had barely lain down before he was asleep.

RJ watched the sleeping man in the light of dawn. She liked the way he looked. He was dark, well tanned, with black eyes and hair. He was tall and well built, and his features were strong. In short, he was the kind of man that made stupid women shit all over themselves. Yeah, she liked the way he looked; she liked it a lot.

"R.J.—What does that stand for?"

Her focus shifted immediately to his face. His eyes were open. She'd been caught off guard, staring, confident that he was sleeping. How long had he been awake? Had he noticed her looking at him?

"Huh?" she responded intelligently.

"What's RJ stand for?" David asked again, stretching.

Her eyes were drawn back to watch the play of his starved muscles. "It's not important." She almost spat the words as she got up and walked over to the fire, where she tried her best to look busy.

"Roxanne Jones," he suggested, his voice still thick with sleep.

"That's close enough," she said on a final note.

David sat up and let out a groan. All that running was taking its toll. He hurt everywhere. RJ stuck something in his hands. A bowl of oatmeal. Now, he had never been too keen on oatmeal, but after that gray shit they fed him in prison, oatmeal seemed mighty fine. He ate till he was stuffed, then he started with his questions.

"What do you plan to do with all these supplies?"

"Keep them." She poured herself a cup of coffee. "Why were you sent to prison?" she countered.

David grimaced. Vagueness and questions. Well, you could take the girl out of the Reliance, but...Still, it was a fair question.

"I tried to raise supporters to fight the Reliance, but everyone is either too scared, too stupid, or both," he said bitterly. "Someone, or maybe all of them, turned me in. Probably all of them. Self preservation."

"I'm not afraid of the Reliance," RJ stated quietly.

"No, I suppose not. But believe me, most are." David paused, then plunged on. "Not to make light of what you've done, but no one believes you're real. They believe you're a story the Reliance made up to flush out people like myself. Ask yourself what good all this is," he gestured at the crates, "if you don't have people to use them."

"I don't pretend to have all the answers, Mr. Grant."

"Just David," he said.

She smiled, shook her head and went on. "I'm a soldier. All I know how to do is fight. I don't know how to win a people's love or loyalty. I can give orders, but that won't work on rebels very well. All I know about people is that if you strike them correctly, with sufficient force, here, here, here, or here,"—she pointed to his head, heart, solar plexus, and throat—"they will probably die. I'm not too overly good with people, and I don't think anyone would want to follow someone who thinks life is so cheap. I could lead an army, but I can't lead people. My wisdom is in this blaster, my poetry in this chain. Killing I know."

David looked into the fire thoughtfully then he looked at RJ. "What if we formed an alliance? Worked together?"

"To do what? You said yourself, the people are too scared, or too stupid..."

"Attacking the Reliance on deserted stretches of road is all well and good, but it's not very visible. If the people could see something, witness it with their own eyes...if they could see that one person really can make a difference...I almost had them convinced. If I'd had proof that you were real, I think that would have made the difference. You're a legend, RJ. Everyone is talking about you. The Reliance hates you, but the people love you, and they secretly hope that you really exist. But you're not very visible. They can't see you."

"Like I said, I'm not very good with people. I do OK with my own kind, but right now I'm number one on the hit list with the army, so I can't very well get in and infiltrate. I'd have to be really stupid to do something visible, and I'm not stupid. Crazy, maybe. Stupid, no..."

"Not to be egotistical, but I am good with people. I think I have a way with words. If we could do something visual, make the Reliance see just how unhappy we are..."

RJ interrupted him with her laughter. "The Reliance doesn't give a shit if their work units, or even their soldiers, for that matter, are unhappy. They have what they want, and they aren't going to give us what we want because it would mean that they would have less."

"Then we'll get an army and fight them. It's got to be worth a try," David paused. "So what do you say? We could give it a shot. You and me against the Reliance." There was a lilt in his voice, and a fanatical gleam in his eyes. He held his hand out to her.

RJ stared for a second at his outstretched hand. "Ah, what the hell." She took his hand and shook it. "I don't know what we'll do, but we might as well do it together." She retrieved her hand, walked over and rummaged through a box of K-rations. "Ah! Here we go!" She pulled out two small glass bottles.

"A toast," she said, tossing one to David. They pulled off the tops and clinked the containers together solemnly.

"To the New Alliance," she offered.

David nodded approvingly. "To the New Alliance."

# Chapter Two

In the weeks that followed, David started to feel more like his old self. He was back to his fighting weight, and his hair was starting to cover his prison baldness. What wasn't going to change was the brand burned on his forehead. A circle with an X through it served as a constant reminder of his hatred for the Reliance and all that it stood for. He ran his hand over it. Darkness had closed in, and the only light came from the fire. RJ planned for them to leave in the morning, but she hadn't told David where she planned to go or why.

"So, I think the first thing we should do is something really big. Something so big they won't be able to cover it up," David was saying. "Like blowing up the Reliance bank in Satis..."

"We'd be killed before we could get out of town," RJ said dispassionately. "I understand the need to do something spectacular to grab the public's eye, and I would love to destroy the bank at Satis. I will do anything to hurt the Reliance, but remember this, David Grant. I don't do suicide missions. I like living. The fact is that I am intensely in love with myself, and fully believe that I am the most important person on this planet, if not the entire fucking universe. So when you talk of suicide missions to blow up banks, then you had better drop the 'we,' because I, for one, have no intention of dying for the cause."

"But Satis is..."

"The kind of thing you need an army for. So until we have that army, I suggest you put all your dreams of conquering Satis on hold." She paused. "In the mean time, I suggest we continue to raid supply trains."

"Why? Why not get right to something that matters?" David asked, with angry disappointment. He had learned that when

RJ made up her mind that was the end of the discussion as far as she was concerned. She proved it now by snoring loudly and feigning sleep.

They loaded the supplies, including the carefully hidden, fully assembled rocket launcher, onto the military-issue dirt bike they planned to ride. It was cold, so they dressed for it. The clothes David now wore, like RJ's, were not Reliance work-issue. Oh, the plain blue jeans and white T-shirts were, but the black leather jackets definitely were not. They were military-issue. He tied a leather headband around his forehead to hide his brand. RJ had already mounted the bike and was screaming at him to hurry up. He looked back at the cave. It had been the first place he had ever lived where he hadn't had the Reliance breathing down his throat. Even though he was eager to get on with the fight, he was reluctant to leave this place.

"Would you hurry it up?" RJ screamed.

He ran over and jumped on the bike behind her. He would have liked to drive, but he had no idea how. The only thing he had ever driven was a farm tractor, and he hadn't been very good at that.

At first, David sat loosely on the back, but as RJ started slinging them down the rough trail at break-neck speeds, he found himself clinging to her for dear life. She seemed to be oblivious to such obstacles as rocks and trees. He wondered if this was the same woman who had claimed to be a lover of her own life just the night before. David took comfort in the idea that the bike couldn't possibly go any faster, and then they hit the pavement.

David was scared shitless. Up till right then, the fastest thing he'd ever been on was the town whore. He was sure he couldn't have been any more petrified, and then he caught sight of a Reliance cop flashing his lights behind them.

"Oh shit! What do we do now?" David said, his panic showing in his voice.

"We pull over and see what the gentleman wants," RJ said. "Just keep cool, and everything will be all right." She pulled the bike over, and they came to a stop.

The police car stopped right behind them.

RJ got off the bike, and David followed suit.

"Any problem, officer?" she asked.

David tried his best to look unconcerned.

"Standard procedure," the officer stated, proving that he had studied his handbook well. "I'll have to see your military free-days pass."

Of course he assumed they were military. They were wearing the jackets, and they had access to a motorbike. Civilians didn't have either.

David swallowed hard, and started to go through his pockets. Very slowly at first, and then more urgently. It was OK that he looked nervous. After all, everyone was nervous when dealing with Reliance police.

David shrugged, raising his open hands in a gesture of frustration. "I don't seem to have them," he said, sounding quite convincingly upset.

"Could you give me your pass numbers then? I'll just run them through the machine," the officer suggested with surprising patience.

"Oh, come on, officer," David whined, "who remembers their pass numbers?"

"I do," the officer said. "I'm sorry—he didn't sound sorry; he sounded bored—"but you know the rules. I must either see your passcards, or you must recite your numbers so that I may run them through the machine."

David assumed an expression of intense concentration. "Seven, seven, two—no. Seven, seven, four—no." Suddenly, he turned on RJ.

"I could have sworn I told you to get the passcards," he said hotly. David, of course, had never seen a pass-card in his life. RJ caught on quickly; she shrugged.

"I'm sorry," she said, assuming an air of total indifference.

"You're sorry." He sounded as if he were barely controlling his temper. Then he exploded. "Sorry! Why, you stupid bitch! This is the first free-days pass we've had since we got married. You did this on purpose because you don't like sex." All David's very genuine terror lent veracity to his assumed rage, and the outlet in turn helped him regain control.

RJ kept a smile from her face only with great effort, and managed to play along. "Oh, please. You're not going to start all that again are you?" she sighed.

David looked at the officer, man appealing to man. "The Reliance gave me three women to choose from. I went for looks, and wouldn't you know it, I wind up with the one that doesn't like to screw."

The officer started to speak, beginning to look uncomfortable, but RJ jumped in first.

"How am I supposed to get turned on by a guy that likes to wear my underclothes? Would you tell me that?"

"That's a lie!" David screamed back, turning to face RJ.

"Go ahead, officer, ask him to drop his drawers, and we'll just see who's lying," RJ demanded, with an air of wronged innocence.

"Oh, that's not fair!" David cried accusingly. "You know I always wear them when we're on the bike." He turned to the officer appealingly. "They keep me from chaffing. You understand, don't you?"

"Oh, really, Howard, you don't expect him to buy that, do you?" RJ asked with disgust. "It's you who purposely forgot the passes so that you could go back to the house and go through my clothes!"

"Lying bitch!" David screamed. The two faced off, totally ignoring the officer. RJ opened her mouth to scream something back, but the officer had obviously had enough. He whistled to get their attention, and threw up his hands as if to ward them off.

"Enough! It's obvious that you two are only a threat to each other, so just go on about your free days. I suggest that you take the time to try to work out your differences. As you know, the Reliance hardly ever sanctions a second marriage."

"Thank you, officer," David started pumping his hand. "Thank you very much!"

"Yes, well, just do me a favor, and try not to kill each other in my jurisdiction," he said.

He shook his head as he watched them drive away. "You meet all kinds on this job."

It was dusk when they reached the town. It was run-down, but still very much alive. The streets teemed with activity, none of which was Reliance sanctioned. Bars lined the roads, far outnumbering restaurants. They stopped at what seemed to be the busiest bar in town. It had golden arches outside, obviously a relic from antiquity, the plastic coating was beginning to flake. Even so, one could clearly see "Billions and Billions served" written below the arches. In answer to David's question, RJ said that no one knew what the "Billions served" were. Some speculated that they were drinks. Some of the hookers claimed it referred to satisfied Johns, but no one really knew—or cared.

David listened with a feeling of relief as the engine died. They got off the bike. David tried to stretch out his weary muscles, but that only aggravated his saddle sores. RJ looked as sharp as she had that morning, and David fought the urge to smack her. He followed RJ inside, where they sat on stools at the bar. The bar was low, and the stools were wooden and crudely made. David would have preferred to stand, but he supposed that would have been too conspicuous.

"What's yer poison?" the bartender asked.

"Whiskey, beer chaser," RJ said, without noticing the strange look David gave her.

In David's experience, you could have a whiskey, or you could have a beer, but you couldn't have both at one time. That was against Reliance Law. But then so was most of what he had seen since they drove into town.

"And what can I get for you?" the bartender asked David.

"Ah, just a beer," he said. He was given a beer, and one sip told him that this was not Reliance-approved beer. It was too strong for that. This was more like the "whiskey" they had back home. David took a look around the bar. The other customers, like he and RJ, were wearing non-regulation clothing. There wasn't a proper uniform in sight. You couldn't tell whether these people were farmers, ranchers, cloth makers or military. Where the hell had RJ brought him? As if reading his mind, RJ started talking in a low whisper that was barely audible above the constant din.

"Welcome to Alsterase, David. Nothing in this city is up to Reliance code. This is where escaped prisoners, tax evaders, politicos, and riffraff of virtually every type come to escape the Reliance," she explained.

"I've never heard of it," David said. "Why doesn't the Reliance just come wipe them all out in one fell swoop?"

RJ smiled, then ordered another drink. When it came, she explained. "Like you said, you've never heard of it. To attack the town would be to admit that such a place exists and draw attention to these rebels. Besides, Alsterase plays a very important role in Reliance politics."

"What's that?" David asked. By now, he was thoroughly confused, and looked it.

"If a rebellion ever starts, it's a fair bet that it will start here in Alsterase, the home of the malcontents. If you know where your enemy is, you know where to go to crush them quickly and completely."

David nodded his understanding.

"As long as there's a place for the malcontents to go, they'll go there. As long as they're here, they can't be in the towns stirring others into a rabble. As long as they're not stirring up any trouble, it's in the Reliance's best interest to leave them here to attract those rebellious souls who slip through the system." As RJ finished, she picked up the whiskey and downed it, then started on the beer.

David allowed his brain a few minutes to soak up what he'd just heard. "OK, I think I get it. But if all that is true, what are we doing here? This place is no doubt crawling with Reliance spies." David glanced nervously around the bar as he spoke.

"Oh, no doubt about that at all. Which means that nobody asks any questions or gives out any information. See, everyone's either afraid that you're a spy, or afraid you'll think they're one. Spies in Alsterase are more or less useless."

David nodded slowly. "But that still doesn't answer my question. Why are we here?"

"A little reverse logic. You see, the Reliance knows that Alsterase is the festering place for a rebellion, but then so does anyone with half a brain. So, they don't really expect anyone to try. Oh, there's talk—there's always talk, but nothing ever comes of it. Therefore, this is the perfect place to start a rebellion. A town full of people who all hate the Reliance is the perfect cover, because only an idiot would seriously try anything here. Therefore, a really intelligent person who plays her cards right can march right into a ready-made army. Or at least a unit," she gulped her beer down.

It took several seconds for all of that to soak in. When it did, David still didn't understand, and he didn't like not understanding. He didn't like her drinking, either. While he sat sipping on his single beer (which was making him giddy already), RJ put away six of the combination drinks. Her speech wasn't slurred; her movements weren't clumsy. In fact, the only indication that she'd had anything to drink at all was that her right arm was flopping around like a fish on a pier.

He'd noticed the arm thing before. She seemed to have a habit of jerking it at odd moments; it could be a little distracting. Right now, the damned arm thing was enough to drive him crazy. When she started to order another round of drinks, he decided she'd really lost it.

"Don't you think you've had enough?" David asked quietly.

RJ laughed and patted him on the back, none too gently.

"More than, probably. Bartender! Do it again!" she yelled.

Just as the bartender set her drinks on the table, she felt a hand on her shoulder, and hot breath in her ear.

"Hey, baby, why don't you and me blow this dump?" The man was huge, six-foot-eight if he was an inch. He was gigantic, humongous, fantastically enormous, and damn near as blond as the woman he was coming on to.

"Well," RJ drawled slowly, not even looking at the man. "For one thing, I'm not your baby."

David gulped, and decided to give RJ charm lessons as soon as he got the chance.

"You could be," the big man said.

"You could be well-mannered, too. But you're not," RJ said coolly. "Any man can see that I am with this gentleman."

David looked around for several seconds before he realized that RJ meant him. The smile he gave the big man was sickly at best.

"Oh, I'm sure he wouldn't mind," the big man said, and added menacingly. "Would you, buddy?"

David gulped again. RJ had strapped a gun under his arm before he put his jacket on, but he didn't know if he could get to it—or if he should even try. He wasn't ready for this situation; he wasn't exactly sure how he should react, or if he should at all. Goddamn RJ! She was just sitting there, grinning at him, as if waiting for him to do the right thing. Whatever the hell that was.

"Actually, I do mind," David tried to sound cocky, but somehow, just didn't quite make it. He went for the gun, which turned out to be the wrong thing to do. Someone—he never knew who—hit him in the head with a beer bottle before he could clear leather. His head spun, his vision blurred, and he hit the floor just seconds after his gun.

RJ came off the stool, bringing a knee up into the big man's groin. He let out a howl and bent double. RJ brought her cupped hands down on the base of his skull, and he hit the floor shortly after David.

Some guy took exception to his friend's nose-dive and slung his fist into RJ's gut. It hit the chain-now hidden under her jacket, and he jerked his hand back, screaming. She delivered a well-placed kick to his head, and the second man fell beside his friend.

David kept trying to get up, but couldn't figure out which way that was. He didn't even know where he was, or what had happened. He didn't feel the blood running down his face. The noise around him registered, but it was just that—noise—no words, no sense.

RJ turned just in time to deliver a roundhouse kick into the ribs of yet another attacker. When the girl fell to the floor holding her ribs, she yelled out, "Elite! She's a fucking ELITE!"

"No doubt she remembers the boots," RJ said in the sudden stillness. She announced, "I used to be an Elite. I have been well trained, and I don't have any qualms about killing anyone. So if you're feeling froggy, go ahead and jump."

With this said, she proceeded to kick every willing ass in the bar. She threw one poor man out the window, and another down the bar. In ten minutes, anyone who had thought it was a good idea to kick this stranger's ass had either rapidly changed his mind and left, or was suffering from some degree of bodily disrepair.

RJ stood up straight and took a deep, cleansing breath. Then she walked over to the bar where, by some miracle, her drinks still stood, and slung them down. Turning to David, who lay practically comatose on the floor, she picked him up, threw him over her shoulder, and started for the door.

Pausing in the doorway, RJ turned, "I'm not paying my bill. I didn't have a good time, and I don't think my date had a very good time either. What's more, the atmosphere in this place stinks." Having said her piece, she stomped out the door, slamming it behind her so hard that the rest of the glass fell out of the broken window.

When they reached the bike, RJ tried to set David's limp body on it. She put her hands in his armpits and sat him up, but as soon as she let go, he almost fell.

"Oh, come on, David," she said in exasperation. "It's been a long damn day."

After several unsuccessful tries, she finally got David to hold himself up long enough that she could get on the bike. At which point he promptly collapsed against her back.

"Can you hang on?" A gurgling sound was her only answer. "Oh, I can tell that this is going to be a fun evening." She jammed David's limp body against the sissy bar with her back, and somehow managed to drive to the motel across the street. Not being in the mood for formalities, she drove the bike right inside and turned it off.

"Hey! Hey!" The fat, greasy, chrome-dome of a manager popped up from his seat behind the desk and waved his black-market nudie magazine in an apparent attempt to shoo them out. Clamping his huge, smelly cigar firmly in his teeth, he screamed, "No pets and no motorbikes in the lobby. That there's the rules. I'm trying to run a classy joint here."

RJ got off the bike and headed for the desk. David fell unceremoniously to the floor. She opened her jacket so that both chain and plasma blaster were visible.

"Lady, I don't care if you have a fucking rocket launcher, you can't bring your filthy motorbike in my lobby." Gun-toting customers were nothing new to him. The sight of a plasma blaster, even a big one, didn't impress him.

RJ didn't feel like dealing with points of etiquette at the moment. She reached across the counter, grabbed the man by his collar, and lifted him off the floor with one hand. Then she drew her blaster and stuck it up one of his nostrils. Now he was impressed. She didn't even have to mention the fact that she did just happen to have a rocket launcher.

"Me, this pistol, and my incredibly bad attitude all say that I can park this bike up your ass if I like. Do you have a problem with that?"

"All right, all right," the manager huffed. RJ set him down slowly and removed the blaster. He straightened his dirty collar and tried to straighten his now bent cigar. "I swear, you girls are all alike. Give you a gun, and you turn into thugs."

"I need a room for tonight," RJ said.

"Just for tonight?"

"If the room is suitable, we'll be staying longer."

"Oh! How lucky for us!" The fact that the blaster was back in the holster seemed to restore some of his self-confidence, not to mention sarcasm. "Is your friend dead or alive?"

"I don't know. Why?" RJ asked, glancing at the pile of David on the floor.

"Charge more for stiffs. People leave them in the rooms. It makes an awful mess," he said.

RJ nodded. She could relate to that. So she yelled across the room, "David, are you dead?"

The pile of David made that gurgling sound again.

"See, he's not dead."

"He's pretty bad. May die tonight," the manager speculated.

"If he does, I'll take the body out myself." RJ shoved some credits at the man, poured David back on the bike, climbed aboard herself, started the engine and headed for the stairs.

"Hey, you crazy bitch...!" The rest of the man's obscenities were lost in the roar of the bike.

They reached the sixth floor in a few minutes. The top two floors of the old eight-story building were in such bad repair that even a "classy joint" like this had them closed off. A few people stepped out into the hall to see what all the noise was, but quickly lost interest. Just another crazy asshole riding a bike in the hall. Nothing very unusual about that. Not in Alsterase.

Outside the room, RJ stopped and shut the bike off. When she got off, David hit the floor again. He had this falling bit down pat. This time, however, he gurgled and stirred and seemed to want to get up. That he didn't do quite so well—not at all, in fact.

RJ opened the door and pushed the bike into the room. After she was sure it was OK, she went back for David. After all, first things first: men were a dime a dozen, but a good bike was hard to come by. She kicked the door shut and tossed David over onto the bed.

RJ bent over David, looking at the cut in his scalp. It was deep, and about four inches long, but the skull seemed intact. "You stupid jackass. Anyone with half a brain knows better than to pull a gun in Alsterase unless you have a death wish, or full body armor."

She cleaned and stitched the wound, berating David the entire time. "And another thing, never start anything unless you know what's behind you, you stupid prick." She covered him up after stripping him down to his shorts. "You'll live. You won't enjoy it for a while. Not with the headache you're going to have come morning, but you'll live."

Finished, she sat down on the edge of the bed and unwound the chain. Taking a coin from her pocket, she bent it double around a link, adding it to the small collection of change already bent into its folds. She smiled and let the chain fall to the floor.

He felt as if the sun were trying to drill its way through his eyelids. His head was pounding, but the soft, warm, and undeniably female contents of his arms temporarily distracted him from his pain. He smiled. It had been a dream. Prison, RJ, the brawl, all a dream. He was home after all, safe in his own bed with some delectable hometown girl. Jane? Or maybe Susan. He wanted to go back to sleep, but the pounding in his head became more insistent. Why did his head hurt? He put his hand to his head, and found the stitches.

OK, so it wasn't a dream. He couldn't decide if he was relieved or sorry. Without thinking, he pulled himself closer to the woman, and felt himself drifting off into unconsciousness again. Then it hit him. He was in bed with a woman! But who? He opened his eyes slowly. RJ sat in bed, wearing only her pants. She was cleaning her blaster as if it were the normal thing for a half-dressed woman to do while sitting in bed with a man wrapped around her waist.

David couldn't help realizing just how really built RJ was. Not that he hadn't noticed before now, but clothes did tend to screw up the view.

She blew some debris out of her gun, and it hit him in the face.

"Hey!" He wiped at his face.

"Well, I'm glad to see you're still alive. They charge extra for stiffs around here. Real classy place," she said with a smile.

David let go of her and rolled onto his back. It was the wrong thing to do. The room wouldn't quit moving, and he felt instant nausea.

"You're all heart, RJ." He held his head in an effort to keep it from splitting open. "God, I feel like I've been hit by a tractor."

"Actually, I believe it was a beer bottle," RJ offered. She stood up and grabbed her shirt off the chair where she had put it. She pulled it on and started wrapping the chain around her.

"Do you always have to wear that thing?" David asked making a face.

"Yes," RJ said simply, as she continued wrapping. She strapped the blaster, now in its holster, around her waist, and tied it down to her leg.

"Why? I mean, it must be heavy. And it looks kind of stupid."

"Because I like it," RJ replied dismissively.

David didn't take the hint. "There has to be a good reason for it. I mean, you don't do anything without a good reason." It was obvious that she had no intention of answering his question. "You know I was damned near killed, and the why of it completely eludes me. You'd think you could answer one simple question."

"Well, you should be just thrilled because there really isn't a good reason for me to wear it," RJ drew in a long impatient breath and then blew it out. "This chain helped me to escape from the Reliance. We were sent on a mission to cleanse this village...Do you have any idea what that means?"

David shook his head no. He was so ignorant that it was a real pain in the ass to have to tell him anything.

"It is Reliance policy that when an area becomes over-populated, when there are more people than necessary—you know, when they're using more than they're producing—then the Reliance sends in troops to 'cleanse' a village or two. They say they are just weeding out spies. At least, that's the official story that goes out over the viewscreen. But they kill everyone, David. Every man, woman, and child. I was a major in the Elite Guard. I was trained to fight armed soldiers: men, women, or aliens who were trying to kill me. I had crossed galaxies to battle aliens on distant planets, and now they wanted me to slaughter children. To cut down unarmed civilians and leave them to rot in the streets. To make a long story short, I refused. And I wasn't going to stand there and let *them* do it, either."

Her smile wasn't quite human as she continued. "So, I put a blaster bolt right through my CO's head. The troops stopped shooting at the civilians and started after me. I evaded them easily at first, but then I lost my blaster and took a plasma hit, and things started going downhill fast. Just when it looked as if my chances of survival were nil, I saw this chain. I picked it up, and with it I made a hole in the wall of soldiers that surrounded me. And so, I escaped."

She fingered the chain absently. "I have always looked at everything with a very analytical eye, but this chain...It's part of me. You see, I have this feeling that as long as I hold this chain, I will win against the Reliance. It's a stupid, romantic idea, and how it got into my purely logical and unromantic brain is a mystery to me. Still, it's what I believe."

David nodded. Now it made sense. Maybe not to her, but it did to him. "So, as long as I'm on a roll, what does RJ stand for?"

RJ shook her head and half grinned.

"Ruby Jean," David suggested.

RJ laughed, then sobered and looked right at David. "Why do you feel compelled to have all your questions answered? Some questions have no answers. Others are best left unanswered. Ignorance is not always a bad thing."

"Aw, geesh! It's just a name. How bad..."

"I'm going to check things out. I'll bring you something to eat." She walked to the door and was gone.

David held his hands to his head. The throbbing seemed even worse now. He tried to stay awake because he had heard somewhere that it was bad to sleep if you had a concussion. What he hadn't been told was that it was all but impossible to stay awake.

RJ kicked a rock down the street as she walked in her Elite boots, carrying her Reliance-issue blaster—so blatantly Reliance that everyone knew instinctively that she wasn't. She kept her hands in her pants pockets and had the air of one who was totally unafraid.

News traveled fast in Alsterase. After all, it didn't have the Reliance to slow it down. Most had heard of the platinum blonde goddess who had whipped Whitey Baldor and half the clientele of the Golden Arches. People stood clear as she walked by. She smiled and nodded her head in a friendly way that served only to further terrify them.

Derelicts, merchants, Reliance spies, rebels, prison escapees and hookers. Alsterase had its share of all of these, and none of them passed RJ's eyes unnoticed.

The roads were narrow and steep and in a state of total disrepair. The rails that once flowed down the center of the street had been removed long ago for the metal. This had once been a great and beautiful city. The city by the bay was now the city of the discontented and outcast. Its golden gates were long fallen into the sea. It was Alsterase now. Alsterase, where you went when you had nowhere else to go.

It would take a great deal to make this lot into an army. The very things that had driven them to Alsterase and made them the sworn enemies of the Reliance would make them hard to train and harder still to lead. They were a rebellious, undisciplined lot, who had grown out of the habit of taking orders. Still, they had the fighting spirit that RJ was looking for.

She walked down to the wharf area. It was full of cheap thrills like whorehouses, dirty movie parlors and bars, but RJ's attention was immediately drawn to a small island in the bay. It seemed to be almost entirely covered by structures. Structures obviously dating from antiquity and yet, from what she could see of them, they seemed to be in good repair.

She walked over to the edge of the pier, totally ignoring the rotting timbers, to see if she could get a better look. The architecture was at least as old as some of the buildings now laying in heaps around town, yet she could see no signs of wear. She pulled a small telescope from her pocket to help her get a better look, and still she could see no sign of decay. "Curioser and curiouser," she mumbled.

"They say is haunted," a voice said behind her.

RJ spun around, but she saw no one. Then there was a jerking on her pants leg.

"Down here!"

It was a little man, about three-foot-three. RJ smiled broadly at him. "Ah, but I don't believe in ghosts."

"Don't, either. Said *they* say, not *I* say." He craned his head back so he could look at her. His glance took in both chain and laser, but he didn't seem bothered. In fact, he looked relieved. "What interest in island?"

"So, who says I'm interested in the island?" RJ asked.

"I do," he replied with an impudent grin.

RJ laughed. "Well, I am a little interested. Do you know anything about it?"

"Only what hear." He walked away, and RJ followed.

"And what do you hear?" she asked, somewhat impatiently.

"Man said been there once. Said evil things chased away. Lightning struck brother down before could get to building." The little man looked sideways at RJ and said, "Of course, know for what is—fishermen's stories. Have seen lights though, sometimes at night. Reason, don't know."

He had a strange habit of omitting words from sentences that RJ found mildly annoying.

"Sometime on very foggy nights lighthouse will come on. Fisher folk say is kindly spirit on some day, and on other say it demon."

"So, to whom am I speaking?" she asked.

"Name's Willie, but they call Mickey," he announced.

RJ nodded seriously, as if there were perceptible logic in his statement. She'd noticed for some time that the little man's eyes kept darting around. He seemed unusually worried, even for Alsterase. Had he sought her out as protection? Even in Alsterase there was safety in numbers. Especially when one of the numbers carried a blaster.

"OK, shorty. What kind of trouble are you in?" she asked.

"Bad," he said with a smile. "See, am bit light-fingered. Lifted man's wallet today. Reliance. Badge in wallet. Now know spy. Soon all Alsterase will know. Unless kill first. This man and another have been chasing all over. Am tired, running out of hiding places," he explained. "Won't dare attack while in such company." The words had no sooner left his mouth, than blaster fire tore up the pier beside her. "Of course, could be wrong."

RJ glanced back quickly. There were two men, one holding the blaster, another with a more primitive projectile weapon. The man with the blaster would be an Elite, the other a secondary. Both were of course Reliance spies. It wasn't incredible intuition that told her this—although she possessed incredible intuition. It was common knowledge. Elites got lasers, secondaries got projectile weapons, and first-class soldiers made do with swords. At least, that was the way it was here on Earth.

RJ didn't wait around to give them time to aim. She picked up the little man, stuck him under her arm, ran for the nearest pile of rubble, and jumped behind it.

"Oh, come on, little man, we don't want any trouble. I just want my wallet back. Why involve your friend?" The Elite's attempt at persuasion was ruined by the obvious threatening tone in his voice. He was enjoying this. If he had to shoot her, too—even in front of the half-dozen witnesses that were scattered around, it didn't bother him. "You might as well come out. We're going to find you, anyway."

Mickey looked at RJ. "Better go. No sense getting hurt."

"Honey, the day I let some dick with a hand blaster intimidate me, that's the day I hang up my chain." RJ pulled her own blaster and handed it to the midget. "Here, hold this for me." She stood up in full view of the Reliance men.

Mickey pulled at her pants leg urgently. "What doing, trying get killed?"

"Just shut up and stay down." RJ moved away from the pile of rubble unwinding the chain as she walked.

"I don't have any quarrel with you, lady, just tell me where the midget is," the Elite said.

The Elite, he was the real threat. She finished unwinding the chain with a jerk and a flip of her wrist. It snaked out hitting the Elite in the head. *Fawapp*! *Thunk*! He hit the ground—dead. His blaster skidded across the ground to rest against a dead fish.

The secondary was in deep shit, and he knew it. He could think of only one possible explanation for what had just happened, and he didn't like it one bit.

RJ slowly and deliberately rolled up the chain.

Seeing her take no defensive action, the soldier aimed.

Mickey fired, missing the soldier completely. But the force from the plasma blaster sent him flying into a wall which he skidded down to land with his butt in a bucket.

"Freak!" The secondary hoped he was wrong about that. The midget had distracted him, but he was ready now. Unfortunately for him, the moment of hesitation was more than she'd really needed. He fired, but he lost all interest in the result of his shot. Out of the corner of his eye, he could see the chain coming at him—almost in slow motion, like a nightmare. He even seemed to scream in slow motion, "B-i-i-t-c-h-h-h-f-f-f-r-r-r-e-a-k!"

The chain caught the soldier in the left side with such force that he was pitched sideways and slammed face-first into the pavement, his nose shoved into his brain. His death was, if not painless, at least mercifully swift.

"Men really just don't know how to talk to a lady anymore," RJ mumbled to herself. "It's a crying shame what this world is coming to." She picked up the weapons of the two dead men, and then retrieved her own blaster from where Mickey had dropped it. She took a few moments to wrap the still bloody chain around her waist, then went to pull the little man out of the bucket. This proved more difficult than eliminating the Reliance spies.

"Thank you. Thank you very much," Mickey said.

"Tell me something. When you kill people around here, are you expected to clean up your own mess?" asked RJ, ruefully surveying the destruction she had wreaked.

"Killing Reliance spies considered community service work. Someone else will clean mess. You saved life." Clearly, this meant a great deal to the little man.

"Well, I do expect something in return," RJ admitted.

"Anything," Mickey promised earnestly.

"First, I think it might be a good idea if we put a little distance between ourselves and these corpses," she said.

Mickey nodded his agreement, and they went on their way.

Strapped to the wrist of the former Elite, and hidden by his cooling corpse, his comlink glowed and pulsed.

# Chapter Three

RJ walked in and threw a bag of food on David's chest. He started awake and was instantly in a bad mood. He looked in the sack and made a face.

"You were expecting maybe veal?" RJ asked sarcastically.

"What's that?" David looked around him. It was almost dark. He'd been asleep for hours, and apparently RJ had been gone all this time. "Where were you? What were you doing?" He was a little angry. He could have been lying here dead for all she cared.

She sat on the end of the bed and smiled at him. "Always with you it's questions." She shrugged. "I believe I have found a good ally, among other things."

David stiffened. "You can't just go about the streets stopping people and asking them if they'd like to help us destroy the greatest power in the universe!" he said hotly. "Some people might not like that. Not to name names, but the Reliance, for one."

RJ shrugged, as if the Reliance bothered her only a little. "If they were the strongest power in the universe—and please try to remember that the universe is a very big place—they wouldn't still be fighting with the Aliens, now, would they?"

"Uh, I really hate it when you do that, RJ." David got out of bed and stormed to the bathroom. Once inside, he held his head in the hope that it would stop that rocking motion. He closed the door and screamed at her. "I hate it when you get technical about shit like that!" A few minutes later, he walked out of the bathroom looking fairly relieved. "One thing's for damn sure, the Reliance can sure as hell tromp our butts. And if you're going to run around telling them right where to find us..."

"Relax already, David," RJ said lightly. "The man was a midget."

"So?" David obviously saw no significance in this. "What's a mij-jet?" He fumbled over the unfamiliar word.

RJ looked at him in disbelief. "Are all civilians so ignorant? A midget is a little person."

"So. It's a little person," he shrugged. He didn't believe in fairy stories.

"Why do you think you don't know what a midget is? Can't you ever just put two and two together?"

"A work unit's ability to think is not overly important to a Reliance overlord. I think I do pretty well considering that I didn't have anywhere near the education that you had. I didn't get the breaks that you did..."

"Excuse me, ass-bite, but in my job I got shot at..."

"Just tell me the significance of this man being a midget."

RJ nodded. He was right. The key to the Reliance's power was ignorance. They gave the people just enough knowledge to do the jobs the Reliance wanted them to do—no more and no less.

"All people with what the Reliance has classified as 'defects' are hunted out and killed. Being a midget is a birth defect. Usually such 'defective' persons are convicted of rape, theft, or murder, and then executed. If they are allowed to reach adulthood at all, that is. Obviously, defective babies are usually stillborn. The people just stand back and let them do it, because they don't trust anyone that's different. That's human nature."

David nodded slowly in reluctant agreement. He remembered how the villagers had reacted to his new ideas.

"This Reliance policy will help us out quite a bit here in Alsterase," RJ announced. Clearly, David was lost again. RJ sighed. For an intelligent man, he could sure be dense at times. "If the Reliance is out to exterminate anyone who's different, then those who are different aren't going to feel very charitable towards the Reliance, now are they?" She sighed.

Light dawned, and David nodded. "So they'll be more likely to join us."

"Well, at least we can trust them not to hurt us." Suddenly, RJ's head jerked towards the door. She tensed. David noticed that the arm started to jerk more, and suddenly she was on her feet.

"What's wrong?" he asked, puzzled.

RJ pulled her blaster.

"What's wrong?" Alarmed, David stood up from the bed.

"Quiet!" RJ ordered. The door flew into splinters, and the biggest man David had ever seen stepped into the room. He dwarfed the man they had encountered in the bar last night. The giant threw a piece of the door at RJ, and her blaster went flying.

David had never seen a GSH, but he knew instinctively that this was one. He'd heard stories about them most of his life, but he hadn't really believed them. The stories were of manufactured beings capable of great feats of strength. Stories told by the same people who talked about gnomes and fairies. Yet here it was, the monster behind the stories. David was terrified. He knew his life was over. Then he realized that the man wasn't paying the slightest attention to him; he was after RJ.

RJ went for the second blaster, but before she could free it from the loops of chain, the giant was upon her. He bashed her head with his fist, the blood flew, and RJ fell to the floor. He lifted the still dazed woman up by a loop in her chain, and threw her against the wall, and still he paid no attention to David.

David saw only one hope for them. He started across the room for the bike. The GSH pounced on RJ once again. David had no idea how much punishment RJ could take, but it couldn't be this much. She had to be unconscious, maybe even dead. He was, therefore, stunned to see the GSH fly across the room and land at his feet, effectively blocking the way to the bike.

RJ ran at the man.

"Are you nuts!" David yelled, jumping smartly out of her way. "He's going to kill you!"

RJ wasn't listening. She hurled herself headlong into the monster's stomach.

"He's going to kill you, and then he's going to kill me," David mumbled as he resumed his trek towards the bike.

All mumbling stopped as David was thrown to the ground by the impact of an incredible weight. He lay where he'd landed, and dazedly watched as RJ jumped up off him, quickly disengaging the chain from her body. She whipped it out at the GSH. It hit the monster's head with a thud. David heard the thing fall, although he didn't really see it, and he was sure it wouldn't be down long.

David crawled the short distance remaining to the bike, where he fumbled to free the rocket launcher. Apparently, RJ had been more worried about losing the damn thing than about having to actually use it. He wasn't having much luck getting it off. She had the chain around the monster's neck, pulling on it for all she was worth. David fumbled with the strings holding the weapon, and the next time he looked up, RJ was being choked with her own chain. David pulled frantically at the launcher, and it came loose with a jerk that set him on his butt. He aimed, but RJ was in the way. Then the giant made a fatal mistake; he threw RJ across the room. David fired. The kick sent him crashing into the front wall of the apartment. He saw the rocket hit the monster square in the chest and propel him through the exterior wall before it detonated. When the smoke cleared, there was a gaping hole in the wall, and no GSH.

David tossed aside the launcher and crawled to where RJ lay, the chain still around her throat and blood running from her nose and mouth.

"Don't be dead," David prayed. He poked at her to see if she would move. "Are you OK?" he asked.

RJ opened her eyes and stared at him in disbelief as he unwrapped the chain from her neck. "Oh, yes, I'm fine," she croaked out. "Never felt better. In fact, think I'll go dancing!" By the end of her speech, she was screaming at him.

David sighed with relief. She'd be fine. David got unsteadily to his feet and reached down to RJ. After a moment, she let him help her up and tilted her head back to slow the nosebleed.

The fat manager finally managed to shove his way through the small crowd that had gathered at the now door-less doorway. Shaking his head and clicking his tongue in obvious disapproval, he surveyed the room.

"The use of rocket launchers in the rooms is strictly against the rules—ten unit penalty." He crossed to the hole in the wall, and looked out. "As for that," apparently indicating the remains of the GSH which were on the street below, "it will cost you fifteen units to be paid immediately. After all, we can't have a corpse plastered all over our doorstep. I'm trying to run a classy place here, you know."

"Why you..." David raised his fist threateningly.

"Get the man his money, David," RJ ordered.

David lowered his fist reluctantly, and dug the money out of the pack on the back of the bike. He walked over and counted out the coins.

"And two units for dripping blood all over the room," the fat man said, his hand still extended.

"I ought to..." David started to raise his fist again.

"Take your money, and these people, and get out," RJ said as she took the two units out of David's hand and handed them to the manager.

Satisfied, the manager scurried out, herding the crowd out as he went.

"Come on, people! Party's over for now," he urged.

"We're going to have to leave Alsterase for a while," RJ said almost conversationally as she disappeared into the bathroom.

"Why not leave it for good?" David asked. "Last night I almost got killed; today you almost got killed. I think we should take the hint and get the hell out while we still can." He followed RJ as he spoke, but she shut the door in his face, and the lock clicked. "RJ, you need help."

RJ's voice floated out the door. "The last thing I need, my friend, is an amateur trying to help me."

David looked around the room helplessly. The devastation was complete. The bed, dresser, and footstool were broken, the door was gone, the walls were busted at irregular intervals, and a big chunk of the back wall was missing. They, especially RJ, were damned lucky to be alive.

RJ didn't feel very lucky. She looked in the mirror. Her nose was set to one side, and the angle was all wrong. She checked to be sure that the door was locked because she would never be able to explain this to David. She grabbed her nose between her thumb and forefingers, and with a twist, re-broke it. Ignoring the fresh gush of blood, she forced it into place and held it several seconds.

The bleeding stopped, and when she removed her hand a moment later, her nose was as good as new. Grimly ignoring the pain, she moved on to her other injuries. She took the two teeth she held clenched in her left fist and forced the roots back into the already-healed gum. When the bleeding stopped and the teeth were firmly rooted, she moved to the cracked ribs—six at least by the feel of it. Fortunately, they seemed to be in place, or close enough, and were already healing, so she left them alone. Her injuries cared for, she started to wash off the blood, but thought better of it. It was going to be tough enough to explain her miraculous recovery. She left most of the blood.

Satisfied, RJ pulled a black wallet out of her hip pocket and opened it. Inside were three tubes, each four inches long and filled with small white pills. On the other side were a small knife and a syringe. She took one of the tubes out and dumped a pill into the palm of her hand, then threw it down her throat. She took meticulous care to return the wallet to her pocket precisely as she had found it.

She hurt more than she would ever admit, and her damn arm felt like it was about to jerk out of its socket. By morning, though, she would be fine; all thanks to that little white pill.

When RJ came out of the bathroom, she flopped straight down onto the broken bed.

David gave her a worried look.

"Ask me if I'm OK again, and I'll split you," she said. She covered her face with her hands, as if still warding off blows.

Silently, David pulled her boots off and covered her with a blanket. It was dark now, and the temperature was dropping. It was going to be a cold night, especially since they were practically sleeping outside.

"RJ, that was...was that a GSH?" David asked hesitantly.

RJ started to make a flip remark, but decided it would take too much energy. "Yes, David, that was a Genetically Superior Humanoid—a GSH."

David sat heavily on the end of the fallen bed. "I always thought they were made up. You know, old wives' tales. Like the little people, but you said there are little people, too."

"Take my word for it, they're real enough." She spoke through her hands, the warmth felt good on the new tissue.

"They say that they don't feel heat or cold as we do," David said.

"They don't," RJ agreed.

"They say their bones are as strong as steel, their skin impervious to almost anything."

"Except rockets." Her small attempt at humor fell flat. "True."

"They say that they never get sick, that they don't age."

"They don't."

"Why are they after us?" David asked in a frightened whisper.

RJ thought that was a very good question. Why had the GSH come after them? It was a sure bet that it hadn't just happened to single them out for abusive treatment. They didn't have the emotions necessary to carry out free thought. Then she realized her error. The dead Elite. Elites had wrist coms. All Reliance enforcement personnel did. He was in pursuit, so his would have been on—SOP. Naturally, he would have been linked to someone in Alsterase. Of course, that other person would be another Elite. GSHs were classed as Elites, and while they very rarely wasted a GSHs talents on Earth assignments, it would probably seem necessary in Alsterase to have a backup that could handle almost every situation. The dead Elite would have given his backup a complete description of her. The com would have provided a complete blow-by-blow of the action, and RJ knew the conclusion the GSH would have drawn. Even the Secondary had known, just before he died. That's why the GSH had ignored David; RJ was the target, the problem. And she wouldn't have been hard to find.

Impatient, David asked again, "RJ, why did that thing come after us?"

"I...I made a mistake. I was careless. I should have known he'd be linked. I...was...careless. I...made...a.... *mistake*." She repeated herself in a tone of total amazement. It was as if she had made an impossible discovery.

"You sound surprised," David laughed. "You aren't infallible. No one is."

"I *have* to be." RJ took her hands from her face. Her expression was grim. "I just don't make that kind of stupid mistake."

David could have understood it if she was mad at herself. She wasn't. She seemed confused, as if she just really couldn't accept that she could have made a mistake at all, much less a stupid one.

"Oh, come on, RJ," David laughed in disbelief. "I don't know what this mistake was, but I'm sure you've made mistakes before, and I'm sure you'll make them again."

This enraged RJ. "What makes you so damned sure of that?" She demanded hotly. "People like you make mistakes, not me!"

"You know, I haven't said this before, RJ, but you are, without a doubt, the most pompous, egotistical jackass I have ever known." David stood up from the bed.

"I love you, too," RJ said, and blew him a kiss.

David ignored her and started to pace. "You made a mistake anyone could have made..."

"Well, I don't think just *anyone* could have made it," RJ said with a grin.

"That's exactly the kind of shit I'm talking about!" David steamed. "God, don't you ever listen to yourself? Have you always been this arrogant, or did you have to work at it? That...thing...almost killed you tonight." He stopped pacing suddenly, obviously struck by inspiration. After a moment, he continued, "I saved your life tonight!"

"You saved yourself," RJ said flatly.

"Yes, all right. But, by saving myself, I also saved you," he repeated smugly.

"OK," RJ conceded. "I admit that things looked pretty bad." She shrugged and rolled on her side, trying unsuccessfully to get comfortable.

"Bad!" David repeated in disbelief.

"I still had a trick or two up my sleeve," RJ stated calmly.

"I can't believe you! The thing was strangling you with your own chain. You were bleeding out of every opening in your skull. How were you going to get out of that? This I want to hear!"

She didn't answer. She was asleep, or at least pretending to be. "Bitch," David swore. He dug through the rubble till he found the sack of food RJ had brought him. In spite of the way it looked and smelled, it tasted pretty good. After eating, he threw the sack across the room, shut off the light, and slid into the bed beside RJ.

"Thanks for maybe saving my life," RJ mumbled.

"Bitch," David swore again.

She just laughed and went back to sleep.

He wondered just how badly she was hurt. RJ tossed and turned and moaned in her sleep, and David felt helpless. He didn't know what to do for her, and wasn't sure she would let him do it if he did. She was such an insufferable hardhead.

In her tossing, RJ rolled against David, reminding him again that she was female. Still, David felt nothing even close to desire. It wasn't that he was a gentleman, or at least no more than any other red-blooded man of his age and health. If she were any other woman, he would have done everything in his power to seduce her. But she was RJ, and he had no urge to possess her. To him, RJ was just a guy with an extremely attractive body and a great set of tits. For David, sleeping with RJ was like sleeping with your dog. It was warmer than sleeping by yourself, and gave you someone to turn to if you had a nightmare.

What they had was far more important to David than sex, even more important than love. He made a silent vow to whatever powers might be listening that he would never let anything come between them. That he would not let friend or foe, man or woman, or even their cause, separate them.

When David woke up he heard the shower going. He was freezing cold, and that damned woman was taking a shower! He knew from experience that there was no hot water.

"You're insane!" David screamed at her.

The man in the apartment next to theirs apparently didn't appreciate the noise.

"Keep it down, you assholes!" he yelled, throwing something solid against the wall.

"Bite me!" RJ screamed back. She walked out of the bathroom drying herself. Modesty was not one of RJ's strong suits. But then, having been in the military all of her life, she was used to showering in communal, coed showers.

David took a good look at RJ. She looked to be in the peak of health, not a scratch, not a bruise, not so much as a skinned elbow. Even the sparkle in her eyes seemed genuine.

She wasn't hurt, not even a little. That just wasn't possible. Was it?

"You'd think you'd never seen a woman before," RJ mumbled.

"I've never seen anyone heal so quickly," David said defensively.

"Oh. Well, now don't you feel like an ass?" she mumbled to herself.

David smiled. It wasn't very often that he got the better of RJ. He enjoyed it when he did.

"Part of my training included learning how to take a hit, to roll with a blow, how to pull out of a punch so that it does the least damage." She watched David from the corner of her eye. Was he going to buy that?

At first he frowned. Clearly, he was finding that hard to swallow.

"There was a lot of blood coming from my nose and inside my mouth where he loosened a couple of teeth. But besides being a little sore"—which was a lie; her only symptom this morning was a dryness in her eyes which was caused by the drug—"I feel fine. I have taken worse beatings." That was a lie, too.

This time David smiled; he believed her.

RJ sighed with relief. She dressed quickly, topping her ensemble off—as usual—with the chain, oblivious to the dried blood which now covered it, and was coming off in flakes as she wrapped it in her usual fashion. She took the bag off the back of the bike and went through it, checking the armaments inside. Satisfied, she added the pistol gleaned from the dead secondary to the assortment of weapons and explosives.

David helped her, and they dug through the wreckage till they found both blasters. RJ put hers in her holster, then helped David to customize the shoulder harness he'd used for the gun he'd lost in the bar, making it fit the blaster. They grabbed their jackets and bag and left. They were halfway down the stairs when David realized they had forgotten something.

"What about the bike?" David said, stopping in his tracks.

"What about it?"

"You don't plan to walk, do you?"

"I've got a truck." RJ started walking again, and David followed.

"Where did you get that?" David asked.

"We'll find one," RJ said with a shrug.

"You mean STEAL one!" David shrieked.

"Shush," RJ hissed. "Only Reliance bigshots get to own cars. The rest are used by the military or in farm work. Not even an Elite can buy a car or truck. They're too rare, and too expensive. There are several vehicles in Alsterase. Now, use your head, where did they come from in the first place?"

"They must be stolen," David answered.

RJ clapped.

"Well, it's different stealing from the Reliance," David said in a harsh whisper. "You're going to steal from someone who stole from the Reliance, and that is altogether different."

"Then consider it borrowing," RJ said in disbelief.

"It's only borrowing if you ask," David pronounced self-righteously.

RJ decided to ignore him.

But David didn't want to be ignored. "It's wrong. That's all. Anyone who steals from the Reliance is on our side, and we shouldn't take from them..."

"If this is too big a moral dilemma for you, perhaps you would prefer to walk!" RJ screamed, fed up.

"Shush, shh!" David slapped a hand over her mouth. He nodded his head. "All right, we'll do it your way, but I don't like it."

"No one says you have to," she said with a shrug.

They walked up and down the streets for what seemed like hours to David. By the time RJ found what she was looking for, the streets were already filled with people. She walked around the red Reliance farm-issue truck, kicking the tires and checking out the paint job, then she popped the hood and checked the engine.

"Damn it, RJ! You're stealing the damned thing, not buying it," David whispered nervously.

RJ slammed the hood. She gave David a wicked grin. "I like to know what I'm stealing." She took hold of the driver's door handle and gave it a heave. The door opened. She jumped in and opened the passenger door, setting the bag and rocket launcher on the seat as David crawled in. He closed the door and looked around in awe. He had never seen such a machine from the inside.

RJ was under the dash, taking her time hotwiring the vehicle.

"Could you please hurry up and do whatever it is you're doing?" David said anxiously. "We're going to get caught."

"So?" RJ sneered. She had never hotwired a vehicle before, and while she understood the principle, she was having a little trouble putting it into practice. It was made more difficult by the fact that the new "owner" had attached several safeguards to stop people from doing just what she was trying to do. "If someone comes, I'll just kill them." She might have been ordering lunch by the tone of her voice.

"I'd rather not have to kill someone over a car, if you don't mind, RJ. Did anyone ever tell you that you can't just kill every one that pisses you off?"

"Yes." She had finally succeeded. She touched the two wires together and the engine roared. "I killed them." She laughed at her own joke.

"Very funny, RJ. Now, could we just go?"

"OK, OK, don't get your shorts in a knot." She got into the seat, closed the door, and they were on their way. As they pulled out, RJ saw the owner come running out of one of the buildings. She waved wildly at him and roared off.

Whitey Baldor chased after them, screaming till he ran out of breath. He finally gave up. Hands on knees, he watched till they were out of sight. He recognized that pair. Two nights ago that woman had kneed him in the balls so hard that he still hurt. Then she'd knocked him cold. He'd been out for something close to three hours. Whitey laughed, shaking his head he turned back toward his apartment. He laughed again and looked back in the direction she had gone. "God-damned gutsy bitch."

"I've always wondered how they could see out of these things," David ran his hand over the glass. "I still don't have any idea."

"Keep your hands off it; you're smearing it up. It's one-way glass. Because of the way it's made, the driver can see out, but from outside you can't see in."

"When I was a kid I used to think they drove through some form of magic. Later, when I stopped believing in magic, I thought they used something like a view screen," David said. "It's kind of a letdown to see it's something so simple."

RJ nodded. It was funny what people would make up to explain things they didn't understand. The Reliance didn't tell them anything, so they had to make up their own answers. In a way it was ingenious, even if they were mostly wrong.

"I still don't understand why they do it this way," David said. "I mean...what's the purpose?"

"Ah, my friend, that is because you have yet to understand the Reliance. The glass in Reliance vehicles is one-way for the same reason that Reliance police wear masks over their faces. Intimidation. People fear the unknown, the unseen. From outside how do you know whether there is one man in this vehicle or five? You don't. When a man covers his face with a mask, how do you know whether he is in a good mood or a murderous one? You don't. How do you even know he's human? You don't. The point is that people expect the worst. Therefore, there are always five men in the truck, the men is always in a murderous mood, and you're never sure that they're quite human. They scare us, so we imprison ourselves."

"Slaves to our fear." David's voice sounded far away. He himself was scared. He crossed his arms and put his fists in his armpits to hide his nervousness. He didn't know exactly what RJ had planned, and as she said, you tended to fear the unknown. *Slaves to our fear*, he reminded himself. *I won't be afraid.* It wasn't as easy as it sounded.

He imagined a whole patrol could swarm down on them at any moment. His palms were sweaty, and his mouth was dry. RJ sat there as they traveled along through the maze of David's imaginary policemen and hummed a tone-deaf tune which seemed to be in time with the jerking of her right arm. Humming and jerking, jerking and humming. After an hour, David could stand it no more.

"Would you please stop it!" he screamed.

"What?" she asked, obviously not understanding what he meant.

"All that humming and arm-jerking," he said.

RJ was momentarily taken aback; then she was mad. "I can stop the humming, but I can't stop the arm jerking. I wish I could. It's a side effect of battle fatigue. Unless I concentrate on it, it jerks. Not enough to be debilitating, just enough to be annoying."

Now David felt like a real ass. "I...I'm sorry," he stammered. "It's just that...well, do you have to be so damned...happy?"

"I'm sorry, David; in future, I will try to be more morose." With that said, she started right back humming again.

It wouldn't have been so bad if she could carry a tune, but she couldn't have carried a tune in a bucket.

"Hum hum hum hum huuum huum hum hummm."

He couldn't take it any longer. Two hours of RJ's offensive humming was enough to drive a man to suicide.

"Shut up!" David screamed at the top of his lungs.

RJ clicked her tongue. "My, my. Are we feeling a bit testy today? Humm?" She smiled pleasantly. She was infuriating.

"You are without a doubt the worst hummer I've ever heard in my life. In fact, I've blown farts that were better," David said truthfully. To his surprise, RJ seemed upset by his criticism.

"Yes, well, there's not much chance to hear music standing in mud up to your neck or crawling through a jungle on your belly on some plague-infested outer world," she hissed.

David was intrigued. It suddenly dawned on him just how much RJ must know. She had the answer to every question he had ever asked about the Reliance. She had told him that she had fought on the outer worlds, but he had never realized just what the meant till now. RJ had traveled through space in a spaceship. She'd walked on other worlds, come face-to-face with aliens.

"Tell me about the outer worlds." His voice was as eager as a child's.

RJ hesitated only for a moment. No one had ever really been interested in where she'd been or all that she had seen, and she found herself willingly spouting all she remembered of the outer worlds. She told him of Trinidad, the planet with five inhabitable moons. Of Ufora, the jungle world where the rivers could change daily, and where new plants could spring up in a single day, making it impossible to follow the same trail twice or to locate a missing man. She told him of Urta, Deaka and Sheows and the ultra-modern cities Earth-descended humans had built there. She did her best to explain about their seasons and their different plant and animal life. She even explained the customs and fashions of the native intelligent life forms which had been encountered on two of Trinidad's moons.

"They believe that these moons were once one planet, and that it was split in two. That's how they explain that the same primitive being wound up on two different worlds. Their cultures are identical. Their language is even almost the same. From what the archaeologists can dig up, both cultures are the same age. So, it's a sure bet that no one transplanted them from one moon to the other. The experts maintain that the two moons were once one planet that split somehow. I find that difficult to believe, however. The likelihood of anyone's surviving such a cataclysmic event is pretty slim."

"So, how do you explain it?" David asked curiously.

"I don't," RJ said with a broad smile. "What's the point? They exist as they are. The Ingits don't ask why, so why should we?"

She spoke on, telling him about Deakard, the planet of their alien enemies. The Aliens called themselves Argys, meaning "Peoples of the Red Star." They held four planets called Arg, Varg, Garg, and Farg. She explained to him that the Reliance didn't want Deakard, and that the Argys didn't want Earth.

"See, they're in the same spot we're in. They've used up all their home planet's resources. Deakard isn't even fit to farm. We don't have any metal ore left, no petroleum products, nothing of real value as far the Reliance is concerned, but we still have soil and air. Deakard doesn't even have that. They manufacture their own air, and grow all their produce on another planet, importing all their food. On Earth, we may import metals and plastics, but we *export* wool, cotton and wood products. Not to mention the occasional shipment of meats and vegetables that can't be grown on the outer worlds. Deakard sucks its worlds dry."

"So why do they stay there, why don't they move to their other worlds?" David asked.

"For the same reason a good share of the Reliance bigshots stay on Earth. They're safe on Deakard, just like we're safe on Earth. Because they've got nothing there that we want, and we've got nothing here that they want, the home worlds are safe worlds. The fight is over the colony planets that are still rich in mineral content. Mostly, they fight over a planet called Stashes, because both planets claim it."

"What's so special about Sta...ashes?" David asked, stumbling over the name.

"It's got the highest mineral content of any of the planets, and that's about it." RJ sounded far away. "It's a big, hot rock of a planet. Very little water, and half of that's poison. The animal life is aggressive—so is most of the plant life. The air is barely breathable. Breathing it for a period of three months cuts your life expectancy by ten years. Some can't breathe it at all. I saw one man die after being exposed to the atmosphere for less than ten minutes. On Stashes they say that if the enemy doesn't get you, it's a sure bet that the planet will."

She saw she wasn't boring David, so she kept talking.

Stories unwound of battles fought on worlds so distant it was hard for David to fathom. She told him of technology he had no idea existed. She opened his mind to a new and wondrous universe filled with fantastic machines, horrid alien beasts, and beautiful and dangerous places. Battlefield after battlefield was spread before him. Battle after battle. RJ had seen it all, up close and personal, and he began to understand why human life was so cheap to her. Sometimes he could see a picture of it so vividly in his mind that he was almost sick. Other times he seemed to be drawn into the fever of the battle, to feel the adrenaline of those who fought.

She had been so many places and done so many things that he found himself wondering just how she had squeezed all of it into her short life. Even if he stretched his imagination to its fullest he couldn't believe that RJ was any more than twenty-five.

RJ was a good and articulate storyteller. There was, however, one thing she hadn't talked about that David was intensely curious about.

"Just what is a GSH?"

"As you already know, GSH stands for Genetically Superior Humanoid."

Clearly, while David knew what GSH stood for, he had no idea what a Genetically Superior Humanoid was.

RJ sighed. "Well, they take a human embryo...Do you know what an embryo is?"

David shook his head no.

RJ sighed again and went on indulgently. "It's a baby before it's born—when it's just first made."

David nodded, but made a face that said that this was the most gruesome thing he had ever heard of.

"Anyway, they take this embryo...by 'take' do you think I'm saying that they take it out of the mother?"

David nodded his head.

"Well, they don't. God! You're hard to explain anything to! You don't even know a simple word like embryo. What the hell do you call them, little baby seeds?" RJ said, her patience wearing thin.

"We don't talk about making people," David said with equal disgust. Didn't she understand that the populace had been deprived of any but the most basic knowledge for centuries?

"OK. They take the Mommy stuff, and the Daddy stuff and mix them together in a petri dish; embryos result. Then they use a process called gene splicing." She wasn't even going to *try* to explain gene splicing to David. "Through this process they take out qualities they don't want, and put in qualities that they do want. They use chemicals, too. To put it simply, they shape this embryo into the person that they want it to be. In the case of a GSH, they build the perfect soldier. They grow them in a special solution in vats, and when they are old enough they're born. In other words, they take them out of the vats. Then they feed them growth hormones and information till, within a year, they are fully grown and know all that they will ever need to know."

Something still puzzled David.

"How does the Reliance control them? What's to keep them from doing whatever they like?"

"Good question. It would seem that such beings could easily take over and probably would, but they can't. When they are still in an embryonic state, their minds are altered. First, all emotions except loyalty are removed. They are then brainwashed so that their only loyalty is to the Reliance. They aren't capable of anything else. They eat, sleep, live, breathe and kill for the Reliance. Obeying orders, and completing their assigned task gives them a sense of accomplishment which is as close as they get to happiness.

"Then there's the box planted in the base of their skulls. If they show any signs of rebellion at all, this control box can be detonated. It literally blows their brains up inside their skulls. The box blows of its own accord when the GSH reaches the age of fifty. The Reliance is afraid that after that, their conditioning might wear off. They couldn't have that. There is no escape for them. They must serve the Reliance. So you see there is really nothing superior about them at all. They are slaves just like everyone else. Worse, really, because they have no free will."

"You sound like you're sorry for them!" David said in disbelief.

"I...just think it's wrong, that's all. Here is this thing that could have everything and the way it is it has nothing. Take for instance the GSH who tried to kill us last night. He went after me exclusively, because logically you posed no major threat. So he ignored you and never realized that *you* were the real threat. If I were the GSH, I would have killed you first, because it would have been easy. Then I could have given all my attention to the Elite without having to worry about where you were. Sometimes the most logical thing to do is something illogical. Emotion causes you to think illogically." RJ finished with a shrug.

David laughed. "You're twisted."

She took it as a compliment.

Towards nightfall, the fuel gauge cranked over to empty, and RJ pulled into a Reliance fuel station. David thought he would die, but RJ acted as if she belonged there. The attendant filled the truck while she went inside and got a couple of sandwiches and some bottled soft drinks. David didn't dare breathe till they were three miles down the road.

"Are you crazy?" David breathed at last.

"Where did you think we were going to get the alcohol to run this thing, David? Squeeze it from a tree maybe?" RJ asked sarcastically.

"I thought we'd steal it late at night when no one was around. I had no idea that you would be blatant enough to pull into the damned Reliance fuel station in broad daylight! You even went inside to get sandwiches, for God's sake!" David screamed.

RJ just grinned.

"It's not funny, RJ."

"I guess you'll never understand, will you? Those people who run that station are just class-two work units. Only authorized Reliance personnel drive vehicles. Therefore, if a vehicle pulls in, it must be Reliance. Right?"

"OK. But the way you're dressed...."

"They wouldn't care if I were buck naked and had 'The Reliance Sucks' painted in bright red letters across my butt. Don't you see? They service the vehicle, not who's driving it. All they do is fill the cars and trucks, and give you a sack lunch if you need it. They're not expected to think, so they don't."

"But what if another Reliance truck had pulled in while we were there?" David asked.

RJ started to say something.

"No, wait, don't tell me. Let me guess. We kill them, right?"

"You're getting better," RJ cooed.

"You're sick, you know that, RJ? Real sick."

"Hand me a sandwich," RJ said, pointing at the sack.

He did.

"That's your answer to everything, isn't it? Just kill it!" David said hotly.

"Hand me my drink," she said, through a mouth full of sandwich.

He handed it to her after opening it.

"What happens when you don't kill someone? What happens when they kill you?"

"You quit worrying about it," RJ grinned crookedly.

David shook his head in disbelief. Not a damned bit of sense arguing with her about it, she wasn't about to change her mind.

They drove for another hour then pulled off the road and parked. RJ pushed a button on the dash and almost gave David a heart attack when the seat flipped out of its own accord to make a bed. He and RJ marched in separate directions to relieve themselves, and returned almost simultaneously.

RJ took off her chain and boots and lay them in the floorboards. Then came the blaster.

David just sat there.

"What's with you?" RJ asked, wondering if he was still mad over the fuel station thing.

"I thought I'd take first watch," he said with a smile. "After all, you did all the driving."

"No one needs to take watch, David. No one's going to find us." She took off her shirt and hung it on the steering wheel.

It was a strange thing to notice, made even stranger by the fact that he hadn't noticed till now. The golden-brown color of her skin, which he had attributed to time spent in the sun, wasn't a suntan at all. There were no tan lines on RJ's body. Her color was natural, and he had never knowingly seen anyone naturally colored this way.

"Is that your natural color?" he asked, thinking perhaps it was a side effect of being exposed to something on some alien world.

"My hair?"

"No, your skin." To his surprise, RJ looked nervous.

"Why?" There was a suspicious tone to her voice.

"I've just never seen anyone colored like that. I thought it was a tan, but it's everywhere." He blushed as he said it.

RJ sighed with relief. Just farm boy curiosity, nothing more than that. "Where I come from a lot of people are colored this way." She turned off the lights and lay down, covering herself up with her jacket.

David was satisfied with her answer. He just didn't understand why it had made her so uptight. She must have thought he was coming on to her. Now he was really embarrassed.

He took off his own boots, weapon and shirt, then lay down and covered up with his jacket. He purposely lay as far away from her as possible. If she had thought he was coming on to her, she could stop thinking so now. David knew he wouldn't be able to sleep. RJ had filled his head with too many things to think about. He looked out the window at the full moon.

"RJ?"

"What?" It was obvious, from the tone of her voice, that she wasn't ready for more questions.

"Are there people living up there?" he asked.

"Up where?" RJ asked with an indulgent sigh.

"On the moon."

"There's a spaceport there. All spaceships dock and take off from there. Everything goes from here to there through a matter transporter, and vice versa. It saves the ships having to use the energy and fuel to break away from Earth's gravitational pull. Not to mention the stress of re-entry." She was glad she had already explained matter transporters to him, otherwise she would have, no doubt, had to explain it now. "The station itself is really very impressive. It spreads across the surface of the moon like some great spider, its tentacles occasionally catching and holding a ship so that it can be loaded or unloaded." For someone who had been reluctant to answer his question, she now seemed only too happy to fill him in on all the details. "You can see Earth from up there. It's quite a sight. I've seen grown people weep when seeing it for the first time. It is lovely, but it's the space view of Deakard that I have imprinted on my heart. It lies there in the heavens cold and black and distant. At just the right angle, you can place it so that both of its red suns are behind it. The light catches on the silver of the buildings that cover its surface, and makes for a glittering effect which almost, but not quite, overcomes the sinister look of the planet. I've never been to the surface of the planet of course, but someday I hope...I would like to see it again."

When she spoke again, her voice was wistful. "There is something in seeing it that I can't quite explain. It stirs the senses. You seem to smell things you have never smelled, see things you have never seen, hear things you have never heard, and want things you have never wanted before. For me, it was as if I had never really been alive before. As if I had been asleep all my life, and then I woke up and realized that I hadn't really done any of those things. It was as if a new day had dawned, and I could do anything I wanted. I guess it was at that moment that the seeds of rebellion were planted in my heart, because I knew I wanted more from life. And I knew the Reliance wasn't going to let me have it." RJ suddenly seemed to realize she was rambling. "We'd better get some sleep."

The next day, shortly after noon, they reached their destination. The road had been cut through the mountain so that it ran between two cliffs. They made their camp at the very top of the cliff so that the whole roadway could be seen. They hid the truck in a clump of bushes. RJ set the weapons out in a pattern on top of the ridge. David helped her as she tied a rope around a tree and went down the side of the cliff to set explosive charges; this process took the rest of the day.

Then they waited. One day passed, then two, then three. When, on the fourth day, David was eating yet another burnt dead animal and crunching on some weed RJ said was wholesome, he'd had enough.

"Are you sure that this is a supply route?" David asked for the five-billionth time in four days.

"Yes, and don't ask me again." If David was getting tired of waiting, RJ was just as tired of his constant bitching.

"We've been sitting on this cold-ass mountain for four days, and not one truck has gone by. Not even a small one," David said. He threw down the rest of the meat. "Just what the hell was that before you burnt it to a crisp?"

"Some sort of bird," RJ picked the meat up off the ground and started eating it—bone and all.

"I really hate when you do that," David said, making a face.

"I know. That's why I do it," RJ said flippantly.

David stood up and started stomping away. "That's it! I've had it with waiting for nonexistent convoys in the middle of nowhere. I've had it with trying to live on things that weren't even good before you burned them, and I have really had it with you!"

RJ said nothing; she ignored him.

David turned abruptly around. "Did you hear me?"

"No. I was trying to listen to the convoy." She pointed down the road.

He could see them.

There were a few moments of pandemonium as they went to their respective positions.

The two topless four-wheel-drive vehicles were positioned one before and one behind the huge cargo truck. The vehicles held a full company of soldiers.

"Must be some good shit," David said excitedly.

"Shush," RJ ordered, and there was no doubt that it was an order. She held the detonators in her hand, waited for just the right moment, then—*BOOM!* The first two charges sent rocks as big as the vehicles raining down into the road. Now they couldn't go forward. The mountain shook so hard that for a second David thought they were going to go down with it. *BOOM!* She blew the second set of charges. Now the road behind the convoy was blocked as well.

David saw RJ pick up the rocket launcher. That was his cue. From behind his rock, he started firing. Not at anybody, just firing. That's all he had been told to do, and he soon found out why as the bullets and blasts started to bounce off his rock. He tried to make himself as small as possible behind it as shreds of rock rained down upon him. "Holy shit!"

While they were all shooting at David, RJ made her move. She jumped out of hiding, aimed, and fired. The rocket hit the uncovered vehicle in the front. There were no survivors. RJ hit the ground before anyone had a chance to fire at her and crawled on her elbows and her knees over to where David was.

"You knew they were going to shoot at me," David accused.

RJ gave him one of her crooked grins.

"You did a very good job. Being a target isn't as easy as it sounds." She jumped up and took off running.

He wished that she would tell him what the hell she was doing. David didn't know what else to do, so he shot his gun, although all he was hitting was the trees above him.

RJ fired, but this time all but one man jumped clear before the rocket could hit the uncovered car. RJ discarded the rocket launcher, and pulled out her sidearm. She checked quickly to be sure that David wasn't watching. In an apparent suicide attempt, she took a running leap off the top of the cliff. Landing with both feet on top of the truck, she shot three men before the truck stopped shaking, then jumped to the ground. RJ calculated quickly that there were seven men left.

The first three were easily dealt with. They had taken cover from the "snipers" on the ridge, but hadn't counted on fire from behind. RJ had no qualms about shooting a man in the back. Dead was dead—it didn't matter how they got that way. The fourth man stumbled into her, and wound up with a face full of fist. The fifth heard the fourth's cries and came to help. He got a blaster bolt in his scalp for his pains.

David couldn't see RJ. Even up here the smoke was getting thick. No one was shooting at him anymore, so he crept out of cover on his knees and elbows. He traded his blaster for the rocket launcher when he came to it. In his opinion, bigger was always better.

The man had lost his weapon after one of the blasts. He felt helpless; the smoke stung his eyes so that he couldn't see. If he coughed, they'd find him. He wasn't sure, but he thought one of them was down here with them. If he could just get his hands on a gun! How many of them were there? How many of his people were dead? He didn't know. He had a bad feeling that he was going to die today, that they were all going to die today. When he saw the woman, he did what any good Reliance man would have done. He pounded the metal bar—his only weapon—into her head. She went down to her knees. Then he put a stranglehold on her and waited for her to go limp, but she didn't. Instead, she stood up, with him hanging on for dear life.

She plucked him off her back and pitched him against the truck as if he were a toy. The dazed man looked up into the laughing eyes of his opponent. He was gripped by cold fear; the thing he fought wasn't human.

"Go ahead, freak, kill me," he spat at her. "Some day they'll do away with all of you, and people like me...."

She went ahead and killed him.

David peered cautiously over the edge. Through the smoke he saw RJ, then he saw the man crouching behind what was left of one of the four-wheel-drive vehicles, his weapon aimed at her. David didn't think, he aimed the rocket launcher and fired. It's safe to say he didn't get the result he wanted. He missed the man and hit one of the vehicles. The man fell back, temporarily stunned, and a big hunk of the vehicle landed on RJ pinning her underneath it. David dropped the launcher and ran down the mountain as quickly as possible.

"RJ! RJ!" he screamed, running towards her. He knelt beside her. Only her head, shoulder and one arm were sticking out. Her eyes looked blank. David buried his head in his hands. "Oh, my God! What have I done?" He wept.

"You mean besides throwing a piece of car on top of me?" a pained voice cracked. Her eyes blinked.

David was only a little relieved.

"RJ! You're alive!" Clearly, from the tone of his voice he was sure she couldn't remain that way for long. Maybe the kindest thing would be to give her the blaster and let her end it.

"I'm not squashed, David, I'm just pinned," she said, ignoring the look of doubt on his face. "Push on that corner up there, maybe you can rock it enough so that I can pull myself free."

David put his weapon down. He put his shoulder to the chunk of twisted metal and pushed for all he was worth. "It's not budging," David said frantically.

"Keep trying. If you could just move it a little, I could get out," RJ was insistent, so David kept trying.

RJ felt him before she saw him.

"David." She pointed with her free hand.

David saw the wounded man trying to sneak away, but he didn't care. The important thing now was to free RJ.

The man started to run.

RJ was frantic. "Leave me, I'll be all right. Get after him."

"But, RJ, what could it matter? Let one get away."

"You don't understand, he knows what I am. He'll tell the Reliance..."

David didn't have to hear more. If RJ thought it was important, it must be. He nodded and took off after the man.

When David was well out of sight, RJ put her hand on the edge of the chunk of metal. She braced herself, took a deep breath, and threw it off of her. She stood up slowly. "Ugh! That smarted." She rubbed at her ribs and back, took one of the pills, and sat down to give it a few moments to catch. In a matter of seconds she felt fine.

She was torn. If she left David to catch the man, he might lose him, and then the man would get back to the Reliance and tell them what she was. If she got up and went after him herself, David would become suspicious. There was no way around it; she'd have to take her chances that David could catch the man. Besides, it wasn't really very likely that they would believe what the soldier had to say anyway.

The man had been hurt by the blast, and David easily overtook him. David leaped, caught hold of the man's heels, and the man fell to the ground with a thud, face first into the dirt.

The man kicked out of David's grasp and jumped to his feet. David got up as quickly as he could. He expected the man to flee again, but he didn't. David didn't see where he got it, but suddenly the man had a knife in his hand. He lashed out at David and David barely stepped out of the way in time. David silently thanked RJ for not listening to him when he said he knew how to fight. She had taught him some basic martial-arts techniques, and one of the things she had taught him had just saved his life. Another trick she had taught him allowed him to use the soldier's failed attack to bring him down. As the man passed, David brought his knee up, kicked out and landed his foot just below the guy's knee. The soldier hit the ground hard.

"Why fight for the Reliance?" David asked. "Why not put down your weapon and join us?"

The man rolled quickly into a sitting position. He looked at David. David had no weapon, but he did. "Die, Rebel." He jumped up and ran at David.

David wasn't ready. He managed to grab the hand that held the knife and keep himself from being stabbed, but he wound up on the ground with the soldier on top of him.

The soldier smiled. He smelled blood—David's.

They wrestled with the knife, but David realized that the man was much stronger than he was, and better trained. In a minute his strength would give out, and the man would stab him. David knew he wasn't going to get out of this through strength or skill. That left only one thing.

"RJ! RJ!" he screamed, looking at an imaginary personage. "Go ahead! Shoot him!"

The man's head swung around to look and his grip slackened just for a second.

A second was all David needed. He forced the knife back into its owner, and blood poured from the wound like water from a faucet. Quite by accident, David had managed to sever the man's external carotid artery.

The soldier looked at David, a look of sheer terror on his face. He knew he was dying, and it was because he had fallen for one of the oldest tricks in the book. His limp, lifeless body pitched forward, landing on David like a bag of wet sand.

David had to work at getting out from under the body. When he did, he couldn't hold what little lunch he'd eaten. He couldn't believe what he'd done. True, he had cut Cobal's dead hand free of the manacle, and he had shot the GSH with a rocket launcher sending him flying through the wall, but nothing had prepared him for this. Nothing could have. The man had looked at him as he died. David had seen his life drain from him. He was covered in the man's blood. It smelled sickeningly sweet; he'd never forget that smell. He watched where the blood pooled up in the dust at his feet as it dripped off his clothes, and then he threw up some more.

He had hunted this man down, and he had killed him. Nothing could be the same now. The man had run, and he had chased him down and killed him. Why? Because RJ had told him to, that was why.

RJ! RJ was still trapped under the chunk of car.

He raced back as fast as he could, sighing with relief when he saw RJ sitting on a rock, rubbing her ribs, a pained expression on her face. He ran up to her.

"How did you get out?" he asked.

"Did you get him?" she asked, not looking up. If she had, the answer would have been obvious.

"Yes," David said hotly.

"Good," RJ replied.

"Good," David repeated, sounding sick. "A man is dead." He looked around him in disgust. "A lot of men are dead."

RJ's answer was to get up and limp over to the truck. "Don't you feel *anything?*"

"Hungry." RJ sighed as she turned to face him. "We are fighting a war, David. It's us against the Reliance. This was partly your idea, if I remember correctly. These men fought for the Reliance. That made them our enemies. You can't win a war unless you kill the enemy. That's just one of the rules of this game."

Logical. David gave her an angry look. How could she be so damned cool about the whole thing? People were dead, and the hard, cold fact was that his companion didn't give a damn as long as she got what she wanted. Sure, RJ had killed a lot of people, but that didn't excuse her complete detachment from the whole thing. David knew that no matter how many men he killed, he would never get used to it.

RJ opened the doors to the truck, then smiled. She was apparently very pleased. "A shipment of the new Z-27 Laser sidearms."

She looked at David. "So, now what do you say, David?"

"I don't know if it was worth it," he said, looking at his blood-covered feet and the carnage all around them.

RJ snorted angrily. "OK, Mr. Conscience. Why don't you jump on your high horse, ride up to the top of the cliff and get our equipment and the truck. I'm sure your conscience wouldn't allow you to dig through the pockets of these dead men and take all their units."

David nodded and left gladly. RJ placed some charges at the bottom of the rubble pile, got behind the truck and detonated. She was good at this. A path was cleared wide enough to get their truck through.

"God damn it, RJ! Tell me when you're going to do that!" David screamed from atop the cliff. "I might have been in the blast area for all you know."

"Oh, bitch, bitch, bitch," RJ grinned. She went about the tasks of picking pockets, making sure the dead bodies stayed dead, and picking up the soldiers' fallen weapons. She had just finished when David arrived with the truck.

"You sure you can load these crates?" David asked indicating her leg.

"I'll have to, won't I?"

"I could do it myself," David offered.

"It would take too long. I'll be fine. When the convoy doesn't call in, the Reliance will send a reconnaissance team, and they'll no doubt be Elite. May even have a GSH with them."

David had never worked so fast in his life. The truck bulged with its load. They covered it with a tarp.

"Maybe we shouldn't take all of them."

"Ah, you worry too much," RJ took a can of spray paint and started to paint her name on the roadway.

"Do we have time for that?" David sounded worried and more than a little irritated.

"Always," she said with a smile. Finished, she threw the spent can down, got in the truck and they sped off.

"I still say we shouldn't have taken them all. It looks like we're carrying something we shouldn't be," David said.

"Our first drop is close. We'll leave the top layer there. That should make us less conspicuous and get some weight off the axle." RJ obviously wasn't worried. She started to hum.

David gave her a hard look, and she grinned.

"OK, OK, I'll stop."

"RJ, just how did you get free?" David asked curiously.

"One of the alcohol tanks on one of the vehicles exploded. By a stroke of luck, the explosion pushed up the piece I was trapped under just enough so that I could get free." It was so absurd that he bought it without further question.

RJ took a coin from her pocket and bent it over yet another link of chain. Coins on her chain, like trophies on a shelf.

David shook his head and looked at the blood on his clothes.

The Z-27 Laser sidearm was smaller and, unlike the bulky plasma blasters, had no kick. It was deadly accurate, and RJ was very pleased to have them to add to her hidden arsenals. David was surprised and impressed by the piles of supplies RJ had scattered across the countryside. In old mine shafts, under the floorboards of abandoned buildings and in holes in the ground covered with plastic tarps and tree limbs. Apparently she had planned to do more than raid supply trains long before she met him.

By the time they returned to Alsterase, they had hidden all but one crate of the weapons.

They struggled up the stairs with the crate.

"I still say you're nuts," David whispered. "If we get caught with this crate of lasers..."

"We're not going to get caught," RJ said as they struggled around a corner.

"We're carting them around in broad daylight. Any one could see us," David whispered back urgently.

"How will anyone know what's in this box?"

"Oh, I don't know, RJ," David said sarcastically, "but they might read the side of the box right here where it says 'Reliance Arsenal, Z-27 Laser sidearms'."

"No one pays attention to what's written on a box," RJ said, shrugging it off. Just then, they met the manager. His immense bulk made it all but impossible to get up the narrow stairway.

"Oh, how lucky for us! You're back!" he said flippantly. "You'll be happy to know your room's just like you left it, no door, gaping hole in the wall, etc. So, what's in the box?"

"Just what it says, Z-27 Laser sidearms," RJ answered.

David squirmed. If he could have reached her then, he would have punched her in the mouth.

"Yeah, sure, everybody's a wise guy." The manager gave her a patronizing laugh. "I'm telling you right now, if that's a dead body..."

"What if it is?" RJ said, poking him in his fat stomach with a finger of her free hand.

"I'm not cleaning it up," the fat man said heavily.

"Our room is well enough ventilated that it shouldn't bother anyone."

Turning to David, RJ continued in the same sarcastic tone, "Come on, honey, let's take Irving home." They continued their trek up the stairs.

The manager shrugged and started back down.

"Do you delight in making me squirm?" David spat.

"Well, you are kind of cute when you do it," RJ answered with a smile.

Finally, they reached their room and gratefully set the crate down. They looked around. As promised, their room was just as they had left it. Gaping hole in the wall, everything totaled, door gone. What David couldn't believe was that the bike was there, and seemed to be in one piece. He supposed they had gotten their bluff in. David ran and threw himself on the broken bed.

"Guess there really is no place like home."

# Chapter Four

They took the bathroom door and hung it in the front doorway. It was about five inches short, but beggars couldn't be
choosers. Of course, this meant they had no bathroom door.

RJ had just taken a shower and now she was drying off.
David found himself watching her. Just for a second, he got
an uninvited picture of those long legs wrapped around him,
those breasts pressed tightly against his chest. He shook the
thought from his mind, and made a conscious effort not to
watch her.

It had been an incredibly long time since he'd had a woman.
Too damn long if he was looking at RJ. A woman should be
soft, sweet, and gentle. Someone to be protected. Any woman
who would break a man's neck with her bare hands and then
eat a sandwich was not the girl for David.

RJ started to dress. First she pulled on straight-legged black
pants, then a white tank top. She pulled on her boots, strapped
on her blaster, and then started wrapping the chain around
herself. This time, she just wrapped it around her waist. David
preferred this to the way she had been wearing it. She threw
on her jacket.

"Sure you won't change your mind and come with me?"
she asked.

"No, I think not." David rubbed his head. He still
remembered catching the beer bottle with his skull and remembered stopping alongside the road so RJ could pull the
stitches out.

"I'll stay here and guard the lasers. Bring me something to
eat."

"OK, but I can't promise I'll be right back." RJ started for
the door.

"Why not?" David wanted to know.

"Don't wait up." She grinned and went out the door.

First she took the truck back to the exact spot where she had "requisitioned" it. Then she walked back the five blocks to the Golden Arches. It was just twilight, and the air was cool and filled with the smell of food being prepared. The smell from one restaurant was particularly sweet, and RJ decided to come back there to eat and get David's dinner.

Whitey Baldor sat at a table with a brunette in his lap. He'd just eaten dinner, had a few drinks, and was planning to take this girl and do what he wanted with her. He couldn't have been happier. He didn't even notice the hush that fell across the bar till some jackass had the utter gall to sit at his table and flop his boots right next to Whitey's drink. He quit kissing the girl and looked up to see who had dared to interrupt his space.

"You!" he said in disbelief.

"Me," RJ smiled broadly.

"Get up," Whitey ordered the girl in his lap.

"But, Whitey..." she started to protest. Whitey dumped her on the floor.

"What do you want?" Whitey growled at RJ.

"Want?" RJ repeated innocently. She watched the dark-headed girl walk away in a snit. "I don't want anything. I've brought your truck back with a full tank of alcohol." RJ found the barrel of Whitey Baldor's gun pushed firmly against her head. "It pulls a little to the left, and it's not very good on fuel, but nothing that couldn't be repaired with a few minor adjustments."

"I could blow your brains out right here Lady, crowd or no crowd. You're in Alsterase now. No one gives a shit. I could..." He cut his speech short. Something very cold, hard and sinister was nestled against his balls. He looked at RJ, who just smiled.

"You might blow my brains out, Mr. Baldor, but not before your balls bounce off the far wall," she said, still smiling.

She moved the pistol against him. "I don't see any reason that we can't talk civilly."

"You got this thing about my nuts, don't you, lady?" Whitey withdrew his pistol, wiping the sweat from his brow as she took her weapon away from his privates.

"Could I get a beer!" she yelled. She was quickly brought one. The usual bar noise started up again. The moment of tension was over. She sipped at the beer.

"What do you want from me?" Whitey asked again with venom.

"I think it's fair to say that we got off on the wrong foot," RJ said.

"Your foot, my balls," Whitey said harshly.

"Knee," RJ corrected with a smile.

"Your brains for my nuts is looking better and better," Whitey hissed. "You made me look like a fool in front of the whole bar."

"You *did* start it," RJ reminded him gently.

"You stole my truck," Whitey continued.

"I *borrowed* your truck. For which I am willing to pay you," she said with a crooked grin. Now she had Whitey's full attention. "Is there somewhere we could go?"

Whitey was game. The owner, a personal friend (well, maybe not a personal friend, but someone who believed that Whitey could shove him into a beer bottle, butt first) had an apartment in the back of the bar. Whitey wasted no time in dragging RJ—under the watchful eyes of all the patrons of the Golden Arches—into the back room and shutting and locking the door.

"OK, baby," he took off his shoes and flopped down on the bed. "I'm ready to be paid."

"Fine." RJ reached into her jacket pocket and pulled out a laser pistol. She tossed the pistol onto the bed beside him.

"What's this shit?" He picked up the weapon. He wanted the woman, not a damned laser. Then he noticed the design. He stood up. "This is the new laser Z-2-11!"

"Z-27," RJ corrected.

"Where did you get it?" Whitey asked.

"I stole it—God! Men ask stupid questions."

"It's very nice, but not exactly what I had in mind," he smiled. "Let's call this laser the first installment." He reached out and touched the side of her face. It felt good, but she pulled away before he could get any further.

"Let's call it payment in full," she stated firmly.

"Does it have any trade-in value?" he asked hopefully.

RJ laughed. "Think of it this way. Sex lasts only a few minutes, but a good laser side arm is forever."

"You only say that because you haven't been with me," he bragged. He knew from the look on her face that he wasn't going to talk her into anything. He didn't understand any of this. "Why?" He held up the laser. "I mean, you had already gotten away with it."

"My friend and I have decided to take on the Reliance. Having done this, the last thing we need are more enemies."

"You know, we could do wonderful things for each other," he said with a sigh.

RJ laughed. "I'd better go."

"No! Wait a minute," he jumped in front of the door. "If you walk out now, they'll know we didn't do it. I have a reputation to protect."

RJ smiled.

"If you could maybe make a little noise?"

She grinned and nodded.

"Thanks."

She groaned. "Like that?"

"A little louder. I don't think they can hear you." He went over and started bouncing on the bed. "So, tell me more about this suicide rebellion of yours."

"Are you interested?" she asked.

"It depends on what the membership package includes," he said with a smile.

She groaned again.

"Oh, that's much better; that does credit to our race."
She gave him a look.

"Sorry, is it supposed to be a secret? It's obvious to anyone with half a brain, but hey, my lips are sealed. You know,
taking on the Reliance isn't like beating up a bunch of drunks
in a bar. No one can beat the Reliance." A statement of fact
with undertones of bitterness.

"You've done a very good job removing the mark," RJ said.

"Don't get any ideas, lady. I wasn't a political prisoner,"
Whitey informed her.

"And I'm no lady," RJ said.

"Then why are we faking it?" Whitey asked with a broad
smile.

*Why indeed,* RJ asked herself, but she knew why. Want,
need and desire, were old enemies of hers, and the hardest to
fight. Still, she managed an answer.

"You don't have to be political to hate the Reliance. You
don't need to be political to fight them." As she finished she
let out another long moan.

"Say yes," Whitey prompted.

"What?" she asked in disbelief.

"Say 'yes.' Scream it ecstatically," he begged.

"For the life of me, I don't know why I'm doing this," she
said, and then said "yes" just in the way he had requested.

"Beautiful," Whitey said with a sly smile. "Before you try
to win me over to your cause, I think you ought to know that
I was sent to prison for killing my wife."

RJ looked at the way he jumped up and down on the bed.
"No doubt you fucked her to death," she guessed.

Whitey laughed. "No, I just hated her guts. The damned
Reliance demanded I marry her. I hated that cunt. So, one day
she burned dinner, or some damned thing, and I planted a
hatchet in her brain." He had hoped to shock her.

"Hey, a man can only be expected to take just so much,"
she said. "Well, that's the last moan you're going to get out
of me."

"Too bad, I was just starting to enjoy this." He quit bouncing, and put on his boots. He picked up the laser and stood up. "Keep this hidden?" he questioned.

"That would be best, yes," she said.

He walked over to her and messed up her hair. When she started to protest, Whitey commented, "You have to look authentic." He looked at the chain. On impulse he grabbed one of the loops and dragged her against him. He kissed her on the mouth quickly, then released her. "Now you look like you've just been kissed."

Her protest died unspoken. She groaned. "I like you. You're incorrigible."

Whitey nodded and reluctantly opened the door. He held it for her as she walked out, then he followed. When he caught up to her, he put an arm over her shoulders. She put her arm around his waist, and he walked with her out of the bar.

She stopped just in front of the door. "Whitey," she protested, "how far does this charade have to go?"

"I was hoping it could go back to my place," he said with a roguish grin.

"I think we've gone far enough," she said.

"Not for me."

"You're pushing it," she hissed.

"Well, at least kiss me goodnight. For them, not for me."

"For them, not for me," she said.

He took her in his arms and kissed her. He didn't find her all that unwilling. It was a good three minutes before she even attempted to push him away.

"Whitey," she protested. "Whitey!" she said more urgently.

"What, what?" he asked angrily. "You like it, I like it. Let's go back to my place..."

"I hardly know you," she said quickly.

"So that never stopped anyone," he said. "At least not here in Alsterase."

"I kicked you in the balls," she reminded him.

"I forgive you," he said with a shrug.

"Then I'll do it again," she said with a sly smile.

He took a step away from her.

"OK. All right."

She started to walk away.

"Wait a minute." He caught up to her.

She looked at him suspiciously.

"I just want to know your name, then I'll leave you alone."

"Why?" she asked.

"Because I'm a sensitive guy. I like to know the names of women I'm going to have explicit sexual fantasies about."

"RJ. My name is RJ." She left.

As promised, Whitey didn't follow. He watched her till he could see her no more, and it was only then that he realized what she had said. RJ! She said she was RJ. He decided right then that if she was *that* RJ, he would follow her. Of course, at that point if she had been Dogaretha, the Death Whore of Valgares, he would have followed her.

RJ sat down in the restaurant, ordering for herself and something for David. She smiled when she thought about Whitey Baldor. He'd be a good ally if he could ever get his head out of his pants long enough. The food was good, and after her own cooking, she ate it with pure delight.

She saw the man walk in, and watched the waitress walk over to him. The waitress made the mistake of looking up at RJ, giving them away.

No doubt, the man had been looking for her.

She remembered seeing the waitress leave earlier. It had only been for a few seconds, so RJ hadn't though too much of it. Apparently she'd been gone long enough to contact this man. As RJ watched she saw the man give the girl money. A lot more than he'd have to pay for the cup of coffee he bought. She ate her dinner as if she didn't know she was being watched. When she finished, she paid, picked up the sack for David, and left. As expected, the man followed. No doubt hoping she would lead him to her friend. She turned a sharp corner, her shadow following quickly.

He saw nothing. The alley was a dead end. Then he heard something behind him.

The shape that separated itself from the shadows was obviously female. She held a weapon.

He moved to draw his own.

"Oh, I wouldn't," she said coolly. She walked over and took his weapon from inside his jacket. "So, why follow me?"

"I don't know what you mean." No doubt he thought that he could bluff his way out.

"Then I'll tell you." She pulled up his sleeve and ripped the communicator off his arm. This time she checked to be sure it was off.

"It's just a watch," the man said.

RJ crushed the communicator in her fist and let the pieces fall to the ground. "And I'm just a girl. Come on, man. You can't kid a kidder." She smiled at him, her white teeth shining in the darkness of the alley.

"What are you going to do to me?" The man had gone from cocky to terrified in a few short seconds.

"That depends on what you tell me." She rubbed his chin with her laser. "Why were you looking for me?"

"You and your friend killed a GSH. The Reliance wants to know how," he answered.

"Nothing about the Elite and the secondary on the pier?" she asked curiously. The man's eyes got big. "Oh, so you didn't know who did that. People in Alsterase are pretty tight lipped. Still, I guess blowing a GSH through a wall and making it go splat all over the ground is the sort of thing people tend to talk about." She paused to laugh at him. "So, did you find out what you needed to know?" She laughed again.

"A bitch freak," the man mumbled it, but RJ still heard him.

He shouldn't have said that. He shouldn't have said that at all. She grabbed the man by his collar and lifted him off the ground. "I can't help what I am," she hissed. "You *chose* to be a Reliance spy." She holstered her weapon and dug the wallet out of her pocket. She carefully replaced the wallet after extracting one small pill. She held her palm flat and showed the pill to the man.

He pulled his head back.

"Do you know what this is?"

He didn't answer.

"Do you?" She hissed the words with venom, and shook him till his teeth rattled.

"It's Pronuses," the man answered with a gulp.

"Do you know what happens to a normal human when he takes Pronuses?"

He knew. He tried to squirm free, kicking her in the process. It was a futile attempt, it didn't even phase her.

"Interesting statistic on Pronuses. Did you know that the suicide rate is incredibly high among Reliance spies? Guess the job gets them down. You'll never guess what they use almost exclusively." She held out the pill. "Pronuses."

"They'll never believe I committed suicide," the frantic man whined. "I've got no reason to kill myself."

"Oh, that's lame, desperate and lame. The Reliance doesn't give a damn about you or anyone else. Do you really believe that they know whether you're a candidate for suicide or not? Do you really believe that they care?" She shoved the pill in his mouth, past his closed teeth, and down in his throat. By the time she let him go he was dead.

She picked up David's dinner from where she had set it on the ground and marched back to the restaurant. The waitress was obviously surprised to see her back so soon, or at all for that matter. Reliance spies usually killed the people they were spying on as soon as they found out what they needed to know. It was just tidier that way. RJ ordered a cup of coffee. When the waitress brought it, RJ grabbed her arm in a vice-like grip.

"A Reliance man followed me when I left here," RJ said accusingly.

"You're hurting my arm," the girl protested in a whisper.

"Good, good," RJ grinned wickedly. She forced the girl's hand to lie flat on the table, then dumped cup of hot coffee on it. The girl let out a scream.

The guy behind the counter started to come to her aid. RJ pulled her blaster with her free hand and aimed it at him; he stopped in his tracks.

"A small accident," RJ explained making it sound like a threat.

She didn't let the girl's arm go. She gave the girl a menacing look.

"That's a bad burn. Could have been worse; could have been your face."

The girl started to whimper.

"I don't want anyone to know you talked to that man. I don't want anyone to know he was looking for me. I don't ever want to turn around and see that anyone's following me, ever again. If I do...do I have to get vulgar, or do you get the idea?"

The girl nodded her understanding.

"Good, good," RJ said with a happy smile. "I hate to waste good coffee." She finally let go of the girl. She stood up, and picked up David's dinner. "Notice that I am not leaving a tip." She laughed wickedly as she left the restaurant.

RJ woke him up to eat. Having eaten, David now found he couldn't go back to sleep. He looked at RJ where she lay. Even in her sleep the arm jerked. That must be irritating as hell. He imagined she was probably used to it.

For some reason, David couldn't quit thinking about his family. When he had been ten, his younger sister died of a disease which RJ had recently told him was easily cured. Two years later, his mother died in childbirth. He now knew that this, too, was uncalled for. The Reliance had the medicine and the technology, but why waste it on work units? In the Reliance, people were an expendable commodity.

One day, not long after David's mother died, the Reliance came and took his father away. He had done something, but they never told David what. His father was sent off to a prison camp, and David was moved into the home of another family. A family that couldn't afford him any more than they wanted him. They made sure he knew he was an inconvenience for them and delighted in telling him that his father's selfishness would ruin them all. It was during this time in his life that he first started to harbor the idea of overthrowing the Reliance.

Somewhere in David's mind, he had long cherished the fantasy that his father was alive. That someday they would be reunited. But after David's first week in prison, he had to admit that his father was dead, that he was an orphan.

He wondered about RJ. Did RJ have a family somewhere? Did she have parents who loved and worried about her? He couldn't see RJ with a family, couldn't place her as sister or a daughter. If she still had family living, she never talked about them. Perhaps they had a falling out. David got the impression that if you fell out with RJ, you fell all the way out.

Suddenly, he was feeling melancholy. He missed his family. He wanted to wake RJ up and ask her about her family, but if he did, she would no doubt rip his arm off and beat him to death with the bloody stump.

He could vividly remember playing with his sister in the road in front of their cottage. His mother would walk out every few minutes and tell them not to play in the road. Stupid advice; there was no place else to play, and the only traffic was the Reliance evaluation team which drove through once a month.

There was never much time to play. When their work shift came up, they would go as a family to the fields and work. Even this was a fond memory for David, because at least they had been together. When their last work shift ended, they would go home and eat a quiet meal. Sometimes, after dinner, they would walk down to the village viewscreen and watch the carefully regulated Reliance programs. Most of them he realized now were little more than Reliance propaganda, but at the time it had served as their only form of entertainment, their only link to the world outside their village. Each day was pretty much like the one that had gone before.

That was not the case in Alsterase, not the case anywhere where people were free.

# Chapter Five

He really couldn't be bothered. As head of Reliance's Sector 11-N, he had more important things to do than worry about such trifles as this.

"So, this RJ person has raided another shipment," Jago said blandly. "So what?"

"She had help this time, Excellency. We found one set of civilian footprints. There may have been more. After all, we know she wears Elite boots herself," General Right explained.

"So?" Jago sighed out.

"We lost an entire convoy, Sire. The shipment stolen was of the new Z-27 laser side arms," Right said with urgency.

"So?" Jago still didn't get it. What did any of this have to do with him? Didn't the military take care of this sort of thing? He stretched out on his giant pillow, looked around the sheik-like elegance of his surroundings and sighed yet again. "Can't you take care of this without bothering me?"

"We need your guidance, Excellency," the General said. Jago lay there like a great beached whale. Beautiful women hurried around working hard to fulfill his every obese desire. Right hated Jago, but Jago had power, and Right was smart enough to know that he had better not wipe his own ass without written orders from Jago.

Jago was infamous for blaming anything that went wrong on his underlings. He also had a bad habit of having the people he blamed executed. So Right, who was a perfectly capable individual, never did anything without orders in triplicate from this stupid, obnoxious blob.

Jago was busy playing with the right tit of one of his lovelies, and was totally ignoring Right. "Excellency, I really think you ought to take these rebels more seriously. This is the sixth convoy that has been attacked, and the sixth shipment stolen in the last ten months."

Jago snorted in disgust, oozed to an upright position and picked up the report. Without so much as glancing at it, he ground out, "OK, we've got six convoys lost to this RJ person. Now you say this rebel has help, but you don't know how much. What the hell *do* you know?"

"We know she's female because she saw fit to write that out for us on her first raid. We have deduced that she must have been an Elite at some time. We don't know anything else. We haven't been able to pick up enough DNA to make any sort of test. She's not stupid, that's for damn sure."

Jago moved his immense bulk to a standing position, and began to pace back and forth. This was very bothersome. Rebels used to be happy to hide during their work shifts, take more than their share of food and cheat on their taxes. Why did they suddenly find it necessary to pick up weapons and blow up convoys? And why did they insist on stealing weapons that Jago was completely unfamiliar with? They were ruining his day. He flopped into his throne with a great dispatch of blubber, and tapped his chins with his finger in a very discontented manner.

Life could be a real bitch. This whole episode had done nothing for his heartburn. Rebels looting supply trains, as if it were perfectly normal and above-board, troops that couldn't stop an old lady from jaywalking, and a General who wouldn't ball his wife without orders in triplicate. There were days when running all of Sector 11-N could be a real drag.

"OK Right, I'll bite. What do you want me to do about it?"

"If we could shift some of the GSHs off their regular assignments and put them with all the important..."

"Get the papers, Right, and I'll sign them. I'm tired of all this." Jago waved his hand dismissively.

"As you desire, Excellency." Right clicked his heels and went off to do the necessary paper work. Putting GSHs with the supply trains might be a little extravagant, but it would certainly be effective.

The young man stepped into the laboratory and was silent. He waited patiently at the old man's shoulder.

Finally, the old man sighed and looked up from the sophisticated electron-escalating light-infused microscope he was using. He didn't like to be disturbed. "Yes, what is it, Poley? And make it quick. I'm very busy."

"You wanted information on the random unit?" Poley asked.

Suddenly, the old man's eyes sparkled with interest. Professor Stewart clasped his hands together in an excited manner. "So, what has the little devil done this time?" he asked with anticipation.

"She has destroyed another convoy," Poley smiled a small smile. "It was carrying some of the new Z-27 laser pistols. All Reliance Personnel were killed. All Reliance vehicles destroyed."

Stewart broke into a bout of hysterical laughter. He patted Poley on the back. When he finally quit laughing, a fanatical gleam entered his sky-blue eyes. "Do you realize what's happened, Poley?" He didn't give Poley a chance to answer. "She has taken it upon herself to fight the Reliance. And, as if that's not good enough, she's winning!" He turned back to his work at the microscope. "Despite all her training, all the years she fought for the Reliance, she's rebelled. She's turned her hand against them," Stewart said happily.

"You sound as if you hope she will win," Poley said.

"Who cares one way or the other?" Stewart said with a shrug. He looked up from the microscope. "We're scientists, Poley. We're not political. The important thing is that the experiment is a success."

"Of the twelve units, only this one still lives," Poley reminded him.

"One out of twelve isn't that bad," Stewart said defensively.

"Those are not very good odds. I calculate that if this one does not stop her fight against the Reliance, she will not live beyond six more months," Poley said. "Then the experiment will be a..."

Stewart pulled a box from his pocket and pressed a button on it. Poley became totally immobile.

"Damned cocky machine," Stewart humphed. "Give a robot a personality, artificial intelligence, and the best years of your life, and what do you get? Back talk. That's what." He looked at the deactivated Poley for only a moment. "Uppity robot." He reactivated him. "What do you say?"

"I'm sorry, Dad," the robot looked down at his feet. "I'm just worried about RJ, that's all."

Stewart just stared at him. He shook his head and laughed. "Really, Poley. Sometimes you surprise even me. I'm sure RJ will be just fine. After all, you are only my *second*-greatest creation."

# Chapter Six

RJ heard someone pounding on the door, so she got up and pulled on her pants. The knock became more urgent, so she picked up her blaster.

"Who the hell is it?" She tried to sound alert, but the truth was that she didn't feel up to a fight just now.

"It's Whitey Baldor."

RJ sighed with relief. "Come in," she lowered the weapon only when she saw that he was alone. "I'd ask you to sit, but..." she shrugged around the room.

Whitey was not a man who closed his eyes to the obvious. Yes, he saw the hole in the wall, but that was not what caught his eye. There was only one bed. The man slept on one side, and the covers were pulled back on the other. Obviously, RJ and this man were lovers. He wondered for a moment what someone like RJ was doing with a wimp like that.

"So, Mr. Baldor..." she started.

"Whitey," he corrected with a smile.

"So, Whitey, what can I do for you?"

He smiled broadly.

"Let me rephrase that question."

"As long as your friend is asleep..." Whitey winked.

"Don't you ever give up?" she asked with a grin.

"Not till I get what I want," he said. "Right now, you're at the top of my list."

It was at this time that David woke up, but he preferred, for the time being, to pretend to be asleep. He wasn't sure that he liked what he was hearing.

"You may have a considerable wait. Care to fight a war while you're waiting?"

"Ah, why the hell not? If you're really RJ," Whitey said.

"Don't I look like an RJ?" she asked.

"As a matter of fact, yes." He looked at David. "You know it's all over town that you and I" he coughed, and RJ smiled. "I, of course, love the publicity, but aren't you going to get in trouble with him?"

By now, David was positive that he didn't like what he was hearing.

"I'm not afraid of David," RJ said, dismissing the whole thing.

"Oh, is that his name?" Whitey smiled. "That's cute. So, tell me, is it love, or just mutual lust?"

"None of your business," RJ replied with a sly smile.

David could pretend no longer. He sat up and rubbed his eyes. When he opened them, he took a double take. "Him!" he screamed angrily. "You slept with him!"

RJ didn't like the tone of his voice. "I'll do as I damn well please." She wrapped the chain around her waist and over her shoulders.

"Do you think you could quit panting long enough to help me patch up this wall?" she asked Whitey.

Whitey smiled broadly. "I could give it a shot." He followed her out of the room, but paused before closing the door to look back at David.

"You might as well accept it. I'm going to take her away from your scrawny ass." He swung the door closed with an air of self-confidence that made David fume.

"Smug fucker," David cursed the door. The vision of RJ with this great hulking lummox drooling all over her made David's blood boil. He felt very much the way a father feels towards his daughter; he didn't want RJ himself, but he didn't want anyone else to have her, either. Especially not this giant blond jerk.

David got up walked to the hole in the wall and looked out. What was that? He saw it again. Someone had moved down there. Behind the old dumpster. He couldn't see anyone now. The funny thing was that David was sure that whoever it was had been watching, looking for signs of activity. It might just be paranoia, but he decided to tell RJ when she returned, just to be on the safe side.

Willie Jones, who preferred to be called Mickey, ducked quickly behind the dumpster. He didn't know whether it was a good idea to be seen or not.

It hadn't been difficult to find out where the platinum blonde goddess was staying. Not after she had blasted the GSH through her wall. He had been watching, waiting for her return. Now she was back, and he wanted very much to get in touch with her, but he would wait till she was alone. Mickey'd had no cause to trust anyone save himself, but now he trusted the woman. She had gone out of her way to save him when she'd no reason for doing so. All his life, no one—not parent, grandparent, aunt or uncle—had gone an inch out of their way for him. They had shoved him back and forth like a hot potato. When it became obvious that he wasn't going to grow, the Reliance had sent a message to his family saying that they would be coming for him. Even at twelve Mickey had known what that meant. He left home and went into hiding.

It hadn't been too hard to pass himself off as a child. What was hard was earning a living. Since Mickey couldn't risk Reliance involvement, he just sort of fell between the cracks. No one was going to take on an extra kid unless the Reliance ordered them to. To stay alive, he had learned to pick pockets—a career at which he excelled. Eventually, like most who have fallen out of grace with the Reliance, Mickey wound up in Alsterase.

He wanted very much to belong to something. This woman's interest in him had given him hope that he wouldn't have to spend the rest of his life alone. If being with her meant going up against the Reliance, so much the better.

RJ and Whitey scavenged the streets of Alsterase gleaning materials from structures long ago abandoned. When they came back to the apartment with their haul, David looked at it skeptically, but it soon became apparent that RJ and Whitey knew what they were doing. In less than two hours, the hole was patched.

While it couldn't be said that it was as good as new, it would keep the cold out and the warmth in. At least you couldn't see out of it.

David hadn't helped much. In fact, he hadn't helped at all. He was mad, and didn't even attempt to hide the fact. He did offer to go get lunch.

"Good idea, I'm starved," RJ said.

"Fine," David huffed. "Money, RJ?" He held out his hand, and she gave him a fistful of units. "Well, I'll just be going then." He left, being sure to slam the door good and hard on his way out.

"What in hell is wrong with him?" RJ said hotly. Whitey just shrugged. If she didn't know, he was damned if he was going to tell her.

"So, RJ, want to make the walls go thump?" Whitey asked, flopping down on the bed.

RJ laughed and shook her head.

"No, huh? Well, then how about I jump up and down on the bed, and you can groan," Whitey smiled broadly.

RJ laughed louder.

"I'm serious."

"What was your military specialty?" RJ asked.

"You're changing the subject. I was talking about sex," Whitey told her.

"Humor me," RJ said with her best crooked grin.

"I was Elite. I specialized in small arms and gorilla warfare. You?"

"I've been a colonel—temporary battlefield promotion. Lieutenant mostly." She played with a link of her chain. "Also Elite."

"Most of us are. So why did you leave the Corps?" Whitey was more than a little curious. Being Elite was a privilege.

Elites rarely decided to just defect. There was no reason for them to rebel; they had everything they could want. Except real freedom of course. He wondered what could have made her leave her post and go after the Reliance with such a vengeance. He would have stayed right where he was and probably never noticed what was wrong with the world if they hadn't made him marry that fucking bitch.

"Simple enough. I don't like their tactics. I don't like the idea that some people are better than other people just because they were born into a high-ranking Reliance family. I like to fight; I won't lie about that. But I can't feel good about fighting if I don't think I'm on the right side, and cleansing missions aren't really my idea of sport. To make a long story short, I shot the CO in charge of the slaughter, ran like hell, and here I am."

Whitey nodded his head, satisfied with her answer.

They were laughing by the time David got back, and he practically threw their food at them.

"I ran into a man at the restaurant who was only too happy to tell me that you slept with him," David said hotly, pointing at Whitey.

"So?" RJ shrugged.

Whitey turned away so that they couldn't see him fighting his laughter.

"So? Is that all you have to say for yourself? So?" David shouted.

"I *didn't* sleep with him, but I don't see why it should matter to you if I did." RJ did not even do him the courtesy of being defensive. Hell, she didn't even stop eating. "Really, David, why should you care who I fuck?"

In spite of himself, Whitey let out a laugh. He couldn't help it. David gave him a hot look, and Whitey shrugged. "That's the problem with a military bitch, Mac. Very cold, very calculating, and not very compassionate."

David was silent. He started to eat, giving RJ dagger-filled looks the whole time.

Finally, she could stand it no more. "Why are you looking at me like that?" she demanded.

"Like what?" David asked innocently.

"Ugh!" RJ growled in anger. She tried to ignore him, but he wouldn't be ignored.

"If you want to fuck everyone in Alsterase..." he started.

"I didn't fuck him, but even if I had that would hardly be everyone in Alsterase," RJ said through gritted teeth.

"...I don't care. I mean, it's certainly none of my business," David said haughtily.

"I'm glad you understand that. Now, will you just let it lie?" RJ went back to eating.

"Fine!" David said on what was supposed to be a final note. Of course, it wasn't. "It's bad enough that you did it, but then to lie about it."

RJ murmured a curse. "You're sick, David," she said. "You're a sick man, and you obviously need help."

Whitey unceremoniously kicked off his shoes and lay down on the bed as if he belonged. He was for the most part, forgotten at this point.

"Everyone thinks you're living with me and sleeping with him," David said indignantly.

"Oh, and you must uphold your reputation," RJ mocked.

"Fine," David started for the door.

"Where are you going?" RJ asked.

"Out to get laid," he said bluntly.

"You better take some money with you," RJ said in a hateful tone. For some reason, the thought of David's having a woman distressed her, but she hid it well.

"I don't need money, smartass," David stomped out of the room.

Whitey looked up at RJ. "You know, as long as he's going to condemn you, and he's gone, we might as well..."

RJ shook her head.

"Are you having trouble understanding 'no,' Whitey? Has it got too many syllables for you? Thanks for the help. Don't be a stranger."

He was being dismissed. She opened the door, Whitey got up, grabbed his boots, and walked out. He turned briefly. "You really don't know what you're missing," he said, winking.

"Yes, I think I do," she smiled. "Take care, Whitey." She shut the door.

RJ sighed, and leaned against it. "God, men are assholes."

Her eyes were still dry from the Pronuses, and she was going to have to do something with her hair and nails before the rapid growth was detected. She went to the bathroom and washed her eyes with water, then she dug the kit from her pocket. First she pulled out the knife and cut her nails. It was no easy task. The toenails were especially hard. She dumped the clippings into the toilet and stood in front of the mirror. She hated to cut her hair. She never seemed to be able to get both sides to match. As a result, she usually wound up cutting it shorter than she had originally intended. Unfortunately, this time was no different, and she had her hair a good inch shorter than she wanted it. She dumped the hair into the toilet with the nail clippings and pumped the handle. She had a moment's anxiety when it looked like the toilet wasn't going to flush, but after a few curses and some tinkering, all was clear. She gave her hair one last disgruntled look, and went into the other room.

For the first time she really looked at the room. She was living in a pigsty. David was off fucking some bimbo, and she was living in a pigsty.

Without really thinking about it, she started to clean up the mess. Originally, she thought that she'd just remove the obvious junk, but before she knew it, she was searching the building for cleaning supplies. The janitorial supplies were practically nonexistent, so she decided to bring it up the next time she saw the fat man with the corpse fetish. Every time she thought about David, she scrubbed a little harder. By the time she admitted that she was mad—about what, exactly, was unclear—the whole place was spotless, and the smell was gone. She sat down on the crate of lasers and surveyed her handiwork.

"It's still a dump, but at least it's a clean dump," she muttered to herself. "No place like home," she added on a sarcastic note.

Then it hit her like a brick. Home. She'd never really had a place to call home before. A sleeping bag in a barracks full of people she had no desire to know. Alone with no privacy; the worst possible scenario. Never any place she could call home.

Then her thoughts turned to David. He had been gone a long time. She wondered what he was up to, and if she was pretty. She stood up and started to pace. The longer she paced, the faster she went. The faster she went, the madder she got. Why did she care if he had a woman? It was certainly none of her business. Hell, let him have a dozen for all she cared! Except that she *did* care, and that was, of course, what made her the most angry. She knew that logically she should kick back and spend the rest of the evening contemplating anything except what David was doing, but all she really wanted to do was track this whore down and rip her face off. When a knock came on the door, she snapped.

"Now who the fuck is it, and what the hell do you want?"

"Is Mickey," a small, unsure voice choked out.

It took only a second for the name and voice to register. She mentally chastised herself.

"Wait a second, buddy," she took a deep breath, and then went and answered the door.

Mickey looked reluctant to enter.

"I'm sorry, Mickey, it's been a rough afternoon."

He gathered his courage and entered. "If a bad time..."

"Not at all, why don't you sit down?" RJ said, waving towards the box of lasers.

Mickey waddled over and sat down.

"It's good to see you."

"I watch island. Find out things...don't know name?"

"RJ."

His eyes lit up with recognition, and he stared at her as if expecting the spectacular at any moment.

"So, what have you found out?" she asked as she sat down on the bed.

"About island, not much. Fishermen swear is haunted. Say see ghosts and hear strange sounds. I watch. Many times see lights." If he'd had a tail, he would have wagged it.

She looked thoughtful for a moment. "If there are lights, then someone is over there."

"What I thought," he said.

"What about recruits? Would any of these assholes fight? Would they join us?"

"Most think fighting Reliance useless."

"At least we know they're not stupid," RJ said with a grin.

"Not cowards, either. If prove can win, might be inclined to join." It sounded like he was telling her so little, and he had worked so hard to find all this out. He hoped it would be enough to get him accepted. He had no way of knowing that RJ would have recruited a dog if she thought he was loyal.

"Stand up and look in that box you're sitting on," RJ said. He did so, and his eyes grew wide with delight and awe. He was a thief, and such a theft as this obviously impressed the hell out of him.

"They're the Reliance's newest hand-held weapon. I want you to take one."

Mickey was excited. He knew that the offering of the weapon meant he had been accepted, but...

"Remember what happen last time?" Personally, he hadn't been happy with the results. He rubbed his behind and grimaced

RJ smiled at the memory of the midget with his butt jammed in a bucket.

"This is a laser, not a blaster. It has no kick. That's why it's the new, improved weapon. Take one, you'll need it."

He picked it up reluctantly, but once it was in his hands, he smiled.

"Keep it hidden."

He nodded.

"Needless to say, I'm not supposed to have them." She showed him how it worked. "Come on, let's go have a look at those lights."

Mickey held on for dear life as RJ drove the motorcycle down the stairs.

The fat man met them in the entrance hall. "Hey, how many times do I have to tell you? No riding motorcycles in the building. It's in your lease..." He kept screaming as she roared out of the building.

RJ's driving didn't scare Mickey. He felt as if nothing could happen to him as long as he was with her. It was a feeling of security the likes of which he had never before experienced.

RJ parked the bike beside the rickety pier. She got off and, much to Mickey's amazement, picked him up and put him on her shoulders. She walked onto the pier. The boards creaked under her feet. She stopped. Sure as hell, there were lights on the island. She clicked her tongue.

"I wonder who's out there, and, more to the point, why?"

"All the time watch. No boats come. No boats go. No helicopters," Mickey informed her.

RJ nodded and looked thoughtful. "Could it be some Reliance thing?"

"Don't know."

She looked at the lights again. It was no trick of the water and the city lights. It wasn't a reflection. There were lights on out there.

"It's certainly curious."

"Want me keep watching?" Mickey asked eagerly.

"Yes, but quit asking questions. It wouldn't do for people to know that we're interested." RJ turned and started down the boardwalk.

"You hungry?" she asked.

"Always." Mickey liked the view from RJ's shoulder. For once, he was looking down on people instead of up. Life could be a real drag when all you ever saw was people's asses.

They went into the first restaurant they came to. Both RJ and Mickey ducked as they came through the door. RJ took Mickey from her shoulder, and they found a table.

"What ya want?" the waitress asked shortly.

RJ looked up at her and smiled a satanic smile. The waitress cringed. "A little respect, for one thing," RJ said through gritted teeth.

"Sorry, ma'am," the waitress said quickly. "It's been a long day. What can I do for you?" It had been a long day, and the last thing she needed was to get her ass kicked. This had to be her. This had to be the woman who had kicked Whitey Baldor's ass in the Golden Arches.

RJ ordered and the waitress placed the order promptly. She brought the beers at once. "Your order will be ready shortly."

"Thank you," RJ said with equal politeness.

Mickey lit a cigar.

RJ shook her head. "Didn't anyone ever tell you that smoking will stunt your growth?"

Mickey smiled and stuck the cigar in RJ's outstretched hand.

She took a long drag and handed it back.

"Hear you and Whitey Baldor are having a thing," Mickey said conversationally.

"Don't believe everything you hear," RJ said with a smile.

"Whitey Baldor's a nasty piece of work," Mickey told her.

"So am I," RJ took another drink of her beer. "He hates the Reliance. That's the only credential you need to join my army. I don't give a damn about his manners."

"So, are you and Whitey having a thing?" Mickey asked with a mischievous smile.

RJ shook her head and smiled. "Mickey, it would shock you to know just how virtuous I am."

David experienced no trouble at all picking up a woman, getting her to take him back to her place, or having his way with her. He certainly felt a hell of a lot calmer than he had in weeks. He'd needed a woman's attentions, and this one had been good. But it was late, and he wanted to go home now. He sat on the edge of the bed, getting dressed.

"Do you have to go, lover?" the woman asked, as she rubbed against him in a provocative manner.

"I'm afraid so," David stood up and finished pulling up his pants and zipped them. "It's been nice."

"Can I see you again?" she asked.

David looked at her. She was a dark-haired beauty. He smiled and nodded.

"Yeah, sure...sometime." He pulled on his boots, blew her a kiss, and was gone.

When he returned to the apartment, it was obvious that RJ had been busy. It was even more obvious that she wasn't home. No doubt she had gone off somewhere with that giant person. He went into the bathroom, stripped and started the shower. He heard the front door open.

"RJ?"

"Ax murderer," RJ answered.

"Where's the bike?" he asked.

"I decided to make lard-ass happy and leave it in the lobby," RJ started to take the chain off.

"The apartment looks nice," David told her.

"Thanks," she finished taking off the chain and let it fall to the floor. She sat down on the bed.

David really had no idea what possessed him at that moment, but the words were out of his mouth before he could stop them.

"Where were you?"

He heard the curses as he turned off the water. Damn it, he couldn't help it. He'd never really got to be a big brother to his own sister. Now, he wanted to protect RJ, but damn her, she didn't want or really need protecting.

He was just stepping out of the shower when RJ stormed in, obviously ready to let him have it. He cringed in anticipation. He knew from past experience that RJ wasn't likely to pull any punches. She'd call him every choice word that came into her head.

RJ was prepared to let him have it. *Hypocrite* came to mind; so did *slut* and *miserable-mother-fucking-pencil-dicked-moron*. She took one look at him standing there buck-naked, and didn't say a word. It didn't make any sense. How many men had she seen nude? A hundred, two hundred, a thousand? She'd never felt like this before. Her heart was pounding, her breath seemed to come in gasps, and her palms were sweating. Must be some new reaction to the Pronuses. She should have called him a stream of profanities that would make a whore blush, but the words wouldn't come.

Finally she said, "Everyone in Alsterase is getting fucked except me. If you don't believe that, I don't give a shit." She left him in the bathroom alone, but didn't quit looking at him. She wondered if he'd had a woman, then knew, instinctively, that he had.

"Fucking whore," she mumbled.

"What's that?" David was brushing his teeth, and hadn't heard what she'd said.

"Nothing," she took off her pants, and hurled them against the wall. It was irrational, but she felt better. When he came out of the bathroom, she went in. The shower didn't make her feel any better.

She could see David lying in bed, smiling stupidly at the ceiling. He was nice and content. She wasn't. She turned out the lights and got in bed beside David.

"RJ, I'm sorry that I made such a scene. If you want to sleep with that fellow, that is your business, and I had no right to..."

"Jump to conclusions. I told you I didn't sleep with him. You and I aren't lovers. Why should I lie to you about it, and why should you care what I do?" She rolled over so that her back was to him.

David put a friendly hand on her shoulder. "I'm sorry, RJ. I guess I got a little overzealous in my role as big brother. You forgive me?"

She made a noise that might or might not have meant yes.

David was in too good a mood to assume that it was anything but agreement. He lay back to get comfortable. "RJ, what were your parents like?"

"I was raised Elite," RJ said quickly.

"Huh?"

"I was an orphan, or a bastard, or something. I stood out from the other kids. So, instead of being sent off to the work camps, or farmed out to some other family, I was raised Elite. If you're raised Elite, you go right into service. You never really know anything else, and you can bet on going in as an officer."

"Do you ever wonder about them?" David asked.

"Who?"

"Your parents."

"No." There was a final note in RJ's voice.

For once, David let it lie.

# Chapter Seven

The next week RJ stayed more or less at home. She wanted to give the side effects of two doses of Pronuses so close together a chance to subside. Mickey took up residence with them, feeling very privileged to have a moth-eaten twin-sized mattress on the floor.

David found a way to occupy his time. He took to going out on a nightly quest, the object of which was to bed everything with hips and tits in the entire city. So far, things were right on schedule. He had everything it took to impress the local women; he was tall, good-looking, breathing, and had a dick. The girls of Alsterase were neither too particular nor particularly moral. Anyone, anytime, and anyplace. If they were attached you might have to give them a second to get rid of their current mates.

David was out, bent on yet another conquest, so RJ decided to go out as well. Whitey and Mickey were only too glad to tag along.

They sat at the corner table after persuading a young man and his girlfriend that they didn't want to sit there. The place wasn't packed with atmosphere nor was it particularly clean, but both Whitey and Mickey assured RJ that the food was the best in Alsterase. The three of them were a sight to see, so it was no wonder that they were looked at with a certain amount of interest. This lot stood out even in Alsterase, which was quite an accomplishment.

After eating, they relaxed over their first round of drinks. RJ went so far as to plop her feet in the middle of the table. Whitey draped a huge arm over her shoulders.

"I really don't see why you put up with it," Whitey said, playing with a lock of her hair.

"What? You slobber all over her?" Mickey asked lightly. Whitey gave him an angry look, and he shrugged.

Whitey returned his attention to RJ and repeated. "I don't know why you put up with it."

"OK, Whitey," RJ said in an exasperated tone. No doubt he was going to hit on her. After all, it had been almost twenty minutes since his last attempt. "What?"

"David's gallivanting all over town, poking anything that will stand still long enough," Whitey said.

RJ shrugged. "I don't care what David does," she said with a flip of her head. Both Whitey and Mickey laughed at the lack of conviction in her voice. "I've told you both before, and I'm telling you again. David and I are not now, nor have we ever been, lovers. I really don't care what he does."

"All right, RJ. Then, if everything between you and David is so..." Whitey paused in thought, "what's that word?"

"Boobs!" Mickey said.

Whitey gave him a confused look.

"Look at boobs on waitress." He pointed.

RJ hit his hand.

"Oh!" Mickey protested, and rubbed his hand.

"RJ, if everything between you and David is so...ARG, what is that damned word?" Whitey hissed.

RJ had no idea what compelled her to fill in the blank for him. She knew damn good and well what he was up to. "Platonic," she said, helpfully.

"Exactly. If you and David are so platonic, why can't you and I..." he whispered something particularly wicked in her ear.

"No." RJ said quickly.

"You're a cold bitch, RJ," Whitey whined in mock despair.

David staggered home. The woman had been a disappointment. Her looks had promised so much, and she'd had so little. It wasn't fair. It really wasn't. Sometimes it seemed to him that the more beautiful a woman was, the lousier she was in bed.

He'd had far too much to drink. That, he admitted, hadn't
helped. The combination of bad sex and too much liquor
had given him the granddaddy of all headaches. All this fun
was wearing him down. He wished RJ were home, but she
wasn't.

"Off with the boys again, you bitch." He laughed at his
own joke, then held his head. RJ's jacket was lying on the bed.
It was a stroke of luck, because she usually wore it. He'd seen
RJ take pills out of her pocket. No doubt they were pain pills.
He rummaged through her pockets till he found the leather
pouch, pulled it out and opened it. He saw the pills. Smiling
with the anticipation of relief, he walked into the bathroom
and filled a glass with water.

RJ had been about to suggest that they leave when the stranger
walked in. "You ever see him before?" she asked her companions.

They both said no.

"He doesn't look like trouble to me," Whitey didn't understand her curiosity. He wondered whether he should be jeal-
ous or not.

"He also doesn't look like your typical Alsterase riffraff."

He was a tall, thin, good-looking man. No growth of beard,
his clothes were well cared for, and he was clean. Militarily
clean.

"You think he's a spy?" Mickey asked.

"If he is, he's being awfully blatant about it," RJ said.

"Whitey and I will create a diversion. You pick his pocket."
Mickey nodded eagerly.

"Why, you two-timing slug!" RJ screamed, standing up
and slinging the rest of her beer in Whitey's face. Whitey didn't
have to act shocked. He jumped up, slinging the beer off
himself. As every eye in the place turned on them, Mickey
slipped away.

"You platinum blonde bitch," Whitey screamed back. "I
ought to knock the crap out of you."

"Do it and die, fuckface," RJ said, poking him in the chest.

"Oh, I love it when you talk dirty to me," Whitey said with a broad leer.

RJ fought her smile. "Fuck you, Whitey Baldor!" she screamed.

"I wish you would," he grabbed her and kissed her full on the mouth.

When he let her go, she whispered, "What the hell are you doing?"

"Creating a diversion," he grinned. He bent and kissed her throat.

She gave up and laughed. She kissed Whitey on the cheek, and they both sat down. Mickey crawled out from under the table, as if he had been hiding there till the fight was over.

"Get it?" RJ asked him.

He looked hurt.

"Would I not?" He took the billfold from a pocket, and handed it to her under the table. She opened it and began to examine the contents.

"Well?" Mickey asked eagerly. Whitey, on the other hand, was totally occupied with chewing on RJ's earlobe.

"Three hundred units, a picture of a naked woman..."

"Let me see," Mickey moved so that he could look over her shoulder. Apparently he wasn't impressed, because he sat down again.

"Ahha!" RJ said in a pleased-with-herself tone.

"Ahha, what?" Whitey came up for air long enough to ask. Without waiting for an answer, he moved to her neck.

"Discharge papers, *dishonorable* discharge papers. Our stranger used to be an Elite Captain. It gets better. He was a pilot—starship class," RJ said. She looked thoughtfully back at the man. "He could be useful to us." She was trying to decide whether she should approach him or not when three of the local bully-boys decided to hassle him. "Shit!" RJ said.

Whitey gave up on her temporarily.

"What?" he sighed.

"Oh nothing. It's just that I've had such a pleasant evening, and now I'm going to have to kill those men," RJ said coolly.

"What ya want here, stranger?" the lead bully-boy asked.

"To live a quiet life," the stranger was obviously scared, but trying not to show it.

They laughed at him.

"Live a quiet life," the lead bully laughed. "In Alsterase?" He kicked at the man's stool.

"Leave him be," RJ ordered.

"Keep your woman out of this, Baldor. We got no beef with you," he said, turning toward Whitey. He wasn't afraid. The three of them could take Baldor, and he saw nothing to fear in either the woman or the midget.

Whitey laughed. "Zero, no one owns this woman. You'll see why if you persist in starting trouble."

"The name is Zant." Losing interest in the stranger, Zant motioned to his buddies, and they moved toward the table where the three were sitting. "I don't mind kicking your ass, Baldor, or screwing your woman while you're unconscious. So why don't you just stay out of this?"

"It's a shame that a man who is such a prick doesn't have any balls," RJ said coolly. She didn't move. Not even so much as to take her boots off the table.

One of Zant's boys got antsy waiting for the fight to start and pulled his knife.

Mickey swung his arm out from inside his jacket, and fired the laser he clutched in a white knuckled fist.

The man fell dead.

RJ moved quickly. She jumped up, taking the midget with her.

Whitey overturned the table, throwing it with a growl.

The other customers either fled, ducked into safe spots, or donned protective headgear.

RJ dumped Mickey on the floor, and he ran to hide behind the bar. As far as he was concerned, he had done his part.

Zant and his pals were joined by two more who had stayed in the background until then.

RJ looked at Whitey, and smiled. "Well, at least it's a fair fight now."

"Shall we?" Whitey asked, bowing slightly and motioning RJ forward.

"You first, dear," she offered with equal politeness.

"I'll use you, you smug bitch," Zant promised.

"You'll have to get it up first," RJ chided.

The fight was on. Zant drew a knife and ran towards RJ. She simply grabbed the wrist that held the knife as it came at her. She pulled the arm out of its socket, then slung Zant into the floor, face-first before he had time to scream. Then she stomped on the back of his neck, successfully putting him—and everyone else—out of his misery. One of the other men grabbed her around the throat with his forearm. She slung him over her shoulder and looked up in time to see another thug getting ready to hit Whitey in the head with a table.

Whitey was occupied at that moment with throttling a man against the far wall.

"Whitey!" She screamed the warning as the man she'd just thrown down got shakily to his feet.

Whitey let go of his man and turned, drawing his sword. He plunged it through the tabletop into the man's chest, and pulled it out in less time than it takes to tell it. The man with the table staggered and paused, but didn't fall. Whitey immediately returned to his interrupted labors.

As RJ's slightly dazed opponent pounced on her again, she hit him in the chest hard enough to stop his heart. He gasped once and hit the floor at her feet.

The man with the table was still staggering. Whitey took a finger and pushed on the tabletop. Man and table both went down.

"Whitey, grab them and let's go," she pointed to the pilot who was hiding with Mickey behind the bar.

Whitey grabbed the man by the collar and unceremoniously pulled him to his feet.

"Come on, Mickey," Whitey ordered.

Mickey ran to RJ, and she put him on her shoulder. They left the bar, Whitey pulling the discharged captain along by his collar.

"Ah, thanks a lot," he stammered. "Sorry I didn't help, but I'm not really much of a fighter."

"Pilots usually aren't, Captain Levits," RJ said simply.

"How..."

RJ held up his wallet.

He slapped his pocket. "Why, you...!" He reached for it, and she jerked it out of his reach. "Why did you stop them from beating me up? So that you could take my wallet?"

"I don't want your money." RJ tossed the wallet in his general direction.

"What then?" Levits asked while deftly plucking the wallet from the air. Nothing wrong with his coordination, at least.

"You're a pilot. You're a coward, but you were an Elite. So, in spite of what you say, you know how to fight. My friends and I are going to overthrow the Reliance, " RJ explained.

"Good luck," Levits laughed in disbelief.

"Did I say something funny, Whitey?" she asked him in an ominous tone.

"Not at all, dear," Whitey said, tightening his grip on Levits' collar just a bit.

"I don't like to be laughed at, Mr. Levits. Call it a weakness, a flaw. I have absolutely no sense of humor where that is concerned." She stopped and folded her hands behind her back.

Mickey quickly repositioned himself.

"Now, either you want to help us, or you don't. It's that simple."

Suddenly, the sight of the woman standing there calmly with a midget climbing all over her like she was a tree didn't look funny. Not funny at all.

"And if I say no, you kill me," Levits said.

"That is the Reliance's way, not ours. We don't want anyone with us who doesn't want to be here. We are fighting tyranny, Mr. Levits. I won't fight it with more of the same."

She motioned for Whitey to release him.

"Take some time, Mr. Levits. Think about it. If you have come to Alsterase, it's because you have nowhere else to go. Alsterase is a hard place, especially if one is 'not much of a fighter.' It's not the sort of place to be friendless, and it's not easy to make friends here." She tapped his cheek sharply.

"Come on, boys, let's go."

Levits watched them leave. He shook his head and laughed—quietly. "Fight the Reliance! She must be mad." He laughed louder. "Crazy bitch."

He looked down the long dark street. A cool breeze blew, and he pulled his jacket tighter around him. He set his mouth in a firm line. He didn't need anyone, and he certainly wasn't going to join her in her suicide rebellion.

David looked for some instructions in the leather pouch. It would be nice to know something about dosage, but several minutes of search turned up nothing. He put one into his hand. If one would do it, another would be better. He popped another into his hand. He was about to take the pills when he heard the door open.

"RJ?" he asked.

"Ax murderer," she answered. Mickey jumped down and retired to his mattress.

"That was only funny the first fifty times you did it, RJ," David replied testily. He was in no mood to deal with her questionable sense of humor right then. He walked out of the bathroom and held out his hand.

"How many of these do I take?"

RJ looked at them in panic. "Where did you get those?" she demanded.

For answer, he held up the leather pouch. Whitey saw the pouch. He'd seen them before; he knew what they were. Moreover, he knew what it meant.

RJ was across the room in a heartbeat. She grabbed the pills from David's hand and flung them down the toilet.

"Wash your hands, wash your hands!" she ordered.

When he didn't move, she pulled him into the bathroom and forced him to the sink. She turned on the faucet.

"Wash your hands." There was no denying her tone.

"What the hell is going on?" David asked, as he began washing.

"Those are poison, David. Lethal poison," she said.

"But I saw you take them," David said as he scrubbed even harder.

That confirmed it. Whitey had no doubts left. He didn't know how she came to be, but she was, and he knew what she was. Surprisingly, it didn't change the way he felt about her. One thing was for sure. She hadn't lied. She wasn't David's lover. Somehow knowing what she was made him feel better. Now at least he knew the reason she wouldn't sleep with him.

"I saw you take them," David said again as he scrubbed at his hands.

Whitey laughed. "Now, she would have to have an amazing constitution to do that. That's Pronuses."

"What the hell is Pronuses?" David demanded.

"It's a lethal drug." He looked at RJ in admiration and shook his head. "Only you could get hold of a freak kit."

She looked at him expressionlessly. He couldn't tell what she was thinking. He prayed he could block her as easily as she seemed to block him.

"My God, my hand's blistering!" David exclaimed.

"It's all right," RJ said, handing him a towel.

"Don't tell me it's fucking all right! I damn near get myself killed over a goddamned headache, and you say it's all right?" David wasn't feeling overly understanding at the moment. "Why are you carrying around lethal poison anyway?"

"It's a weapon." She shrugged. "You never know when you might want to poison someone. It's a lot more subtle than shooting, clubbing or stabbing. If you work it right, you don't even have to be there when they die."

David was more persistent than Whitey deemed to be safe at this moment. But then, he had two things up on David. First, he was relatively sure he knew why she had them, and second, he hadn't nearly eaten the damned things. For once, Whitey sympathized with David's reaction.

"I saw you take them," David persisted.

Whitey just laughed, as if he thought David were the world's biggest fool and flopped down on the bed.

RJ sighed in exasperation. "I had some pain pills; they're gone now. Want me to run out and get you some?"

"No thanks," David turned to the bed to lie down, but Whitey was lying in the big middle of it.

"Do you mind?" he asked sarcastically.

"Well, actually, I do, but..." Whitey got up. David lay down. "You know, David, someday I'll be staying and you'll be going."

"In your wet dreams," RJ said, not without a smile. "Good night, Whitey."

"Ah, but Mom, it's early yet," Whitey whined, then ducked out the door. "Good night, my love!" He waved flamboyantly, and was gone.

RJ sighed and started to unwrap the chain. It had been a long damn day.

"David, I'm really sorry about the Pronuses."

"I feel very, very lucky. Another second, and I would have eaten the damn things. Next time you're going to carry poison around, you might at least tell me." David was still sore. He wasn't really mad at RJ, it was just this damn headache. "I think Whitey is serious about you," he said in the best bantering tone he could muster.

"The only thing Whitey Baldor is interested in is getting a piece of ass," she said, although she knew it wasn't quite true.

"If all wanted was piece of ass, wouldn't hang round." This piece of wisdom from Mickey, whom RJ had believed to be asleep.

"What's that supposed to mean?" RJ asked indignantly.

"I think what he means is that if all the man wanted was a piece of ass, he could get that anywhere. Believe me, it's easy. If that's all he wanted, why on earth would he continuously hit on the only woman in all of Alsterase who actually has the word 'no' in her vocabulary?"

"Because I'm a challenge, I guess," RJ snorted and dismissed the subject. She finished undressing and went to bed. After several moments of trying to achieve a comfortable position, she decided it was impossible and gave up. She looked at the ceiling. Then she looked at David. *Wonder where you were. Idiot! You know where he was. Off with some slut making the beast with two backs.* An angry scowl crossed her face, and she resumed looking at the ceiling. *I don't care. I could have anyone I wanted.* She started counting cracks in the ceiling. *I wonder if she was good-looking...Well of course she was, David's too shallow to even look at a woman for any other reason.* She frowned. *I wonder if she was any good?* She looked at David again. He couldn't sleep either; he was frowning. RJ smiled and looked back at the ceiling. *I'm guessing that means no. Good. I would be amazing, because, after all, I'm good at everything...Provided of course that I didn't crush my lover during orgasm. Damn, now look what I've done...I'm depressed and horny.*

She sighed and looked over to see that David was asleep. She had half a mind to wake him up. *That's right, you bastard, sleep. God knows you get laid plenty. Hell, I don't even think you realize that I'm a girl most of the time. All the guys I used to shower with in the service...they used to get boners in spite of all the saltpeter the Reliance put in everything.*

David rolled over—so he wasn't asleep. What was more, from the look on his face, the headache was getting worse. *Good! I don't care if I am being illogical and petty. When you're as old as I am and you still haven't gotten laid, you're allowed to be illogical and petty.*

She tried not to think about David with other women,

because for some reason the thought was very distressing to her. Of course, the more she tried not to think about it, the more she did. And the more she thought about it, the madder she got.

Just then, David was unwise enough to speak to her.

"RJ?"

It took her several seconds to suppress the urge to scream interesting things at him, like, *You miserable whoremongering, womanizing little piece of shit!*

"Ugh." That was the only sound RJ could make when she was biting her tongue.

"Are you awake?" he asked.

"Ugh," RJ said again.

"Is that a yes or a no?" David asked with a laugh.

"That's a maybe," RJ said, trying to keep the angry tone from her voice.

"What's RJ stand for?" he asked.

RJ muttered a few choice curses.

"Ah, come on, RJ."

"Let it lie, David. Even if I told you, it wouldn't mean a damn thing to you. It doesn't mean anything. It doesn't stand for anything. My name is RJ. It's just something to call me instead of 'hey you!' Who cares what it means or what it stands for? Your questions will be the death of us all."

# Chapter Eight

It had been a long and tiring drive across half of the country.
The truck had suffered multiple breakdowns, and they'd been
stopped several times by the Reliance cops. Sometimes they
could bluff their way out. But when they couldn't, there was
always RJ's special way of dealing with people who became
annoying.

Now, it was just him and RJ. Getting ready to face God-
only-knew what, armed only with blasters and a cock-and-
bull story. David didn't really understand why they were here
or why what they were doing was important. RJ said do this,
do that, she explained what to do and how to act, but what she
had never explained was *why*.

"I don't know. It doesn't seem right waiting for
them...tricking them like this," David said.

"Right shmight," RJ said, checking to make sure her uniform was straight. "You wanted to do something that everyone would notice, and this can't go unnoticed, David. After
today, they're going to know we mean business. Don't get
squeamish on me." She straightened her uniform yet again.

"I don't know why you're bothering so much with looking
just right when you refuse to take that damned chain off,"
David said, then added in an exasperated tone. "Reliance cops
don't wear chains around their waists."

"I'm not a cop. I'm a freedom fighter," RJ said with mock
fervor, hands on hips, chin up staring into the distance.

"It's not funny, RJ," David said in disgust.

"Chill out, will you? I only have to look like a cop for a few
minutes. It just so happens that I'm not worried about my
disguise. I just want to look my very best when I assassinate a
governor. I've never done that before, you know."

"You're sick, RJ. I swear, sometimes I think you're really as warped as you make out to be." He gave RJ a contemptuous look.

She just grinned. "What can I say, David?" She shrugged and the grin left her face. "I am what the Reliance made me, and I love my work."

Jack Bristol was the governor in charge of military affairs for the area that was known by the Reliance as Zone 2-A. As such, he lived and traveled in luxury with an armed escort.

Four first-class soldiers armed with swords and riding motorbikes surrounded his armor-plated limo. He shared the limo with four laser-carrying Elites. And the driver, who was a second-class soldier, was carrying a projectile weapon. Because of this—and because Jack Bristol had never seen real combat in his life—the governor felt as safe as if he were in his mother's womb.

Jack was the first to see the barricade. "What the hell is that?" He didn't like to be delayed. As governor, he hardly ever was.

"It appears to be a barricade, sir," the driver informed him helpfully.

"I can see that, you fool," the Governor blasted. "What's it doing there?"

"I don't know, Your Worship," the driver replied, and stopped himself from saying. *No doubt it's there to annoy asshole bureaucrats in armor-plated limos.* He smiled at his thoughts and said over his shoulder, "No reports have come in over the radio, sir."

The entourage came to a halt. The only alternative would have been to turn around and go back the other way. That would have served no purpose. There was no reason for them to think that they were in any danger because there wasn't anything particularly strange about surprise road-blocks in the middle of Reliance territory.

The woman—obviously the commanding officer—walked purposefully over to the lead motorcycle.

"See what's going on," Jack ordered one of the Elites. The man got out, making sure that the door was closed securely behind him. He walked over to the woman, they spoke, and he returned to the limo.

"Well?" Jack demanded.

"There was a threat made that someone would try to assassinate your person on the stretch of road ahead," the Elite said. "They are checking the road for mines or ambush parties. It should only take them a few minutes."

"This is ridiculous! How could any rebel know our travel route?" the governor asked hotly.

"It was on the viewscreen that you would be arriving at Greenside base to do an inspection. This is the only route to Greenside Base..."

"Stupid PR people. They really don't understand the importance of security." Jack pulled a face. "Why didn't they contact us by radio?"

"They said that their equipment is acting up."

"Oh, that's par, isn't it? The viewscreens work, but our radios don't." Jack pulled a face. "All this talk of rebels makes me tired. Tell them to move. We can take care of any trouble we come up against."

"Sir, the threat came from RJ," the Elite warned.

"So? She scares me no more than any other rebel. Tell them to move their stupid barricade. I'm in a hurry. I've wasted enough time already," Jack ordered.

The Elite nodded and got out of the limo again.

As the Elite reached RJ, David joined her.

"The Governor says to move the barricade," the Elite informed them.

"Sorry," RJ said, and added on a final note. "My orders came down from Jago. We were told to keep this road blocked till they've made their sweep. I'm keeping it blocked."

"Between you and me, Jack Bristol is a real prick," the Elite informed her. "If you don't move that barricade, your butt's going to be in a sling."

"If I move it, and the Governor gets killed, I can put my head between my legs and kiss my ass goodbye," RJ said hotly. "You know Jago's policy. If it fucks up, kill it...I'll take my chances with Bristol any day."

"It will only be a few more minutes," David said calmly. "Surely, it's worth a few minutes of time to make sure that he arrives at Greenside Base in one piece."

The man looked at David and smiled. "I know that, and you know that. But the governor is in his armor plated limo, his god is in his heaven, and you would be hard-pressed to prove to him that he is anything but perfectly safe. Truth is, I doubt Ole Ironguts Bristol has ever seen open combat."

RJ and David both laughed.

"If you could just see fit to let us through..."

"Sorry," RJ said flatly.

The Elite mumbled a curse and returned to the limo.

"Well?" Jack demanded when the Elite returned.

"They refuse to move the barricade," he reported. "They are under orders from Jago."

"I can see I'm going to have to handle this myself. Oh, why must Jessy surround me with idiots?" Jack got out of the limo, ignoring the Elite's protests, and marched up to RJ.

"I want this barricade moved immediately!"

"Sorry, sir," RJ said.

The governor stopped just inches from RJ. "Do you have any idea what kind of trouble you're going to be in..."

"I don't think you are aware of just how dangerous these rebels can be." RJ posed purposefully. "Why, they could even pose as Reliance police officers and set up a barricade to stop impatient governors."

The look on Jack Bristol's face told her that he was only too aware of the laser pressed against his stomach.

"Keep your hand away from your gun, and I might, *might* being the operative word, let you keep your mid-section."

"This is an outrage," the Governor sputtered in an angry whisper.

"I'm a rebel. Outrages are my specialty."

She nodded at David. He moved into position, pulled the pin on the gas canister and lobbed it into the open door of the limo. Then he ran and kicked the door closed to keep the gas in.

One of the first-class soldiers pulled a projectile weapon he shouldn't have had, and RJ blasted him. A second went after David with his sword, and she bored him through the head. The other two fell before they even knew what was happening.

Governor Bristol stood there in stunned silence.

RJ smiled, removed his laser, tucked it into the folds of her chain, and put her own sidearm away.

"What is all this?" Bristol was scared. This bitch meant business.

"This is rebellion, Governor," RJ announced.

She looked at David. "Get it."

David nodded and went to the stolen police car. He emerged with a silver briefcase. The governor knew what they wanted now, and he shook with the magnitude of their crime.

"You can't open it without my help, and I won't help you," the governor announced.

"Oh, I think you will." RJ pulled the laser and pressed it against his head.

"You're going to kill me anyway," he scoffed.

"Use your brains. As long as you have hostage value, you're safe," she said. "As long as you don't give me any trouble, you're worth more to me alive than dead."

"The gas should have dissipated by now." She motioned towards the limo. "Of course, if you're not going to be cooperative…"

The governor moved over to the limo. The door was geared to his finger prints, and those of his entourage. No one else was going to be able to get in. He opened the door, and RJ smiled broadly. "Very good."

She motioned David towards the open door.

David threw in the dummy case, and pulled out a similar one. He coughed. "Damned shit! Damn you, RJ," he coughed again.

"Don't be such a wimp, David. A little sleeping gas never hurt anyone." She took the case, smiled, walked over to the hood of the limo and set the case down. Then she looked at the governor expectantly.

"Open it."

"And if I won't?" he asked.

"Then I kill you and take my chances. And yes, I know that the wrong combination sets off a charge that can blow up everything for a ten-foot radius. Therefore, my friend and I are going to stand way back here while you open it. Just in case I've read you wrong, and you are the hero type." She held the laser on him.

Jack hesitated. He looked at the combination buttons. He was a loyal Reliance man. Press the wrong buttons and he did them out of their trophy. Of course, he also blew himself up. Damn it, if he opened this case for them, he was putting a Pandora's box in their hands that would take the Reliance months to close, and they might kill him anyway. He keyed the first sequence of numbers.

If he opened this box, he was betraying the Reliance. He did the second sequence of numbers. Again he paused. He keyed in the third and final sequence and the lid flew open to reveal his personal computer. RJ smiled, walked over and closed the lid. The combination was now a permanent part of her memory. She picked up the case and smiled at the Governor.

"I thank you and the people thank you," she said.

She looked at David, and he came over took the case, and started for the police car.

She grabbed Bristol and started pulling him along.

He was surprised at the direction they were suddenly going in—not towards the stolen police car, but back towards his limo. She had no intention of using him as a hostage or for ransom purposes. Bristol's attention was captured by the body of one of the first-class soldiers that had fallen across the hood, his sword still clutched in his hand. If he could just stall her, there was a chance.

"Why me? What have I done to you? What have any of us done to you?"

"It's not what you've done to me, Bristol," she spat, stopping and turning to face him. "It's what you asked me to do to others. I was sent on a 'cleansing' mission. The order for the authorized slaughter of unarmed civilians came across your desk. You ordered it."

"The thinning of the population is necessary..."

"Then you should understand everything I do." There was a noise in the brush; nothing dangerous, probably a rabbit, and she turned only for a second, but it was long enough for him to pick up the sword and sling it into her side. Apart from a nasty tear in her shirt, nothing happened. She slung off the face shield and helmet in anger, and when she did a look of total shock crossed Bristol's face.

"You...But why? Why?" Total confusion. He obviously knew too much, so she shot him in the head before he could say anything else.

David came running up. He had seen the sword hit her. "RJ...!"

"And you didn't want me to wear the chain," she said lightly.

"Why'd you kill him? I thought you said he was insurance..."

"That's what I told him. I knew he'd consider himself to be too important to kill," RJ said grinning smugly.

"You planned to kill him all along!" David shouted in disbelief.

"It's not like I didn't tell you that I was going to assassinate him. If it makes you feel better, he did try to kill me," she said. "Think of it as reflexive. When someone tries to kill me, I kill them back."

David threw up his hands and stomped back to the car as RJ dragged Bristol's body over and loaded it into the limo.

She flung in a grenade and closed the door. She was in the police car before the grenade detonated. She looked back and grimaced.

"Yuck! What a mess."

David refused to look back. Just the thought of blood and various body parts thrown against unbreakable glass was enough to make him sick.

"Was that really necessary?" David protested.

"Dead people don't talk," RJ said, by way of an explanation.

RJ hit the siren, and they roared off. She patted the case and smiled.

"Now there will be no stopping us. We will be invincible." She let out a stream of maniacal laughter just to mock his moral concern, but the fanatical gleam in her eyes was real enough.

"I don't know, RJ," David said in a troubled voice as he shoved the case into a backpack to conceal it from view. "I'm beginning to wonder if the end justifies the means."

"Always! Always, if the end is freedom," RJ said sternly.

"What gives us the right to kill?" David asked hotly. "What makes us any different from the Reliance?"

"We are right, and they are wrong. That is all the difference I need." RJ was beginning to lose patience with him. David was the poop at every victory party.

David looked at the bag that held the case. "I just find it revolting that this little box is worth nine lives."

"Ten, but who's counting? Sit there and condemn me, David. I really couldn't care less. You talk like it's a game, at which you believe I'm cheating. This is not a game, David. It's a war. In war, people die. Whoever kills the most people wins. That's the only rule that counts."

She took the news of Governor Jack Bristol's death very hard.

Jessica Kirk was senator of Zone 2-A, but it wasn't because she had lost the head of her military that she ordered Reliance flags to be flown at half-mast. That wasn't why she had locked herself in her room and refused all visitors. Nor was it why she had flung herself across her bed and broken into tears.

Jack Bristol had been her lover, and she had loved him. She hadn't believed he was truly dead till she'd seen the body. Or, rather, what was left of the body. It had been all she could do to keep her composure intact till she got back to her room. Now she cried.

She cried for the empty feeling in the pit of her stomach, for wasted time and nights spent alone that could have been spent with him, and she cried for all the things she should have said, and never quite got around to. When she had finished crying, she decided to go after RJ.

She dried her eyes and went to her terminal. She punched up every bit of data on RJ, and then she called her new temporary head of the military.

"Fools, you are looking for the out-of-the-ordinary. Look for the ordinary. Look for a military or police vehicle. I want everyone checked out. If one of them doesn't belong, then you've found RJ. She couldn't have gotten more than a hundred miles away by now. Don't fuck up this time. I want her, and I want her dead. If anyone spots her, they are to wait for backup. I don't want her to get away. Do you understand, Perkins?"

"Yes, Senator," he said, "but...we have no idea what she looks like or..."

"She looks like someone tough enough to kick the asses of several Reliance soldiers at once. She looks like someone smart enough to make elaborate plans and carry them out successfully!" Senator Kirk yelled. "She looks like an Elite. Find a female Elite in that sector who isn't supposed to be there, and you've found her. Now get your asses in gear. If she gets away, heads will roll." she turned off her terminal.

She fought the tears.

"Fat, incompetent fool!" she screamed in rage. This was all Jago's fault. All her requests had been denied or overlooked. She talked daily with Right, and he was trying to do his best for her, but getting Jago to take any action more exerting then scratching his own ass was close to impossible. Now Jack was dead. Was it her fault? Was there anything that she could have done that she hadn't? She could think of no stone she had left unturned.

Till now, Jessica Kirk the senator had let the chain of command deal with this. In fact, Jack had more to do with the RJ thing than she had. But now, Jessica Kirk the lover wanted revenge. Suddenly it had become personal.

"Oh, you are clever, RJ. Very clever. But this time you have met your match. You can not fight me and hope to win," Jessica muttered into the emptiness of her office.

Jago and his band of fools had more or less ignored RJ, hoping that she would go away. RJ hadn't gone away, and now Jack was dead. Eventually, they would all pay, even that malignant tumor they called a sector leader. Yes, even Jago. They'd all pay for her grief—for Jack's death. But first she had to deal with the main perpetrator of the crime. First, she had to kill RJ.

She stood up. "I can be clever, too." She walked over to the mirror. "Let's see you match wits with a master." She stared at the image in the mirror. Her eyes were bluer than blue, and already clear of any signs that she'd been crying. She ran a comb through her platinum blonde hair and checked the makeup on her dark skin.

RJ was humming in her usual tuneless fashion. David was chewing his nails. He had quickly joined that group of people who firmly believed that people who couldn't carry a tune shouldn't try to sing, whistle, or hum. *Especially* hum. He was about to lose his cool and scream rather loudly at her, when she abruptly stopped. He immediately wished that she would start up again. The lack of humming no doubt meant that there was something a lot worse about to take place. His fear was confirmed when he saw RJ looking in the rear-view mirror.

"Don't look now, but we've picked up a military patrol," RJ announced cheerfully.

David turned to look, and a laser blast hit one of their tires.

RJ managed to put the vehicle into a controlled skid, and they stopped. "Damn! I told you not to look." She grabbed the pack that held the case. "Let's move!"

David didn't wait around for further instructions. He got out of the car and rushed to catch up with RJ.

"They're going to kill us," David whined.

"They're not going to kill us," RJ said. "Just keep your head, and do what I tell you. Here, take this." She handed him the pack, and he put it on his back. She started to unwind the chain.

The damned patrol was almost on them, and she was playing games. It wasn't a small patrol, either; a topless vehicle, three motorbikes and a three-wheeled ATV. The ATV was in front, and that turned out to be a bad place. As the three-wheeled contraption roared in for the kill, its driver met with the killing end of RJ's chain. The driver fell, but the vehicle kept going.

RJ jumped on the trike, and ordered it to stop. She quickly slung the chain around herself as David boarded, and she was off before the rest of the patrol realized what had happened. They recovered quickly, however, and the chase was on.

The trike wallowed like a pregnant cow. It had never been designed for more than one rider. Their pursuers were closing in, and the laser blasts they fired were getting closer and closer to their mark.

"They're going to kill us!" David moaned, close to hysteria. "They're going to kill us. You shouldn't have killed our hostage!"

"They're not going to kill us," RJ stated flatly, gunning the machine for all it was worth. She knew there was only one place that this beast was going to be able to stay ahead of the patrol: off the road. The problem being that there was no place to get off the road right here. RJ took a quick shot at their pursuers. Surprisingly, it hit one of the motorcyclists square in the chest and sent him flying.

Fortunately, RJ had driven these things before. On some of the outer planets, three-wheeled ATVs were the most popular mode of transportation. David had never been particularly happy with RJ's driving, and at this moment it seemed to him that if the patrol didn't kill them, RJ would.

"They're going to kill us! They're going to kill us!" David's whine was beginning to sound like a chant.

"They're not going to kill us!" RJ shouted over her shoulder, as she finally swung off the pavement and onto a dirt road. This gave her an edge. She still couldn't find a place to get into the woods. If she could find a small trail they wouldn't be able to follow. A laser blast clipped the trike's fender and showered David with sparks. RJ jerked the trike sideways and swung it down an even more primitive road.

One of the bikes skidded out in the gravel. The rider was thrown into a tree, and the bike slid on down the road.

RJ nearly lost it on a sharp corner, and the patrol gained precious ground.

"They're going to kill us...they're going to kill us...they..."

"They're not going to kill us!" RJ didn't need his pessimism. Just then, something tugged at her leg. She glanced down quickly. Nothing serious. Still, even a glancing shot from a laser hurt like hell. Now she was pissed.

The last bike made a bad move, slipped just a bit, and the car hit it. RJ sighed with relief and satisfaction. The ATV could easily outrun the car on this terrain. No sooner had this happy thought flashed by than the engine started to cough. A glance at the fuel gauge showed why.

"They're going to kill us...they're going to kill us...they're go..."

"David." RJ's voice was dangerously calm. "If you don't shut up, you won't have to worry about them, because *I'm* going to kill you. I AM GOING TO KILL YOU!"

The ATV uttered a final splutter and died. RJ jumped off the bike. "Someday you'll laugh about this." She gave his neck a quick, precise chop and caught him as he went limp. As she lay his unconscious form on the ground, the vehicle was almost on them.

"That's right, come on." She fingered the chain and smiled smugly. "Come on, motherfuckers. Let's get this over with, once and for all."

The soldiers stopped firing. One of the rebels was dead, and the other was obviously giving up. Live rebels were valuable. But suddenly, the woman wasn't standing still anymore.

"What the hell...open fire!" the captain screamed.

RJ ran at them full speed. Just as it seemed sure that she would make impact with the vehicle, she jumped and landed in the vehicle with them. The chain lashed out. In seconds, all five men were dead. RJ stopped the car and unceremoniously tossed the bodies out. Then she walked over to David.

"David."

No response.

She slapped him lightly on the face. "David. David, come on."

He stirred. "Ugh, what happened?" He opened his eyes slowly. "Was I hit?" Then he remembered. He jerked into a sitting position. "I *was* hit. By *you*," he accused.

"You were hysterical," RJ explained.

"I most *certainly* was *not*!" David said indignantly.

RJ raised her eyebrows.

"OK, so I was a little on edge. Couldn't you just slap me?"

"Not nearly as effective," RJ said with a crooked grin.

David gave her a hard look.

"I'm sorry, OK? I lost my cool. It was the first thing that popped into my head."

"Knocking me out! That was the first thing that 'popped into your head?'" David screeched.

RJ walked over and got into the car. "Are you coming?"

He hesitated, so she started to leave without him. He ran to catch up.

"Why are we going back this way?" he asked.

"To pick up one of those bikes. They must have been on the road looking for us a long time, and this damn thing's almost out of fuel, too. We ought to be able to siphon out enough to get us a full tank on a bike."

"Why did they just start shooting at us? I mean, they didn't even pull us over and question us!"

"Well, like I said, they had been on patrol for awhile. They were probably hot to shoot at something, and when we couldn't be reached over the radio…when we weren't on their frequency…" she shrugged.

"But what if our radio was broken, or…"

"The Reliance deals in statistics, David, not people. Odds were that we were their target. They were right."

"But what if they hadn't been?"

"I thought that was what the war was all about."

"Lost them?" Jessica screamed. "Lost them?" Her eyes blazed fire. She checked the map. "They've taken one of the bikes, but they still can't have gotten far." She drew a circle on the map. "Concentrate the search here."

"First thing in the morning, Senator," Perkins confirmed, saluting.

"*Now*, fool. Bring in fresh troops. They're running, but they'll try to rest. They'll have to. Now is the time to find them, and we're not going to stop till we do."

"As you wish, Senator." He bowed and left her office, happy to escape her presence.

RJ threw David a carton of the K-rations she'd found on the bike.

"I'm not eating. Not this crap, anyway." He set it on the ground beside him and lay back on his bed of leaves.

"It's all we have and could be all we have for awhile," RJ said. She sat on a pile of leaves she'd raked up and started to eat. "They weren't planning to be out long. No camp gear, no extra ammo. They didn't pack much food, either."

David sat up and watched RJ eat in disbelief.

"You're eating a dead man's food," David said with a note of disgust in his voice.

"Well, then he can't bitch, can he?" she asked with a smile.

"If you hadn't killed that man, he'd be eating that food right now," David said in a faraway voice. A shiver went up his spine.

"God, I hate it when you're morbid. It's just *food*. Peel off the foil top, pick up the fork on the left and eat," RJ said.

"I can't." David lay back down.

After a few minutes he sat up, picked up the tray, peeled off the top and started to eat.

RJ smiled smugly, but said nothing.

"I'm hungry," David growled defensively. "So, what's next? Satis?"

"God no!" She tapped the pack with the case in it. "This should tell us our next move." She'd finished eating and tossed her tray aside. She took the case out and started to hammer out the code.

"Careful, careful!" David said, flinching.

RJ just grinned as she opened the case.

"Damn it, RJ, why don't you write the combination down somewhere? One wrong number and you blow us both into tiny, bite-sized David and RJ pieces."

RJ just continued smiling as her fingers flew across the keys. "You worry about the damnedest things." She looked away from the screen just long enough to see that David was not at all happy with her cavalier attitude. "David, do you know what 'total recall' means?"

"I don't know, and I don't give a..."

"It means that I remember everything I ever saw, everything I've ever heard." She went back to the keyboard. "I don't forget *anything*. I'm certainly not likely to forget something as simple as the combination to this case."

"That must be great!" David said, impressed in spite of himself. "Hell, I can't remember my name half the time."

"Most of the time it's more a curse than a blessing." RJ's voice dragged. She didn't stop working with the computer, but she wasn't smiling any more. "There are some things that are better off forgotten. It can be real hell being able to remember in detail something you would just as soon forget." She smiled then. "A wise man once told me, 'Be careful what you wish for, you just might get it.'"

David finished eating. His curiosity aroused, he moved to sit behind RJ. He looked in awe at the print out screen. It was like the viewscreen in his village, except much smaller. Instead of pictures, there was a steady stream of letters and numbers. He understood that by hitting the keys, RJ was making the numbers and letters appear. Beyond that, he was lost.

"What do all those letters and numbers mean? Are they important?" he asked.

"Yes," RJ replied shortly.

"Well, what do they mean?" he asked again.

RJ sighed, then said in the most patient voice she could muster. "It's computer lingo. This computer is tied into Zone 2-A's military computer. All the data on military operations in the zone are stored there. With this portable model, I can access the main computer and extract any information I deem necessary. Because it is tied into the system, it won't show a break-in. It can tell us about any shipment of arms or anything else in detail. How many troops are in the convoy, how many vehicles, what sort of material they are transporting, et cetera., et cetera."

David understood now why the box was so important, and why they had gone to so much trouble to get it.

RJ stopped the scrolling on the screen. "Hum."

"Hum, what?" David asked.

"That's very interesting."

"What is?" These letters and numbers didn't look any more interesting to David than the others had.

"Most of the more important shipments are being accompanied by GSHs. Still, with this we ought to be able to avoid those. I wish I knew where we were. I could see if there are any troops close to us," she added thoughtfully.

"You mean you don't know where we are?" David asked in disbelief.

"Haven't the vaguest," RJ answered, obviously unconcerned.

"I thought you said you had total recall," he said.

"I do. I also have a lousy sense of direction. I can tell you this: we are somewhere north of the point where the patrol started chasing us." She shrugged. "There are no road markers on these pig trails we took. I know where we are in relation to where we were, but I can't put it into anything that I can use in the computer. I'm not too worried. They won't try anything till morning." Suddenly, she looked up and seemed to be listening. "Of course, I could be wrong." She packed the computer back into the pack, jumped up and ran for the bike.

David had learned to trust RJ's instincts. He got on as she started the bike. "What is it?" he asked.

"I hear bikes." She roared off into the woods, choosing not to return to the road. She also didn't bother to turn on the headlight. This was none too safe considering that it was now pitch black.

"RJ, the lights," David reminded her, thinking that perhaps it had slipped her mind.

"No!" was all she said.

David didn't argue. Actually, considering the way RJ drove, he'd just as soon not be able to see.

The Elite Captain got off his bike. The infrared scan showed where the bike had left the road. He got on his comlink. "Senator Kirk, this is Captain Sikes."

"Here, Captain," she said, but made him look at the back of her head.

"We've found where a cycle left the road."

Now he had her attention. She turned to face him. "Then don't stand there, imbecile. Get after them! I want those rebels dead!" she almost screamed.

"Yes, Senator."

"And Captain..." she added.

"Yes, Senator?"

"If you fail, I will not feel very charitable towards you."

Her tone made Sikes shiver. "I won't fail, Senator." He cut the link. "Let's move out." He started out with his four men on the trail of the bike. He had to kill these rebels or face the wrath of Senator Kirk. For some reason he didn't feel confident. He shouldn't be feeling uneasy. He had the scan, and with that he couldn't lose them. Surely, four secondaries armed with projectile weapons and an Elite with a laser ought to be able to overpower two tired rebels who'd been on the run all afternoon with no food and no rest. If nothing else, their bike should be running low on fuel.

They drove up on RJ and David's rough camp. Gone— damn it! Sikes saw an empty food tray and the piles of leaves. Damn! They'd eaten and probably rested—so much for *that* part of his fairy tale. He got off the bike, retrieved the food tray and looked around quickly. There was nothing to indicate that he was dealing with any more than two rebels. Good, he didn't need any more surprises. He stuck the tray in his pack and took off again, following the heat trail the rebels had left.

The bike lugged up the hill. It hadn't been designed for the kind of abuse it had endured since RJ seized it. The patrol was closing in on them. She now not only heard them, but she could see their lights. The bike reached the top of the hill, sputtered and died. RJ's attempts to start it were futile. She quickly jerked the battery off the bike and stuck it in the pack.

David just sat there.

"Come on, get off and let's go."

"What's the use, RJ?" David said. "Couldn't we just accept defeat gracefully?"

"I am a six-foot-two-inch woman. I don't do *anything* gracefully." She took a timed charge from her pocket, set the timer and stuck it to the bike's fuel tank. "Coming?"

David jumped off the bike and ran after her. They heard the explosion, and turned just in time to see one of the Reliance bikers thrown through the air. A split second, later the newly damaged bike exploded.

"One," RJ said in a satisfied tone. She started to run again, and David followed, shaking his head. RJ's sense of timing never ceased to amaze him. Somehow, she had calculated to the second when the patrol would come even with their abandoned bike.

Captain Sikes stopped just short of catching the blast. Now they were four. Sikes' illogical sense of doom mounted. He looked at the picture on his comlink—once again he was privileged to view the back of Senator Kirk's head.

"Senator."

She turned.

"Senator, I..."

"I take it that you do not have good news for me, Sikes," she said angrily.

"I've lost a man," he said. "But the rebels are on foot now, and we should have them shortly."

"How did the man die?" she asked curiously.

"An explosive device was set up on the bike. I see no tripwires, so I assume that it was a timed charge. They must have estimated how long it would take us to arrive at this point."

"She must know that you're tracking her with infrared," Jessica thought for a second. "OK. Stay to one side of their trail and be careful. She'll no doubt set more traps. You can't kill *them* if *you're* all dead. This RJ is no one's fool. From the data we have on her, it is more than likely that she used to be a high-ranking Elite. So, Sikes, help is on the way. All you have to do is keep a bead on them. In a few minutes, that whole area will be so full of troops that a fart couldn't get out. Just don't lose track of them."

"I won't, Senator," Sikes said. Communication ended.

He looked at his men. Two of them were busy with the body of their fallen comrade. "Leave him. If we don't catch RJ, what happened to him will seem like child's play."

They started off, but without their former enthusiasm, and using much more caution.

Sikes' lower lip trembled. His hands inside his gloves were unnaturally sweaty. He was an Elite. He'd seen combat before. Hell, the odds were in his favor, and more troops were on the way. The rebels were on foot now. The odds were all in his favor. Still...

He wondered how well they were armed. Hell, they had to be pretty well armed. They had killed the governor and his entire entourage, not to mention the patrol that had first spotted them. Another charge went off on the trail beside them. One of the men was startled and almost went down. This explosion wasn't as spectacular as the first, because it didn't have the added attraction of the alcohol tank exploding, but it still scared the shit out of them.

Sikes bit his lip to stop the trembling. He knew now that he was fighting something the likes of which he had never fought before. These two fanatics were fighting for a cause. How could men who fought for a paycheck and the dubious glory of plastic medals match their spirit?

Sikes was a Reliance man. He had a Reliance wife and two lovely Reliance children. All his loyalty belonged to the Reliance. After all, he had been raised Elite. He knew in his heart that the Reliance protected and nurtured the people it served. But he couldn't help but respect the people he hunted. They fought with a fervor that he didn't have now, and probably never had possessed.

The thought of a rebel Elite intrigued him. He knew he had never had the inclination. He really couldn't conceive of any Elite rebelling. Elites had it made in the Reliance. They got the best of everything.

He did know one thing. For whatever reason, she had to believe that she was right. Just like Sikes knew *he* was right. After all, that was the way wars got started, and *this* was *war*.

"Damn! I missed!" RJ stopped, and David tried to catch his breath. "They must have figured out what I did, and started to follow the trail to one side." She thought about it for a second, then grinned. "OK, assholes, try this." She took more charges out of her pocket and planted one on either side of the trail, taking care not to disturb the ground too much. After all, she didn't want the infrared to detect that they had done any more than walk by.

"I can't...believe it! You're actually...enjoying...all of this!" David gasped, exhausted. RJ grabbed his hand and started to drag him along. "I...don't know...if I can...go on," David said between gasps.

"Of course you can," RJ said. "You have to. That was the last of the charges."

"Great! No cycle...no charges...What do...we do...now?" he puffed. This had all ceased to be fun for him about two miles back.

"Now we improvise, David," she said simply. "Now we use our heads."

Sikes got on the comlink again. This time, Kirk was facing him, and he decided that this was worse.

"Well?"

"I've lost another man, and yet another needs medical attention. Two bikes were destroyed," Sikes informed her. He didn't know how he managed to sound so cool with his heart stuck somewhere in his throat. The wounded man was screaming in the background.

"What happened this time?" Jessica demanded.

"She must have figured out what we were doing. The second charge missed us—it was on the trail, we weren't. She set charges on both sides of the trail this time."

"Imbecile! You should have known that she would change her tactics to match yours. She's obviously timing you. Change your pace. Set no patterns. Go back and forth, on and off the trail. That should throw her off. If she had mines, she'd have used them by now. I will not tolerate failure, Sikes."

"Yes, of course, Senator." This time, it was Sikes that cut the link. He looked at the smoldering remains of the bikes and the rider.

"You, ride with him."

The man did as ordered, in spite of his barely functional leg.

"What can you do to me, Senator?" Sikes mumbled. "If we fail, there won't be any of us left to punish."

Sikes was following the other bike, so it was that bike's driver who screamed out in pain. Not Sikes.

The lead bike fell. Sikes stopped short and jumped off, laser in hand. He scanned the area, but saw nothing. The man held his upper arm. It was a nasty wound, and the blood flowed freely. Sikes helped him to bind the wound then he looked at the trap.

The limb of a small tree had been sharpened into a spear. The top of the tree had been tied down, and a rope wrapped half way around the base of another tree. The rope was then stretched across their trail at chest height, and carefully placed on the small limb of another tree. Crude, but obviously effective. The secondary was lucky. If he'd been any further away, the spear would have struck him in the head. Any closer, and it would have hit him with enough force to penetrate a limb or his body cavity.

Sikes once again called the Senator. This time, he was in no mood for pleasantries. "I've got good news and bad news." Was that hysteria in his voice? He couldn't be sure, and he didn't really care.

"What do you mean?" Kirk asked.

"The good news is that she's out of charges. The bad news is that she doesn't need them." Sikes moved his arm in an arc, so that Jessica could see the trap. "So, tell me how I plan for that. I don't have enough men to go on."

This attitude did not please Jessica. "They are only two people on foot in the dark..."

"And I am the only one in this troop that isn't badly wounded. We can't go on. If you send us on, you send us to our deaths, Kirk."

"If you come back here without their heads, Sikes, I will kill you myself. Now quit wasting time. Don't you realize that you are giving her time to set another trap?"

Sikes moved out. This time he took the lead. He moved cautiously, slowly. He was resigned that he was riding to his death. He had no doubt now. That was why he had felt strangely from the first. That was the reason for his dread. He was going to die. *It's true*, he thought, *foresight is real. Too bad I'll be dead before I can tell anyone.*

She'd set another trap. This one took even less time. They really couldn't afford to rest, but David's labored breathing told her that they must. She was tired, and she knew that this meant that David must be on the brink of total collapse. The fact that he had held up this long was a credit to his strength and his force of will.

The Reliance would be deploying more troops. At any moment, their running could shove them right into another patrol. These men were just the dogs sent in to tire them out. To bark until the others were in position, and then point the way.

Plans formed in her mind, and were discarded. She needed to know more about the situation to make any real plans. If she had time to fiddle with the computer, she could figure out what they were sending in. She would have been able to call up maps and try to figure out where they were in relation to the troops, but that could take as much as thirty minutes. That was thirty minutes they didn't have. She was running out of tricks, and they were running out of time.

Sikes barely saw the rope in time to stop. If he hadn't been looking so carefully, he wouldn't have seen it at all. This time, the rope was just inches above the ground. Sikes got off the bike. He picked up a rock, slung it at the rope and watched in horror as the area he would have occupied burst into flame. The stench of battery acid bit his nostrils, his eyes teared, and he retreated to a safer distance, coughing. It was clear, now. She was a devil. This trap was the worst thing Sikes had encountered in all his years with the Reliance. Apparently, she had rigged a tree as before. Instead of a spear, however, she'd attached the opened battery in the improvised catapult. When the rope was tripped, the highly volatile acid was slung over the target area.

Sikes was old enough to remember a time when batteries contained a much more stable acid, but like everything else, the Reliance had been forced to start using a cheaper and less stable alternative. This stuff was less efficient in some ways, but much more lethal. Instant combustion—what a horrible death!

Slowly, it dawned on Sikes that this trap was even more subtle. The recent drought made the forest a tinderbox. Already the fire raged out of control. In a few hours, it would successfully block the deployment of troops from the east, and that was where the roads were. He got on his bike quickly and passed the flames before he, too, was blocked off. Sikes called Jessica on the move. "She's set the forest on fire," he reported calmly. "You'd better send in some extinguisher planes, or we'll be completely cut off."

"Immediately. Just get after her," Jessica ordered.

*Damn it, they were going to fart around and let her get away!* She quickly checked her map. She already had troops deployed in the area. A quick check of wind direction and velocity told a story she didn't like.

"Damn!" She checked again to be sure. "They're heading right into the fire." She got on her communicator. "Captain Fry, the rebels have started a fire and it's headed your way."

"We see it, Senator," the Captain said. "I think we can beat it and join Sikes."

"No, you don't have time. If you don't retreat, you will be stuck in that box canyon. You have to go west," Jessica ordered urgently.

Captain Fry beat his wrist communicator against a tree. "What's that, Senator? Can't hear you." He hit it again, "We've got a bad link—must be the fire."

"Damn it, man..."

"You're fading, Senator," Captain Fry hit his wrist unit hard enough to break it. He looked up at the secondary soldier who stood beside him.

"Oh, dear! My wrist com seems to have broken." He nudged the man, and said jokingly, "Give a woman a title, and she right away thinks she knows everything. Come on, let's go give Sikes a hand."

The extinguisher planes didn't arrive in time to save Captain Fry and his troop. Seventeen soldiers burned to death in the box canyon. Death by fire was terrible. Terrible to hear, terrible to see, but the most terrible thing of all was the smell.

It was an even more terrible thing to live through.

Alexi pulled himself through the flames. How he had escaped with no more than the equivalent of a bad sunburn was nothing short of a miracle. His sleeve was on fire. He stopped, dropped and rolled, then jumped up and ran again. He couldn't stop long. To stop was to die.

The smoke made him cough, and his brain was a blur. Too much horror. Dead, all dead. He'd been with some of those people since he'd made it to third class. They hadn't died like soldiers. They hadn't died in battle. They had died screaming like terrified children as the flames engulfed them.

He'd worked hard to make it to third class. He'd seen quite a bit of action. But none of his experience or training had prepared him for this.

Alexi was ambitious. He wanted to make it to Elite, then on to governor—maybe even Senator. It was a wild dream, a dream of power. He'd worked hard.

Then he'd almost died in a fire.

Till now, he had never seen how intangible his dream was. Now he realized the absurdity of it. He'd been third class for six years. He'd been passed over for promotion to Elite twelve times.

Who was he kidding? He was forty-five years old. At his age, if he hadn't been promoted to Elite, it wasn't likely that he would be. Hell, they hadn't even offered him a wife yet. Governor Alexi, Senator Alexi, what a fool he'd been.

He'd seen how the high-rankers lived. They had everything a man could dream of. He had nothing. He had busted his hump for the Reliance, and they sent him to die. *No reward in that.* And if he'd died, who would have cared? *Who would even notice?*

*Well, 1-Z-2678-11 bit the big one today.*

*Anyone to claim his ashes?*

*No.*

*No? What a shame.*

*Yes, what a waste. Do you have any idea how much energy it takes to reduce a body to ash?*

*Oh, this one was mostly done when it got here.*

*No one to claim the ashes?*

*That's right.*
*Well, then put him with the others on the public gardens.*

"No!" Alexi screamed out loud and doubled his pace. He wasn't going to die in this damned fire and become fertilizer. He wasn't going to die a nobody.

RJ and David came to a river. The water ran hard and fast. RJ stepped in and David followed. At this point, he was too exhausted to do anything but follow dumbly. The current was strong, and the rocks were slippery, but worst of all, the water was frigid.

"The infrared won't be able to track us in the water," RJ told David, though for once he didn't ask.

The water got deep, up to David's waist. The current was strong, and David no longer had the strength to fight it. He collapsed from shear exhaustion.

David had been holding on to her for the past three hours, so she felt his grip on to her chain loosen. She turned just in time to see David go under. She didn't think; she just dove in after him. It wasn't easy, but she caught hold of him and pulled his head out of the water. He was OK, or at least he was still breathing. She wrestled him out onto the bank, caught her breath, and pulled her laser. She looked at it in a defeated sort of way, and poured the water out of it. It would be useless till it dried. She was sure she didn't have time to strip, dry and reassemble it now. She quickly checked the case to make sure it hadn't leaked. It would be the shits to have gone through all this for nothing. The case was tight, and the computer was dry.

She was exhausted; running on empty. No wonder David had collapsed. She couldn't afford the luxury of rest right now, however. That meant only one thing. She reached into her pocket, pulled out the leather pouch and extracted one of the pills. She swallowed it dry. As always, the effect was almost immediate. She took a deep breath; she'd be good for hours now. She began to replace the pills, but stopped. Smiling wickedly, she dumped one into her palm, replaced the cap and carefully stowed the pills in her kit. The she took a cup from the pack and filled it with water into which she crushed the pill. Using the knife from her kit, she cut several three-foot lengths of straight limbs from a nearby tree. Sharpening each stick, she dipped the sharpened end into the Pronuses solution and set them carefully aside to dry briefly. She poured the remaining solution over the sharpened spearheads for good measure, then tossed the cup across the river. She packed up quickly, tossed the pack over one shoulder, David over the other, picked up the spears and started off again.

"They went into the river. The infrared won't..." Sikes found himself on the defensive again.

"I don't want your excuses, Sikes." Jessica had lost any sign of patience hours ago. "All I asked was that you not lose them, and now you tell me some story about the water. Find them. Now!"

"Yes, Senator," Sikes grated out. Transmission ended.

"Captain, look!" The man pointed to something on the trail ahead of them.

They stopped beside the cup. A quick scan showed that the rebels had crossed the river at this point. Somehow, Sikes didn't share the secondary's enthusiasm. The people they hunted didn't make mistakes; she'd left the cup for a reason. Still, they crossed the river, leaving the man with the wounded leg behind. There was only one set of footprints on the other side, but the depth showed that one was no doubt carrying the other.

"One of them must be wounded," the secondary said.

"Or just exhausted. Remember that they have been on foot all night," Sikes said. "Come on, we should be able to catch them easily now."

They had traveled only a minute or two when the screaming started. They ran back, weapons pulled. But when they arrived it was obvious that the wounded man hadn't died of any direct attack. Even from across the river, they could see that the man's face was bubbled and misshapen. Sikes saw the cup in the man's hand. Only one thing could do that. Sikes looked away.

"God damn her! Is there nothing she can't get her hands on?" Sikes cursed.

"What happened to him?" the secondary asked, sickened.

"Pronuses poisoning. She must have laced the cup with it," Sikes said.

"Pronuses! But only *freaks* have Pronuses!" Obviously, the man was now terrified.

"Don't be a fool, man. Only Elites wear Elite boots, but she's got a pair of those, too. Come on. Let's go before the trail gets cold."

RJ found a clump of brush and put David into it. She covered him with leaves, partly to keep him warm, and partly to hide him. It was time to get rid of the dogs. They were following her footprints. If that told them where to find her, it also told *her* where to find *them*. She walked back down her own trail then crawled into a tree with her spears to wait.

Sikes stopped. He held up a hand, and the secondary stopped, too. He could feel it. She was watching him. The spear hurled through the air to land with a pounding thud in the secondary's chest. Death came so instantly that he didn't have a chance to scream. He fell backwards, his body arched once, and then he was still. The boiling of his flesh told Sikes that such a direct hit was unnecessary.

"Go ahead! Kill me! I can't see you, I can't stop you! Go ahead!" Sikes screamed. He spread his arms wide. "Come on, kill me! But at least have the guts to show your face."

RJ was never one to deny a man his last wish. She jumped down from the tree.

Sikes' reaction to her appearance wasn't quite what she'd expected.

He stared at her in horror and confusion, mouthing words he couldn't get out. His reason, already stretched tightly, snapped.

RJ raised the spear.

"How? Why?" Sikes gasped.

"The answer to 'how' is easy," she smiled broadly. "I'm a freak. 'Why?' Because I want to topple the Reliance. Is that all? May I kill you now?" Actually, she didn't wait for his answer.

He fell to the ground and rolled. The spear missed, but his blast hit her square in the chest and sent her reeling. He took the opportunity to run, but he knew that a blast to the chest wasn't going to slow the freak down for long. He turned on his comlink, and there was Kirk.

"You're not killing me!" he laughed maniacally.

"Sikes, what's going on?" Jessica demanded.

"They're all dead. But not me. You're not going to kill me, you freak!" He threw his comlink against a tree, where it shattered. He'd lost her for the time being, but she'd heal. Then she'd come to kill him. He laughed hysterically. "You won't kill me!"

RJ had taken the full blast in her chest. She stopped and leaned against a tree. She tried to catch her breath, but ended up slumping down to the ground. She had to catch him, but it would have to wait. Hell, she could see her breastbone through the hole in her chest.

"Oh, bother." She took another Pronuses and waited for the effects. "Pride goeth before a fall. Father always said that." She felt better. Glancing down, she saw the damage rapidly repairing itself, so she got up and continued the chase.

The hunter had become the hunted, and as was so often the case, the hunter couldn't handle the role reversal. RJ found her quarry hanging limply in a tree with a rope around his snapped neck. She quickly took his jacket—he'd ruined hers, after all. She took his shirt and sidearm, too.

Addressing the corpse, RJ commented dryly, "You know, if you start killing yourselves, you're going to take all the fun out of this little war."

On the way back to get David she stopped just long enough to take the dead secondary's clothes and weapon. Then after she uncovered him, RJ traded David's wet clothes for the dry ones. Oh, the pants were a little wet from wading the river, but nothing compared to the wet, muddy mess that David had been wearing. David groaned as she changed his clothes.

"Oh, just shut up and go back to sleep. A lot of help you are." She picked David up and started out again. Right now, her only plan was to keep moving.

Jessica tried desperately to reach Sikes. She couldn't. She played back his last communication. The word "freak" echoed through Jessica's brain. She quickly erased the communication from the terminal's main memory.

She was tired of playing. It was time to get serious. She put on her combat fatigues. If you wanted killing done right, you had to do it yourself. She wanted RJ dead, and if Sikes wasn't dead already, she had to kill him, too.

It took all of RJ's skill to continue dodging the ever-increasing number of patrols in the area. Now there were helicopters, and that made it decidedly more difficult.

After two hours of carrying David, she sat down for a rest. She slapped him a bit. Till then, all the bouncing and trouncing and tossing from one shoulder to the other like a feed sack hadn't made him so much as stir or mutter. Therefore, RJ was surprised that the gentle slap had any effect at all.

David stirred.

"Yes, it would be nice if you woke up now," RJ commented sarcastically. She rubbed her Pronuses-dry eyes as David rubbed the sleep from his.

He was awake, and he looked around in a disoriented way.

"Have a nice nap?"

"What happened?" David asked. He felt nauseous and his ribs and stomach hurt.

"You passed out." She got up and helped him to his feet. "Can you walk now? We've got to keep moving, and I'm tired of carrying you."

He nodded, although he held his head when he did so, and looked a little green.

"The water," he mumbled. It was like he was remembering some horrible nightmare. "Under the water..." He remembered hands grabbing him, pulling him out, a gasp for air, and then all was dark. He knew only that RJ had pulled him out of the river. If she hadn't, he'd have surely drowned. "Thanks, RJ."

"Don't thank me yet. We've just been spotted." It wasn't her imagination, either. The helicopter flying just above the tree tops tossed out two brightly colored smoke bombs.

"What the hell did they do that for?" David coughed out. "Now they can't see us."

"Now every troop in the area knows where we are. By the time the smoke clears, we'll be surrounded. Come on." She ran, pulling him after her.

Alexi saw the colored smoke, but he went towards it for a different reason than his fellows. If RJ died, almost everyone would know, and everyone who knew would care. Pro or con, no one would be indifferent.

RJ and David broke into the clearing. "Hit the ground and stay there."

"Why?" David wanted to know. "What are you going to do? What can you do?"

"Just stay down." She didn't have time to explain.

She ran into the clearing. As she had expected, the helicopter spotted her. It swooped down for the kill. RJ waited till the runners were dangerously close. Then she jumped for all she was worth and caught hold of one of them.

"Where'd she go?" the gunner asked the pilot.

The pilot shrugged.

"Where did who go?"

Both men turned to look at the woman standing on the runner. Their mouths hung open in disbelief.

"Oh, you meant me." She grabbed the gunner and jerked him out of the helicopter.

The pilot drew his gun and fired point-blank.

RJ looked from the hole in her jacket to the stunned pilot and frowned. "Damn it, I just got this jacket."

The man screamed as she grabbed the front of his shirt in one hand. His scream rose to a shrill soprano as he was hurled out of the chopper, and didn't stop till he hit the ground with a wet thud.

RJ finished climbing in, took the controls, turned the chopper around and set it down close to David.

David didn't have to be told twice. He ran and jumped in, thinking that RJ would take off immediately.

She just sat there.

"What are you waiting..." then he saw the Elite with the rocket launcher.

"Turn the bird off, and get out—slowly."

There were three others with him, all holding lasers pointed directly at them.

RJ turned off the helicopter.

"OK, get out. Hands up!"

RJ and David did as they were told. They stood before the group, arms held high.

"So, you're the great RJ. You don't look so tough to me." He raised the rocket launcher, and aimed it at her.

"In all fairness, you're not seeing me at my best," RJ replied dryly.

RJ was probably the only one there to notice the badly battered trooper stumble into the clearing. One part of her mind processed his presence, and decided that he had come in for the kill.

"Die, traitor!" The Elite's finger tightened on the trigger.

RJ prepared to throw herself to the ground. Her laser should be dry by now, and with it, she could give these four a run for their money.

Then two unexpected things happened. First, David flung himself on her, knocking her to the ground. Second, the soldier who had stumbled into the clearing shot the Elite before his finger could close on the trigger.

In the pandemonium that followed, two of the remaining Elites fell to RJ's laser, and the third to a second bullet from the stranger's gun.

The three looked at each other for only a second. No word was spoken.

RJ grabbed the rocket launcher, slung it into the chopper, jumped in and started the engine.

David grabbed up RJ's spears and got to the chopper only seconds after the stranger got into the back and sat behind RJ.

They lifted off just as troops started pouring into the clearing.

David had never flown before. He found the feeling exhilarating.

"We're flying, RJ! Flying like a fucking bird!" He jerked on her shoulder in an excited fashion.

"If you don't quit pulling on her, we're going to be dropping like a fucking turd." Alexi had flown before; he'd even had a few chopper lessons once upon a time, but he still didn't like it.

RJ saw the chopper coming up on their tail. "Buckle in."

For once, David complied without question. Alexi fastened himself into the gunner's harness. RJ swerved, but the blast came so close that it shook the chopper.

"That was fucking close," Alexi said.

"Hang on." RJ flipped the chopper upside down and came in behind the other bird.

"All right!" David said, like a kid on a carnival ride.

"Fire," RJ ordered.

Alexi hesitated. That was a Reliance chopper. The chopper opened fire on them. One bullet shattered the windshield in front of RJ. She kicked the safety glass out all the way so that she could see.

"Fire! Fire, or I'll kick your ass out of this chopper," RJ said with a hiss.

Alexi had no doubt that she meant it, nor did he doubt that she could do it. He took careful aim and fired. Then he watched as the chopper exploded in flames, and knew that there was no going back now.

The next chopper to come in pursuit was newer and better equipped. Their first rocket missed. RJ was a superb pilot, but she couldn't outmaneuver the super-chopper indefinitely.

"Can you fly?" RJ asked Alexi.

He nodded reluctantly. "A little."

"Take over." She didn't give him much choice. She unstrapped herself, grabbed the rocket launcher, and stepped out on the runner.

"Are you nuts?" Alexi asked, taking the controls.

"She's nuts, but she's OK," David assured him.

RJ braced herself and prepared to fire. The pursuit had the same idea, and the two rockets hit simultaneously. RJ's rocket hit them squarely, and there was no more pursuit. Their rocket hit the tail of the rebels' chopper, and blew off a piece. It rocked and spun the chopper violently, and RJ fell.

"RJ!" David shrieked. He unbuckled himself, and moved quickly to the door. RJ was hanging on the runner. David hung on to his safety belt and with his other hand reached out and grabbed RJ. "No sense hanging around down there." He pulled her back inside as she cursed his sense of humor.

RJ took the control seat, throwing the rocket launcher off her arm.

"Out of rockets," she said as Alexi started to grab it.

"So, now what? Here comes another one." Alexi pointed. He was beginning to wish he'd stayed on the other side.

"Hand me one of those spears, David. Be careful not to nick yourself; I've poisoned the tips." He handed her one. She took firm hold, positioned the spear and slowed the chopper.

"What the hell are you doing!" Alexi screamed in disbelief and terror. "We've got half our tail shot off. That means that we have damn little sideways motion. They've got a fully operational bird. Machine guns, rockets…"

RJ slung the spear.

"Yes, but they don't have a pilot." RJ said smugly, as the other chopper raced towards the ground.

Alexi just sat there with his mouth hanging open.

"Isn't she neat?" David asked lightly.

RJ fled as another chopper came in. She was beginning to lose her cool. Enough was fucking enough. She was strung out on Pronuses. Her eyes felt like her lids were made of sandpaper, and her arm was jerking so much it was becoming increasingly hard to control. It had been a hard couple of days on the front, and she was starting to take this all very personally.

"I want a bath," she said longingly.

"What?" David asked.

"Nothing," RJ said with a smile. She looked at David. "Ever wish we'd gone into another line of work?"

David smiled and put a reassuring hand on her shoulder. "Know what you mean, partner. The hours are a bitch, and the pay sucks."

RJ patted his hand.

"We can't outrun them, can we?"

"No," she said. "But we're not going to give up, either."

"Never crossed my mind." David looked at the rocket launcher, then he saw the smoke bombs. He was so excited, he couldn't speak. He picked both up. "RJ?"

She smiled. "Find the rest."

"It could work," Alexi said.

"Of course it will. You load and prepare to fire. Get it in the cockpit."

Alexi nodded grimly.

David dumped eight smoke bombs on the floor between RJ and Alexi.

"Fire on my command," RJ ordered.

Alexi nodded.

RJ slowed and dropped so low that it looked like they would crash into the treetops. As she maneuvered, she took time to be grateful that Earth had no War Birds. They would have been dead long since on one of the outer planets where the equipment was all-new and lethal.

The chopper swooped in for the kill.

"Fire!"

Alexi's aim was right on the money. The first smoke bomb landed in the cockpit of the attacker, which immediately filled with smoke. The pilot was flying blind, and was too close to the trees. It crashed, and RJ pulled up.

"Reload."

The order was unnecessary, as Alexi was already doing so. There was one chopper left that they could see. They could run, but then they would be chased.

"Fuck you," RJ swung around, heading straight for the last chopper.

"What the hell..." Alexi was as shocked as the pilot of the other chopper.

The chopper pilot couldn't believe it. Hell! Their tail was shot off, and they were coming after him. He didn't know whether to attack or to run away. While he was wondering, a smoke bomb landed in his gunner's lap. Suddenly he couldn't see.

"Get rid of it!" he screamed.

The gunner was trying to do just that, but it rolled off his lap and got lost on the floor. The pilot knew of only one thing to do. He went up. There shouldn't be anything to hit up there. The smoke was choking him and making him dizzy, sick. Something hit his gunner. He never knew what. The gunner fell from the craft screaming, still tied to the chopper by his half-fastened safety harness. The pilot's head was pounding. Who would have believed this shit could fuck you up so badly? No sense calling for help, there wouldn't be any. The rebels were getting away. Well, he thought, at least he wouldn't have to face Senator Kirk's wrath. He passed out, and the chopper went down, making him just one more of the casualties.

# Chapter Nine

By the time Senator Kirk arrived, all she could do was assess the damage and try to figure out what had happened. To do this, she decided to go to the beginning and follow the rebel's trail. She took General Sacks with her, although at this moment she wasn't sure that she really wanted company—especially Sacks.

"I really can't see what good following this trail will do us," Sacks grumbled.

They stopped their bikes at the spot where RJ and David had set up their rough camp. Jessica got off her bike and started to look around.

"We should be after them. We should be trying to find them."

"And how would you suggest that we do that, Sacks?" Jessica asked hotly. "Should we ask them nicely? Yoo-Hoo! Oh, Rebel Terrorist! Could you please set off a smoke bomb or something so that we can find you?" She saw something on the ground, and moved towards it. "We must see just who we are up against. Obviously, these two people are a lot more capable than our soldiers, since a large number of them died out here trying to catch two Rebels. AH!" She reached down slowly and moved the leaves aside. She carefully lifted the discarded food tray with two fingers. "So, RJ, you do occasionally make mistakes." She put the tray into her backpack. Then she got on her bike and they started out again. The next stop was the booby-trapped bike. Jessica seemed oblivious to the body of the man who had died here.

From here, the rebels had gone on foot. She got off her bike again, this time taking her pack and the infrared scan with her.

"Let's go," she ordered.

"On foot!" the general shrieked. The three first class soldiers with them didn't seem any too pleased either.

"You'll join me, General. You men will follow on the bikes." She was not in the mood to argue with the arrogant jerk, and with her rank, she didn't have to.

"Whatever for?" Sacks whined.

"Because I said so," she spat with venom. She turned cool eyes to him. "And, in case you've forgotten, I'm in command. If I tell you to shit, you had better drop a turd. Do you understand, Sacks?" she screamed.

"Yes, of course, Senator. A thousand pardons." He got off the bike and got his pack.

"Double time," Jessica took off. She expected him to keep up, and he did—just. They followed the path RJ had taken as well as they could. The fire had wiped out part of the trail. She stopped and studied the ground.

"Doubtless, you've noticed that one of our rebels is wearing Elite boots," Jessica said to Sacks.

Actually, he hadn't, but he nodded anyway. He didn't have the breath to talk.

Jessica looked at Sacks and frowned. She didn't like the implications. Sacks was a strong, healthy man at the peak of physical health and strength. As an Elite General, he couldn't have been anything else. He was damn near done in, but the rebels had continued from here. Had, in fact gone on to wreak devastating havoc. How could they, if Sacks' condition was any indication of what theirs had been...Add to this that they probably hadn't slept for twenty-four hours, and that it had been night, and Jessica started to form a picture of her adversaries that she did not like at all.

They came to the river, and Jessica waded in.

"You've got to be kidding," Sacks groaned.

"In," she ordered. Sacks complied.

Thirty minutes later, Sacks had had it. "I can't believe they walked in the water this long. I'm freezing."

So should they have been. Jessica had a sinking feeling. Ten minutes later, they came to Sikes' discarded bikes.

Sacks only had to take one look at the body to know what had happened to the man.

"Pronuses." He swallowed hard.

Jessica nodded, and picked up the cup. She sniffed it.

"She laced the cup with it. This fool must have used it." She put the cup in her pack. "Come on, this is where they crossed over." On the other side, Jessica found where RJ had pulled David out of the water. From the amount of water still on the ground, Jessica deduced that they must have both been drenched from head to toe. She looked fleetingly at Sacks. He was huffing and puffing, trying to catch his breath. He was on the brink of exhaustion. Likewise, one of the rebels had been in worse shape than the other. She scanned the footprints, and puzzled out the prints left by the rebels.

"One of them had to carry the other one from here. The one with the Elite boots."

Sacks nodded silently. He didn't find that too hard to believe. Ten minutes later, he collapsed. Jessica left one of the men with him, and took the other two with her.

She found the body with the spear sticking from its chest, the face twisted and distorted.

"Very clever. Pronuses-laced spears." She put her foot on the man's chest and pulled the spear out, oblivious to the gore that oozed out of the now-open wound. Both soldiers swallowed hard. Jessica shook her head.

"A direct hit was unnecessary. You were showing off, RJ." She was talking to herself.

There were two sets of Elite boot-prints on the ground now, and they were going every which way. It was obvious that RJ had lost the dead weight of her partner at this point. Jessica followed the clearest set of prints. One set of Elite prints followed another. Sikes and RJ were apparently about the same size, because she couldn't distinguish between the two. Still, Jessica had no doubt who was chasing whom.

Even so, Jessica was not prepared for what she found. She stopped short with a gasp. Sikes was dancing there in the air like a puppet on a string. This explained Sikes' last hysterical outburst. He had cracked. She really couldn't blame him. His troop had been meticulously picked off. One by one, each had fallen. He had been alone, and he knew there was no escape. He hadn't given RJ the satisfaction of killing him.

"Oh, Sikes," she sighed a deep and heavy sigh. If he had lived, Jessica would have killed him herself, but she still hated to think of him dying like this. Sikes had been a brave man, a strong man. But he couldn't fight RJ. Jessica thought she knew why. She assessed the damage, and her worst fears were only confirmed. There just couldn't be any other explanation for all that she saw.

At the end of the trail, she talked to a third-class soldier who had been on hand to witness the slaughter in the air.

"What did they look like?" Jessica asked.

"What?" The man was in shock. He'd been hit in the arm by a piece of shrapnel. It wasn't a bad wound, but it hadn't been anything but field-dressed, and he was in a great deal of pain.

Jessica didn't care. She was out of patience with the whole damn lot of them.

"The rebels, man. What did they look like?" She demanded.

"I wasn't very close. They were both over average height. The man was very dark, average build. The woman was...well, she was blonde...as blonde as yourself, Senator, and her skin was about your color."

"A hybrid," the third-class Captain—the soldier's commander—said.

Senator Kirk stiffened. She turned icy blue eyes on him, and his blood ran cold.

He shrugged. It wasn't like it was any secret that Kirk was a hybrid.

"They were joined by a third man," the soldier said.

"He had to be one of ours," Jessica said thoughtfully. "He must have sympathized with her, and gone over. God, if she builds an army, there will be no stopping her." Again, the Senator was talking to herself.

"I don't believe that for a minute," the captain said. "He must have been one of her men."

Jessica slammed the palm of her hand into her head. Partly because she couldn't believe that a man with so little in the way of brains had made it to third-class captain, and partly because after all that had happened, hitting her head felt good.

"It's no wonder they got away. There is not a whole brain in the entire Earth-based Reliance army. RJ and her friend were alone, being chased all night and most of the day. You want me to believe that this fellow just happened to stumble upon them here at the exact moment that all this"—she made a flamboyant hand gesture—"happened? Do you have any idea what the odds of that happening are?" She was yelling in rage by the end of her speech.

The Captain stood there silently. Obviously, he was trying to do the math in his head. "No, Senator. I don't know," he said at length.

Jessica ripped his captain's patch from his shoulder. "Think about it, private. Think about it long and hard. Save all your money, and maybe someday you'll be able to buy a brain. They are doing wonders with artificial intelligence these days. Wait around and maybe technology will catch up with you."

Jessica stomped over to the chopper that was waiting for her and boarded. "Take me back to Capitol. Get me the hell away from all these incompetent fools."

"At once, Senator."

# Chapter Ten

General Right walked into Jago's Throne Room and bowed as was required.

"Oh, what is it now?" Jago sighed. He popped a grape into his mouth, and then said around it, "Well?"

"RJ and the rebels..."—Somehow, that sounded better than *RJ and one other rebel*—"...have assassinated Governor Bristol. Troops were deployed to exterminate them, but with no success. Senator Kirk is reporting the destruction of numerous pieces of Reliance hardware, as well as the deaths of more than fifty soldiers, including Elite Captain Sikes, who apparently went mad and hanged himself." Right tried to report it in the bland, emotionless tones he had been taught at the academy, but it was difficult. This was the most excitement they had seen on Earth in centuries.

"Oh, damn! And this started out to be such a nice day." Jago rested his fat chin on his pudgy-fingered hand and looked at the wall with a pout. "I suppose you want me to do something about it." He sighed heavily. "I'm starting to dislike this RJ person immensely. She is interrupting my life. I want her dead."

"We all want her dead, Excellency. As Governor General of Sector 11-N, I feel it is my duty to go to Capitol 2-A and assist Senator Kirk in putting these rebels down," Right said.

"Then why are you bothering me? Why don't you just do it?" Jago asked hotly.

Right cleared his throat and handed a paper to Jago. Jago read it carefully.

"What is this, Right?" Jago asked suspiciously.

"Sir?"

"This states that you will report directly to Senator Kirk—that you would take your orders from her, and not me. That I am to give you and that hybrid absolute control in matters concerning the rebel RJ," Jago paraphrased: He didn't really understand what it all meant, but he was sure that he shouldn't like it.

"For your protection, Excellency," Right said.

"How so?" Jago asked with the lift of an eyebrow.

"Well, Sire, you couldn't possibly be blamed for any mistakes that we might make since we wouldn't be consulting with you."

Jago thought about that for a moment. He finally decided that he liked the sound of it.

"I wouldn't have to hear any more about who this horrid RJ person was killing or maiming?" Jago asked hopefully.

"Of course not," Right smiled on the inside.

"Or what she's stealing?" Jago asked, still suspicious of anything that sounded this good.

"That's right."

"And I wouldn't have to deal with you until this thing with the rebels was all cleared up?" Jago asked, beginning to get excited.

"Regrettably, no, Sir. I will be leaving General Zaks in control here," Right said.

Jago laughed happily. Zaks was known for his meekness. He wasn't likely to be as brash about interrupting him as Right was. Jago signed quickly and handed the paper back to the general.

"There you go, Right. I wish you luck in your endeavors." He motioned towards the door. "Have a good trip. Give my love to the hybrid bitch of Capitol."

Right bowed quickly and left. When the door closed, Jago gave vent to his joy.

"No more RJ! No more Right! No more Right bugging me about RJ, who's always stealing weapons that I have no knowledge of!" He shoved a nectarine in his mouth, and looked like a pig stuffed for baking.

They'd ditched the chopper and were now hoofing it. RJ spotted an unguarded farm truck. She decided that this meant that the owners wanted her to have it.

"I think this is where we part company," RJ said to Alexi. "You'll have to find your own way from here."

"Now, wait a minute!" Alexi started in disbelief. "I'm going with you!"

"I don't think so," RJ said plainly.

"I saved your wretched neck!" Alexi exclaimed.

"Maybe," RJ said, shrugging it off.

"Maybe!" Alexi was incredulous. "Undoubtedly!"

RJ sighed heavily. "Why do men always assume that they have saved my life? Is it some male thing? Does it make you feel good to think that I am so helpless that I must be saved?"

"He had a rocket launcher pointed at your head," Alexi reminded her harshly.

"And from that one little fact, you assume that I was having trouble?" RJ just shook her head in disbelief. "Thank you for maybe saving my life. Now, goodbye."

"Listen, lady..."

"Ladies don't carry guns," RJ informed him shortly.

David listened to RJ. He had been watching her. She was having trouble walking straight, and her arm was jerking ferociously. She obviously wasn't thinking straight, or she wouldn't be trying to get rid of such a valuable ally.

"RJ, this man can help us."

"What's your name?" David asked Alexi as RJ snorted her disapproval.

"Alexi. I'm a third-class soldier. I want to join the Rebellion."

"No," RJ said decisively. She was only too aware that she wasn't thinking clearly. But she didn't think she was wrong about her ill feelings concerning Alexi.

"RJ, he's a fighter, and he wants to join..."

"Ah, but why does he want to join?" RJ rubbed her Pronuses-dry eyes. She looked at Alexi. Oh, he had no intention of turning them over. He wasn't a plant. He meant what he said. But he wanted to join them for all the wrong reasons.

"For God's sake, RJ, you recruit a pickpocket and an ax-wielding wife-murderer, but *this* man makes you uncomfortable. You're strung out, that's all. You're not thinking straight." David was a little aggravated with her.

"I know what I'm doing," RJ said hotly.

"Do you? We are fighting the Reliance, and we need every man we can get." David tried to keep the anger out of his voice. After all that had happened, RJ was more than entitled to a little paranoia.

"David," RJ motioned with her hand, and David followed her out of Alexi's hearing. "He's no good. If he joins us, eventually there will be trouble."

"RJ, we're supposed to be partners, aren't we?" RJ nodded.

"Then I want Alexi."

"Then you shall have him, David," RJ hissed. "But know this. If that man stays, he will be trouble. If he stays, eventually I will have to kill him. His blood will be on *your* hands, not mine."

David smiled reassuringly. "You're just tired."

They walked back to Alexi, who was looking at David hopefully.

"You're in," David told him.

The smug smile Alexi gave RJ only confirmed what she already knew about him. Alexi was a weasel, but she'd be sure that he was a useful weasel for the time being.

Jessica met Right as he stepped out of his plane. They embraced, then headed for Jessica's car. It was a short trip from the airstrip to the interior of Capitol.

They sat in the back together while an Elite drove. They were silent for a long time, then Right ventured condolences.

"I was sorry to hear about Jack's death. He was a good man, and a good friend."

Jessica's lip quivered a little, but that was her only sign of emotion. She was still silent.

"The whole of the Reliance grieves with you."

"Not that fat bastard." Her mask of calm crumbled to be replaced by rage. "Jack asked for help months ago, and Jago did nothing. You tried, Right. I don't blame you. I know how hard it is to get that slug to do anything except bed some poor unfortunate wretch of a girl, or stuff his face. Jago is as responsible for Jack's death as RJ is." She turned to face him, and the rage he saw there was more than a little frightening. "I tell you, Right, when I am done with RJ, I will deal with Jago in the same fashion. I mean to have their heads."

"Shh," Right warned, motioning towards the driver.

"I really don't care who hears. Jago would be a class-B worker if his brother weren't World Commissioner, and even he thinks Jago's an idiot."

"I realize that you're upset, Jessy. But threatening to kill Jago is dangerous."

Jessica laughed, then sobered. "Not nearly as dangerous as this RJ we face. I don't mind telling you that I fear her much more than Jago, or anyone else for that matter." She ran down, in detail, all that had happened, excluding only what she was sure RJ was. "There's no body, Right." She choked a little on her words. "Just pieces smeared all over the inside of the car."

"His box?" Right questioned.

"It was there." She fought to control her tears. "The only thing keeping me going is the need to have this RJ dead."

"Where do you suppose she got the Pronuses?" Right asked curiously. Trying to take her mind off her loss.

"I imagine she could get anything. Do you know that she has the utter gall to wear Elite boots?" She had calmed herself by sheer willpower. "We aren't up against a dissatisfied work unit; she's one of our own. At one time, she was probably a high-ranking Elite with combat experience on the outer worlds. Her army grows daily. Today she gleaned a third-class soldier—a man with an otherwise flawless record. If loyal soldiers will leave the ranks to join her, think what will happen to work units."

Right's eyes grew huge as the implications hit him.

"And she could do it, Right. I have no doubt about it. We could have our first real rebellion since the Reliance seized control four hundred and ninety-four years ago."

While Right was busy getting himself settled in to his new office, Jessica was sitting alone in hers, tapping her fingers on her desk impatiently.

The man walked into her office.

"What took you so long?" she demanded.

"Sorry, Senator," he said, depositing the two small disks on her desk in front of her. "The DNA on the items was sparse and contaminated by other organic material. It took some time to sort it all out and get a true reading."

"Go away," she said ungraciously.

He was only too happy to comply. Senator Kirk had never been the best person to work for, but lately she was impossible.

When she was sure he was gone she locked the door. Then she put the first disk into the terminal. This was the man. Not bad looking. David Grant, Class D work unit. Imprisoned for acts of treason against the Reliance. Died in a logging accident. The computer droned out dates and other unimportant data. Jessica removed the disk.

"Someone was covering their ass." She hissed the words, her jaw tight with rage. It wasn't the first time a prisoner had escaped and been marked dead. It was easier that way—less paperwork. Jessica picked up the second disk carefully. She looked at it for several long minutes. She had a gut feeling that her worst fears were about to be confirmed.

"So, RJ, let's see what you look like." She put the disk in with trembling fingers, then sagged back in her chair and closed her eyes against what she saw.

She might as well have been looking in a mirror.

"Senator Jessica Kirk, Elite..." before the computer could say more, she ripped the disk from the terminal and crushed it in her fist.

Several hours later, Jessica woke with a start. The dream she'd been having hadn't been a pleasant one. Sleeping alone had never bothered her before. Perhaps because it had never seemed so permanent. She got out of bed and put on her robe. She took a cigarette off the bedside table, lit it, and took a long drag. Then she started pacing.

The thought of RJ curled around her lover, safe and snug, ate at Jessica's soul. It wasn't fair. Jessica felt lost and miserably alone.

"OK, Stewart. You've got some explaining to do." She put out her half-smoked cigarette, and got dressed.

Poley ran into Stewart's lab. He shut the door heavily.

"Oh, whatever is it now, Poley?" Stewart asked without looking up from the microscope.

"It's the random unit, sir," an edge of excitement to his synthetic voice.

Dr. Stewart abandoned his microscope and started pacing in anticipation. "So, what's she done now?" Stewart asked happily.

"She's assassinated Governor Bristol..."

Stewart started laughing, and didn't stop until Poley had given him a full report on all the damage. Suddenly, he stopped pacing and a worried look replaced the laughter.

"Damn," he said in a put out tone.

"Is there something wrong, Doctor?" Poley asked.

"She used Pronuses to poison the tip of those spears." Stewart was thoughtful.

"So," Poley didn't understand the problem.

"So, tin head, how long can it take them to realize what RJ is, if they haven't already? After that, how long before they realize that I'm the only one with the brains to have created her?"

"Dr. Preston..." Poley started.

"Oh, don't make me laugh." The professor looked far from laughing. "Preston is a smug fool."

"His endeavors in both robotics and genetics equal yours." Poley was trying to ease the professor's mind, but Stewart didn't take it that way.

"Ha! Preston! Equal to me! Never! Has Preston created anything to equal RJ? NO! Oh, no he hasn't. And do you know why, Tim Pants?"

"Because he wasn't concerned with perpetuating his own genes," Poley answered excitedly. He thought he'd done well, so he didn't understand the doctor's wrath.

"Because, you great metal fool, I have more brains in my little finger than that idiot Preston has in his whole body!" Stewart screamed.

"Oh," Poley said. "That was my next guess."

"Preston could never duplicate one of my creations. Only a complete and utter fool would mistake RJ for one of Preston's abortions," Stewart hollered like a lunatic. "Why, Preston has trouble making a sandwich!"

"Of course, sir," Poley said, making it obvious by his tone of voice that it was a humbling experience to be allowed to work in the company of an intellect as vast as Dr. Stewart's. "I was simply suggesting that the Reliance may mistake RJ for one of Preston's creations."

"Are you trying to patronize me, Poley?" Stewart asked suspiciously. "Any one with a single ounce of sense is going to know that only I have the necessary knowledge and intellect to have created RJ. Anyone with even a spark of intelligence would know that. Preston doesn't have the good sense to dump piss out of his shoe without being told. Preston, make

RJ? Ha! I have studied amoebas with more intelligence." He sat down on his stool, folded his arms across his chest, and proceeded to pout. "Only a complete and total idiot would mistake one of my projects for one of Preston's."

"Of course, sir. But, as you have often told me," he cleared his synthetic throat. "The heads of the Reliance are a bunch of butt-brained buffoons who wouldn't know shit from computer chips without a diagram."

Stewart began to laugh again. He jumped off his stool, and hugged his metal friend. "Oh, quite right, Poley. Only a complete idiot would mistake my work for Preston's. But that defines the Reliance *perfectly*! They will probably assume that RJ is Preston's work, and go bother him." He sat back down at his microscope. "I am quite safe."

Not ten minutes later someone walked into the room. "Tell them to go away, Poley. I don't have time for people today."

Poley was silent.

"Go away," Stewart said irritably. He didn't bother to look up. "Next time you ignore an order, Poley...I'm going to fire you."

"Dr. Stewart?" Stewart's head jerked up quickly. He hit his head on a light fixture, and fell off his stool, holding his chest.

Jessica jerked the old man up off the floor and shook him roughly. "Oh, come on, old man. Who do you think you're kidding?"

"He's an old man. He has a spastic heart." Poley took Stewart from Jessica's rough grasp and helped him back onto his stool.

A quick look told Stewart that this was not the random unit. This had to be one of the others. The random unit had a defect, and she would never have treated him disrespectfully.

"What right do you have to bother me when I'm working?" Stewart asked hotly.

"I am Senator of Zone 2-A." Jessica informed him haughtily.

"And I suppose you think that gives you a right to be rude," Stewart said curtly. Then he started to laugh. "Did you hear that, Poley? A Senator."

"Do you find that amusing, old man? I could have you arrested for what you've done."

"And just what have I done, dear?" Stewart asked innocently.

"I think you know, old man," Jessica spat. "One of your creations is running amok. Destroying anything that gets in her way..."

"And one of my creations is a Senator. I'm so proud."

"Listen to me, you crazy old fool..."

"Is that any way to talk to your father?" Stewart asked, aghast.

"If you don't cooperate with me..."

That sounded like the start of a threat. Stewart didn't like threats. "You'll do what? Tell them that I made RJ? That I also made you? Do you really want all your hoity-toity friends to know what you are?" Obviously, from the expression on her face, she did not. "So, let us dispense with the threats, shall we, J-6?"

"Jessica," she grated out. "My name is Jessica Kirk."

"So, without any unpleasantness. What has brought you back to the fold?"

Jessica cringed. She had never in her wildest dreams ever thought that she would have to deal with Stewart at any level. "How many?" she asked at length.

"How many what?" Stewart asked cagily.

"How many like myself did you make?"

"Oh, that." He played with something on his work bench. "Twelve."

"Twelve!" Jessica held a hand to her head.

"If it makes you feel any better, there are only two of you left."

"How can you be so sure?" Jessica asked.

"I placed a transmitter at the base of each of your skulls that emits only as long as the unit is viable. Of course, RJ's is dysfunctional." He scratched his head as if wondering how he could have made such an error.

"What do you mean?" Jessica asked.

"Well, till most recently, I thought you were the only one left. But when RJ started her little reign of terror..." He shrugged extravagantly. "I knew that had to be one of my girls. Of course, I already knew where you were, and what you were doing, so it couldn't be you. I suppose RJ's unit must have broken."

He gave Poley—who had a very confused look on his face— a warning look. "It must have been one that you assembled."

"Are we...are we all the same?"

"Of course," Stewart answered.

Poley looked about ready to speak, and Stewart fingered the shut off box in his pocket. Poley stood silently.

"So, for all practical purposes, I am fighting myself." She seemed to ponder this.

"It should make for an interesting addition to my experiment," Stewart said, rubbing his chin. "Imagine, if you will, two great minds attached to two superior bodies. Together, you might well conquer the Reliance. Why fight her, J-6? Why not join her instead?"

"Join her against the Reliance! Have you gone mad? You talk treason, old man!" Jessica was enraged at the mere suggestion that she would join RJ.

"Well, it's a sure bet that she won't join you." Stewart answered her rage with careful calm. "Pitted against each other, neither can win."

"I shall win. I will track her down and utterly destroy her." Jessica's eyes burned with all the hate and rage she possessed.

Stewart clicked his tongue. "My, my. Why such malice?"

"Because she chose to kill and mutilate my lover as a sign to the Reliance," Jessica spat out.

Stewart looked shocked, then pleased. "Did you hear that, Poley? J-6 had a lover. And you argued that they could never lead normal lives." Stewart laughed heartily.

Jessica had enough. He was laughing at her. He was laughing at her heartache. She grabbed his shoulder in a vice-like grip, and he stopped laughing.

"J-6, you're hurting my arm," Stewart said, angrily. "Let me go at once!"

Jessica surprised herself; she let him go. "My name is Jessica...Senator Jessica Kirk!"

"Stalemate, Senator. Tell them that I made RJ, and you also have to tell them that I made you. Tell them what RJ is, and if they catch her, don't you think they are going to notice the uncanny resemblance? Don't you think they are going to start to ask questions about you? A few simple tests, and any fool would know..."

"I don't need you alive." Jessica informed him in her most menacing tone.

Stewart just smiled. "You gain nothing by killing me."

"Satisfaction." Jessica hissed.

Stewart laughed. "Satisfaction? In killing me? Why? What sort of challenge would I be? I'm an old man whose days are numbered. The brain is still strong, but the body is tired. You could kill me with the poke of a single finger. I am old and tired of fighting death. So, if it would give you satisfaction to take what little life is left to me..." He stopped speaking and opened his arms as if inviting her blow.

Jessica gave him a black look, then turned and stomped off towards the door. She turned just as her hand touched the knob. "This isn't the end of it, old man. Not by a long shot."

"I didn't think it would be." Stewart watched her as she made her exit.

Stewart addressed Poley. "That girl is a little high-strung."

"Why did you lie to her?" Poley asked in confusion.

"Shush, tin fool." Stewart hissed. He waited till he was sure she was out of hearing. "Perhaps I shouldn't have allowed them to keep their emotions."

"Why did you lie to her?" Poley persisted.

"She was supposed to be dead." Stewart was thoughtful. Her calling unit must have failed. "So, I have two left. A rebel and a Senator." He scratched his chin thoughtfully. "Pitted against each other, there is a good chance they may both wind up dead. I will have to intervene, or the entire experiment will be jeopardized. If Jessica goes after RJ in grief-stricken vengeance...well, neither can win." Stewart got up and started to pace his laboratory. "I must decide which one has the best chance of survival, and then work to help that one."

"I have always been partial to RJ, myself," Poley said.

"You know, my metal-bodied friend, I sometimes wonder if I didn't make you too human!" He sat down and put a finger to his mouth. "So, J-6 had a lover." He moved his finger from his mouth. "And RJ killed him to make a political statement. Allowing them irrational thought; that was my first mistake. I could have altered their minds, but at the time it just seemed like too much bother. Now, I'm beginning to think it would have been well worth the effort. RJ running around in her suicidal revolution. J-6 going after RJ. It's all madness. Madness, I tell you. I don't have the strength, the determination, or the bloody time to run up another batch. I'm an old man, Poley. An old and very tired man. One of them must live. Unfortunately, that means—I hate to say it—that the other must die. Poley, I want you to find out everything you can about both RJ and J-6. I want to know which has the greater chance of survival."

Stewart knew his decision must be based on facts. He had never been political, and now was not the time to start.

Jessica looked over graphs and charts on her computer screen. General Right stood attentively at her shoulder, although she clicked through them too fast for him to actually see anything.

"There is no apparent method to her madness." He grabbed her hand, gently stalling her rapid progress on a map of the zone. He pointed to the red marks on the map to further explain his meaning. "She steals a load of supplies...tents, K-rations, clothing, etc....here. Three weeks later, she steals a shipment of projectile weapons here—clear across the zone. A week later she steals a load of medical supplies just an hour's drive away. A month later, they're back across the country, stealing a load of our new laser sidearms. Two weeks later, and halfway across the country, they steal yet another load of supplies. Two days after that, they're two hundred miles away, stealing a load of plasma blasters. Then yesterday they steal—are you ready for this?—boots! That makes no sense at all. Obviously, these raids are made at random, and without any prior study of the contents. Yet they have not stumbled upon a single one of the convoys harboring a GSH. They must just have the most incredible luck."

"It has very little to do with luck," Jessica said shortly. She had done everything in her power to make RJ's life difficult. She'd doubled the number of GSHs accompanying the convoys. She'd set up random roadblocks. She'd scrambled the shipments and changed shipping routes.

Nothing.

RJ was outwitting her. She didn't know how, but it was obvious that RJ had an edge. Jessica was not as blind to the obvious as Right seemed to be.

"There is most definitely a method to her 'madness' as you call it. An army doesn't just need weapons. It needs food, clothing and shelter. And yes, even boots. She's collecting the provisions for an army." She looked carefully at the map. "These raids are anything but random. How can we prepare any real defense if we don't know when or where she will strike next? RJ is preparing her army to march, and so far our attempts to stop her have been ludicrous."

"There is no reason to believe that she is doing anymore than stealing the supplies. There is no sign of any sort of a rebellion, much less one on that scale. In fact except for RJ, there is no sign of an organized rabble anywhere."

"What about Alsterase?"

"What about it? The entire population of Alsterase couldn't use one sixteenth of the pilfered supplies. Besides, there is nothing to suggest that there has been any kind of uprising in Alsterase," Right explained.

Jessica was silent for a moment. Then she spoke her thoughts aloud. "RJ's got an army. Somewhere. At least, she knows where to get one. I've got to believe that, or nothing she has done makes any sense." She contemplated the ceiling for a moment. "And I believe that she never does anything that doesn't make perfect sense. What I don't understand is how she's missing the GSHs."

"Well, she must just have the most incredible luck," Right suggested a second time.

"There is no such thing as luck in matters of war," Jessica snapped back. "Somehow she *knows*."

"Impossible. She would have to have a box." Right assured her.

Jessica's head snapped up. Her eyes had a carnivorous shine to them. "What did you say?" Her quiet voice made Right's skin crawl.

"I said she would have to have a box." Right's voice was a little more choked than he would have liked, but at least he had been able to fight the impulse to cringe.

"Of course!" Jessica slammed her fist into her palm. "That's it! That's the answer. She's been sitting with a box, carefully picking and choosing which cargoes she wants and which ones are safe."

Right looked at her and shook his head sadly. The whole thing had finally gotten to her. Her cable had snapped. "She couldn't have a box. All of the boxes are accounted for," he said carefully.

"Not Jack's." She got up and started pacing, picturing the whole event as it must have happened. "She got it from Jack." No longer a hunch, she now knew her statement was true.

"But they found Jack's box with him," Right reminded her.

"No! They found *a* box with him." Jessica sat down on the edge of her desk and looked at Right. "You can bet that no one checked to make sure that it was his box—a *real* box. RJ threw a plasma bomb into the armor-plated limo and closed the door. Everything inside would have been covered with a thick, bloody, pulpy coat of what had once been men."

Right swallowed hard.

"Can you see *anyone* digging through that to make sure of anything? If they saw a part of what could have been his box, that would have been all the confirmation they needed." Jessica's features turned into a mask of white-hot anger, cool, but deadly. "That's why she did it. So that no one would notice, so that no one would look. She didn't kill Jack to make any sort of grand point; she just wanted the box. All along, she only wanted the box. It didn't matter who she got it from. She killed Jack to cover up the theft of his computer." She looked out her office window and smiled a sadistic smile. "So, RJ, you're using the box," Jessica looked at Right. "Anything that can be pushed can be pulled. I think it's time we did some pulling, Right ."

# Chapter Eleven

Levits hadn't found Alsterase very hospitable. He had no money and no skills with which to barter. There wasn't a hell of a lot of call for a starship pilot in Alsterase. He wound up with a job gutting fish, which gave him just enough money to eat on, and more or less guaranteed that he wouldn't be eating what he could afford...fish!

Most nights he found a corner in some abandoned ruin and tried to sleep. Whether he actually ever did, he wasn't quite sure. He knew he sometimes approached something very near sleep, but when he did he had the nightmare. After he had the nightmare he didn't want to even try to sleep.

He'd lost at least twenty pounds, and he'd been wrestling with a cold for two weeks.

He had just enough money in his pocket for one half-assed meal, and payday wasn't for two more days. To make matters worse, it was raining. A cold rain.

Things couldn't possibly get any worse.

As he reached this point in his reflections, he realized that a big, burly, rough-looking fellow was following him.

Now, Levits was sure that in his present condition fighting with this guy would be the closest thing to suicide, but he was hungry, and he had worked his ass off for the little money he had. The guy started walking faster, and Levits took off in a dead heat. He had never been much of a fighter, but he had always been one hell of a runner.

A man darted in the door, fighting for breath.

"Isn't that RJ's pilot?" Whitey slurred out.

Mickey barely looked up. "Looks like it."

Levits watched with relief as the goon who had obviously been chasing him ran past the bar. He took a deep breath and started to go get a seat. He had almost reached his goal when someone grabbed his arm and damn near pulled it out of socket. The man was big and dark and looked to be witless, which meant there would be no dealing with him rationally.

"Buy me a beer," the man ordered.

There comes a point when a person has just been pushed one foot too far. Levits had reached that point. He balled up his fist and punched the man as hard as he could in the nose. As blood gushed from the man's face, he let go of Levits. Levits started to flee, only to be caught by the bleeding brute's other hand.

"Let him go!" Whitey bellowed, without bothering to stand up.

"He broke my nose, Baldor," the man hissed back.

"Let him go, or I'll break your whole fucking head," Whitey said in a coolly menacing tone.

The man grudgingly let go of Levits and made a rude noise in Whitey's direction. Then he turned and left the bar trailing a steady stream of blood behind him.

Levits looked over at the odd pair. He remembered his first encounter with them. How could he forget it! A woman had been with them then. Now he realized that her words had been true. Alsterase was no place for a man alone.

He walked over to where they sat. "Thanks."

Whitey nodded his huge head. "Join us?"

"Does the invitation include a meal?" Levits asked as lightly as his belly would allow.

In answer, Mickey called a waitress over to the table and ordered. "Room, too. If you work with us," Mickey told him with a smile.

"Where's the woman?" Levits asked looking around.

"She doesn't love me," Whitey moaned.

"Damn, now you've done it." Mickey said in disgust. "You got him started again."

"Sorry," Levits shrugged. "So where is she?"

"Away on business," Mickey answered simply.

"With *him*," Whitey spat.

"Him who?" Levits asked.

"David! God, how I hate him!"

Food was set before Levits, and all else was forgotten till he finished shoving his face full.

"What can I say? This is too good to be true. Food, lodging...Do I get clothes, too?"

"Oh, yes. And weapons," Whitey said bitterly. "And maybe RJ will come home and..."

"RJ!" Levits gasped in a whisper. "Not *the* RJ! The one the Reliance wants killed at any price?"

Whitey smiled sadistically. "Is that a problem?"

"Damn, I knew it was too good to be true," he mumbled.

"She grows on you after while," Mickey said with a reassuring grin.


They looked out from their hiding place among the trees. Victory had made them overconfident.

Or at least it had made David and Alexi overconfident. Things had gone smoothly. Too smoothly for RJ's liking. She'd learned to be leery of anything that seemed too easy.

There was really no reason for her guts to twist themselves into knots. Everything was in position. She had checked and double-checked. Everything was in order. Everything except her gut. She had set the charges. She had placed her weapons. She had planned her strategy. She had checked and double-checked the box; still...

"We're not going to do this one. Let's pack up," she announced. "It's time to go home."

"Are you nuts?" Time and togetherness had not made Alexi any fonder of RJ, nor had it endeared him to her. "Those Reliance dicks are like fruit for the picking. As long as we have the box..."

"What if they've figured out that we've got it?" RJ asked hotly.

"What could they do then?" David didn't understand.

"Remember in the forest when the Reliance were chasing us?"

David nodded, how could he forget.

"I knew were to plant the traps because I knew they were following us. Same thing here. If they know we have the box, they could enter false data. Scenario...We wind up facing a GSH and a troop of Elites for a shipment of bubble gum."

"But surely we could finish this one. I mean, we're already set up," Alexi said. "Or is everyone's favorite warlord having an attack of woman's intuition?"

"Maybe," RJ said simply. "But it's time to pack it in. We've got enough. It's stupid to let greed get us killed."

"I agree, and no one will be happier than I will to get home. But why don't we go ahead and do this one?" David told the truth. He did want to go home. He found it exhausting to be in the company of two people who hated each other so intensely. "So, what do you say? Let's do this last one, and then we'll toss the box and call it quits."

RJ thought for a moment. Was she being silly? Well, of course she was, but that was her prerogative. She looked at Alexi.

"Troublemaker," she grumbled at him.

He smiled smugly.

They waited in silence. The caravan came into view. The lead vehicle came even with the charges. RJ threw a switch and BOOM! No more vehicle. The caravan came to a halt and well-trained Elites deployed quickly into the surrounding areas, looking for their targets. They ran right past the three rebels and right into a trap. Nothing fancy, just a line of dummies set behind automated projectile weapons controlled by a button in RJ's hand. The troops stormed up the hill towards the fake Rebels and right into a mine field.

RJ whispered to her companions. "Those are Elites."

"So," Alexi whispered back.

"So, there weren't supposed to be any Elites in this caravan. So, what do you think of woman's intuition now, smartass?"

"What do we do?" David asked.

"We don't have a choice now," RJ said. "The men who stayed to guard the shipment aren't likely to sit down there or move on and forget about us. We've got to go on as planned. You know, sometimes—not very often, mind you—but sometimes I hate being right."

They ran in to clean up the remaining personnel. It wasn't difficult. The men that had been left behind were only first-class soldiers. Realizing that the Elites were gone, most of them were too busy deciding whether to bolt, or not to put up much of a fight. They were easy prey for the three rebels, who had killing down to a science.

When the last man fell, Alexi looked at RJ and laughed. He walked to the back of the box-shaped supply truck and took hold of the handle. "See, RJ? I told you. Nothing to worry about."

The door flew open with such force that it sent Alexi flying through the air for twenty feet. He landed on his head and was still.

David looked at the mammoth form that filled the doorway. "GSH," he breathed.

It seemed to survey the situation; then it jumped to the ground.

"Holy shit!" David screamed, then fired the projectile weapon he held in his fist.

It didn't do any good. The bullets hit the GSH, balled up, and fell off, inflicting little more than a few minor bruises. It turned its massive head to face David, and slowly raised the laser it held in its hand to level it at David's head.

"Oh, holy shit! Holy shit!" He continued to fire as he began running backwards as fast as he could.

The GSH was preoccupied with David. RJ watched. Just as the GSH prepared to shoot David, she fired. The laser hit it in the head. It groaned and fell to its knees.

David dove behind a vehicle.

RJ fired again, this time hitting it in the arm.

It swung its weapon towards where she'd been, but she was gone. It got to its feet. It wasn't particularly hurt, but it was for sure pissed off. It looked around for RJ, but obviously hadn't forgotten about David. She was nowhere to be seen. That meant there was only one place she could be. With a mighty leap, the GSH landed on top of the truck.

RJ had anticipated this move. She was lying on the other end of the truck. The moment the GSHs feet hit, she fired the laser. The bolt struck it in the chest, and threw it off the truck. It landed with a thud that seemed to shake the earth. Still the monster got up.

David threw down his projectile weapon. It was useless now. He usually felt more comfortable with it; for dropping humans it was damn near as effective as a laser. Fortunately, he hadn't stopped carrying a laser. It was under his arm in...Where was it? He looked around quickly. There it was, on the ground more than ten feet out of his reach. It must have fallen out of the holster while he was running. With a GSH lurking about, that ten feet might as well have been ten miles. David steeled himself. RJ needed his help. He made a dash for the weapon.

The GSH got shakily to its feet. It saw David and fired just as RJ landed on its back, knocking it off balance.

David's leg buckled and he hit the ground hard. He retained enough sense to grab the laser as he pulled himself back behind the vehicle. The pain finally hit him, and he looked at what was left of his leg. Tears obscured his vision, but he could still see that at least half the flesh of his right leg was gone. The smell was awful. It was all over now—his quest, his part in the rebellion. His life was going to end here, on a dusty stretch of road, at the top of a mountain he didn't even know the name of. He couldn't see RJ or the GSH now, but he could hear the struggle. He would make sure RJ won. He would make sure the rebellion didn't die here on this road with him.

RJ jumped on the GSH, knife in hand. Her intention was to sever his jugular vein.

Not too surprisingly, the GSH objected, and was trying to redirect the knife in question to a similar point on RJ's throat. On most days, it would have been no contest. The GSH was three times RJ's size and much stronger, but it had taken a lot of damage from her laser. Enough that it wasn't repairing itself as fast as it should have been.

They rolled around and around. It on top, her on top, like some bizarre mating ritual which seemed to last for hours. RJ realized that the struggle could go on long enough for the thing to repair itself. She had to make her move, and she had to do it quickly.

David saw his chance. He fired.

The laser hit the back of the GSHs head, the monster lost its grip, and RJ cut its throat. Bright red blood poured out over her. She threw him off, got up and stood watching as its struggles grew weaker and finally ceased. RJ walked over to where David was leaning against one of the vehicles. She patted him on the back, and he collapsed to the ground. After she picked him up and set him against the wheel of the truck, she looked at his leg and said nothing.

"Kill me, RJ," David said, biting on his lip to fight the pain.

"Cure you or kill you," she said thoughtfully. "There isn't any in between," she pulled the black leather pouch from her pocket and extracted the syringe.

"What are you doing?" David asked through gritted teeth.

"For once in your life could you just not ask questions?" She stabbed the needle into her arm and started to draw a syringe of blood.

"What the hell are you doing?" David demanded.

"Something I shouldn't. Now shut the fuck up." The syringe was full; she took it out. "Make a fist," she ordered.

David gave her a skeptical look.

"It will either work or you'll be dead. Either way we're never going to talk about it again. Now just make a fist."

He did, and she shoved the needle into his vein and emp-tied the syringe. She withdrew the empty needle and carefully packed it away.

At first, he felt nothing. Then there was a tingling. Then nothing again. Nothing at all—not even pain. He looked at his leg. The flesh of the wound began to bubble, and—to his amazement—it began to rebuild itself. He didn't know how much time passed, but it couldn't have been long. His leg was healed. New flesh and skin covered the wound. Oh, it wasn't exactly healthy-looking tissue; the muscle tone was nonexist-ent, and the skin was white and bare. But he had a leg again. He looked at RJ and started to speak.

RJ smiled her most rakish smile. "I told you, and I meant it. We're never going to talk about it," she stood up. "Stay still. I'm going to make sure there aren't any more of them lurking about."

"But...how..."

RJ just shook her head and walked away.

He watched her go. She wasn't human. Alexi had said she was an Argy hybrid. David hadn't believed it, but it must be true, because RJ was *definitely* not human.


"They *what*?" Jessica screamed at the messenger.

The man gulped and pulled at his collar before answering. "They killed everyone in the caravan, including the GSH."

"How?" Right bellowed in disbelief. "How did they kill the GSH?"

"What about the follow-up troops?" Jessica asked, ignor-ing Right.

"An extensive search of the area failed to turn up any sign of the rebels."

Jessica gritted her teeth. She definitely would have been all for the ancient custom of running the bearer of bad news through with a sword. "And I suppose that the roadblocks were just as ineffective," she said coolly.

"Correct, Senator." The man cringed as he said it.

Jessica drew a long, shuddering breath, and then completely lost her cool. "Fucking idiots! We had her in our hands, and they let her slip through their feeble fingers!"

"How do you suppose they killed the GSH?" Right asked again.

Jessica knew how, and she didn't want to hear that question again. She stood up and rested her fists on her desk, looking down at Right.

"I don't care how they killed the fucking GSH!" she screamed. "What I care about is that RJ is still at large, and now she knows that we know that she has the box. GSHs are expendable, Right. They are made to fight and die. So one is dead. Does it matter whether they ripped out its throat or shot it a thousand times with a laser?"

"If they can kill a GSH..." Right started.

"What, Right? If they can kill a GSH, what? They're dangerous! Now, there's something we didn't know before!" She sat down heavily and took a deep, cleansing breath. She turned her attention back to the messenger.

"I don't want anything left undone this time. I want every inch of ground for a ten-mile radius analyzed till it's bleached out white. I want everyone questioned—workers, soldiers, pigs, chickens and goats. Do you understand?"

"Yes, Senator," he stood there, waiting to be dismissed.

Jessica lost her cool again. "This week, if you don't mind too much, dumbass!"

The man practically ran from the room.

"What do you hope to find?" Right asked carefully.

"I have no idea. Something that might give us a clue as to where her base of operations is." She looked at the maps placed in front of her, and suddenly it hit her. It was so obvious she could have kicked herself for not figuring it out sooner. She stood up abruptly and started out of the room.

"Jessy, where are you going?" Right asked. She turned to look at him with a wry smile on her face.

"In my grief, I have become as stupid as everyone else. I should be back in a few hours."

Dr. Stewart tapped on his desk, pondering his latest dilemma. "So, Poley, what do you think? Should I have the chicken or the tuna?"

"The chicken looks very nice, sir," Poley answered attentively.

"Think I'll have the tuna." He picked up the sandwich, took a bite and made a face. "On second thought, the chicken does look nice." He put down the sandwich he held and picked up the other one.

Jessica swept into the lab as if she belonged there. Before she could speak, Stewart chimed in, "So, J-6, so good that you could drop in. Sit down and have a sandwich. It's hardly been used."

"I'm not in the mood for your shit, old man..."

"It's tuna," Stewart corrected.

"It has suddenly occurred to me that I'm the one you thought was dead. Your reaction to me was one of shock. So, first that tells me that I'm not supposed to exist, and second that tells me that she and I are *not* exactly the same," Jessica announced smugly.

"Oh, very good, J-6." He set his sandwich down and started to clap. "Slow, but good."

"I'm glad you're amused," she said acidly. "Now, if you'll just tell me everything you know about RJ."

"Come now, J-6. Don't be unreasonable. You know that would be detrimental to my experiment." Stewart clicked his tongue. "You wouldn't want an unfair advantage, would you?"

"She is working against the Reliance. By helping her, you are betraying the Reliance," Jessica reminded him.

"I'm not helping her. Sure you won't have the tuna?"

"Damn it, Stewart..."

"Call me Dad," Stewart said with a smile. Jessica took him by the collar and shoved him against his workbench. She gave him her most terrifying look, and was more than a little perturbed when he refused to be frightened.

"Tell me everything you know about RJ, or I'll pull your head off," Jessica snarled.

Stewart laughed in her face. "So, pull my head off if it pleases you. I'm an old man. It's been a long time since I feared death."

"Tell me!" She shook him till his dentures rattled.

"No." Stewart said as plainly as he could under the circumstances.

Jessica let him go. It was no bluff. He really wasn't afraid of death. Jessica looked at the robot. She smiled, then walked over and grabbed hold of his arm.

"What are you doing?" Stewart demanded.

Jessica's smile broadened. "As I thought. You care more for this metal man than you care for yourself. Tell me all you know about RJ, or I'll rip this thing apart. And believe me, I'll know if you're lying."

"You didn't last time," Stewart said, still cocky.

"I was distraught last time. I'm not now." She twisted the robot's arm. "It wouldn't be hard for me to tear your favorite toy apart."

"I don't know any more than you do. In fact, I probably know less."

"You can do better than that, Stewart. How did you know I wasn't RJ?" Jessica twisted harder on the robot's arm, and this time he yelped.

"She's bigger that you are," Stewart said, grudgingly.

"And?"

"She has a deformity caused by an overdose of growth hormone. Her right arm jerks."

"She's imperfect!" Jessica said in disbelief.

Stewart knew what she was getting at. It wasn't like him to keep anything that wasn't perfect. "I never meant to let her live. I just kept her as part of the experiment. She damn near died. Then she got better. I mean *really* better. Brighter, stronger, more determined than the others. Her empathic powers were much stronger. She also has much better manners. She would never enter my lab without knocking."

"So, what you're saying is..."

"That if the tables were turned, you'd have been dead long ago," Stewart snarled. "In retrospect, it is obvious that you are the imperfect one."

Jessica let go of Poley and slapped Stewart across the face. She could have killed him. She had only bloodied his lip.

Poley went to Stewart's side, and helped him steady himself.

Wiping the blood from his lip, Stewart grinned. "Did I hit a nerve, J-6? It now becomes obvious to me why RJ would choose to fight the Reliance. She's a free thinker. She could never take orders from someone like you."

"The Reliance is the savior of the human race."

Stewart clapped. "Oh, bravo! Recited like a true Reliance zombie. The Reliance is a boil on the ass of the thinking man—a system that you have to get around to get anything worthwhile done. It takes and takes and takes, and gives back nothing but pain."

It was Jessica's turn to laugh. "And to think I have always believed scientists weren't political."

"I wasn't. But after talking to you, it seems that I have become so."

Jessica had learned all she thought she could. She walked towards the door. "I'll be back."

"Any time!" Stewart called out to her back.

She was gone. Stewart sighed with relief. She hadn't asked the one question that could have really hurt RJ.

"Are you all right, sir?" Poley asked with concern.

"Yes, I'm fine..."

"I would have done something, but..."

"She would have crushed you like a tin can."

"That was my thinking," Poley said. "I'm sorry you're hurt."

"You know, Poley, I have given it a great deal of thought. I have studied all the data and assessed it. I say the hell with it. I know that RJ's odds of winning are far less than J-6's. After all, J-6 has the entire Reliance behind her. Damn it all, I love RJ, and I can't stand J-6. It can't be long before J-6 figures out that I know how to find RJ. When she returns, you must not be here."

"What do you mean?" Poley didn't understand. He'd *always* been here; where else should he be?

"You're going to go help RJ."

"But what about you?" Poley was more than a little confused. He wasn't at all sure that he could survive without Stewart, much less Stewart without him.

"J-6 will return soon. When she does, you can't be here, Poley."

"But she'll kill you," Poley said.

Stewart smiled sadly. "You're too sentimental, Tin Pants. I promise that she won't kill me."

"I will miss you," Poley said.

"Go now, Poley. You have a new master and a new mission."

Poley turned and walked slowly to the door where he stopped and turned to look at Stewart.

"Would you go?" Stewart said, wiping a tear from his eye.

"Goodbye, Father." Stewart rushed up and hugged the metal man.

The robot didn't hug him back.

"Goodbye, son, and good luck. Give my love to your sister."

# Chapter Twelve

As soon as she saw the lights of Alsterase, her heart began to lighten, and she was filled with a happy, giddy sort of feeling. They were finally home.

She abandoned David and Alexi and went bounding up the stairs of the hotel. She burst into the room without knocking, and clicked on the lights. "I'm home!" she announced.

Whitey's first reaction was to grab his gun. But the second his eyes adjusted to the light and he saw who had interrupted his sleep, he forgot all about the weapon.

It took him a second to find his voice. "My God! I thought I'd never see you again."

To his surprise and delight, she landed on the bed beside him. She gave him a big smile and started to say something flippant, but then she saw the look in his eyes, felt his feelings, and decided to face what she'd been running from.

"Would it have been that bad if I'd never come back?" she asked quietly.

"I would have missed you." He took her in his arms and kissed her.

She liked the way his love felt. Warm, comfortable and familiar, like an old coat. She responded eagerly to his kisses.

Mickey rubbed his eyes, took in the strange scene, and smiled. The legend had returned.

Levits' response was to roll over on his cot and try to go back to sleep.

When David and Alexi reached the room, Whitey and RJ were still lip-locked in the middle of the bed. If Alexi was shocked to see RJ in the arms of a stranger, he was even more surprised by David's lack of concern.

"You might have helped us with the boxes, RJ," David complained dropping his.

RJ finally pried herself away from Whitey. "I see Levits decided to join us."

"I don't know what good you think he'll do us," Whitey said. "He's a lazy coward."

"We all have our little faults." RJ shrugged and got up from the bed.

She walked over and embraced Mickey. "You're looking well."

"Been getting some sun. Good to see you."

"So, Levits," she shook him till she got his reluctant attention. He finally turned to face her. "Why the change of heart?" she asked with a wry smile.

"Many things, really. Hunger, getting rained on, getting the crap beaten out of me twice weekly." Levits, for all his faults, was truthful.

"That's what we need in our soldiers, David. Men with heartfelt conviction," she said with a lilt to her voice.

David had never seen her like this. In a way it was funny. He smiled broadly back at her, to let her know that he approved of her temporary lapse of restraint. She probably would have babbled on happily making no sense for hours, but Alexi opened his mouth.

"This place is a dump."

Considering how glad RJ was to be home, this was probably the worst thing he could have said.

"Since it distresses you so much, you can clean it up." RJ said in a growl.

"I'm not a fucking house maid." Alexi took an ominous step towards RJ, and found his face in the middle of Whitey Baldor's rather large chest. He looked up at the giant, and swallowed hard. He heard RJ's voice, cool and superior, and wished more than ever that he could slap that smug smile off her face.

"You'll find that you won't get as much leeway here, Alexi. I suggest that you learn to accept that I run things. If I say clean it up, you will put on an apron and ask whether I want the windows done or not. Do you understand?"

Alexi was silent.

Whitey's huge hand went around his throat. "She asked you a question, Jack," Whitey said coolly, and Alexi realized that the man could snap his neck with no trouble and with even less remorse.

"I understand," Alexi choked out. He understood that if he wanted to run things, he was going to have to get rid of RJ. Or at least discredit her.

Jessica sat in her quarters at Capitol looking at the knife in her hand. She sighed, then steeled herself. She had to know. She sat between the two mirrors and pinned her hair up. She knew the spot. She took the knife and began to dig the device from the back of her neck. It was a painful process, but when she cleaned the device off, it was worth any amount of pain. It was broken, and had been for some time. Moreover, it had been more than a vital signs monitor. The old man didn't just know that RJ was alive, he knew where she was.

Poley saw the lights of Alsterase off in the distance. Soon he would be reunited with RJ. Soon he would be himself—Poley, a component of RJ.

Jessica stormed into Stewart's lab.

He looked up and smiled. "I've been expecting you, J-6."

She held out the device for him to see.

"Been digging in your neck, I see. That couldn't have been pleasant."

"Can the crap, old man. Where is RJ?" Jessica demanded.

"I really have no idea. At the moment, she might be any-where." He smiled sweetly.

Damn it all, he wasn't lying. Jessica realized instantly what that meant.

"Where is the metal man?" She looked around in a panic.

Stewart smiled and looked at his watch. "Well, by now, he's probably taking tea with RJ."

"Where's her base? You know where it is, tell me," she commanded.

"You have that tone in your voice, J-6. The sound of someone who's used to getting their way. I've always hated that."

"Tell me." She took one menacing step forward.

Stewart laughed, and she stopped in her tracks. Stewart's features went cold. "I'm not going to tell you, J-6. And I'm not going to give you the chance to beat it out of me or extract it with drugs, either. I'm an old man. RJ is my greatest creation. Her secret belongs to me, and it's the one thing I can take with me."

"No!" Too late, she saw the barrel of the pistol enter Stewart's mouth. She leapt forward, reaching him just as he pulled the trigger. Then watched in horror as his limp body collapsed to the ground, spasmed once, and lay still.

She had watched hundreds of men die. Hell, she'd killed most of them, but this was different. She knelt beside him and gently moved the strands of bloody gray hair out of his face.

"Why?" she asked the inert form. "Why her? Why not me? All I wanted was your help." She stood up and wiped a tear from her eye. "I was just another experiment. What made her different?"

She left without looking back. Yet another lead was lost forever. Still, Jessica would do her best. In spite of the fact that for the first time she doubted that her best would be good enough.

David wasted no time picking up where he'd left off. After all, there were still women in Alsterase he hadn't screwed. He didn't really like taking Alexi with him on his nightly excursions, but RJ more or less insisted. No doubt her way of punishing David for insisting that they take on Alexi, whom she hated.

David didn't understand what was happening. On the raids, he and RJ had been as close as ever. Maybe closer. But since they'd been home, he felt a distance growing between them. She seemed cool to him, at times even argumentative.

He didn't much care for the sleeping arrangements, either. He still slept in the bed, but RJ didn't always sleep with him. She would be in the bed when he came in most times, but as soon as he lay down, she would get up, grab a blanket, and find a piece of floor. This habit was all the more irritating because Whitey Baldor had a way of finding out where she was and moving so that he woke up in the morning with his head between RJ's tits. There was no doubt in David's mind that the giant was tragically in love with RJ. Tragically, because it was just as obvious that RJ was too focused on overthrowing the Reliance to even notice.

RJ, Whitey, Levits, and Mickey were discussing important business.

"So do we eat the lobsters or the crabs?"

There was much discussion, but they finally decided on the crabs. Whitey had his hand down RJ's shirt, and was sucking on her neck. This had become so commonplace that she barely noticed anymore.

"Keep an eye on Alexi, boys. I don't trust him. Not because he'd go to the Reliance, but because he wants to be me."

"He's quite a piece of work," Levits said, taking a drink from his glass. "Last night he informed me that I was sleeping on his piece of floor."

"He damn near got us all killed out there," RJ said making a face as she remembered the sight of David's leg.

"Why not just kill him and get it over with?" Mickey asked.

"Because he's useful for the time being," RJ said, taking a drag off her cigarette.

"If had told me what to do, would kick butt," Mickey said, in Levits' direction.

"Yeah, right," Levits said.

"Well, would if was your size."

"Hey, just because I'd rather move than get my face kicked in…"

"Don't get your panties in a knot, Levits. Cowardice I can tolerate, treachery I can not." She took a long drink, then swallowed thoughtfully. Whitey's hand had found its way to her breast, his lips had moved to her earlobe, and Levits now found it impossible to concentrate on anything else.

"How can you talk when he's doing that?" Levits wanted to know. Whitey pulled away, as if giving up.

"I ask myself that at least a hundred and fifty times a day," he said with a sigh.

RJ smiled and shrugged. "What can I say? After awhile you get used to anything."

"I know what I'd like you to get used to," Whitey said slyly.

Levits laughed heartily. "I've got an embroidered picture of her talking all the way through it, and you being happy."

They all laughed, then ordered another round of drinks while they waited for their dinner. By the time dinner got there everyone but RJ was about half drunk.

David was having a rare night. He had put his hook out in several bars, and hadn't had so much as a nibble. They had worked their way back to the Golden Arches.

"Cheer up, David," Alexi said, rapping him in a friendly manner on the shoulder. "You always have RJ."

"Huh?" David asked, never taking his eyes off a brunette at the bar.

"RJ. You know," Alexi made an obscene gesture which took both hands.

David shook his head decisively. "RJ and I have never…" He made the same gesture.

"Give me a break. I've seen you sleep with her," Alexi said. "Whose virtue are you trying to protect here, David? This is RJ. RJ, who fucks Whitey Baldor, of all people."

David didn't like RJ's name being said in the same sentence as "fucks."

"RJ doesn't screw me, and I don't think she does him, either," David said hotly.

"Ah, come on, David! Get your head out of your ass! RJ is half Argy. Those damned hybrid bitches could screw a mink to death. Literally. I knew a guy had his neck broke by one. They're really strong, and when they have orgasm, they just lose it. I had one myself once...."

"An orgasm?" David said flippantly.

"No, an Argy. It was a trip, like nothing I've ever had before or since."

David didn't know why Alexi was making him so mad. Maybe because he had finally began to see what RJ had seen all along. For instance right now Alexi was trying to belittle RJ's importance by making her into an object for sex.

"Alexi," David hissed the name through clenched teeth. "If it comes to a choice between you and RJ, RJ always wins. You try to hurt her in any way, and I'll stop you myself."

Alexi laughed nervously. "Calm down, old man, I have no designs on our intrepid leader."

"Make sure you keep it that way," David spat.

Suddenly, the bar was deathly quiet. David turned to see who was fighting and why. In the doorway stood a tall, slender man with immaculate, short-cropped black hair and coal black eyes. He wore a two-piece black leather suit and spit-and-polish black boots. He had an air of importance about him, and while it was obvious that he was out of his element, it was just as obvious that he was not afraid.

He looked around the bar for several minutes, then turned and left.

Curious, David followed him with Alexi scrambling behind him. The man was stepping into—much to David's disbelief—a bright red air-car.

The man turned, looked at David and Alexi and smiled. "Ah, you look familiar."

"Kill him; he's Reliance," Alexi said urgently.

"What do you want here?" David asked in his most intimidating tone of voice.

"I am looking for my sister," he said simply. "You are not my sister, so good day to you." He started to get in his car.

"Perhaps we could help you," David said, grabbing the man's arm.

The man looked down at David's hand curiously, but was still unconcerned. There was only one explanation for this man and his attire. It wouldn't be the first time some well-to-do Reliance brat had run off to Alsterase to catch a glimpse of the other side. They usually had to be rescued by siblings or parents. After all, a well-to-do (and therefore military) Reliance family wouldn't want it known that their precious little darling had been consorting with the scum of Alsterase.

The problem was, it explained the man's presence all too well, and was a perfect cover for a Reliance spy.

"What does your sister look like?" David asked carefully.

"I remember, and I'll know her when I find her. Now, if you'll excuse me." He started to pull away, and Alexi started to hit him.

David grabbed Alexi's arm. "I'm going to ask you again. What does your sister look like?"

Suddenly, the man's face seemed to light up. He raised his arm and waved extravagantly. "That's what my sister looks like."

David turned and saw, to his amazement, RJ and her crew getting ready to enter the hotel.

David started to question the man, but he was gone.

He bounded over the car and ran towards RJ.

David went after him. He tackled the man just feet from her.

When she heard the commotion, RJ turned, laser in hand.

The man shook David off, and stood up in a single movement.

RJ looked at him in disbelief. "Poley?"

"RJ!" He clapped his hands together. "I think I am excited."

RJ laughed, then moved forward to hug him. He didn't hug her back. "Poley, what on earth are you doing here?"

Before he could answer, David demanded. "Is this man really your brother?"

RJ looked at Poley and smiled broadly. She nodded her head. "Yes. Yes, he is." She saw the air car and made all the right assumptions.

"Levits, take that thing and park it on the roof."

"Well, that ought to make fatso really happy," Levits mumbled as he went to move the car.

RJ took Poley's hand. "Come on, let's go up to the room."

In the room, David silently fumed as he listened to RJ and her brother talk.

"You never answered me, Poley. What are you doing here?" Poley was more or less a component of Stewart. Till now, she had always assumed that Poley was pretty much dysfunctional without Stewart. Apparently, that wasn't true.

"Our father sent me," Poley answered.

David snorted angrily. Not just a brother, but her father was still living.

RJ ignored David. "Why, Poley? Why did Father send you here?"

"To help you." Poley watched David. He didn't understand the man's reaction, and he found it curious. "Because he doesn't like J-6."

RJ didn't like that term, and she decided the rest of their conversation should be conducted in private.

"What else have you lied about, RJ?" David demanded. He was ignored.

RJ grabbed Poley by the hand and started to pull him towards the bathroom.

"Hybrid bitch," David cursed.

This got RJ's attention. She swung around to face him. "What did you say?"

"He called you a hybrid bitch," Whitey said, helpfully.

"Thanks a lot," David mumbled.

"No problem," the giant said with a smile.

RJ pulled Poley into the bathroom and shut the door, which Whitey and Mickey had replaced in their absence.

David glared at the closed door. He was being shut out. He was slowly being replaced in RJ's life.

"OK, Poley, I'll bite. What's a J-6?" RJ asked.

"Who," he corrected. "J-6 is Senator of Zone 2-A, and she is from the same batch as yourself."

RJ sat down heavily on the toilet seat.

"That explains a lot."

Poley nodded.

"How many of us did Stewart make?" She had always assumed that she was part of a batch. This just confirmed it.

"Twelve. But, as far as we know, you and J-6 are the only ones still operational. However J-6's calling unit was damaged, so who knows? You may all still be operational. You are the strongest, brightest, et cetera."

RJ smiled. It had always been obvious that Poley had been based on Stewart.

Stewart had told her that for some reason, her defect—the jerking arm—was directly related to other, more favorable aspects of her physical makeup. Now it made sense that he had come to this judgment by assessing her against others.

She started to fill Poley in with all he needed to know to function in this new environment. The last thing she told him was. "I want you to monitor Alexi."

"May I know why?"

"Because I don't trust him. That's why."

Poley nodded.

"Now, tell me about J-6."

"What the hell are they doing in there?" David asked in frustration. He moved closer to the door.

"Get back," RJ warned from inside.

"What are they talking about for so long? And why is it such a big secret?" Alexi asked, trying to add to the paranoia. "I don't like it."

"And I don't like you," Whitey growled.

"And I need to use the john," Levits said, uncomfortably.

"Go out the window," David suggested, flopping down on the bed. He had more important things to worry about than Levits' toileting needs.

"I would if I only had to whizz," Levits said, jumping around in an odd way.

"There's probably a charge for shitting on the side walk," Whitey said lightly. "After all, this is a classy joint."

"Ha, ha," Levits said. "It's easy for you to make jokes. Your piles aren't backing up."

"I don't understand. Why wouldn't she come over? What is her tie to the Reliance?" RJ smiled crookedly. "Besides being a Senator I mean."

"Governor Bristol."

"Yes, I killed him. So?" She was growing impatient with him.

"He was J-6's lover..."

"Her what?" RJ shouted. She put her hand to her mouth. "He was her what?" she repeated, quietly.

"You have total recall." Poley didn't understand the necessity of repeating himself. Perhaps she had become partly dysfunctional.

"Humor me," RJ said acidly. She just *couldn't* have heard him correctly.

Poley shrugged. "She said he was her lover. I have no reason to believe that she lied." He went on, "She is very intent on killing you."

RJ was thoughtful. This could change a lot of things, or it could mean nothing at all.

"I have to say that both Stewart and I were very surprised. We had naturally assumed that in any kind of sexual relationship, considering your maternal parentage and your massive strength, that you would crush your mate to death during orgasm."

"Thank you very much, Poley," RJ said with a sigh.

"You're welcome." He smiled his very best synthetic smile. Sarcasm was more or less wasted on the robot.

As they emerged from the bathroom, Levits danced in. He came out some time later, a very relieved look on his face.

There were a lot of things she should have been mulling over, many things that should have been occupying her brain. Important things. Things that needed all her attention. But all she could think about was that J-6 had had a lover. She'd had sex with a human man, and he'd survived. Been quite healthy, actually, before RJ killed him.

Everyone else went to bed long before RJ did. When she finally did, she crawled into bed with David. This time he got up and moved to the floor. Damn, this was just what she needed. He was mad at her. Probably because she hadn't told him about her family. But how could she?

She looked to where he tossed and turned on the floor and smiled. Good, he couldn't sleep either. It wasn't much of a consolation. She didn't want him to be mad at her. He had called her a hybrid bitch! The nerve, the gall of the man! If he was mad, that was his own fault. Piss on him! Three minutes later, she joined him on the floor. She put her hand on his shoulder.

"David, I'm sorry."

He harrumphed.

"Oh, come on, David, quit acting like a baby."

"You lied to me!" he said in disbelief. "You looked me right in the eye and told me a bold-faced lie."

"Ah, come on, David," she said, with equal disbelief. "At worst it was a little white lie."

"A little white lie?" David nearly yelled. RJ put a finger over his lips, and he lowered his voice. "You told me you had no family. You told me you were raised Elite."

"You called me a hybrid bitch." RJ countered.

"Don't change the subject," David said hotly. "You lied to me."

"You called me a hybrid bitch." Suddenly, she didn't want to make up with him any more. She started to get up, and he grabbed her arm. For a moment she froze. She looked at where his hand touched her arm. Then she did something that shocked her at least as much as it did him.

She kissed him.

Because it was a reflex action, he kissed her back without thinking. He found her mouth a warm, wonderful, and wildly erotic place to be. He felt her hands running recklessly over his body. He could actually hear her heart pounding. His hands began their own exploration, almost without direction from his mind. She had an amazingly fascinating body, smooth but not soft. She had great breasts. Suddenly, her kisses became more demanding, he felt her hand at his waist undoing his pants. It came to him all at once. It was RJ's breast in his hand, RJ's tongue climbing down his throat, RJ's hips moving seductively against his.

He couldn't do this. Not with RJ. It would be like doing his sister. He tried to push her away, but RJ didn't want to be pushed.

"RJ," David said, pulling his lips away from her. She still wasn't responding. "RJ, for God's sake."

RJ was confused. Why was he doing this? Had she hurt him? She let him go. She looked at him. He wasn't in pain. He was fine. So, what was the problem?

David could see the confusion on her face. Knowing that hybrids were at least somewhat empathic, he rushed to explain.

"RJ..." How to word this? He ran a gentle hand over her hair. "You are beautiful, and by far the most exciting woman I've ever known. I would make love to you in a minute if you were any other woman in the world, but you're not. You're my best friend. I love you in a way that I have never loved anyone else, but I don't love you *that* way. And I can't just have sex with you because...well, I wouldn't feel right if I did."

She felt like a fool. She felt raw and exposed. What should she say? What could she say? "I'm sorry," she finally ground out.

"Me, too," David said with a shy smile.

"Good night." RJ got to her feet. Damn! She had never felt like this in her life. Well, maybe just that once when she'd been showering with a lot of men on...No, she'd never felt like this. There lay Whitey. Whitey loved her. He would hold her. He would comfort her, and she felt a great need to be comforted.

Besides, J-6 had had sex. Now RJ wanted it. Now that she knew it was possible. Right now. Whitey would be only too happy to oblige her.

She lay down at his back, put her arm around him, and kissed his neck. She ran her hand over his bare back. "Whitey..."

"No, RJ," Whitey's voice was cool, and she could feel his pain even if she didn't understand it.

"Why not?" RJ said in disbelief. "Come on, Whitey." She kissed his back.

"No, RJ! And you know why," he said firmly.

RJ got up and stormed out of the apartment, stopping only long enough to grab her chain.

Whitey went into the bathroom and stepped—with his pants still on—into the shower.

David went into the bathroom. "Was that really necessary?" David demanded. He didn't know why he was so angry at Whitey. Perhaps because he thought RJ should have what she wanted, and he couldn't give it to her. "Excuse me if I sound stupid. But haven't you been trying to get in that woman's pants ever since you met her?"

Whitey turned the water off. He turned to face David, trying very hard to hate him. He couldn't really. After all, it wasn't David's fault. In fact, David was telling him to do something that he wanted to do. "You're a fool, David."

"ME? I don't want to ball her," David said, shaking his head in disbelief. "You know RJ. Do you actually think she's going to give you a second chance?"

Whitey grabbed a towel and started to dry his head. "I don't expect you to understand this, David." He threw the towel on the floor, and looked into David's eyes. "I know RJ and I will be together someday. But when she comes to me, I don't want it to be because you wouldn't ball her first. Call me a romantic, but I don't want her in my bed simply because you didn't want her in yours."

"All well and good, Whitey, but while you're sitting here nursing your wounded pride, do you know what she's doing?"

"She's walking off some steam," Whitey said, without blinking an eye.

"Wishful thinking," David said. "She's out looking for a stud."

"Well, that's her business." Whitey knew better. He took off his wet pants and went and lay down on the bed. He stared at the ceiling. He was hurt. He had fantasized that when she was ready she would come to him. But she hadn't. She'd gone to David. He had been trying to convince himself that RJ didn't love David, but now it was pretty obvious that she did. But David didn't love her. In fact, Whitey wasn't sure David was capable of loving anyone but himself.

Whitey smiled. As long as David stayed out of the running, he could make RJ love him. It was all a matter of time. He decided to sleep. He was going to need his strength.

RJ walked through the dark streets of Alsterase. Most places were still open, and she stopped many times for a drink. The night air was cool, but even shoeless RJ was not uncomfortable. The only weapon she had with her was her chain. It was wrapped around her right shoulder and rested on her left hip. It now had a small fortune in coins wrapped around its links, and she looked at them as she walked along.

She had never been so confused in all her life. She didn't even try to bring reason to her random thoughts. She just let them bounce around in her head. Occasionally, they ran head-long into each other, and caused even more chaos.

This seemed like a good thing to do. The last thing she wanted to do was think real, solid thoughts about sex, J-6, kissing David, or trying to screw Whitey. She surely didn't want to give any thought to having been turned down by not one, but two men in one night! She didn't want to think about how wonderful it had felt to be held, or how awful it was to be pushed away. *Life sucks*, she thought, and kicked a can so hard it went out of sight.

David had pushed her away. That had hurt worse than any injury she had ever suffered. She'd never known defeat. People said it was a humbling feeling, but it just pissed RJ off.

She was horny. She admitted this. So what? Why shouldn't she be? She was a sixty-four-year-old virgin. She shuddered at the thought.

Still, it was probably a good thing that they had both turned her down. After all, just because J-6 had done it, didn't mean that she could.

She saw a man who caught her eye and started to follow him. He was a total stranger. She could sleep with him. If she crushed him to death as Poley had so eloquently put it, who cared? But only seconds after she'd started to follow him, her pace slowed. It just didn't sound like much fun, doing it with a perfect stranger. Especially if there was a good chance that he might also say no. She'd had enough rejection for one night.

She would have gone home then, if it weren't for the fact that she'd made such a total ass of herself. She walked around till about ten o'clock the next morning. Then, realizing that she had to go home sometime, she started back. Maybe they'd all be out.

They weren't. Whitey was still there. For a moment, she thought about turning around and leaving.

"Your brother said you'd come back here, then took off with the others to go look for you." Whitey smiled. "I figured your brother would know you best." He knew damn good and well there was no way that Poley was her brother, but he would play along.

"I'm sorry about last night," she said sheepishly. Then her frustration reared its ugly head, and she screamed. "And drop dead!"

Whitey smiled. "I love you, too, RJ."

She threw herself down face first on the bed. "God, my head feels like jelly."

She rolled over and looked at him. She felt the love radiating from him, and she wanted it. Without a word, he lay down beside her.

She didn't really know who started it. If she kissed him, or he her. But she was in his arms, and it felt good. It felt right.

Whitey had never wanted anything the way he wanted her. It had never been so personal. He had never loved anyone else. They exchanged caresses and kisses. Clothes were discarded like old rags. He wanted her; he needed her. She was everything he had dreamed that she would be, and in a few minutes she would be his. Then she hurt him. Nothing terrible, and he tried to ignore it, till it reached the point that he couldn't. He'd hoped that she'd realize what she was doing and stop, but she wasn't.

"RJ," he swallowed hard. "RJ, you're hurting me."

She recoiled from him like he was hot.

He reached out and moved the strands of hair away from her face. "Don't stop," he kissed her gently on the lips. "Just be more careful."

She looked at him with wide eyes. He knew. Damn him, he knew what she was. She sat up.

He got up on one elbow and looked up at her, unafraid.

"How long have you known?" she asked gently. She was having trouble grasping the fact that he knew what she was, and yet he still loved her. Still wanted to show his love this way.

"I had my suspicions from the first." He ran his fingertip over her lips. "I'd never had any one whip me, not even another hybrid. Then when David tried to take the Pronuses for a headache..." He shrugged.

"And you don't care?" she asked in disbelief.

He shrugged and smiled. "I don't care." He moved to kiss her on the lips, and she jumped up and went to the window. She stared down at the streets below. He moved up behind her, and wrapped his arms around her.

"I can't..."

"You can, RJ. If you just will," Whitey said. "Damn it, RJ, I don't want anyone else. There hasn't been anyone else since the night you gave me the laser."

RJ was only a little surprised by his announcement. "Whitey, if you know what I am, you must realize that there is a very good chance that you might not live through our mating. I thought I could contain myself, but obviously I can't."

"I'm willing to take the risk." He kissed the back of her neck.

"Well, I'm not." She moved away from him, and started to get dressed. "I'm not willing to risk killing you so that I can get my rocks off."

"Damn you, RJ." He put his pants back on, feeling far too vulnerable without them. "I know you won't hurt me."

"I already have," she said sadly, looking at the bruise already welling up on his arm. She walked over to him and took his hand gently. She looked up into his eyes. "You know that I know how you feel about me, and you know that I don't feel that same way about you. I wish I did, but I don't, and for us to lie to each other would be pretty pointless. But I do care about you, Whitey. I can twist a two-inch piece of steel in half with my bare hands. If I lose control, even for a moment..."

Whitey swallowed hard. "You will love me, RJ."

"I'm sorry." And she was.

He took her in his arms, and they held each other.

"Just don't say no, RJ," Whitey whispered. "Don't say we'll never be together, because I can't live believing that's true. Don't shut me out, because, whether you admit it or not, you need me as much as I need you." He laughed nervously. "Would you listen to me? I sound like some love struck third class farm worker." All traces of humor left his voice. "But I mean it, RJ. All of it."

She knew he did.

What did he mean, she needed him? Needed him for what? Then she realized how good it felt to be held by him. To know he loved her. The unselfish thing would have been to wish that he didn't love her. Instead, she was glad he did. She pushed away from him, knowing that her convictions would wane if she didn't put some distance between them.

Just then, David and the others returned. "Thank God, you're all right!" David exclaimed.

"Why wouldn't I be?" RJ said coolly, and started trolling the room for food. She found half of a peanut butter sandwich under a dirty shirt and started to eat it. "Poley, go get me something to eat. I'm starving to death."

Poley nodded and left.

"So, RJ. Find what you were looking for?" Alexi asked sarcastically.

"Cool it, Alexi," David warned.

RJ took a final bite of the sandwich, and threw the crust— which was hard enough to do damage to normal teeth—out the window.

"Alexi, is my...for lack of a better word...sex life any of your concern?"

"No," Alexi said with a smug grin. "It's mostly David's."

RJ hid her embarrassment by starting to search the room for food again. She pretended not to have heard Alexi's answer.

Alexi wasn't pleased at all. "Actually, now that I think about it, I guess it's everyone's concern."

RJ knew what he meant, and she still chose to ignore him. She knew that he was trying to get a rise out of her, and she wasn't about to give him the satisfaction...At least not until he made her mad enough so that she could feel good about killing him. Not that she would feel bad now.

Whitey didn't feel the same way about it, however. His wound was too new and too deep. "Shut the fuck up." He spat at Alexi across the room.

"Oh, that's right," Alexi laughed. "She tried to screw you, too."

That was too much. Whitey had all this pent-up energy, and frustration. Killing Alexi was a perfect way of relieving himself of both. He ran at Alexi, and pounded him into the plasterboard wall with his shoulder. The old plasterboard broke, and clouds of dust filled the air. You could just barely make out Whitey pounding on Alexi's face. RJ continued to hunt for something to eat.

David tried to pull Whitey off, but soon realized he could accomplish nothing alone. Levits quietly snuck out the door, and Mickey scrambled up on the bed and started jumping up and down screaming encouragement at Whitey. Not that he needed any.

"RJ!" David screamed as he hung on Whitey's back. There was no response from RJ. She'd given up on her quest for food and was in the bathroom, brushing her teeth. "RJ, for God's sake!" he screamed.

RJ walked from the bathroom, still brushing her teeth. "What?" she asked, through a mouthful of toothpaste, as if she were really put out.

"What?" David screamed in disbelief. "He's killing Alexi! Do you think you might give me a hand?"

She clapped, and went back into the bathroom.

"That's not funny, RJ!" David screamed.

Whitey took a break from beating Alexi just long enough to throw David off his back. David landed at RJ's feet as she stepped out of the bathroom. "Would you help?" David begged.

David didn't care that Alexi had insulted her, and RJ certainly didn't care whether Whitey killed Alexi or not.

She looked at Alexi. The only thing that was holding him up were the blows which pounded continuously into his head. He'd be dead soon. If he wasn't already. David didn't want him dead. It was time to strike a deal.

"If I make him stop, do you promise never to mention what happened last night?"

David didn't have to think about that offer. It was what he wanted anyway. "No problem."

RJ walked over to Whitey, and put her hand on his shoulder. "Let him go," she whispered gently.

Whitey let go of Alexi, and he fell with a sick thump to the floor. Before Whitey could change his mind, David grabbed Alexi and pulled him into the bathroom. Mickey followed. He helped David put him into the tub. David started filling it with cold water. He took a damp rag, and started cleaning up what was left of Alexi's face.

Alexi coughed. He came to a bit, and immediately spit blood and two teeth from his mouth.

"Well, you've done it this time, Alexi. It wasn't enough that RJ hated your guts. You weren't happy till you made an enemy of Whitey Baldor," David said.

"I don't like you, either," Mickey said, and seeing that Alexi was going to live after all, stomped out of the room.

"You saved me," Alexi said, in a thankful, if somewhat battered voice.

"Actually, RJ did," David said.

"RJ?" Alexi couldn't fathom that. Even in his current state, he was aware that this sounded all wrong.

"It surprised the hell outta me, too." David cleaned Alexi's wounds. He hoped that the cold water would keep him coherent. Some of these wounds needed stitches, and he only knew one person who could do that. He went to get RJ, and found her with Baldor's tongue down her throat. Now would not be a good time to ask her to stitch up Alexi's head, if there really was a good time for that.

Mickey lay in the middle of the bed, watching the couple and obviously getting his jollies, David gave him a dirty look, and motioned with his head towards the door. Mickey just grinned and shook his head no.

David sighed; he was surrounded by animals.

The fat manager waddled into the apartment. "OK, where is it?" he demanded.

RJ pushed Whitey away. "What?" she demanded not bothering to straighten her clothes. "You could have knocked."

"The door was open," he said. "Don't try to change the subject. Where's the body?"

"There is no body," David assured him. The blood dripping from the rag he held in his hand didn't add credibility to his words.

"Mind if I look around?" the manager asked skeptically.

"Be my guest," RJ said with a shrug.

He waddled into the bathroom. A few minutes later, he waddled out. "That man's almost dead."

"Almost only counts in explosives," RJ said with a sweet smile.

"If he dies..."

"You'll be the first to know," RJ assured him.

"There's a charge for stiffs, you know."

"Really? I wasn't aware of that." RJ looked at Whitey. "You're going to have to take better care of your toys."

"There's a rule. You'll find it in your lease." He cleared his throat and recited. "All sex acts involving more than one person must be conducted with the door closed."

He looked at Mickey. "Want to get the door?" Then he looked expectantly at Whitey and RJ.

"Get the hell out of here, or there really will be a stiff in our room," Whitey spat.

He made a face and left.

Whitey watched as RJ moved swiftly away from him. But putting distance between them wasn't going to work forever; it was just a matter of time now, and time was the one thing Whitey had plenty of.

# Chapter Thirteen

Jessica paced back and forth like a caged animal. It had been several weeks since RJ had raided the supply train full of communicators. The train where RJ had come up against trained Elites and a GSH and had destroyed them all. They had found Jack's box at the scene—proof that RJ knew what Jessica had done and that it wouldn't work again.

Jessica was right back at square one. No clues, no edge, flying blind. She had no idea where or when RJ would show up. Jessica was unaccustomed to being helpless. It was a feeling she promised herself she was not going to get used to.

Theoretically, she and RJ should be identical, but they weren't. RJ embraced chaos, while Jessica worked to preserve the Reliance, the pinnacle of order.

Jessica sat at her desk, and once more studied the autopsy report. RJ had beaten the GSH nearly to death, and then slit its throat. It had been no more trouble to her than anything else they had thrown at her. This upset Jessica more than anything to date, because she wasn't so sure that she could live through a hand-to-hand encounter with a GSH.

Jessica had no doubt that RJ planned to build an army. Yet there was no such activity visible, much less activity on the scale that would be necessary to carry off such a coup.

Jessica didn't understand what motivated RJ. The reports indicated that she had refused to participate in a cleansing exercise, but she had no trouble killing Jack and all his guards in cold blood just to cover the stealing of his box. In Jessica's mind, the two things seemed to contradict one another.

RJ was a genuine threat to the Reliance—at least the Reliance here on Earth. Even if that fat idiot Jago didn't think so. His opinion didn't change the facts, no matter how much he might wish the problem away. Her meeting with the self-important Blob of Sector 11-N had been nothing more or less than a humongous joke.

"Come now, Senator," Jago had laughed, his blubber rippling like a hippo doing a hula. "Grant you this RJ person has been a dreadful nuisance, but to suggest that she can be any more that a trivial hindrance?" He laughed again. "Why, it's absolutely absurd!"

Jessica gritted her teeth. If he admitted RJ was a real threat, then he would have to inform the World Commissioner. So when you boiled it all down, Jago refused to do anything drastic to get rid of RJ because to do that was to acknowledge that RJ was a real threat. He didn't want to admit that RJ was a real threat because he didn't want to have to tell his big brother that he couldn't handle his sector and its problems.

"We need more GSHs. The only one who can sanction their manufacture is the World Commissioner," Jessica reminded him.

Jago managed to look thoughtful for all of two seconds before he waved a hand dismissively and declared. "No, we have plenty of GSHs in Zone 2-A. There is no sense in overkill...

Jessica lost it then. "Overkill? Over kill is what we've got right now! Over four hundred men, including Governor Bristol, several troops of Elites and at least one GSH have been killed to date. Not to mention whole shipments of arms and supplies and caravans of vehicles destroyed or stolen. This is just RJ! Can you imagine what will happen if she succeeds in building an army?"

Red faced, his jowls rippling with anger, Jago levered himself upright and cut her off. "Do you have any idea who you are talking to?" he replied shrilly

For one delicious moment, Jessica thought about being honest: a fat pompous idiot. Fortunately, self-preservation pressed the answer to the back of her throat. "I'm sorry, Your Excellency, but this problem with the rebels weighs heavily on my mind."

"The death of your lover weighs heavily on your...mind...Kirk," Jago hissed, then sat down with a plop.

Jessica thought that his legs probably wouldn't hold him up any longer. She inwardly steamed. This fat bastard had a hell of a lot of nerve.

"I understand how you must feel, but it is time you picked up the pieces and got on with your life. You are obsessed with this RJ person, Senator. That is why you are so ineffective against her. You have made her out to be more than she truly is." He laughed. "Really, Kirk. 'Topple the Reliance!' Do you have any idea how ridiculous you sound?"

She left before she could do anything violent. Depriving herself of this pleasure was regrettable, but necessary for the sake of her career. As she left, she could hear Jago saying to Right, who had sulked silently in a corner through the entire meeting, "I thought you weren't going to bother me about this RJ person anymore, Right." He added with near-operatic melodrama, "You are ruining my day. You know how much this nonsense distresses me."

She heard Right mumbling feebly about needing him to get GSHs. He should have saved his breath. They weren't going to get any help. At least not from Jago.

He was a stupid pig. He wouldn't believe RJ was a real threat till she knocked down his door, stuck an apple in his mouth, and roasted the fat bastard.

Jessica put her head down on the desk. She was afraid. Afraid that she was going to lose the battle with RJ. Afraid of being found wanting. She needed Jack. She needed to feel loved and accepted. But Jack was gone. Nothing could bring him back, and she was alone.

She had never felt so inept or so vulnerable. It was RJ's fault. Everything was RJ's fault. Hate moved in rapidly to fill the space that had once held her love for Jack.

All that was important was to kill RJ.

Stewart had killed himself to protect RJ. Jessica still couldn't quite fathom that. Had she been somehow more than an experiment to him? Why should he care more for RJ than he did for her? There was only one logical answer. Stewart must have believed in RJ's cause. He, too, must have hated the Reliance.

Jessica realized, not without shame, that part of her growing hatred for RJ stemmed from the fact that RJ had somehow won Stewart's favor. Perhaps Stewart had loved RJ. But, what did it matter now? Stewart was dead. RJ had killed Jack, and Poley was off to join the Rebellion. Her family, such as it was, had given her nothing but trouble and grief.

She sat up straight, and dried her eyes. She couldn't afford the luxury of being depressed. If she was going to catch RJ, she was going to have to use all her skills and resources.

If she could just clear her mind of random thought, the answer would come to her. Unfortunately some of those random thoughts were of Jack, and she couldn't let him go. Not yet.

David couldn't be sure whether or not Whitey and RJ were actually lovers, but it was obvious that Whitey meant for them to be. If RJ slept on the floor, Whitey curled up beside her. If she slept on the bed, he crawled in beside her, even if it meant pushing David aside to do so. David no longer had trouble with that particular union. In fact, since RJ had all but attacked him in the middle of the floor, David thought it was a very good idea for her to have sex with someone—anyone but him.

As for RJ's brother...That guy was a real weirdo. He hardly showed any sign of emotion, and when he did, it only seemed skin-deep. He had no body language, and David found that unnerving. But David couldn't say that Poley was hard to get along with. In order to be hard to get along with you had to have a personality. If Poley had one, it was well hidden.

David's own relationship with RJ was changing. Times alone were scarce, and it almost seemed to David that RJ avoided situations where they would be alone together. When they were, there was an obvious tension that hadn't been there before.

One day they went for a rare walk alone on the beach. David reached out and put his hand on her shoulder, and he felt her flesh tighten.

"What's wrong with you?" David asked hotly.

"Nothing," she said with a shrug. She walked over and sat down on a rock, looking out at the ocean. "Nothing at all."

David walked up behind her and started rubbing her back. "You're so tense."

"I don't have a right to be?" She laughed. "We are preparing to wage war with the Reliance. I think we should all be a little tense."

"You and Whitey...is that the problem?" he asked, sitting beside her.

RJ sighed. "He loves me."

"So?" David didn't see that as any sort of problem.

"I don't love him. I'm not even sure I know him. If I did, I might not want to." RJ kicked at the sand with her boots. "I like Whitey."

"So, what's the problem, RJ?"

"I can't sleep with him." She almost mumbled the words, but David still understood her.

"Because you don't love him?" If David was shocked that they weren't already lovers, he was even more shocked that RJ might actually have such antiquated morals.

"You know I'm a hybrid?"

David nodded.

"Well, during love-making we...Well, we lose it. During orgasm Argy women have no idea what they're doing. I have inherited this gene."

"I don't understand the problem.

"The problem, stupid, is that I am also incredibly strong. Stronger even than Whitey."

David didn't understand that for a minute, but he was damned if he was going to argue with her. He shrugged, signifying that he didn't understand.

"There is a good chance that I could do him physical damage."

"Oh!" David winced at the implications.

RJ stood up and started to walk away.

David followed her. He put everything she had just told him through his brain one more time, and came up with a startling deduction. "RJ, don't tell me you've never…"

"No, I haven't, and if you ever tell another living soul, I'll rip your lungs out."

"How do you know you'll hurt someone if you've never…" He finished with a graphic hand gesture that made RJ blush.

"Would you want to be the one I find out on? I broke a bed once having a wet dream."

David thought about it only a second. "Damn! No wonder you're so tense."


They called it "the Pier." Actually, it was all that was left of some huge old cable bridge. Flecks of orange paint could still be seen clinging to it. It now lay in the bay and was used to dock boats. The local fishing population ran across it as if it were a smooth and well-kept surface. It wasn't. It was a jungle of fallen rubble, broken cable and snapped steel. Only the very nimble dared come down here.

"You mind my asking what we're doing down here?" Alexi asked testily as he tripped for the third time.

"You always complain," Mickey said accusingly. From his perch on RJ's shoulder, he feared nothing, least of all Alexi.

"Shut up, you little freak," Alexi said with venom. Whitey did little more than give him a dirty look, but RJ had a special aversion to the term freak.

"*You* shut up, dickhead," RJ spat back at Alexi.

The Pier was alive with activity. People ran this way and that, carrying fish, nets, or the like. No one stopped in their labors to give the strange group more than a glance, but they all knew they were there.

David moved up even with RJ. "You know he purposely eggs Alexi on." David gave Mickey an accusing look. RJ just shrugged. "He knows he is the son you and Whitey never had, and he knows one of you will come to his rescue, no matter what he does." It was obvious that RJ was paying him little if any attention. "RJ, are you listening to me?"

"No," she said flatly.

"Poley." The metal man was at her side almost before she finished speaking his name. "Poley, will that boat over there haul all of us?"

Poley looked at the boat thoughtfully for a few moments. "Weight and mass. Weather conditions, condition of the boat..."

"Yes or no, Poley," RJ sighed.

"Yes." The boat in question currently held a crew of three men.

"You there!" RJ hollered. "Get outta that boat."

"For God's sake, RJ. A little diplomacy," David said.

The three men just stared at them, not knowing whether it was a joke or not.

David laughed nervously, and pulled a fistful of units out of his pocket. "We'd like to rent your boat." It was more money than the boat was worth, so the men quickly got out. The leader took the units from David, looked at him as if he had lost all his marbles, and then he and the two others ran down the pier laughing.

"Great, now they think we're cracked," RJ said with obvious disapproval.

"I suppose you would rather have them think we're a bunch of thugs."

RJ just shrugged. She wasn't in the mood to talk about the etiquette of boat appropriation. They had the boat, that was all that was important. They all boarded, and Levits took the controls as RJ ordered.

"I don't see why I had to come along," Levits complained. "Any one of you could have driven this boat. Going to a haunted island in the middle of the night. Excuse me for my lack of enthusiasm, but I had really hoped for more from life."

"Not afraid of ghosts, are we, Levits?" RJ said teasingly.

"No. That's the least of my worries. There are lights out there, and lights mean there has to be someone out there. Since there isn't a huge, flashing sign saying 'Revolutionaries welcome,' I'm just naturally assuming that they want to be left alone."

"Start the boat, Levits," RJ ordered. She set Mickey down on the deck and took a seat.

"There are no such things as ghosts," Poley said with assurance. "To believe that the dead could be animated is absurd."

"We're not talking walking cadavers here, Mr. Take-Everything-Literally," Alexi spat, "we're talking the unquiet spirits of..."

"Bullshit!" Levits sang out. He had some trouble getting the motor to turn over, but it seemed to run fine after that.

David didn't like all this talk of ghosts. He *did* believe in them. He couldn't help it. Having grown up in a farming community, he had heard stories about ghosts all his life, and they had always been told as if they were fact.

"I believe in ghosts," Alexi defended.

"Hear that, Poley? Alexi believes in ghosts. Better revise your thinking," RJ said with a smile.

"Look, look everyone. Did you see that? Poley almost smiled!" David said sarcastically.

"Poley is not the most expressive person you'll ever meet. You might even go so far as to say he's just like Dad."

Poley's eyes almost shone with mechanical joy. He liked the idea that he was like Stewart.

They sped towards the island, and the closer they got the quieter they got. It was obvious that there were many lights, and there was a sinister feel to the buildings that RJ hadn't felt till they got closer. Suddenly, there was a horrible shrieking noise, and before them loomed a giant, twisted figure.

"Holy shit!" Levits screamed, swerving to miss it. Whitey, who had been standing, fell back onto the deck of the boat. David and Alexi shrank in terror, and Mickey climbed up RJ like a monkey and clung to her chest.

RJ looked calmly at Poley. "Poley?"

"Holographic image projection. The scream is the amplified sound of a blue whale fart."

"Well, they obviously don't want company, but at least we know they have a sense of humor," RJ said with a laugh.

David, Mickey, and Alexi were not put at ease.

"I thought you didn't believe in ghosts," RJ said to Mickey, who was still clinging with his head buried between her boobs.

He peeked up at her. "Did not, but cannot deny truth of own eyes." He returned his head to its place of safety.

Whitey hauled himself up off the deck of the ship. "It's a picture, Mickey." Mickey's head stayed where it was. "Like on a viewing screen, except without the screen."

Mickey still didn't move.

David and Alexi weren't convinced either. After all, they only had Poley's word that it wasn't some misguided soul from the netherworld come to devour them.

"Drive through it," RJ ordered.

"I don't know, RJ," Levits said, shaking his head.

"Go on, man. *You* know what a hologram is," RJ said impatiently.

"I know it's a little high-tech for a bunch of fisher-folk. I know that the same people who have that kind of technology probably have lasers and rocket launchers, and all kinds of big ugly weapons just waiting to blow our asses up."

"Go through it, Levits," RJ hissed. Levits still looked reluctant. "Go through, or I'll rip your arm off and shove it up your ass!"

"When you put it in such a charming manner, how could I refuse?" Levits drove on. In a matter of moments, they were through the hologram, and it disappeared into the night.

"OK, Mickey. We're through. It's gone," Whitey told him.

Mickey stayed where he was.

"It was just a picture."

Mickey looked up, smiling stupidly. "I think I'll stay here."

"Why you little lecher!" Whitey grabbed the midget and jerked him off RJ. He made as if to toss him into the ocean, Mickey screamed, and the whole boat rocked.

"Do you have to make so much racket?" Alexi asked angrily. "Why don't you send up flares so they'll know we're here?"

"They already know we're here," RJ said, matter-of-factly.

"That thing?" David asked, nodding back to where the hologram had been.

RJ nodded. "When we activated that, we alerted whoever put it there."

"We'll dock in less than two minutes," Poley informed them.

"Levits, kill the engine," RJ ordered.

"Why bother, if they know that we're here?" he asked in a doomed voice.

"Kill the engine."

"Maybe we should throw down anchor here and swim it," Whitey suggested. "We could wrap the weapons in..."

"No!" Poley said emphatically.

RJ moved up beside him, and patted him on the back. "It's OK, Poley, we'll pull into the dock."

"My feet are wet," Poley said in a nervous tone. "My feet are wet."

"We'll dock in a minute," RJ told him.

"My feet are wet," Poley said again.

"You'll be OK," RJ said. "What do you want me to do, carry you?"

"Yes," Poley said, nodding his head.

"Well, forget it."

"The dock has been very well maintained," Levits announced. "OK. I've seen enough. Let's go home."

"Just dock the boat," RJ ordered.

They docked without a hitch.

RJ helped Poley out of the boat. "Do you detect any life forms?" RJ asked him in a whisper.

The robot stared at his wet feet and appeared to be pouting.

"You're OK, Poley." She sighed. Why couldn't things be simple? "Do you detect any life forms?"

"Shielding makes it impossible to tell."

"Oh, great." RJ stared up the hill towards the building. The lights were on. It looked so inviting, but something told her she was not going to be invited in.

"We are being monitored," Poley informed her.

"Shit! Now?"

"No, but it suffices to say that they know we're here. We'll be scanned again shortly."

"Let's move." They followed her a little further inland. "Poley, can you stop them monitoring us?" she asked again in a whisper.

"I could emit a silent wavelength which should distort any picture they may be getting."

Behind them, where they had been standing only a few moments before, the night erupted in a shower of sparks.

"Do it, Poley," RJ said. "Let's move!" They walked rapidly up the old road that led towards the building. It was well maintained but steep.

Panting for breath, David moved up to walk beside RJ. "What the hell are you doing? Let's go back. Re-think this thing. Come back better armed..."

"How could we be better armed?" RJ asked. "Besides, they know we're here. I doubt they'll let us leave. We're going to have to fight them, or at the very least outwit them." She looked curiously at the building. "I don't think we're dealing with Reliance."

"Well, they're certainly not friendly," David said.

RJ shrugged. "I'm not so sure. After all, how would you react to a bunch of armed gorillas landing in your back yard?"

"I wouldn't just fire lasers on them without talking to them..."

"Ah, but *I* would," RJ said with a smile.

David nodded, although he wasn't sure at all that this was a comforting thought. They passed several smaller structures on their way to the main building, and David expected spirits or worse to jump out of any one of them at any moment. Finally they found an apparently unguarded door. As they approached a light came on, and they stopped dead in their tracks.

Instinctively, RJ held out her arm to stop them going any further. "Poley?"

"I detect an automated defense system."

"What's that mean?" David asked.

"It means we're in deep shit," Whitey answered.

"Are we already in range?" RJ asked.

"If we were, we would be dead. It's triggered to fire upon the breaking of light beams," Poley answered.

"I don't see any light," Alexi said. He was totally ignored.

RJ took Poley and pulled him off a few feet to talk. This did not pass Alexi's eyes unnoticed. He whispered in David's ear.

"Why is she always asking him questions?"

David shrugged. "I don't know. I suppose because he's her brother, and she trusts his judgment," David said with a shrug. "She does ask him some pretty weird shit, though."

"And what's even weirder, is that he always seems to know the answers."

RJ and Poley walked back. RJ took a handful of rocks and threw them on the steps. Lasers flared immediately and the rocks were blown to bits. RJ drew her laser and fired four shots seemingly at the building. There was a loud hiss of fire at each shot, and David realized that she had shot out the weapons. She threw in another fist full of rocks; this time with no results.

"Poley, go and open the door."

Poley nodded and moved forward.

"Now that's a little strange, don't you think?" Alexi asked.

David just shrugged in mild annoyance.

"RJ just sent her brother to open the door. Odd, because she can't be sure that all of the lasers are deactivated. You'd expect her to send me."

"I would never send a hamster to do a man's job." RJ had no trouble hearing him, and she had no time for his shit. She was not unconcerned about the metal man.

"Well?" she asked Poley when he had been at the door longer than she thought he should be.

"It is too simple," he said.

RJ nodded and walked up the steps to join him at the door. "Well, Tin Pants?"

He pointed at the doorknob and she nodded. "Can you detect anything?"

"No."

"Oh, I hate this. You know what Father always said...."

"If it looks too good to be true, it probably is," Poley finished. As always happy that he could answer her question.

"Exactly." She put her hand on the knob. "Cross your fingers."

"We learned many strange things from our father," the robot said as if it were a revelation.

RJ nodded and turned the knob.

In the depths of the ancient prison, a man stared at three blank screens.

"What's happened, Marge?"

All around him, machinery hummed and lights flashed. The noise and the lights didn't actually have anything to do with the operation of the massive computer which lined every wall of the room the man was sitting in, but he thought it added something to the feel of things.

"They're using a sonic wavelength to distort the picture." The voice was obviously a man trying to sound like a woman, and it issued from the computer's speakers.

"Funny. They didn't look the sonic-wavelength-emitting type." The man laughed and spun in his chair. "Anything else?"

"Specific meaning?" the computer oozed.

"Stupid machine," he mumbled. "Are you getting any reading from the weapon system?"

"Lasers at the front entrance were activated, no human tissue was scorched. Suggest infiltrators threw something into the field to check it."

"Hum." The man stroked his chin.

"What, Master?"

"Just hum. Can't a man hum around here without getting the third degree?" He calmed and smiled. "So. I wonder what she's up to now?"

"Suggest that, seeing the sophistication of our weapon system, the infiltrators have left."

"Suggest you are an idiot!" the man screamed at the computer. "If they have gone, why are the cameras still not functioning?" He rubbed his hands in anticipation. "No, she's coming on. I can feel it. It's all rather exciting."

The antiquity of the exterior of the structure did not match the sleek modern brightness of the interior.

"OK, I've seen enough, let's go," Levits said. "We could always come back another time, RJ."

"Quiet, idiot!" RJ hissed. Then she mumbled. "Idiots! I am surrounded, completely engulfed in idiots."

In the bowels of the computer complex, sirens wailed. "Weapons deactivated! Door open! Infiltrators inside! Door open! Unauthorized entry at main door!" the computer squealed in a shrill voice.

The man jumped to his feet and clapped his hands in glee. "They got in! Any audio on them, Marge?"

For answer, Levits' voice came in over the loudspeaker. The man flopped down heavily in his chair.

"RJ." He said the name almost reverently. "So, I wonder if that could be *our* RJ, Marge. Only one way to be sure."

"How's that, Master?" the computer asked.

"You are such a disappointment to me at times, Marge. We simply leave the security system as is. The real RJ will have no trouble getting through it."

"And if she can't?"

"Then we will have enjoyed a pleasant diversion for a time, and we'll have a nasty mess to clean up." He winced. "Turn off that bloody siren."


"We have to keep moving," RJ said. "But we're going to have to move with caution." She put Mickey on her shoulder.

"I detect an audio system," Poley whispered to her.

"Scramble it," she ordered.

"Done."

They were in a long, dimly lit hallway. There were no doors on either side as far as the eye could see, and RJ's worst fears were realized.

"We are in their security system," she announced.

"What do you mean?" David asked.

"This isn't a logical entrance. In other words, this is the security system," she said impatiently.

David had that *I don't get it* look on his face which she was beginning to find increasingly irritating.

"It's a trap, probably a series of them."

David nodded.

They started down the hall three abreast, weapons pulled. When they reached a corner, they went around it with care. On the floor before them for some twenty feet, the floor changed. Where it had been solid white, it was now a checkerboard of black and white tiles. RJ threw out her arm, and David crashed into it. She looked at the floor, then the ceiling. At ceiling level, she saw protrusions. Glancing back at the floor, she asked, "Poley, can you detect any difference between the tiles?"

"Some are black, and some are white," he stated proudly.

"*I* can see *that*." She took a deep breath, obviously restraining her annoyance. "Can you see any *other* differences? Are some of the tiles thicker than the others?"

Poley scanned the floor. "The black tiles are thicker."

"OK," RJ sighed. "See those gas jets?" She pointed. "I think stepping on the wrong tiles activates them. We have no idea what kind of gas that is. Now, I'm thinking that the black tiles' being thicker means that they are the triggering device. Of course, I could be wrong. So, I suggest that Poley walk over first and that we stand back at a good distance."

"I suggest that we all go back to Alsterase before you get us killed," Alexi said. "Who ever we're dealing with is our technological superior. The farther we go, the more devious and dangerous their traps will become."

"Perhaps I should stay here in case we are attacked from the rear," Levits chimed in.

"Oh, good idea," Whitey said, with sincerity.

"On second thought, maybe we shouldn't break the group up," Levits said, nervously realizing that there actually *might* be an attack from the rear.

"We go on, all of us," RJ said authoritatively.

"Oh, the Great Leader has spoken," Alexi said sarcastically. "Where do you lead us, RJ? Do you know? To our deaths, I think."

RJ just smiled smugly. "If you want to be leader, Alexi, go across the tiles first. If you want to leave, then by all means, do so. But who will follow you? You forget yourself, Alexi.

The Reliance may do a lot of things, but they don't overlook leadership qualities. In your former life, you were a third-class soldier; I was an Elite officer. To lead, you have to put your neck out. Go ahead. Take the walk, Alexi. I say walk on the white tiles, but what the hell do I know? Be your own man! Go ahead, chose for yourself and take the walk."

They all moved a good distance back. Alexi walked up to the edge of the tiles. He could see the gas jets, but he couldn't see any difference in the tiles. RJ said walk on the white ones. He started to take the step and broke out in a cold sweat. She thought she was infallible but he didn't. She could be wrong or she could be doing this on purpose to get rid of him. He stepped back away from the tiles, wiped the sweat from his face and turned towards the group. "Why should I go? I want to go *back*. Remember?"

RJ smiled broadly. She moved forward and Poley grabbed her shoulder. "I should go," he said.

"I trust you, Tin Pants." She patted his face and ran across the white tiles. The others followed.

David moved up beside RJ. "You hit him where he lives," he whispered, smiling, "but is there really any purpose for us being here?"

"Someone has worked very hard at making it damn near impossible to get in here. Therefore, whatever is here must be worth having."

David nodded. That made sense.

"Besides, we're not in any real danger as long as we stay sharp."

"Huh?" David was lost again.

"If the owners wanted us dead, we would be dead."

David gave her that confused look again.

"A weapons system such as this indicates a great technology. Great technology indicates great intelligence. Obviously, these weapons are being computer controlled, but would a wise man build such a system without a manual over ride?"

"So, if he knew we were in, he could have emptied the gas canisters into the hall, and we would have walked right into it." David made a face. "I still don't get it."

"Only *some* of the tiles activated the gas. If you have manual override, none of these traps would hamper your coming and going. So why not have *all* the tiles activate the gas jets?"

"It's like some sort of maze. A test!" David said.

"Exactly," RJ said. "And if we keep our wits about us, we'll pass the test and win the prize."

"Master, the infiltrators have passed the gas trap," The computer informed in its mock-female voice.

The man swiveled in his chair. "They're still scrambling audio and visual?"

"Yes, I am tracing them through their body heat."

"Well, they certainly are a persistent lot." He smiled. "I hope they make it. I have been so wanting to meet these rebels."

The pit spread out before them, blocking their way. It covered the whole width of the hall for twenty feet. Five feet below them they could see a lake of bubbling acid.

"So, what now?" David asked.

"They haven't beaten us yet," she said. "There has to be a door or a bridge. Remember, they have to get past it some how."

Nearly fifteen minutes later, Whitey found a loose section of wall. He moved it aside to reveal a door. It was securely locked, but the mechanism was simple.

"I can do that!" Mickey informed them.

RJ put him down, and three minutes later the door was open. The hallway they entered was no different than the one they had been walking in—which was not at all comforting.

"Master," the computer chimed. "RJ has found the secret passage around the acid trap."

"Marge, you called her RJ. Why did you do that?" he asked.

"You said that if she could get through the traps, she must be RJ. She is getting through the traps."

The hall narrowed and shortened, then it started to descend.

"I don't like this," David said. They now had to go single file, and even then it was tight for Whitey.

"We must be getting close to wherever we're going," Whitey said lightly. "This keeps attackers from attacking in force. I've seen this sort of thing before."

RJ stopped for a second and looked at the air vent considering. It was small; too small for her. She pulled the grill off and stood close enough to feel the air being sucked into the vent. "Poley." He joined her. "What do you make of this?"

"It's probably pulling cool air into the computer complex."

"They probably won't be scanning the air ducts. Maybe we could use it to get to the main computer room undetected."

"In case you haven't noticed, none of us can fit into that air duct," Alexi said dryly.

"As you obviously haven't noticed, *one* of us can."

RJ picked Mickey up.

The midget smiled smugly at Alexi.

"Be careful. If you come to a junction, follow the air current."

Mickey nodded and scampered into the air duct.

"The midget! You're sending the midget as our advance party?" Alexi laughed.

Whitey took Alexi by the collar, and Alexi was quiet. "Laugh once more, and we'll just have to see if you *can* fit into the vent."

"Master, I have lost the heat signal on one of the party members," Marge informed him.

"Now, I wonder what they're up to." He shook his head, and sat back to wait.

Just when the hallway became uncomfortably narrow, they entered a small room. In the wall ahead of them was a door. They entered the room cautiously. There were no windows, and there was only the one door opposite the entryway they had just come through. There was a blue button next to the door, but RJ didn't believe for a moment that was the way out. Instead, she started to search the walls for the true opening device that just *had* to be there.

"What the hell are you waiting for?" Alexi strode across the room. Sure, he hadn't walked on the tiles, but he'd show them all now. "Let's just open the door and..."

"NO!" RJ screamed, but it was too late. Alexi had pressed the button. She ran towards the entranceway they had just come through. When she heard the click, she flung herself the last few feet—too little, too late. The door started to fall, and to make matters worse, she caught her fingers in the door just as it slammed shut. She was stuck, not to mention in a hell of a lot of pain.

Then there was a hum of power, and the room started to fill with salt water.

"I'll be damned if you're going to drown with the rest of us," Whitey started choking Alexi.

"Poley, quick! Do you see the opening device for the door?" RJ asked.

"I'm wet." He answered, as the water reached his knees. "Have lost control of audio and visual." Poley was in a robotic form of panic. While water wouldn't actually harm Poley, it made him unable to operate to full capacity, and he couldn't swim. For these reasons, Stewart had built in a strong fear of water as part of Poley's personality.

"I'm stuck!" RJ yelled as the water started to go over her head. She was, too. She couldn't get her fingers free. With her hands tied up the way they were she had no way of reaching her kit. She tried, but she couldn't pull her fingers off. They were just too well-made.

Everyone except Poley—who was dealing with his own crisis—and Alexi—whom Whitey dropped in the water like an abandoned toy—ran to her aid. The water was coming in quickly, and by the time they reached her, she was already under. Whitey and David both dove under to see what the problem was. They came up and looked at each other.

"What now?" David asked in a panic.

"We'll have to lift it up," Whitey said. He looked at Levits, and before he had a chance to order Levits to help, he had dove into the water. Even with the three of them giving it all they could, there was no way of moving it, they just couldn't get hold of the door enough to get any leverage. The door didn't budge. They broke the surface almost as, one gasping for air. They knew this meant RJ was in a really bad way.

They dove under the water again. RJ mouthed something urgently at Whitey, but he couldn't understand her. Her fingers were keeping the door from closing all the way. There was a gap, but it wasn't big enough for any of them to get their fingers under far enough to have a good enough grip to lift the door. If they could lift it at all and get out before they wound up in the same shape RJ was in.

Whitey came up for air at the same time as David and Levits. He pulled his sword. "We can use it as a lever. With all of us, we may be able to lift the door enough to get her free."

David nodded and they dove again. Whitey jammed the sword under the door, and they gave it all they had.

Her chest hurt from holding her breath. She was supposed to be able to hold her breath for twenty minutes. That was what she had been told. But it hadn't been even ten, and already she could feel her strength ebbing away. It was getting harder and harder to withstand the urge to take a deep breath. She tried to get Whitey's attention, and finally succeeded, but it was obvious that he had no idea what she was saying. Now they were trying to open the door with the sword. This just might work, but then the tip of the sword broke off. This time, she didn't even manage to get Whitey's attention.

"She's gonna die," David told Whitey as they broke the surface of the water for the third time.

"We're all going to die," Levits said hopelessly.

"We'll try again," Whitey said, and dove back into the water, which was now up to his chest. The others were already treading water. They followed him under.

RJ could no longer help. She was using all her energy to hold her breath. Finally, she even lost that ability.

They put everything they had into it. The sword was thicker closer to the hilt and—stronger this time—it bent, but it didn't break. The door moved. Not a lot, but enough. Levits grabbed RJ, and swam with her to the top.

As soon as Whitey broke the surface of the water, he jerked RJ's lifeless body from Levits. Whitey started to shake her violently.

David looked on in horror. She was limp, and her head jerked back and forth as if it might snap off at any minute. She was blue, and there was no sign of life in her. In his grief, David forgot that he, too, would soon be dead.

"God damn you, RJ!" Whitey screamed as he shook her. "God damn you, you can't die here  Not like this. Not by fucking drowning!" Whitey started giving her artificial respiration; not an easy thing to do while treading water, but a lot more effective than screaming and shaking her.

RJ coughed, spitting out what looked like half the ocean, then she took a long, shuddering breath. When her eyes focused on Whitey, she threw her arms around his neck and clung to him.

Whitey held her tight. "I thought you were dead," he whispered.

"GSH kit, you moron!" RJ managed to cough out through her raw throat.

"You need Pronuses?" Whitey asked in a whisper.

"No." Even in her current condition, she knew she didn't want any of the others to see her ingesting what was, for them, a lethal poison. "The knife."

"Oh—OH!" Whitey couldn't believe his stupidity, but he was too elated to let it get him down long. "I kind of like you with your fingers."

Having saved RJ, David and Whitey had temporarily forgotten about their present predicament.

Alexi reminded them. "Good. Now we can all die together." Whitey had hurt him, but not so badly that he couldn't tread water. "One big happy family."

"Shut up!" David screamed. He was trying to think. *We have to look for a way to open the door...Poley said he lost control of audio and visual. I assume that means that they can see us and hear us right now. If what RJ says is true, they may let us live.* "Listen, you filthy bastards. We're tired of playing your little game. We've passed all your little tests except this one. The least you can do is *see* us before you kill us. Give us a chance to explain what we're doing here. We don't want to hurt anyone, we just want some help."

"I don't know," a strange-sounding voice said thoughtfully. "I admit that you did rather well. But this last test...Well, it's the easiest of all."

"A member of our party acted against the orders of our leader," David said, giving Alexi an angry look.

"Hum," the voice said.

"What?" David asked.

"Oh, just 'hum.' Every once in awhile I like to do that. So, I take it that the rather limp-looking one is the one you call RJ."

"Are you Reliance?" David asked suspiciously.

"No. Prove to me she's RJ, and we can talk."

"How do you expect me to prove that?" David asked hotly.

"Oh, just anything. Visa, American Express, a major bank card..."

"We are running out of time down here. I don't want to play your games. Why not let us go? If you're not Reliance, what can you gain from killing us?"

"A clean entrance hall." He laughed at his own joke.

"You're a raving lunatic!" Whitey screamed.

"Really? I've always thought of myself as *demented*. Still, I suppose *raving* has a certain ring to it." He paused as if in deep thought. "Well, that *does* help me make up my mind."

"Thought it might," a familiar voice said. "Now, let them go, or I blow out brains."

"ALL RIGHT, MICKEY!" they all cheered.

The water started to recede. In a matter of moments, the "entrance hall" was little more than damp. The door opposite the one they had entered opened to reveal a flight of steps going upwards.

By now, RJ had recovered completely, but she still let Whitey help her. She told herself she did this to keep the others from becoming suspicious. She looked at Poley. He appeared to be undamaged, but still seemed to be having difficulty with the fact that he was wet. She looked at her laser—also wet and useless.

When she looked at Alexi, he shrank from her gaze and looked away.

"You almost got us all killed. I won't forget that, Alexi. The list of your mistakes grows daily. When I feel you have done more harm than good, I will deal with you in an appropriate and extremely violent manner."

Alexi nodded submissively. For once, he had no snappy comebacks. He had almost killed her. It shouldn't have bothered him; she was, after all, a giant pain in his ass. But it did.

They ascended the stairs slowly, weapons drawn.

"Come on, Poley," RJ ordered when she realized he hadn't moved.

At the top of the stairs they entered a long, narrow room. Along its walls—all around them, and ten feet tall, stretching endlessly in both directions—were the components of the biggest computer RJ had ever set her eyes on. Since she had been privileged to see the military computer at Capitol, this was saying quite a lot.

It was better than anything she had hoped for.

David didn't know what it was all for, but with all the flashing lights and whirring noises...Well, he was impressed.

The man sat up straighter in his chair to get a better look at his intruders. They were an odd lot, to be sure. Three held weapons on him, the other three did not. The woman should have drowned. So, for that matter, should the dark man in the leather suit, because when the water had gone over his head he had done nothing to keep himself afloat. He'd been nowhere in sight until the water receded. The giant was the only other one that didn't hold a weapon. Apparently, these three knew their weapons would be useless till dry. The others either didn't know their weapons were dysfunctional, or they assumed that *he* wouldn't know.

"Poley, strip your clothes off," she ordered. The robot started to comply. "Whitey, don't kill anyone till we figure out what's going on."

"But..."

"We *need* all this, Whitey. These people are not our enemies."

Whitey sighed and nodded.

Poley had finished undressing, and now stood buck naked for all the world to see.

"Feel better?" RJ asked.

"Yes, thank you very much," Poley responded.

"Then let us meet our host, shall we?"

"Damn!" Levits exclaimed. "Would you look at the way that weird fuck is hung?"

They all mostly ignored him.

The man sat in the very middle of the room surrounded by what could only be the control panels. RJ kept a wary eye on the two stories of catwalks above them. Behind the catwalks were what must have once been prison cells, and at the end of the row was a gun gallery. If there was to be an attack, it would no doubt come from there. However, she saw not even the slightest sign of life. The only flesh-and-blood creatures about seemed to be the man she faced, her companions, and herself.

"Like a spider in its web," she whispered to herself.

"What?" David asked.

"Nothing." She looked at the man. Even sitting he looked to be tall. He had a medium frame, with bright, wide, staring blue eyes and a large, aristocratic nose. His mouth was filled with straight, white teeth that seemed too large for his face. His curly brown hair framed a face that shone with boyish impudence and great good humor. This in spite of the fact that he was at least in his fifties.

"Hello," he said. Once again, RJ noted the strange quality of his voice. This time she recognized it as an accent, although it wasn't one she had heard before. "Awfully nice of you to drop in like this. Pardon me if I don't rise." He waved his hand towards the midget with the gun.

"Good work, Mickey," RJ said.

Mickey practically glowed.

"Where are the troops?" David asked.

"He *is* the troops." RJ shook her head, hardly believing her own words. She found a blank piece of console and sat down. "I'm right, aren't I?"

"You seem to have solved all my puzzles," he said, putting on his best pouty face.

"Does it do all that I think it does?" she asked, looking around at the huge computer. She was all but drooling.

"Yes...and probably more."

"There is no one else here?" Whitey asked in disbelief.

"Just me," he smiled. "Sorry."

"Sorry!" Whitey boomed. "You cracked little creep! I oughtta..."

"Calm down, Whitey." RJ patted his back. "You know my name, and these are David, Whitey, Levits, Mickey, my brother Poley, and that stupid crawling worm is Alexi." She pointed at each of them as she spoke. "And you are?"

"Topaz."

"That's an odd name."

"I took it from an old Hitchcock movie."

Not only did he speak with a strange accent, he used strange words. "And all this is?" she asked, indicating the computer with a wave of her hand.

"Marge."

"What does that stand for?"

"A girl whose company I once enjoyed," Topaz said with a laugh. These young ones thought everything had to have a reason.

"Who built it?" RJ asked. "And for what purpose?"

"I built it because I was bored, and because I could," Topaz said with a huge smile.

RJ looked around her. He didn't seem to be lying, and he wasn't shielding. That much she was sure of. Still...he might truly believe what he said even if it weren't true. If he were "cracked," as Whitey had suggested, this was a possibility. His having built all of this himself didn't seem logically possible.

"By yourself?" She gave him a cynical look.

"By myself."

RJ wiped some water off her face. She looked again at the computer. "You lie. This could not be built in one lifetime by one man."

He burst into maniacal laughter. "Quite true. Quite true." He quit laughing, and jumped out of his seat, oblivious to Mickey and the laser he still had trained on him. He started to pace back and forth. They all kept a wary eye on him. Finally, he stopped in front of RJ, and tapped his chin with his finger. "It's a rather long story. Do you care to hear it?"

"Yes, please," RJ said as patiently as the situation allowed her to be.

"Well, it all started some time ago, when I used to be a guy called Bob. After the first five centuries, I got tired of being Bob, so I changed my name to Topaz—it being one of my favorite movies, don't you see. It's not my birthstone, if that's what you were thinking."

"See, I told you...cracked," Whitey whispered to RJ.

"Shh!" RJ ordered. He wasn't lying—or at least he didn't *think* he was.

"There was a crash and a ray of light!" Topaz started to ramble.

"So, Topaz. You have lived a long life. Long enough to have built Marge. How and why?"

"You are a very suspicious young woman. Are you married?"

"No," RJ answered with a sigh. It wasn't going to be an easy task to get anything of value from Topaz.

"In that case, how would you like to..."

Whitey interrupted him with a growl. "She's my woman."

RJ temporarily forgot all about Topaz and Marge and the Reliance. She turned and gave Whitey a cold look. "Your woman?" she spat. "*Your woman!*"

Whitey smiled and pushed a strand of wet hair out of her face. "My woman," he said lovingly.

RJ took a deep breath. This had been a very trying day, and it wasn't over yet. "I'm no one's woman," she grumbled.

Turning to Topaz, she resolutely pushed Whitey out of her mind and asked, "Could you please continue?"

"Well, to make a long story short, in 1986, or was it '68? Maybe it was '2002..."

"Please," RJ begged.

"Anyway, I was a biochemist..."

"Biochemist?" RJ asked, looking around the room again.

"Computers are a hobby," Topaz explained. "Anyway, I was looking for a cure for a disease called AIDS. It was being called the 'plague of the century.' Since initially it affected mostly homosexuals and needle users, at first it was vastly ignored by the government and became rampant in this part of the country. See, San Francisco..."

"San...fran...cisco?" David stumbled through the strange name.

"*San Francisco*. That's the real name of the town you live in. When the Reliance came into power, they changed all the place names, often distorting them. Alcatraz. That used to be the name of this island. They distorted the name to Alsterase, and it became the name of the town, not just the island." He had everyone's attention now. He sat down in his chair and felt rather like a father telling his children a bedtime story about the days of his youth. "Anyway, the disease was greatly ignored until it started to affect the heterosexual community. By the time they started to try to really cure the disease, millions had already died. I jumped on the bandwagon early and started experimenting with real cures. It wasn't easy. You see, AIDS – which stands for Acquired Immune Deficiency Syndrome—destroyed the victim's immune system, so I was trying to create a vaccine that would make the body regenerate itself. Everyone said I was mad. They were right, of course, but I didn't like the way they said it. I worked day and night trying to prove them wrong. What I wound up with was something that caused near total regeneration. I gave it to a rat. I cut its leg off, and it grew a new one. I fed him deadly poison, and he got fat and healthy. I kept him up for days on end, and he didn't even get tired. I blew enough smoke into his lungs to corrode them six times, and he didn't even cough. Finally, I cut it in half..."

"And it lived?" David wondered in awed shock.

"No, it died. But I thought I'd never kill the bastard. Hell, I didn't even *like* the bloody thing. Had a dog I loved once, it caught cold and died, but this thing I couldn't kill..."

RJ coughed.

"At any rate, I took the stuff..."

"And became immortal," RJ said.

"I wanted to say that," Topaz said with a pout. "Unfortunately, I couldn't reproduce the drug."

"Why not?" David asked.

"Because apparently it wasn't my genius that created the serum in the first place, but the will of God. To be more specific, somehow something got into it that I didn't put in it. Something fell into it, or the weather caused an unrecorded reaction. Or maybe I *did* do it during one of those sleep-walking stages I drove myself into, and I didn't record it. I don't know. I only know that I was never able to reproduce the shit. And believe me, I have tried many times. It's just as well, I suppose. Man was never meant to live forever." He paused. "Although they used some of my research when they created the first GSHs. So, how mad was I?

"As for why I built Marge. Well, that is very simple. When one lives forever, one is constantly bereft of loved ones. I have watched friends, lovers, even my own children die of old age. Marge can't die. So, I can have a fondness for her without fear of loss."

RJ had no problem knowing what he was talking about.

"There is another reason." He looked at RJ. "I don't like the Reliance; I never have. I don't like what they've done to the world. I have been waiting for you or someone like you for five hundred years. The computer and this base, as well as my services, are at your disposal," he finished with a grand flourish and a bow in RJ's direction.

"You have a funny way of displaying your eagerness to help," Whitey said angrily.

"Letting Marge fall into the hands of an unorganized rabble would have been the same as letting the Reliance have her."

"You would have let us drown if Mickey hadn't shown up when he did?" David asked, accusingly.

"If he hadn't shown up, you would have flunked the test," Topaz said simply.

RJ caught Poley running his hand over the computer's console lovingly, and wished she could crawl under a rock somewhere.

Topaz saw where RJ's eyes rested and gave her a big grin, his teeth shining.

"Rather appropriate, really," he said.

*So,* RJ thought uncomfortably. *He knows what Poley is. Well, of course he does. With this thing on deck he could probably reproduce old Tin Pants. It might even have told him what I am.*

"Am I to be trusted? Before you ask, perhaps I should tell you that Marge has localized armaments. If I had wanted to kill you, all I would have had to do was say the word."

"I never doubted that."

RJ looked at Mickey and nodded her head. He put away his laser reluctantly.

"Come then, let us retire to some more comfortable surroundings. Marge, prepare the viewing room."

"As you wish, Master," the computer cooed.

RJ grimaced.

"I did that voice myself," Topaz explained. "I wanted it to be female, but didn't have a woman at my disposal, so..."

"I understand."

They followed him to a large room. Plush couches and chairs lined the walls. The floor was covered in elaborately decorated rugs. The walls were covered with tapestries depicting forest scenes as well as some depicting ancient forms of battle in which men wore metal suits and fought with all manner of sharp metal objects. On one wall was a huge viewing screen.

"I managed to save a great deal of our old culture by putting movies onto laser disks. I think you will enjoy it. Before the Reliance, we used viewing screens for entertainment purposes. Marge, put something on for our guests, and bring us some drinks." Then as an afterthought he added. "And do bring our friends some dry clothes. I'm afraid I find the nakedness of this young man," he pointed at Poley, "to be quite intimidating."

"As you wish, Master," Marge responded sweetly. In a matter of seconds, the wall lit up with an ancient movie about warriors like the ones depicted in some of the tapestries hanging on the walls around them. The men were immediately captivated. RJ had seen something similar at the pleasure station in Vector 6. Of course, the satellite in orbit around the planet Deaka was strictly off-limits to anyone who wasn't high-ranking Reliance personnel, so it was all new to the men.

A drone hustled in carrying a stack of khaki-colored clothing. RJ went through the clothes, sorted them by size, and handed them out. Poley dressed as she, Whitey, Alexi, Levits and RJ stripped. Mickey and David looked at each other and then at Topaz.

Topaz smiled indulgently. "There's a room right down the hall and to your right," Topaz said.

RJ looked up from where she was finishing wrapping the chain around herself.

"Oh for shit's sake," RJ said, a bit disgusted with them. "Look, I'll turn around and close my eyes."

When she did, Mickey and David quickly changed. Of course even the smallest clothes Topaz had on hand didn't fit the midget, but he was used to having to modify his clothing, and after a few rolls and tucks he wasn't tripping over them any more.

"All right," David said when they'd finished dressing.

RJ turned around, mumbling something about the stupid modesty of civilians.

A second drone rushed in carrying a load of bottles and glasses. It went to Topaz first, and he grabbed a bottle and a glass and poured. He set the bottle back down, and took a sip.

"Ah," he smiled in pleasure. "Nothing quite like seven-hundred-year-old Scotch."

The drone stopped next in front of RJ, who was the only one who still hadn't sat down. She took the bottles one by one and read the labels. Topaz wasn't kidding. Some of this liquor was hundreds of years old. She finally settled on the bottle of whiskey and took the whole thing.

RJ took a seat somewhat removed from the others and was joined by Topaz.

"So, now that the others are busy, perhaps we can talk."

RJ nodded, but said nothing, waiting with interest for him to start the conversation.

"The Reliance is an unholy abomination. I would have thought there'd have been an uprising long before this. But I guess humankind sort of lost all its spirit." He got off the couch, and started to crawl around on the floor on his hands and knees.

"Can I help you?" RJ asked, intrigued.

"Do what?"

"Look for whatever it is you've lost."

"I haven't lost anything yet. I just want to be prepared when I do. You know, make a list of places to look. Did you ever wonder where those little balls of lint that get under everything come from?" he asked seriously.

"No, I really can't say I have. You were saying something about human kind losing its spirit?"

Topaz got up and sat back down on the couch next to her. "Well, the trouble all started with Earth's not having enough countries..."

David was enjoying the movie until he saw RJ and Topaz talking. He didn't want to be left out, so he got up from where he'd been sitting and moved to sit down beside RJ.

"Anyway, each country had its own government. This usually worked out OK, except that some countries got bigger than all the rest. Now the big countries tried to get along, but they never really did. We called them Super Powers. The reason they didn't really get along was that they couldn't agree on how you should run a country. They had lots of things called cold wars, where no one really fought, but it was really more scary than when they were fighting..."

While Topaz talked to David and RJ, the others watched all of the first movie and a second one about a guy who wore a loincloth and fought with a really big sword. When it finished Topaz had Marge play something non-violent. The men watching didn't seem to care what was on. Topaz got the idea that they would enjoy a documentary on dirt as long as it wasn't sanctioned by the Reliance. Even the robot was watching intently. What was more, he seemed to be enjoying it.

But what Topaz found most interesting was the reaction of the hardened military bitch. While she had totally ignored the first two pictures, she could hardly keep her eyes off this one. Amusingly, this one was a romance.

RJ tried to pay attention to what Topaz was saying, but she found that her eyes kept straying to the viewing screen. The first two movies hadn't interested her. She had lived battle all her life, and she didn't find it particularly amusing to watch. But this one enthralled her. The woman was singing part of the movie, and there had been very little song in RJ's cold, realistic life. It was an entertaining story, and she had to work on listening to Topaz.

"It was fear that allowed the Reliance to come to power. Fear that let the monster rear its ugly head. See, the Super Powers had created a weapon capable of destroying the entire planet. Nuclear warheads."

"What's that?" David asked.

"It's a bomb..."

"You mean an uncontrolled nuclear explosion?" RJ said in shocked disbelief. He had her full attention again. The concept was outrageous. Nuclear power ran many starships. It ran many electrical generating stations on the outer planets. She knew the power they contained; she had seen it at work. "Such a weapon would destroy everything for miles wherever it was dropped! It would make the soil infertile and cause mutations. Who can win a war fought with such weapons?"

"Exactly. And they didn't have just a few of them. They had many. Hundreds of thousands of the damn things. Unknown numbers were detonated as tests. At least two were actually deployed. Thousands were killed, and others were left scarred and diseased. The land was infertile for generations, and there were mutations. Still, they built more. Knowing that to use them would mean the end of our race, nuclear winter, and the destruction of the planet, didn't keep them from building more bombs in great numbers. Everyone was scared. The possibility of nuclear holocaust was something that generations grew up with, but that no one ever got used to. Someone might fire a rocket, and someone else would retaliate, and before you knew it—no more world. Some fool could push a button, and..." he snapped his fingers, "...BOOM! Instant Armageddon. Then, as one of the Super Powers started to collapse it caused even more tension, because no one was sure who had control of their buttons anymore. Just when they thought they had everything figured out and they could relax, the smaller countries—the ones run by all the crazies and religious fanatics—started to make weapons of mass destruction. They started playing with stuff even more frightening than the atomic bomb: chemical and biological weapons. While the Super Powers had been experimenting with the same crap for years, no one trusted these morons to even be able to keep their experiments contained. When you're talking about biological weapons, all it takes is one leak, one mistake. In a global economy, within days everyone's infected. In a few weeks—maybe less—everyone's dead."

"And into this uneasy climate crept the Reliance," RJ said, putting all the factors together.

"Precisely!" Topaz clapped his hands, delighted with his new pupil.

"I don't get it," David said. "What does one have to do with the other?"

"Everyone was so afraid of the threat of total annihilation that they would have done anything not to have to live with that terror over their heads," RJ answered.

Topaz nodded. "Exactly. Moreover, the truly ironic part of it is that the Reliance was behind the whole thing from the beginning. They had infiltrated the central governments of both Super Powers, and the news media as well. Therefore, when the Super Powers had their famous 'peace talks,' the Reliance was there—firmly planted in both houses behind the scenes—making sure peace didn't break out. The powers would make progress toward peace one minute, then back-slide the next. This went on for decades, and the whole time the Reliance grew stronger. Like a sore, it festered and grew. It was nurtured on fear and discord. It was as secret and silent as cancer; then, early in the twenty-first century, it burst to the surface."

"What happened?" David asked.

"I would think a major assassination or two," RJ said, matter-of-factly.

Topaz looked at her in disbelief.

"A calculated guess."

"And a correct one. Mind you, it didn't look like it, but I'm sure it was the Reliance. First, Air Force One took a nose-dive into the Florida Keys, killing the American President. Then several key leaders of the former USSR died of an unknown and virulent disease that they contracted while attending a conference that was supposed to resolve the problems caused by the dissolution of the Soviet Bloc. China had so much internal discord that it was an easy mark. Their own citizens tossed their leaders out of power."

Topaz realized that the place names were lost on these two. Foreign words to them, but he couldn't tell the story without them. "People stepped in to take over the positions of the dead or ousted leaders, and amazingly they immediately signed peace accords. They compromised on a few ideological points, and with a little red tape here and there, good media coverage, some politicking where necessary, and one or two more assassinations in the former Soviet Bloc countries...Wham! Bang! Boom! You have the Reliance."

"But you said *one* of the Super Powers dissolved. Didn't you just say that the people of the other Super Power were self-governing and free? Why didn't they fight?" David couldn't fathom this. Here they were busting their asses to have freedom, and these people had willingly given it up.

"No, I said that was the principle that the government had started with. They let their officials make so many laws that there really were no freedoms left. Somewhere between the far-Left that passed laws to give lots of things to people who didn't work and let criminals run free, and the far-Right that made everything enjoyable illegal, the working class lost its freedom. People forgot that it was their duty to stay informed about what was going on at all governmental levels, and so these laws passed undetected. One day they woke up trapped; they had lost most of their personal freedoms. The saddest thing is that most of them either didn't recognize the trap, or simply didn't care. By the time the Reliance came to power, they no longer knew what freedom was. They'd forgotten that freedom isn't ever either free or easy. They had forgotten how to fight. The Reliance did away with the threat of war and death, and that made everything OK. By the time the people realized what they had settled for, it was easier – and safer— to go along with it than to fight."

"Once—only once—a small group of people tried to buck the Reliance. They might even have won; who can say? But we found Trinidad, and not long after that made contact with the Aliens. At the behest of the twin gods Economics and Security, the people bound themselves to the Reliance forever."

"Huh?" He'd lost David again. "What did the Aliens have to do with anything?"

"With the threat of an alien race, the people had a common enemy," RJ explained. "No matter how they might feel about the Reliance, they would stand united against this common foe. You see, the devil you know is better that the devil you don't know."

Topaz was startled again. "Where on Earth did you hear that one? I haven't heard that expression in...well, over five centuries."

"My father used to say it," she smiled, remembering him. "Come to think of it, he used to say a lot of strange things." Suddenly, all her attention was drawn to the screen where a couple was kissing passionately.

"RJ? You OK?" David asked, slightly concerned.

RJ's thoughts scattered like leaves in the breeze as she watched the couple on the screen. This was something she could never have.

"RJ?" David tried again.

"I'm feeling a bit tired..."

"Of course, how rude of me! Almost drowning would make anyone tired." Topaz stood up and helped her to her feet. "Come on, I'll show you to a room."

He had obviously knocked out walls and made three cells into one room. In the middle of the room was a king-sized bed covered in black satin sheets. Such elegance was usually reserved for high-ranking Reliance personnel, but RJ hardly noticed it. Topaz turned to leave then turned back.

"Are you OK, child?"

"Just tired."

Topaz nodded and left through the curtained doorway.

RJ unwound her chain and let it fall. She pulled her laser from its holster; it still wasn't dry. She sat down on the bed and started to break it down. It wasn't that she feared attack; she simply needed something reassuringly routine to do.

What a mess! How had she ever allowed herself to do something as stupid as to desire something that she could never have?

Romance, she decided, was not logical. She hated it.

Life sucked! No one ever got what they wanted. Well, maybe she shouldn't generalize.

My *life sucks and I never get what I want.*

She finished stripping, drying and reassembling the laser. She lay back on the bed and stared at the ceiling. As usual, as soon as she wasn't using it, her right arm started to jerk. Funny, it had never really bothered her before. Now it did. It was just one more obstacle on the road to normalcy.

She felt vulnerable again. God, how she hated that.

She'd almost died. So what?

Whitey had saved her. That must mean something.

Poor Whitey. She knew now a bit of what he'd been going through.

As if thinking of him had called him up, he appeared in the doorway. He smiled, and she felt like the world's worst bitch.

"How ya feeling?" he asked.

"Like an idiot. I never should have tried to catch that door. Thanks." She wasn't able to scrape up more gratitude than that. Not for *her* life.

He crossed the room and lay down beside her. She didn't have the heart to send him away. He ran his hand over the sheet.

"What's this?"

RJ shrugged. Fabric wasn't her forte.

"It feels good." He ran his hand over her arm. "I thought I'd lost you. We could have all died. Anything is possible, RJ." He was out of his clothes faster than RJ could protest. He covered her lips with his finger. "Look me in the eyes, and tell me you don't want me."

She looked him in the eyes, and prepared to tell the worst lie of her life. But she never got to it. He kissed her, and she responded. He moved his mouth away from hers.

"You couldn't say it," Whitey said smugly.

"It's hard to talk with your mouth full," RJ said with a crooked grin. "Besides, it's hard to look a naked man in the eyes."

He ran a finger over her lips. "I'm not afraid of you, RJ. I never have been. I love you. Let's try again. After all, if anyone's going to be able to do it, it's going to be me."

He wasn't very good with words, but he *did* love her. She could feel it radiating from him. It felt good. *He* felt good. She wanted him, wanted his love. Jessica had a human lover, and Whitey wasn't entirely human. She wrapped her arms around his neck and kissed him.

He held her tightly for a second, then let his hands slide down her body, seeming to have not much more trouble getting her out of her clothes than he'd had getting out of his.

She loved the smell of him, the feel of him, the way he touched her. She could do this. She started to relax. This time, things were going to be different.

She'd surprised him in many ways. He knew she'd be different from human women, and she was. He had expected her to be demanding, and she was. What he hadn't expected was that she would be so giving or so loving.

He lay on his back in the exhausted and ecstatic state she had left him, and this time it was she who clung to him.

For RJ, it was as if she now knew where she stood in the world. Suddenly she had some normalcy. Whitey was her lover now, and she admitted to herself that she loved Whitey in a very comfortable, if less-than-romantic way. He loved her, and she—Argy bitch that she was—loved sex.

"I have never felt...so relaxed...so at peace with the world. I feel fabulous. I love sex."

Close enough, Whitey thought. As close a RJ was likely to get. He kissed her and found his second wind.

David was enjoying the cartoon with talking dogs and mice. He decided that, in ancient times, mice must have been bigger than dogs. It must have something to do with the mutations that RJ and Topaz had been talking about. It finally occurred to him that RJ had been gone an awfully long time. With an effort, David pulled himself away from the viewing screen and went to check on her. He asked Topaz where he'd taken her, and was pointed in the right direction.

David hadn't seen Whitey leave, so it was safe to say that he wasn't prepared for what he found. He heard strange sounds coming from the room, and doubled his pace. When he flung the curtain open, ready to kill, one thing was crystal-clear. Whitey and RJ were lovers. There was no other interpretation for the tangle of flesh under the black sheets. He shut the curtain quickly and stood there in stunned silence. RJ started screaming in ecstasy, and David hurried off down the hall, his face beet-red.

"She OK?" Mickey asked when David re-entered the room.

"Huh?" David asked, startled.

"RJ. She OK?"

"She's, ah..." He started to laugh. "She's sorta busy." The others looked around quickly, and noticed for the first time that Whitey was missing.

"I guess she really *is* his woman," Topaz commented dryly.

"She is now, that's for damn sure!" David laughed.

"Way ta go, Whitey!" Mickey cheered.

"Father will be so pleased," Poley commented.

"Your father would be pleased that your sister is fucking a huge albino? You come from a weird fucking family," Levits said in disbelief.

Suddenly, it all melded in Topaz's mind. The robot, the girl: it all made sense now. "*Stewart's children?* You're *Stewart's* children!"

Poley's head snapped quickly around to face him.

"I'm not authorized to give out that information."

"Ha! Then I'm right!" The triumphant smile left Topaz's face. "I was sorry to hear of Stewart's death."

"My father is not dead!" Poley said emphatically.

Knowing what Poley was, Topaz was a little shocked at this show of irrational behavior.

"I saw his obituary. It went into the Reliance files some weeks back. I'm sorry. I assumed that you knew."

"My father is not dead," Poley insisted.

"I'm sorry." Topaz looked at David.

"How did he die?" David asked.

"They said that he had some terminal illness. He shot himself. They found him in his laboratory."

"That's a lie!" Poley screamed. "My father would not shoot himself. Therefore, he is not dead!" With that, he sat down on the floor and covered up his ears.

David motioned for Topaz to follow him, and Topaz complied.

"RJ's father really killed himself?" David demanded.

"Yes, but I doubt now that it was because of any illness."

"What do you mean?"

"Well...when I read the report, I had no way of knowing that RJ was Stewart's child. She is, and therefore that changes everything. If they knew she was his, they might have tortured him to death. The autopsy could be nothing but a lie. Or, more likely really..."

"What?" David prompted when Topaz hesitated.

"He probably killed himself to protect RJ."

David nodded. That made a horrible kind of sense. He looked at where Poley sat, still covering his ears. "I don't see any reason to tell RJ. If Poley wants to tell her..." He shrugged. "Well, I don't think any of the rest of us should. I can't see that it would do any good."

"Of course," Topaz said. He looked at Poley in a troubled way. "I'm going to turn in. Make yourselves at home. You'll find sleeping quarters just about anywhere you look, some big and fancy, some small and simple. Take your pick. Makes no difference to me; the drones do all the housework." Without further ado, he left.

Topaz walked through the halls of the old prison. The echoes of his footsteps resounded off the walls till it sounded like a small army was walking with him. He liked that. He always had.

Most nights, he liked to imagine that he could hear the voices of those callous prisoners from centuries past. The mutterings going from cell to cell. They'd even used the toilets as a kind of telephone system. Kind of gross, but it had apparently worked. Still, the vision of one man listening to a toilet while another talked into one always brought a smile to his face.

Then he would think of the generations of tourists who had walked through here. Not long after the Reliance took power, the tours stopped. For one thing, such leisure-time activities were discouraged. For another, next to a Reliance prison, Alcatraz seemed like the Holiday Inn.

Not long after the tours stopped, the earthquake hit. It was the worst one to hit in all the shaky history of the Bay Area. It left the city in ruins. The Golden Gate Bridge crashed into the sea, but not till after the Bay Bridge collapsed. The Reliance saw nothing worth saving, so they condemned the "City by the Bay" and relocated the survivors. Topaz, however, did see something worth salvaging. The prison was not only in one piece, it had been virtually untouched by the quake. Besides, all available information indicated that the fault had settled without sinking the entire state, as many in his day had believed it would.

He had worked diligently to prepare for this moment. He'd built a fortress for a revolution. A foundation for a rebellion that would topple the Reliance and bring back a way of life that only he now remembered.

He'd watched through the centuries as San Francisco had become Alsterase, and Alsterase had become the capitol of the discontented. Happily, he had watched as he saw the once-great city become a home for refugees of every type. RJ's crew was a prime example of the variety of misfits that the city attracted. They developed their own values and their own laws. They built up businesses and homes. They were a community unto themselves. Granted, they were mostly undisciplined and unruly, but at least they had spirit.

He'd been monitoring RJ's progress from the beginning. Marge had calculated that there was a sixty-percent chance that she would wind up in Alsterase. When he heard of the death of a GSH, he'd figured she was here. He calculated she would be lured to the island by the lights. He counted on her being able to get through his traps.

He hadn't counted on her being Stewart's child.

He'd never been one to believe in predestination. He didn't believe that the Fates ruled a man's life. Or at least he never had before. Now he wasn't so sure. After all, if he had never made the acquaintance of a rather dark beauty in an even darker tavern...

It didn't bear thinking of. It was speculation at best. It was a coincidence, that was all. Nothing so supernatural about coincidence, right?

Serendipity, a happy accident. He smiled. He was happy. The old place was alive again.

He roamed on down the halls. Clint Eastwood had made a movie here, or was it two? He couldn't remember. Perhaps he'd ask Marge later if it still bothered him. Somewhere on the grounds outside Tyne Daley had done a magnificent death scene.

How many movies had used Alcatraz as a backdrop? How many actors and actresses had listened to their footsteps echo through these dank halls as Topaz was doing now? Were they even now playing out roles? Shakespeare had said that all life was a stage, all men and women merely players.

He looked out a barred window at the City by the Bay. "The City that Rocks, the City that Never Stops," he mumbled. It was true. Battered and weary, it was still very much there, and very much alive. Through earthquake and hostile takeover, the city still stood. Though decay reached to overtake it, it hung on to the last vestiges of its pride and cried out, *I AM A CITY!*

In point of fact, it was the most important city in the world.

The inhabitants of Alsterase had broken the rules and condemned themselves in one way or another. They were wanted men and women. Their lives weren't worth spit outside of Alsterase.

And yet they were the only free people in the Reliance.

Right now, they were nothing but a discontented rabble. But with RJ's leadership and David's charisma they could soon become a force to be reckoned with.

Yes, he and this old city had been through a hell of a lot together.

But the party was just starting.

# Chapter Fourteen

"Senator Kirk," Right finally said after coughing quietly. He'd been standing in her office for nearly five minutes, and she had given him no indication that she noticed him. "Senator Kirk."

"I heard you the first time, Right," Jessica grated out. She stared dispassionately at the shelves that lined one wall in her office. "Anything on RJ?"

"No, but Parker's here."

"Good, good." She didn't look away from the shelves. "Well, don't just stand there, Right. Bring him in."

Right left and returned shortly with a man Jessica assumed was Parker. She had never met him before. In fact, she had only this morning pulled his file.

He wore a gray Reliance suit that showed his rank to be Elite Scientist. His youthful round face shone with eagerness. His blond hair flopped onto his forehead and had to be constantly pushed out of his eyes. He offered his hand, but Jessica ignored it.

"Please sit down, Parker," Jessica said formally. "Right." Both men were seated. "I suppose you've heard of this RJ person?"

"Yes, of course, Senator." Parker said in a squeaky voice that could very quickly get on your nerves.

"I need you to make a GSH for me."

"Well, of course. If you'll just get me the proper papers, and the specifications..." Parker was all cooperation.

"I don't have the proper papers. Here are the specifications." She handed him a paper. He took it, read it, and his eyes got huge. He gave the paper back.

"Even if you had the proper papers, this would be illegal."

"I am well aware of that, Parker. But try to understand. What I am asking you to build is possibly the only thing that has a chance of ridding us of RJ."

Jessica looked at Right. He knew nothing of her plans. His face showed his horror at the idea of going over the heads of not only Jago but also the World Commissioner. She looked him right in the eyes as she said, "Governor General Right and I have discussed this at length, and our conclusion is always the same. Without this creature, we cannot hope to capture RJ."

"If you had the proper authorization...this thing...it would be capable of random thought! A full range of emotions! Its only loyalty would be to you..."

"Is it possible?" Jessica asked.

"Well, yes. But..."

"No buts, Parker. I need this, and I'm willing to do whatever I have to do to get it," she said hotly.

"I'm sorry, Senator, but you know what would happen if I were caught. I would be the one in trouble. No offense, but you military types have a way of not being around when they start asking questions." Parker shook his head. "I'm sorry. Without the proper authorization, I'm just not willing to take the chance."

Jessica smiled, not something that put a man at ease. "I'm not asking, Parker. You *will* do this for me."

"I will *not*. If you try to force me, I'll go straight to Jago." He stood up as if to leave.

"Funny," Jessica leaned forward over the desk and folded her hands in front of her. "That's just what Stewart said.

Parker stopped and turned to face her, a frightened look on his face.

"You remember Stewart, don't you? A brilliant geneticist. They found him dead in his lab just sort of lying there in a pool of blood, cold and very dead. They say that he killed himself. How sad."

Parker sat back down. He had no doubt that she had had something to do with Stewart's death. He could go to Jago, but it would be his word against hers, and she was both military and a Senator. Besides, Jago was more likely than not to blow him off without even giving him audience. He cleared the frog from his throat. "It takes time, you know," he said with a resigned sigh.

"A year and two months. See you then, Parker," she said dismissively. Parker stood and started for the door. "Don't forget this." She handed him the paper. "Enjoy your stay at Capitol."

He left without a backwards glance.

"What the hell are you playing at?" Right asked as soon as the door closed behind Parker. "You're toying with a death sentence. You know that, don't you? Making an illegal GSH is bad enough. But making one without any papers..."

"Do you want to get RJ?" Jessica stared again at the shelves.

"Of course, but..."

"If we're going to stop her, we're going to have to break a few rules. Don't you get it, Right? That's why she's winning." Jessica looked at him and smiled. "RJ's not playing by the rules."

They spent several days on the island, absorbing what information they most needed at the moment. The computer and its creator were only too happy to help them.

What RJ had gleaned she started putting to work as soon as they returned to the mainland.

With a list of political and military refugees, they set out through Alsterase to gather new recruits for their cause. Some were more easily convinced than others, but in the end, they had all willingly joined. Marge and RJ had chosen well.

Among the most eager of their new recruits was a pretty, red-haired woman named Sandra. Her bright green eyes shone with mischief, and she always wore a wide, sincere smile. She wasn't a very big person, barely five-foot-six, and she probably didn't weigh a hundred and twenty pounds soaking wet. Her looks didn't fool RJ. Sandra could hold her own with the best of them, and she had the right attitude.

Sandra had been some bigshot Reliance general's private secretary—a cushy job with a lot of benefits. For years she'd been using the computer at her disposal to divert shipments of supplies from military installations to needy civilian villages. Finally, she got caught. Despite the protests of the general, with whom she'd been carrying on an illegal affair, she was shipped off to a work prison—one that dealt primarily with the raising and shearing of sheep.

Sandra's memories of sheep were less than pleasant. "They're homely, disgusting, filthy little bastards, that will go out of their way to shit on, or preferably, *in* your shoes. They simply delight in getting drenched, so that they can exude the foulest stench known to man, and they do this five minutes before you're supposed to shear them. I hate sheep!"

The only thing that Sandra hated more than sheep was the Reliance. The girl possessed a burning, passionate hatred for the Reliance that rivaled even that of David and RJ.

She'd slept her way into her position as the general's secretary, and she'd slept her way out of prison, and she was damn proud of the fact.

They took over the entire fourth floor of the hotel and made it their base of operations. Their new members were given weapons and communicators set to a closed channel and monitored by Marge.

Now they were ready for the next stage—secretly replacing every Reliance spy in Alsterase with their own personnel. They began this task at dusk one day, and by the first light of dawn on the following morning all twelve spies had been replaced. Poley's skillful hands fixed their Reliance communicators so that there would be no detectable changes in voiceprints.

They returned to the hotel in broad daylight. It had been a long night of hunting, killing, and disposing of bodies. They were all tired. David followed Whitey and RJ into the room, and Whitey gave him an odd look. It took David's tired brain several seconds to realize the significance of that glance. This was no longer his room. He lived next door.

But this had been his room. Back in the beginning, when it had been just him and RJ. That seemed ages ago, now. The rebellion was growing, and that was good, but...Well, he had to share RJ with more and more people. There was less and less time for them.

"Something wrong, David?" RJ asked as she started to unroll her chain from her torso.

David looked at RJ and suddenly felt a great loss. "No...I just...Guess I'm more tired than I thought. Good night...ah, good morning." He shrugged, at a loss for once, and RJ laughed.

"Good night, David," she said dismissively.

David left, closing the door behind him.

In his own room he felt truly alone for the first time. More alone than he'd felt at any time since meeting RJ. He lay down on his bed and stared up at the ceiling. He felt chilled by the thought of the deaths they had dealt just that night. Had it all become this easy? When had he stopped seeing them as people and started seeing them as targets? People had become problems that could only be dealt with one way.

He felt guilty and afraid. He longed for the security he had felt sleeping in a room full of people. More important, he longed for the security and the warmth he had shared sleeping with RJ, knowing that there was nothing expected. They had spent hours just talking. Their days had been filled with idle chatter. Now they rarely got a moment alone. RJ had Whitey now, and Poley. She didn't really need him anymore. But he realized with an aching in his heart that he still needed her.

The women came and they went, and he needed none of them for any longer than it took to satisfy his dick. But RJ was different. She was the only person he had shared any real closeness with since the loss of his father. She had become his family.

They were building an army, which is what he wanted. An army to fight the Reliance. But in the process he was losing RJ.

The noise from the next room became impossible to ignore. He had chosen the room next to RJ's so that he could stay close to her. At times like this, he wished he hadn't. Apparently RJ came if the wind blew, and when she did, she didn't care who knew it. David was sure that there were people on the outer worlds who heard her. Therefore, it was ludicrous for him to even try to pretend that he didn't know what was going on next door.

It was all Whitey Baldor's fault. Everything had been just fine till he came along. He had ruined everything. David snarled at the ceiling. So much for her crushing him to death. He seemed as healthy as ever. Oh, admittedly, Whitey had the occasional bruise, but nothing more serious than that.

David wondered if RJ loved Whitey. He knew Whitey loved her. But he wasn't sure that she loved him back. She acted much the same way towards Whitey as she always had. He continued to hang all over her, she more or less ignored him and went on with whatever she was doing. But sometimes she would reach out and take his hand, or return his kiss. Sometimes she would look at him and smile for no apparent reason. She might love him. It was hard to say with RJ.

It had been Whitey that had saved her life at Topaz's. Oh, David had helped, but it had been Whitey's idea, and Whitey's strength that had opened the door and freed her hands. Maybe she felt grateful to him.

A loud, ecstatic moan emanated from the room next door. David grimaced. Such gratitude was extravagant in his opinion. David was aware of being flushed at the thought of what was going on next door.

The idea hit him from out of the blue, and did nothing for his morale. RJ had come to him. She had wrapped herself around him and showed him just a tenth of what she was showing Whitey right now. He could have been the man sharing her warmth, drinking in her passion. He could have been the man running his hands over her warm, tan, flawless flesh. He could have kept her all to himself.

But that wouldn't have been right. You didn't have sex with someone just so you could keep that person to yourself. *Why the hell not? I've slept with women just because I liked the way they smelled.*

David had thought that making love to her would drive a wedge between them. But so had Whitey Baldor.

He put it out of his mind. He had done the right thing. Whatever else one might say about Whitey, he loved RJ. There was never any doubt about that. David smiled. Besides which, RJ probably *would* have killed *him*. What were bruises on Whitey would have translated to broken bones on David.

No matter how illogical or selfish, David still missed his friend. He didn't understand why everything had to change. Why couldn't it be like it had been in the beginning? The way he knew it could never be again.

Except for Sandra, none of the new recruits were even told about the island, much less taken there. Usually, when the members of the original party went to the island, they all went. This time, it was just David and RJ. Why she chose to do this, David had no idea. But he was glad to have the time alone with her. It was dark, of course, and the hologram rose out of the ocean to meet them.

"Hello, ugly," David waved. He'd become accustomed to this ghostly form and would have thought there was something amiss if it had failed to appear.

After their third visit to the island, Topaz had taken David to a private room away from the others and had Marge show him some old film clips. Ancient forms of government and the history of the same unfolded before him. The names were odd, and sometimes the language made it hard to follow, but he got the gist of it.

He watched as the history of his ancestors flowed onto the screen. He learned that Zone 2-A had once been the country called America. He learned that history almost always repeats itself. That if rebels aren't careful, they could wind up

bringing to power the same, or sometimes worse, form of oppressors than what they had just overthrown.

Topaz came in periodically to check on him. He answered
any questions David had, subtly planting his own ideas in
David's head. David wasn't so blind that he didn't see what
Topaz was doing, but what the man said made sense, so David
listened carefully.

It was obvious that Topaz favored a quasi-democratic form
of government with mild doses of socialism thrown in.

"...so you see, RJ. In America, anyone could grow up and
be President. There was this man named Lincoln. He came
from a very poor background, but he went on to become one
of their most famous men. Imagine it, RJ! People picked their
own mates, their own careers, chose where to live, and how
many kids to have. They even picked their own leaders. When
Lincoln was President, there was a big war, and America split
in two. After the war, they joined back. Lincoln said," David
cleared his throat, 'We are highly resolved that these dead shall
not have died in vain. That this nation shall have a new breath
of freedom.'"

"Very pretty," RJ said vaguely as she steered the boat.

"Don't you get it, RJ? America is Zone 2-A. Ameri-
cans have always fought for their freedom. It has to be
more than coincidence that the fight against the Reliance,
the fight for freedom, has started here." He spoke with
fervor and conviction.

"Maybe," RJ said noncommittally. She had more on her
mind at the moment. Among other things, she wondered
whether she should have brought David with her. She had to
do something. Something she didn't want anyone to know
about. If she was going to bring anyone, she should have
brought Poley. But she hadn't spent any time with David recently, and she sort of missed their talks. Of course she was
really too preoccupied to be good company.

"Don't you find it intriguing?" David asked in a hurt voice.
He finally had RJ alone, and it was as if she were a million

miles away. She didn't answer him. She just stared out at the island, even though it could barely be seen through the dark and fog.

"RJ, are you listening to me?"

"Not really," she said truthfully.

"What?" he said in hurt disbelief.

"Sorry, David. My mind...I think I love Whitey," she lied. She couldn't believe she had lied so easily to him. She'd tried to lie to Whitey a dozen times with no success. Yet it was so easy to lie to David.

David laughed and shook his head. "Well, that would explain why you're so distracted." He hid his anger. He finally had RJ alone, and all she could do was think about Whitey Baldor.

"He deserves better that some half-breed Argy bitch..."

"Isn't he a half-breed, too?" David snapped his fingers. It all seemed too obvious now. "I know what RJ stands for!"

RJ gave him a disbelieving look, but said nothing.

"Well...don't you want to hear it?"

"If you're right, and I seriously doubt it, then I already know." She sighed.

"Argy—RJ," David said.

She shook her head. "They sound nothing alike."

A horrible thought came to David. "Whitey knows, doesn't he?"

"Well, of course he does," she said matter-of-factly. Then added with immense satisfaction, "He guessed."

"If Whitey guessed, it must be pretty obvious," David said, thoughtfully.

"David, they don't make men Elites unless they have a very high IQ. Whitey is not just another pretty face." She docked the boat and jumped onto the pier. As she tied the boat off, she continued. "Besides, Whitey's made love to me. Any man who is my lover would know what RJ stood for." There, that ought to confuse him for all eternity. She started off down the pier with David right behind her.

"I don't get it. Extremely loud is EL, not RJ," David said and laughed. "Come on, RJ..."

"Forget it, David. It's a secret. You hate that, I know, but that's what it is." She turned around and grinned a triumphant grin, before taking off down the walkway. He deserved to squirm.

RJ looked around. Topaz was off with David showing him some more films and trying to indoctrinate him. It was just she and Marge.

"Marge?"

"Yes, RJ?"

"Patch me through to Senator Kirk's private terminal at Capitol. Make sure that no one else can intercept it."

"As you wish, RJ. Do you wish to have visual?"

RJ thought only for a moment. "Yes."

Jessica paced her room. She did that a lot these nights. It beat lying in bed staring at the ceiling.

"Pick up on line one," the computer announced.

Jessica almost jumped out of her skin. "Who is it?" she asked hotly.

"It's RJ."

Jessica heard her own voice call back and she froze in horror. Then she moved slowly to her terminal. She knew what she would find there, but she still sat down in her chair with a thud when she saw the screen. RJ smiled back broadly.

"So, Poley was right. You *are* smaller than I am," RJ said smugly.

"You..." Jessica spat, and started pushing buttons.

"You're wasting time. Do you really think I would be doing this if you could trace this call?"

"Not really, but one must hold onto one's dreams." Jessica took her hands off the terminal. "So, what do you want?"

"Join me, J-6. Together we would be irresistible," RJ pleaded.

Jessica laughed. "Are you mad?"

"I don't know. Are we?" RJ asked with a twisted smile.

"I am not the same as you," Jessica hissed.

RJ leaned back in her chair and folded her arms across her chest, letting her elbows rest on her chain. "Quite right. Poley tells me I am superior in every way. Come join us."

"You killed Jack...He was my lover. You blew him into so many tiny pieces that...Now you want me to join you!"

"One little mistake..."

"You killed my lover!" Jessica stormed.

"He can't disapprove then, can he?" RJ stormed back.

"You've made my life empty and meaningless..."

"I killed an unscrupulous man who sent me to slaughter children," RJ defended. "I'm sorry that you loved him. I'm not sorry that I killed him. He deserved the death he received. Many people did not deserve the deaths he dealt them."

"Jack Bristol was a good man. Villages must be cleansed..."

"You know that is trash," RJ hissed.

"You can't win, RJ!" Jessica screamed. "You can't wipe out the Reliance. You are nothing but a thorn in our side..."

RJ fixed her with a stare that made Jessica's blood run cold.

"I will win, J-6. I know I will. I have calculated that I shall. If you do not join me, then sooner or later, I will have to kill you. That would be sad."

Jessica managed a laugh. "You won't find me so easy to kill." Jessica noticed the jerking of RJ's arm. Something which she was obviously trying to conceal by crossing her arms the way she was. "I am perfect. It would seem that you have a deformity."

RJ just smiled more broadly.

That really made Jessica's blood boil. If someone had said something like that to her, she would have been furious. But RJ just sat there with an impudent grin on her face. "Look at you. Beat the Reliance! I bet it's been weeks since you combed your hair properly, and what is that getup you're wearing? What, for instance, does that stupid chain represent?"

J-6 was almost hysterical. RJ liked that. "Death to my enemies," RJ answered with a smile.

Jessica swallowed hard. She pulled her wits in about her. "I am Senator of Zone 2-A. I can summon..."

"America," RJ corrected.

"What?" If RJ was trying to confuse her, she was doing a good job.

"America. Zone 2-A used to be called America. When we take over, we plan to reinstate all the old place names."

This time, Jessica laughed without any effort. "You can't win, RJ. A grubby rebel with a chain and a fistful of dreams cannot topple a galactic empire."

RJ's eyes gleamed fanatically. "Quite right, dear sister. But vengeful gods can, and do at will."

Jessica smiled broadly and shook her head. "You talk of fairy stories. Who is this vengeful god of yours, RJ? How is your god going to save you from the mighty hands of the Reliance?"

The smile left RJ's face. She leaned forward in her chair, resting her weight on the arms of it. "You are looking at a god, J-6. We should not exist, and yet we do. We are capable of great good or great evil. I don't believe that Father created us to be tools for the Reliance's hands. I don't think it was his wish that we should grow up and be good little Reliance lackeys. If it was, he could have easily altered our brains. He didn't. He left us free to choose. He left it up to us." RJ leaned back in her chair, and the feverish intensity left her voice. "Can't you see? The Reliance is wrong. Its practices are evil. It uses people, then tosses them out. There is no joy or purpose to their lives. The Reliance serves itself. Even you must answer to a fat idiot named Jago, and he to the World Commissioner, and he to the Council of Five, and they to the Council of Twelve. Everything that our father gave us, the Reliance reaches to take away."

Jessica didn't care spit about RJ's pretty speech. Only one thing intrigued her. "Why do you call Stewart Father?" Jessica asked curiously.

RJ knew then that J-6 would never join her. "Because he is," she paused. "And because he prefers that I do so."

"A father raises a child; he helps it develop. He doesn't spit it into a petri dish and be done with it," Jessica said.

"I don't know about you, but Stewart *did* raise me. Stewart is my father, in all meanings of the word. I love him, and he loves me."

If Jessica had hated RJ before, she hated her doubly now. She smiled hatefully. "I guess you haven't heard, then."

"Heard what?"

"Your *father* is dead."

"You lie!" RJ screamed hotly.

"He shot himself in the head. I was there; I saw it." Jessica enjoyed seeing the distraught look on RJ's face. "He did it to protect you. It was really quite touching."

RJ looked at her. Her eyes were cold; her mouth curled into a snarl. "Thank you, J-6. Now I shall not only kill you, but I shall enjoy doing it!" She closed the transmission.

"Marge, is there an autopsy report on..."

"She wasn't lying, RJ," Topaz said in a gentle voice.

RJ turned to face him. She didn't have it in her to be mad at him. "How long have you been there?"

"I already knew who and what you were." A tear came to his eye. "I knew your father. I was very fond of him."

RJ felt a strange tightness in her chest. When she spoke, her voice sounded funny. "He was a very intelligent man." She stood up. "I need to go home now. He used to say that you could never really trust a human. I would remind him that he was one." She smiled. 'My point exactly,' he'd say. He used to say that a lot." She started out of the room. "My point exactly."

David didn't understand why they were leaving so early, but he could tell there was something bothering RJ. There was silence, and silence bothered David. He waited for her to say what was on her mind. Finally he realized that she wasn't going to volunteer the information. "What's wrong?"

RJ didn't answer. She just stared out at the ocean as if it would disappear if she looked away, stranding the boat on dry land. Her voice didn't want to work.

"What's wrong?" David asked again. There was still no answer. "Damn it, RJ, what the hell's wrong with you?"

"My father is dead!" she screamed back at him. She was mad at him because he had made her say it. The madder she got, the faster she drove the boat.

"I'm very sorry, RJ." David didn't dare get up and move towards her. Not at this speed.

Her eyes hurt, and her chest was tight. "I feel so...empty. I...I...like part of me is missing."

"I know how you feel. I felt that way when my father died." She wasn't listening to him, and he understood that, too.

David, under Topaz' guidance, had studied all the great orators at length. Hitler, the Kennedys, Franklin Roosevelt, Ayatollah Khomeini, Martin Luther King, several popes, and a host of celebrities and politicians from several different ages. In short, anyone who had been capable of moving the masses by the use of the spoken word, and that Topaz had on disk. But even with all that preparation, David looked at the growing crowd and felt unprepared.

The crowd was getting restless. They had been lured here by flyers promising great and wonderful things. So far, they weren't impressed. Where were the booze and the naked dancers?

David looked at RJ and gave her a panicked look.

She smiled reassuringly back. She had no doubt that he could pull this off.

Topaz actually left the island for the event, and he stood at RJ's side. The rest of them were scattered through the crowd. Topaz looked at David and nodded. It was time.

David swallowed hard and jumped onto the hood of a nearby wreck. The crowd was so loud you couldn't hear yourself think.

268 Chains of Freedom

"Shut the fuck up!" Whitey bellowed from somewhere in the bowels of the crowd.

They grew quiet.

David searched for his voice and found it missing. He searched for RJ and found her looking at him expectantly. He couldn't let her down. "Citizens of Alsterase. Let me start by saying that we have disposed of all the Reliance spies, and that no one need fear reprisals for being here." A mumble moved like a wave through the crowd. They were no doubt debating whether or not they believed him. Several obviously didn't, and they left. But the bulk remained.

"We, the citizens of Alsterase are the spurned and the outcast. We are the prisoners and the deformed of a repressive society. For our beliefs or what the Reliance chooses to call our crimes, we are forced to hide in the ruins of a forgotten city. Like lizards hiding in the rocks to escape the noonday sun, so do we hide here from the tyranny of the Reliance. But why should we hide? Are we not more righteous than our chained brothers? Are we not better than those who would willingly serve an oppressive and cruel system of government? A government that serves only itself!"

The murmur that went through the crowd now was one of agreement.

"When the Reliance took power centuries ago, they promised peace and prosperity, happiness, and good health. As each of us knows, the only peace, prosperity, happiness, and health are hoarded by a few. All at the top of the Reliance ladder. I ask you, is it peace to kill those who have a defect?"

"No!" RJ prompted, and the crowd followed.

"Is it wealth when you know if your crop doesn't come in, you'll starve? Or worse, be exterminated because you aren't earning your quota?"

"No!" This time, they didn't have to be prompted.

"Is it good health when the Reliance saves only those they find deserving? To hide from the masses the technology to save lives?"

"NO!"

"As for happiness. Find it for me. Can it be found in the face of a class-one farm worker who works the fields every day of his life and goes to bed every night hungry? Is it to be found in the life of a class-three cloth worker who sits at a loom all day with holes in his clothes? How about the class-two lumber worker whose roof leaks when it rains and whose walls let the winter winds blow through. Are they happy?"

"NO!"

"What of the Reliance soldier? The one who is expected to go to other worlds and fight for Reliance glory, yet will be imprisoned for any act of decency towards his fellow man—Is he happy?"

"No!"

"But the *Reliance* is happy."

The crowd roared with enthusiasm, and he had to wait for the noise to die down before he could go on. "They sit in their fine homes with their uncalloused hands, eating their fill like fat ticks. All at our expense. As a people, we have become weak and afraid." Before they could turn on him, he added quickly. "But you, my brothers and sisters, are neither weak nor afraid. If you were either weak or afraid, you would not have lived to reach Alsterase. But, if we are not weak and afraid, why do we hide here? Why do we not take up arms and fight the Reliance? I'll tell you why! Until now we have been without leadership, without supplies, and without arms. To take on an empire without these things would be pure lunacy."

From the mumbling which took place, it was obvious that they thought trying to fight *with* these things was none too smart, either. He was losing the crowd.

"No one can defeat the Reliance!" someone yelled.

"No one can do anything if they don't try," David answered. "The Reliance exists because of man's cowardice, and it will continue to thrive as long as we all run in fear. We can win; I have no doubt of that. But we will never win as long as we hide here in our safe little places. You say no one can beat the Reliance. What about RJ?"

"So? You're not RJ!" someone screamed out.

"No," RJ stepped forward through the crowd. "But I am."

The crowd went wild for a moment, and then there was absolute silence.

In that silence, David continued. "We have supplies. We have weapons. We have leadership. We have a cause, and we know our enemies. The Reliance tells us we are free..." Damn it, he had nothing to follow that up with. He looked around in a panic, and his eyes rested on RJ's chain. He smiled. "If we are free, then I say that it is time that we break these chains of freedom." In that moment, David won them heart and soul. "Who is our enemy?"

"The Reliance!"

"Who will we destroy?" He took a deep breath and waited. "The Reliance!"

"Zone by zone. Planet by planet. We will trample our oppressors till all that remains of them is a black mark on the pages of history. Down with the Reliance!"

"DOWN WITH THE RELIANCE!"

"Long live the New Alliance! Strength to the Rebellion!"

"LONG LIVE THE NEW ALLIANCE! STRENGTH TO THE REBELLION!"

David's face was hot and sweaty. He looked out at the enthusiastic crowd. He drank in the power and began to change.

# Chapter Fifteen

At RJ's command they began to fortify the city. Rubble was stacked into barricades in strategic areas all over the city, and the people were armed. In what was left of the foundation of an ancient building, using rubble and whatever could be stolen or scrounged, they constructed a training area. One of RJ's design.

Then the training began.

The training ground was a maze of sorts. Traps were built into it. None, of course, were deadly. But to fall prey to one was to admit to simulated death.

RJ changed the configuration of the maze and the traps on a daily basis, so that there was no way to benefit from knowledge gained the day before.

She split each group into three groups of ten. Each group was given the same goal, but began at a different door. If you ran into another group, you had to fight them to the "death." Death was indicated by a mark on the head or torso with a marking pen. The group that made it to their final goal with the most party members alive won free dinner and drinks for the evening. This not only gave them incentive, but promoted teamwork.

Part of the maze had once been an Olympic-sized swimming pool, and RJ watched the goings on from her perch on the high-diving tower. Every once in awhile, if she thought a group was taking too long at a particular spot, she would throw a rubber ball into their area. If they didn't move on in sixty seconds, she counted them all dead.

RJ called it a training center.

The people called it "The Maze Of Death."

The maze was not their only form of training. Recruits were also given classes on the use, care and repair of their weapons, and they were trained in hand-to-hand combat. Those training as soldiers got up with the sun, and their day started with a brisk, three-mile run. It always ended with a speech from David.

It had been two months since David gave his first speech. Now there was not a man, woman or child that was not in some way contributing to the cause. Those who weren't training to become the fighting force were helping to build barricades and scrounge materials. Those unable to contribute in any other way were given the job of cleaning up.

RJ never quite got over her military training. She believed in order and cleanliness. She believed that pride in community would strengthen their spirit. She believed that working together towards a common goal would help them fight together in the future. Watching them working together also gave her an idea of who would make leaders, and who would not; who could work together and who couldn't. This was as important in civilians as it was in troops. After all, when she took her troops off to fight, the others would be left to hold down the fort should it prove to be necessary.

It was midsummer and hotter than blue blazes. If it were possible, tempers were hotter still. The troops were tired of training. They thought they were ready to fight.

RJ looked down on the streets below. It would be dark soon. Already the streets were teeming with the night time crowd. These people were ready to go. They were ready to fight. The problem being that she wasn't.

She looked at Whitey and smiled. He slept soundly, no problems and no worries. He was with her, and that was all he needed to be happy.

She wished it were that easy for her.

RJ walked over and sat on the edge of the bed. Whitey stirred and all but uncovered himself, but he didn't wake up. She looked at him and smiled wickedly. He deserved the rest.

She frowned then, and pulled her robe tighter around her although it was far from cold.

Her feelings for Whitey confused her more than anything else. She liked being with him. He made her feel good. She enjoyed making him happy. But in a way she resented his love, because it made her feel obliged to return it. She did love him, but she wasn't sure it was the way he wanted to be loved. She knew he wanted her to tell him she loved him, but for some reason she just couldn't. Like it would hurt her to do it, put her in a position of vulnerability. To love someone was to give them power to control your emotions. To tell them that you loved them put that power into their hands, and she had never been big on giving anyone power over her.

Love caused pain. She tried not to, but as it had so often in the past few weeks, her thoughts turned towards her father. She hadn't felt quite right since she had learned of Stewart's death. David was the only one besides Topaz who even knew, and she had successfully avoided David's attempts to talk to her about it. She didn't want to think about it. She sure didn't want to talk about it, at least not with David, who, of late, couldn't order breakfast without giving a sermonette.

She had told Whitey things she never thought she would tell anyone, and yet she hadn't tried to talk to him about this. There was something about saying it that made it feel so final. It was as illogical as her reasons for not saying 'I love you.'

It was all so stupid. Stewart had been an old man, and he'd led a more than full life. Hell, it had been three years since she'd last seen him, and the way things were going now, she probably wouldn't have been able to see him again anyway.

None of that mattered. It had somehow been comforting just to know that he was around, and now he wasn't. She was never going to see him again, and her only family now consisted of a selfish bitch who wanted her dead and a robot.

Her troops were ready, but she just couldn't work herself into a good killing mood. She couldn't seem to erase from her mind the picture of her father putting a gun in his mouth and blowing the top of his head off. She was reluctant to leave Alsterase. This apartment was the first home she'd had since leaving her father's laboratory, and that hadn't exactly been homey.

If the experiment had gone as planned, she wouldn't have had a childhood or a father. She probably would have grown up and been just like J-6. Having a father had made her different, and now her father was dead.

Stewart hadn't deserved to die like that. He should have died quietly in his bed in his sleep one night. Kirk would pay for his death, but it wouldn't bring her father back.

RJ put a hand to her forehead. Her chest felt tight. Her eyes filled with water until they overflowed and tears ran down her face. She touched her damp cheeks in disbelief. She was crying! Never before, in all her long years, had this happened. She buried her face in her hands and tried to breathe calmly, to stop this nonsense, but she couldn't.

Her sobs woke Whitey. For a moment he thought he was still asleep, dreaming.

"RJ?" He sat up and put a hand on her shoulder. "My God, RJ, what is it?" To his amazement, he found a sobbing woman in his arms. He held her tightly. He was scared; he couldn't imagine what could make her cry like this. "What's wrong?" he asked again.

"My father's dead!" she choked out. She buried her face in his shoulder and cried even louder.

"Oh, babe, I'm so sorry." He held her tighter and rocked her back and forth. RJ was crying, and not just a little bit, either. He didn't know what to do, what to say to make her stop. He felt his own chest tighten.

"It's my fault," she said in a gasp. "Because I'm a freak!"

"Come on, baby. If you're a freak, whose fault is that?" Whitey said gently.

She lifted her head up off his shoulder and looked at him. He was right of course. She felt a wave of relief begin to wash over her, but her grief and guilt pushed it back.

"It's still my fault." She buried her face in his shoulder again. "He's dead because I had to take on the Reliance." A fresh assault of choking sobs shook her. "He's dead. He's dead, I'm never going to see him again, and it's all my fault."

"It's not your fault. Don't blame yourself." His own voice sounded choked. He held her tightly enough to have broken a normal person's ribs. He had never had any desire to see that RJ had a vulnerable side. He didn't want her to hurt. He didn't want her to cry. She was in pain, and there was nothing he could do but watch. He felt useless. He rested his head on top of hers. "Please don't cry, RJ. Please don't." His own tears started to flow. "I can't stand it if you do."

RJ couldn't stop. She didn't even try. Nothing that had gone before had prepared her for this. She'd seen death and misery, often wading through countless bodies of the dead and dying. But she had never lost anyone she cared about before.

There were things she supposed she should have cried about in the past. It was going to be a long time before she did this again, so she might as well get it all over with at once. She didn't really understand it, but crying like this made her feel better. It felt good to purge herself of her grief and frustration. It felt good to know that Whitey was there. That he cared for her, and that he would not leave her side until she'd made it through this. Slowly, she began to realize that she was not the only one crying. She pulled back and looked at Whitey. He was crying, too.

"Whitey, you didn't even know him. Why are *you* crying?" She dried the tears from her face, then started to dry them carefully from his.

"I don't know. I think because you're crying and you hurt, and I can't fix it." He shrugged.

RJ looked into his eyes. Eyes almost as blue as hers, but devoid of the hardness hers had acquired over the years. He was a good man, a beautiful man, a gentle man who deserved a good and gentle woman. Unfortunately, he loved her.

She kissed him gently on the lips. "You're wonderful." She ran her hand over his stomach. She liked the way he felt, all warm and hairy. She kissed him again. "Make love to me?"

He didn't have to be asked twice.

It was different this time. All the passion was there, all the intensity, but it was more emotional, more intimate. Unbelievably, it was better.

Afterwards, she lay curled up against him, her face lying on his chest. He ran his hand down her back, and watched her body rise and fall with the rhythm of her breathing. "I love you," he whispered. Then wished he hadn't, as the silence roared in his ears.

Then she spoke. "I love you, too." There, she'd said it, and she was glad. She meant it, too. "Very much," she added for good measure.

Whitey looked at her in disbelief. He had waited so long...had she really said it? "What did you say?" he asked carefully, almost convinced that he'd imagined the whole thing.

"I said I love you. Here..." Suddenly she got up and strode to the window. She threw it open, leaned out and screamed, "I LOVE WHITEY BALDOR!" She leapt back to the bed, and looked at Whitey impishly. "Are you happy now, butthead?"

"Very." He took her into his arms. "I was beginning to think you never would." He leaned against the wall, she moved to lean against his chest, and he wrapped his arms around her.

"I'm beginning to think I always have." She settled more comfortably into his arms. "I really don't understand people yet, Whitey. I especially don't understand me." She felt as if she couldn't get close enough to him. He must have felt the same, because he pulled her tightly into his chest. "I wish I could stay right here forever. Right here with you." But she couldn't, and she knew it. He was normal. Sooner or later she would lose him, too. She had only just realized how much he meant to her. She'd wasted all this time with him. Then she smiled. If she had felt this way about him before, she never would have let him make love to her. Things had a way of working out.

The next day RJ started working on a plan of action.

# Chapter Sixteen

They took the target completely by surprise, and in thirty minutes the more than eighty men who had manned the installation lay dead. The New Alliance had taken very few casualties. Their dead and wounded were carried out in one of three top-of-the-line helicopters they claimed as part of their plunder.

The attack was so clean and so well executed that they were back in Alsterase swilling down beer and crowing over their victory before the Reliance was even aware it had been hit.

"What did she get this time?" Jessica asked in a hiss.

"Three WH-11 helicopters, seven antiaircraft lasers, 2000 laser sidearms, 300 gross of power packs, 4000 B-Q-56 land mines, 600 cases of K-rations, forty thousand square feet of urban camo-netting..."

"In other words, everything." She tried to calm herself. "In broad daylight, Right!"

"It would appear that way, Senator." Right worked on not flinching.

"How many men did she have with her?"

"Footprint analysis shows five, but..."

"Five!" Jessica screamed. "Five men couldn't have driven the trucks necessary..."

"If you will allow me to finish, Senator...We had five confirmed Elite-type boot prints. All other footprints on site were normal second-class issue. But, if you remember, RJ stole a load of boots..."

"Fine, Right." She stood up slowly. "I want the area cordoned off. I want roadblocks. I want big guns to blast her ass away. But I won't have it!" Jessica lost it. "By now, she's sitting around soaking up beer and laughing. And do you know who she's laughing at, Right? ME!" Her eyes grew large and fanatical. "She's laughing at *me*! And do you know *why* she's laughing at me, Right?" She twisted her head around on her neck at an odd angle, resembling a bird of prey eyeing its victim. Not a shred of sanity evident. "I'll tell you why. Because I am *ridiculous*, that's why." She raised a fist and brought it down on her desk, smashing it in two.

Right looked at the broken oak desk in disbelief for a moment, then he shook as realization filtered into his brain. Fear replaced surprise as Jessica's blue eyes bored through him.

"The real problem, Right," she said punctuating her words by hitting her palm with her fist, "is that you can't fight yourself." Then giving him a contemptuous look she added, "You only *think* you know what I am, Right." Jessica spoke slowly, succinctly and quietly, but Right had never been more terrified. "You're only close." Without warning she jumped over the remains of her desk, grabbed him by his collar and lifted him out of his chair with ease. "Don't *ever* pretend to know what I am, Right. Because whatever you guess, you will be wrong." She did that odd thing with her head again, and Right knew just how a rabbit felt. "I am much more than you can ever hope to guess, and not *at all* sanctioned by the Reliance." She visibly struggled to calm down. Then she set Right down in his chair with precision and carefully straightened his collar. "The only thing you need to know," she whispered in his ear as she finished straightening his collar, "is that RJ and I are the same, and that if you tell anyone what I am, I'll kill you." As she said "kill" she gently wrapped her hand around Right's throat. She held that pose for a moment that seemed like an eternity to Right. Then she released him and stood up briskly. "You may go." She waved her hand dismissively towards the door.

Right couldn't get out of the room fast enough. As he practically ran down the hall away from her office he looked at his hands. They were shaking. He had underestimated Jessica Kirk. Not just because of what she was, but because of what she had become. She was obsessed. She didn't give a damn about the Reliance anymore. It was simply a pawn in the game she was playing with RJ. It had gone far beyond wanting retribution for the death of her lover. Jack Bristol was a hundred years ago, and had very little to do with what was driving Jessica now.

She couldn't win. She kept playing the game, doing everything right, and RJ kept winning. That was what was really bothering Jessica, the fact that she was losing. If she didn't get a piece of RJ soon, her brain was going to snap like a twig. If she was what he thought she was, God help them all when it did. Right felt trapped. He couldn't go crawling back to Jago now. He was stuck. Stuck with Jessica Kirk and RJ.

They sat around a table at the Golden Arches, celebrating their latest victory. All around them they could hear stories of the battle being told. Some of the stories were true, some were highly embellished, and some were out-and-out lies. It was the stuff of which legends are made.

David sat on one side of RJ, Whitey on the other.

"Oh! I almost forgot." She pulled a coin from her pocket and wrapped it around a link of the chain.

The inner circle looked on, cheering approvingly. All except Alexi that is. He had watched her do this every time they won a battle. It never seemed to occur to anyone else that she shouldn't be able to do that. Alexi had seen hybrids before. Hell, he had fought beside them. None of them had been as strong as this single feat proved RJ was.

RJ wasn't just a hybrid. There was something else. He had become even more convinced of this since Poley's arrival. The dude just wasn't normal. He didn't talk much, and when he did, he was always deadpan serious. He didn't sweat. He didn't use his hands when standing up from a sitting position. The list of weirdnesses just went on and on. Whatever Poley was, he was not human. Probably didn't even have any human origins. Since he was RJ's brother, there was a good chance that she didn't either.

Alexi took a good, long, hard look at RJ. He found himself doing that more and more these days. He didn't seem to be able to help himself. In spite of his utter contempt for RJ, he found himself almost uncontrollably aroused by her. He would like to have her out of the way. He would also like to hump her till his brains fell out. No matter how hard he tried he couldn't stop fantasizing about her. He couldn't remember the last time that he'd bedded a woman and didn't pretend that she was RJ.

There was something very sensual in the way that RJ moved. Something in the shape of her mouth that seemed to promise pleasure. Her eyes shone with superior intellect and savage energy, a strange combination, and one Alexi found distractingly alluring. There was something uniquely feminine about RJ. Something that couldn't be hidden with guns or chains or even the fact that she could snap a grown man like a twig.

Sometimes, when he was so close to her that he could smell her, sweet and salty and pressing all the right buttons, he would have to remind himself that she was the enemy. RJ was all that stood between him and his goal of power. With RJ out of the way he had no doubt that the position of warlord of the New Alliance would fall to him.

If Alexi hated RJ, he hated Whitey Baldor even more. Hated him, in fact, more than he had ever hated anyone in his life. Not so much because Whitey had beaten him senseless, but because he had RJ. He knew that Whitey did to RJ all the things he only dreamed of doing. He hated Whitey a little more every time he saw him touch her. Sometimes he thought Whitey did it just to taunt him.

As if to give fuel to his thoughts, he looked over and Whitey was running his filthy hands all over her. *Damn him*, Alexi thought. *Why can't he keep his fucking hands to himself? I could handle it if he just wouldn't touch her. If she were my woman...* His thoughts trailed off. He hated RJ, didn't he? And even if he didn't, she hated him. But his mind wouldn't let the thought go. *If she were my woman I wouldn't give a damn about power. I would hold her and make love to her, and that would be all the power I would need. To feel her legs wrapped around my waist. To feel her hips thrust longingly towards mine. Pulling me in and spitting me out. To hear her cry out for more and be able to give it to her. For that I would gladly give up any dreams of conquest and follow her blindly. Just like that great giant oaf does.* He had hated RJ long before he realized that he loved her. By then, she hated him so much that it didn't matter. No matter what he did, he could never win her love, so his hatred grew and festered. A strong hate nurtured in the putrid remains of thwarted love and sexual frustration. *You've got a secret, you platinum blonde bitch. I'm going to find out what it is and use it to take your ass down.*

RJ had been talking to David, but her head suddenly jerked up, and to his dismay, she was searching him out. She didn't know what he was thinking, but she could feel the hate and defiance in him as sharply as a knife.

"If you have something to say, Alexi, why don't you just say it?" she spat icily at him.

Alexi got quickly to his feet, glaring unblinkingly at RJ. "Stay out of my head." He stomped away from the table. From the corner of his eye, he could see RJ pulling Whitey back into his seat. Alexi sat down at the bar and ordered a drink. "Damned freak," he mumbled. His eyes grew large, and he turned around quickly in his seat. He looked at RJ, and then quickly looked away. *That's it! That's the answer! She's a freak!* He didn't know why he hadn't thought of it before. If he could prove this to the masses, no one would follow her into battle—or anywhere else for that matter. But how to expose her...? He could turn right now and fire a laser blast at her head. But then if he was wrong, she would be dead, and seconds later so would he. He would have to be damn sure that his theory was correct before he executed any plan.

"I wish you and Alexi could get along," David said in a pleading tone.

"When are you going to realize that he doesn't *want* to get along with me?" RJ asked in disbelief.

"You're paranoid," David accused.

"And you're naïve," RJ countered. "Alexi hates me, and he has only contempt for you and everyone else."

"Alexi is my friend," David said angrily.

"Alexi has no friends. He cares only for power," RJ said simply.

"Are you saying I'm a lousy judge of character? I think *you're* my friend; am I wrong about that, too?"

"I'm your friend," she said, answering his anger with calm. "I didn't say you were a lousy judge of character. You're wrong about Alexi, but then he is a very clever deceiver."

David couldn't remember the last time he had been this angry with RJ. "Alexi is my friend!"

"Only as long as you're useful to him," RJ said, still refusing to get angry.

"You need me, too, RJ. Am I to believe that you wouldn't be my friend if you didn't need me?" David all but hollered.

"Need you? What the hell are you talking about?" RJ was more than a little confused.

"You need me to be your mouthpiece..."

RJ was grinning one of those God-damned smug-assed grins of hers, and David sputtered to a stop. "What?" he demanded.

"I need *someone*, David. It doesn't particularly have to be *you*." She wasn't about to let him get away with this little bout of ego.

"Then get someone else." David got to his feet and stormed out of the bar.

RJ went after him.

"Let him go!"

But she didn't listen to Whitey. She went after David.

"David!"

He ignored her. He didn't even slow down.

"David, I'm sorry!" Although she wasn't quite sure what she was sorry about.

David stopped and turned to face her. His arms were crossed over his chest, his mouth was set in an unforgiving frown.

"Let's not fight over Alexi," she said as she caught up to him.

"This isn't about Alexi anymore. You said that what I do isn't important."

"I never said that!" RJ said in disbelief. "All I said was that someone else could do it. That doesn't mean it's unimportant. We've already discussed the fact that I couldn't do it."

"Thank you very much, RJ." He turned and started off again.

RJ watched him walk away. She didn't want to fight with David. The point to be made wasn't all that important. She swallowed her pride with a sigh.

"You're right, David. I'm sorry. You're very good at what you do. The people listen to you." She carefully left out the fact that the people would listen to anyone who said what they wanted to hear. But who was she to burst his bubble? Let him have a bloated opinion of his own worth. Who could it hurt? "Excuse me for being insensitive. But, as we all know, insensitivity is something I take pride in, and the reason why you are the mouthpiece of the New Alliance instead of me."

"I accept your apology," David said grudgingly.

"Then let's get back to the bar." She put an arm around his shoulders, and they headed back to the Golden Arches.

In the weeks that followed they used their ill-gotten gains to further fortify Alsterase. A minefield was laid in the area surrounding the city. The antiaircraft guns and helicopters were placed on some of the higher roofs in the central part of Alsterase and hidden expertly by suburban camo-netting. Laser sidearms were passed out like candy to the citizens of Alsterase until no man, woman, or child over thirteen was left unarmed. The rest of the haul, including one antiaircraft gun, was taken to the island.

With Alsterase fortified they were ready to begin.

Topaz stood between RJ and Poley and smiled a private sort of smile. He waited with all of Alsterase for David to start his speech. Topaz felt his hands shaking and stuck them in his pockets. He was nervous. He had no idea why, but he was. There was that sickness he felt in his stomach whenever he thought that maybe things weren't going to come off the way he had planed. He swallowed hard and told himself he was being stupid.

David jumped up on the hood of the old car, held up his hands, and all was silent. "We have learned to live together, we have learned to fight together. It is time to put our knowledge to work. It is time for us to march forth and take what is rightfully ours, to destroy the forces of oppression. We must free our brothers, so that they may join us in our great battle. Finally, the time has come, to implement my plan."

RJ moved restlessly beside Topaz.

"You heard him right," Topaz whispered, "he said *his* plan. Power corrupts."

RJ looked from Topaz to David then smiled. "Not David," she said in a reassuring tone.

"It is time to make the Reliance bow to our will. To break them as they have broken us. Our cause is righteous. We shall not fail. We will leave Alsterase as many small units, but will return a great force once more. A force which will have made a horrible scar on the face of the Reliance. For some day, I shall stand before the Council of Twelve and I will say, 'Let my people go,' and they will have to listen. They will *have* to listen to *me*!"

"Power corrupts," Topaz said again, and RJ frowned.

"Are you ready to fight for freedom?" David screamed.

"YES!" the crowed roared.

"Then prepare for battle! Prepare to be victorious!"

RJ, taking her cue, joined him on the car hood and the crowd went wild.

Topaz smiled and patted Poley on the back. "They listen to David, but it's RJ who owns their hearts."

She had no pretty words for them, but she had their trust and their respect. She motioned for silence, and they complied. "You all know what is expected of you. Remember that timing is everything. Let nothing detain you. If you are delayed, scrap your mission and return to base. If you reach your destination late all you will succeed in doing is getting yourselves killed. Good luck." She jumped down, and the crowd applauded wildly.

They looked for a place to stay through curfew. They managed to find a place far enough off the road to make a fire safely.

Poley never left the vehicle. He stayed at his terminal. It was linked not only to the communicators of every other unit, but to the super computer, Marge.

RJ stared into the flames, finding them relaxingly hypnotic.

"Can you believe that Levits?" Sandra asked with a laugh, and it was only then that RJ realized that she was sitting beside her. Not that she minded. She trusted Sandra. In a strange way she trusted Sandra more than she trusted anyone else.

"He certainly has a very active imagination," RJ said with a chuckle. She looked at Sandra, who was staring into the fire. Something was obviously bothering her. "He certainly thinks a lot of you."

"I know," Sandra said, as if the words were dragged from her.

"Is that a problem?" RJ asked.

"He's OK..." Sandra looked up from the fire and her eyes landed fleetingly on David, who stood a few feet away talking to Mickey.

RJ didn't have to be empathic to know what the look on Sandra's face meant. "Oh, no." RJ groaned as if in pain. "Not David, Sandy."

Sandra looked at RJ and saw remembered pain. "You? Were you..."

"No, we weren't," RJ smiled, "but it wasn't my fault."

"Did you love him?" Sandra asked.

RJ shrugged. "I don't really know now, but at one time I was sure. I certainly thought I did."

Sandra laughed. "That doesn't make any sense."

RJ smiled and shrugged then got serious. "Don't set your sights on David, Sandy."

"Why not?"

"Because David is an idiot. At least he is when it comes to women. Remember, always remember, that he is a work unit, not a soldier. They have very primitive needs and desires. David, God help him, wants a woman he has to take care of. You know, a bimbo."

They both laughed.

"On the other hand, Levits likes his women to be able to take care of themselves."

Sandra looked at David. Who knew him better than RJ? Nobody. But it didn't change the way she felt. "I've still gotta give it a try."

Just then Mickey walked up and sat next to RJ. "Be there in morning?" he asked.

"Be there in evening," RJ mocked.

Mickey just smiled broadly.

Sandra doubted there was anything that RJ could have said that the little man would have taken offense at. In Mickey's eyes, RJ was a god to be obeyed and worshipped.

Whitey and Levits returned from a 'walk in the woods.' Whitey sat down behind RJ wrapping his arms tightly around her.

Across the fire Alexi frowned deeply.

Whitey untucked RJ's shirt, then he started to rub his hands on her bare stomach. He kissed her neck. RJ suddenly turned to face him, wrapped her arms around his neck, and kissed him back in a way that promised that soon she would give him all he'd ever desired.

Alexi got to his feet and stomped into the woods.

"What's with him?" Sandra asked.

"Who knows with Alexi?" Levits shrugged and sat down close to Sandra.

"I don't like him," Mickey stated matter-of-factly.

"Something tells me that that's not why he left," Levits laughed. "Maybe he just needs to be alone."

Suddenly, RJ was pulling Whitey towards the woods opposite the point where Alexi had disappeared. Whitey was trying to be discreet, but RJ was past the point of caring.

The others contained their laughter until the couple was out of sight. Then they all started laughing at once. "Did you see who had the hot pants tonight?" Levits laughed. "First time I ever saw her show her true Argy colors...except for that time she tried to have her way with you in the middle of the floor," Levits said as David walked up to join them at the fire.

David's face grew flushed with remembered passion and embarrassment.

"They say they can crush a human lover to death with the force of their orgasm," Levits said then laughed. "What a way to go."

"Whitey's a lucky man," Mickey said, taking offense at the way they were talking about RJ.

"I don't know," David said thoughtfully. "It couldn't be easy to love RJ. I imagine she's a wonderful lover, but being in love with her...That's a different story all together."

"Why do you say that?" Sandra asked.

"Because RJ's a legend—bigger than life. What man wants to live in the shadow of a woman?" David said.

"Work units," Levits mumbled, looking at Sandra who smiled and nodded her head in agreement.

"What?" David asked.

Levits looked at Sandra, and they both started laughing.

"What?!" David demanded.

Alexi wouldn't have found any of it funny. He looked up at the full moon. Hateful bitch! She'd done that on purpose.

Like twisting a knife after your victim is dead. But her time was coming. All he had to do was prove to everyone that she was a freak. Of course, he first had to prove it to himself. He was almost sure that she was, but he still lacked any hard evidence.

Sooner or later she'd slip up, he'd catch her, and then he'd bring her to her knees. Then he could claim her as his own. Make her love him...But somewhere in his mind he knew that was only a dream. He was never going to hold her. It was all madness. Desire was madness.

He wanted to tell her how he felt, but he knew it would change nothing.

He's been walking rapidly, blindly circling the camp. Suddenly he heard something in the brush, and his soldier's training took over. He stopped dead, crouched low, and drew his knife, listening intently for a repetition of the sound. When he was sure of the direction, he crept silently toward the source of the disturbance.

He saw them silhouetted in the moonlight. Two unclothed bodies twisted together on the forest floor. Hungry mouths locked together, probing, searching. Their bodies moving together rhythmically. Rushing to fulfill each other's desires. Hands running carelessly over bare flesh. Her cries of ecstasy were carried on the night breezes to Alexi's tortured ears.

He knew that he should look away. Leave.

But he couldn't.

As much as he hated to see Whitey touch her, he couldn't make himself leave. This was it. This was as close as he was ever going to get to making love to her. In his mind he became Whitey. *It was Alexi's hand that searched out her breast and held it tightly. It was his name that she called out. His hips that her hands rested on, his tongue that probed the sweet softness of her willing mouth. It was his swollen cock that filled her.*

Alexi felt his hands undoing his pants, and told himself to stop, but he didn't. *It was to meet him that her hips thrust upwards, then pulled back only to repeat the process. Faster and faster, harder and harder until they were both consumed. Willing slaves to their lovemaking. When she came, it was for him. It was he who was bathed in the juices of her ecstasy. When it happened again a few minutes later, that was for him as well. When he ejaculated, his sperm filled her, and damn if she didn't come again!*

Alexi came to himself as if waking from a dream, and saw the couple on the forest floor. They held each other tightly, bathed in the afterglow of their love. Becoming all too aware of his hand, he looked at the pool on the ground in front of him, and felt shame. He quickly did up his pants. He wanted to run. To get as far away from here as fast as he could. He wanted to leave his shame here on the ground, but he was suddenly terrified of detection. If he stood still, he probably wouldn't be noticed.

He looked at her again in spite of himself, then quickly looked away from the rapture on her face. He hadn't done that. For her, the only person in the world right now was Whitey Baldor. He couldn't hear what they were saying to each other, but he was sure that it was the sort of thing that could make a strong man puke.

The guilt he felt at what he'd done quickly turned into anger. He had never been a pervert before. She had driven him to this. Is this what he had been saved for? He had been the only survivor of that life-consuming fire, and what for? So that he could hide in the woods and beat off while he watched Whitey Baldor screw the only woman he'd ever loved?

Why was she doing this to him? Didn't she know how he felt? Why didn't she care?

He stared at her. It was her fault. God, how he hated her! He hated her almost as much as he hated himself. *Bitch freak!*

Her head jerked up as if he had yelled it out loud. Alexi took a deep breath and frantically thought of nothing. For a second he had forgotten what she was.

"What's wrong?" Whitey asked.

"I don't know. I felt...something."

"I bet you did," Whitey said with a stupid grin.

RJ laughed, and Alexi allowed himself to breathe again.
Knowing what he'd done was bad enough. He couldn't
stand to be caught. For one thing, Whitey would probably kill
him. He was going to have to control his thoughts. One more
mental outburst like that one, and he was going to cue RJ to
his presence for sure.

He watched with relief as they started to dress, but he
didn't start to move till he knew they were almost back to
camp.

When he was sure it was safe, he left that spot as quickly
as possible. His self-esteem was spilled upon the ground. He
could deal with his shattered pride. He could deal with his
guilt. He could even deal with his very mixed emotions towards RJ. What he couldn't deal with was how good it had
felt, and he knew that if the opportunity were to present itself
again, he would do the same damn thing.

The morning air was crisp and fresh. The one good thing the
Reliance had done—quite by accident—was to save the Earth
from death by pollution. The Reliance had turned the Earth
into a huge farming community, concerned only with the production of organic materials. Clean air and water were a natural by-product of nearly five hundred years of agrarian living
and a relatively small population.

To say the group was wired would have been an under-
statement. Till now, they had only slapped the Reliance in the
face. Today, they were going to pull down its pants, slap it on
its bare ass, and bite its dick. After today, there would be no
going back. The Reliance wouldn't be able to ignore them
anymore.

They broke up into three groups. RJ, Poley and David
made up the first group. Whitey, Levits and Mickey were the
second group. Alexi and Sandra brought up the rear.

They sat in position waiting for the signal—a signal which
would be heard by every one of their units across Zone 2-A.

"Come on!" David whispered impatiently to RJ.

"Shh!" RJ ordered.

"What the hell are we waiting for?" David demanded. He was starting to lose his cool.

"For you to calm down a little," RJ said with a smile.

David tensed a moment, then grinned and relaxed, shaking his head.

"That was a direct hit," he chuckled.

"Are you calming down now?" RJ asked.

"Yes," David answered, pushing her playfully. "Can we go now?"

"Are you calm yet?" RJ asked, still grinning.

"Yes," he said, hanging on to calm with grim determination.

"Then let's dance!" She raised the communicator to her lips.

"Now."

One word, spoken slowly and calmly, and the war began.

As soon as the first report came in, Jessica knew where RJ was going to get her army, and she felt a chill go up her spine at the simplistic genius of it.

Jessica was sitting in her office with Right when her secretary came running in with the report.

"Prison break in installation 7-G!"

The words had barely left his mouth when Jessica bolted out of her chair and started pacing the floor.

Right looked at her warily. Lately, Jessica had taken to drastic and irrational bouts of ill temper. Whatever she might be, he knew one thing—she was more than capable of killing him and probably half of Capitol before they could stop her.

"Quit cringing, Right," Jessica ordered angrily. She started out of the room. "Well, are you coming?"

Right followed reluctantly. There was a computer in her office; there was no need to go anywhere to get all the information that she would need.

"I should have known. Where else would a rabble-rouser find such ready followers?"

Right finally understood what was going on. "Among other malcontents." He added, "Among the prison population...But surely, one prison...."

"Oh, I doubt very seriously that we are talking about one prison," Jessica answered.

As if to prove her right, another messenger met them in the hall before they could get to the war room.

"Senator, there's been another prison break. Installation 6-H."

Before they made it to their destination, they had been stopped a dozen times. Jessica got on the command link immediately.

"All units, this is Senator Kirk speaking. Move at once towards the correctional installation in your immediate area. Kill all non-military personnel. Repeat, all non-military personnel." After a few moments, she added. "You are also to kill anyone in Reliance military issue who does not immediately and satisfactorily identify themselves. Repeat, kill anyone who appears to be suspect."

"That should stop them," Right said, gleefully.

One of the men running one of the stations called his superior over. After a hurried consultation, he called Jessica over.

"Senator, there seems to be a problem."

Jessica walked over, looked at the screen and scowled. "What does that mean?" she asked with a hiss.

"Someone is scrambling our signal," he answered, unable to hide his cringing. "It's going to take us a while to descramble it."

"Then I suggest that you get on it, dunderhead!" Jessica thundered.

It took only fifteen minutes to clear the lines, and Jessica's message went out, but she knew it was too late. By the first rays of the morning sun, RJ would have her army.

There were two guards at the front gate. Neither one knew what hit him. RJ grabbed one and killed him instantly with a quick twist of his head. Simultaneously, David grabbed the other and drew a knife across his throat. As the blood gushed, strangling the man's death scream, David pulled him out of sight behind a bush, oblivious to the blood that covered his shirt, pants, and hands. It had been a long time since he had killed his first man. The guilt he'd felt then was a dim memory. The smell of fresh blood no longer sickened him. It was part of the game. He heard a voice in the back of his head saying, *How can you expect to win a war if you don't kill the enemy?*

RJ had disposed of the other body. Poley joined them, and they opened the gates and hurried in.

Whitey, Levits, and Mickey came in on the west side of the complex, just moments before RJ, David and Poley. They cut a hole in the fence and stealthily made their way towards the guards' barracks. As they started placing the plastic explosives, Mickey saw a sleepy man stumble from the guardhouse. He flattened himself against the ground and drew his laser. If the guy took one more step, he was going to see Whitey. If he shot the guard, that might blow everything. He crossed his fingers and hoped the guard wasn't the only one who would hear him.

"Psst, Whitey!" he hissed in a loud whisper. He wiped the sweat from his forehead as he saw the guard turn away from Whitey's position. Problem was that now he was headed straight for Mickey. He held his breath. A few more steps and the guy would be standing on his head. *Where the hell is Whitey?* Maybe he hadn't heard him. Maybe this was where it all ended. His pitiful little life. He held his breath, buried his face in his arms, and tried to wish himself even smaller.

Then he heard that wonderful sound, the sound he'd learned to associate with Whitey's fist making violent contact with someone's skull. He looked up just in time to see the guy pitch onto the ground beside him. He looked up at Whitey's grinning face.

"What took you so long, you big asshole?"

Sandra and Alexi went over the wall. They moved towards the huddled group of prisoners sleeping on the ground in the open. As Sandra started to leave cover and move on, Alexi grabbed her arm. She looked back at him in irritation. He pointed to the guard tower—it still held two men. Sandra took a deep breath.

"Thanks."

"We'll have to wait our turn," Alexi said with a smile. "No matter what RJ says, I'm really not such a bad guy. Don't dislike me just because your girlfriend does."

Sandra smiled broadly.

"What's funny?" He was perturbed because he thought she was laughing at him.

"It's just that I never thought of RJ as a girlfriend. I mean a girlfriend is someone you share makeup and fashion tips and go shopping with. Not someone you plan to overthrow the Reliance with. You know, someone you share clothes with, not sidearms."

Alexi nodded his understanding. "Get ready; there she goes."

Sandra looked at the guard tower. RJ was on the move.

David and Poley stood at the base of the tower and kept watch as RJ climbed. David occasionally turned to look at RJ. It never ceased to amaze him how she could move. She didn't take the stairs. She went up the framework as quickly and as quietly as if she did it every day. David saw her removing the chain as she moved. Not because it was necessary; she was going to use the chain because it was more personal, because she liked to use the chain. David cringed. Beautiful and deadly. A confusing combination. She moved with such grace, but she moved like that because she was going to kill someone. David saw her go over the rail and steeled himself for the sound he would hear as the chain met flesh. It was an awful sound. Like someone hitting a soaking-blanket-wrapped gong with a dead cat. A dull, hollow and yet ringing, splashing sound which defied a proper description, and put a lump in David's throat no matter how many times he heard it.

This time, he was spared having to hear it. Sandra saw RJ enter the tower and opened fire. Alexi followed suit, and they ran up on the five startled guards, screaming, automatic weapons blazing. Taking his cue, Whitey pushed a button, and the barracks went up.

One guard turned to face the intruder in the tower.

"Say goodbye," she said with a satanic smile. The chain snaked out and hit him in the head. Disappointingly, the sound of it was lost in the automatic weapon fire from below. The second guard fired his projectile rifle at RJ. The shot hit her in the chest, barely rocking her backwards. She looked up at him and smiled. His face crumbled into a mask of hopeless despair. He knew that the thing that confronted him wasn't human. He screamed in terror and froze. He saw the chain coming for him. The end of it closed on his head in nightmarish slow motion, and he couldn't move. There was no pain. He saw pieces of his skull and brain explode out of his head as he fell to the floor. His body bounced as if made of rubber, then lay still. He couldn't move. His one remaining eye stared up at his assassin. A woman. A beautiful woman, not much more than a girl. In what was left of his brain, he smiled. Better to be killed by a beautiful woman than an ugly man. His left leg jerked, then lay lifeless like the rest of his body. The body was dead, but the man remembered a warm spring day, a field covered with wild flowers, and a pretty dark-haired girl's touch. He smiled once more, then died.

RJ looked down at the lifeless husk as she wrapped the bloody chain around her waist. She had felt the man's parting emotions. He hadn't been a bad man; he'd just been on the wrong side. She walked over and closed his eye.

"I'm sorry. Better luck next life."

Below her the gunfire had stopped, and the only sounds were those made by the milling, confused prisoners. They were free, but didn't know what to do with their freedom.

RJ started down the tower stairs and saw that the inner circle was intact and uninjured. Unfortunately, that included Alexi. She stopped three steps from the bottom.

"You prisoners, gather round," she ordered.

The two-hundred-plus men and women were used to taking orders, and they gathered around as they were told.

"The guards are dead. We are the New Alliance. We are dedicated to fighting the Reliance and its oppressive rule. In return for your freedom, we ask that you join us in our struggle. If there is any man or woman here who does not wish to join us, step forward now."

A man stepped out of the crowd. RJ lifted the plasma blaster she was carrying and blasted the guy in the head. He flew back several feet and landed with a thud on the ground. She brought her hand with the weapon in it back to her side.

"Any one else?"

There was some mumbling and shuffling, but no one stepped forward.

"Good," RJ said with her sweetest smile. "Then we may begin." As RJ moved forward, she nodded to Alexi and Sandra who went to get the buses.

"Was that really necessary?" David asked hotly as he approached RJ.

"These people are prisoners, David. Most of them are innocent victims of the Reliance, that's true. But not all of them are victims of the system like you and Sandra. Some of them are cold-blooded killers. We don't need an uncontrolled mob on our hands. The next few hours are vital. We will either pull this off or fail miserably, and it will all be determined by how fast we can move and whether or not they can take orders. Right now, if you were them, would you do anything to cross me?"

"No, but...RJ what if the poor slob was stepping forward to ask if he could use the rest room?"

"I guess I saved him the trip, then," RJ said with a smile.

David threw up his hands and walked away.

# Chapter Seventeen

"Not so bad, Right!" Jessica yelled. She threw something—he had no idea what—and after it hit the wall, there wasn't enough left to tell. "Thirty prisons were emptied. Not one, not two, not ten, *thirty*! RJ's army is now 15,000-plus strong. Armed, and scattered across the entire zone."

"We did manage to stop two groups," Right said on a positive note.

"We stopped *one* group," Jessica hissed. "The second group was all prisoners. Somehow, RJ warned her people, and got them out of there before we arrived. All we did was slaughter unarmed prisoners. That's always a challenge. When our troops actually ran into hers, the rebels killed twelve men and wounded six others before being killed themselves. There were only five of them, Right! FIVE! We only heard from fourteen of the prisons. I shouldn't have to do the math for you, Right. At over half the installations every single guard was killed before they even had a chance to call for help. We don't have the manpower to scour the countryside looking for these rebels. Every aspect of Reliance life on Earth depends on the military to control it. I'll have to pull the troops in and put them back on their regular assignments, or everything will fall apart. RJ knows that! I'll have to go to Jago and ask for more men. Ask him to pull them from other zones."

Clearly, this thought did nothing to brighten her day. She slung some other unknown object against the wall with similar results.

"How the hell do I stop her?" She didn't expect an answer, and Right didn't offer her one. She was drained. She'd been up for eighty-four hours straight. "I don't think I can take much more of this." She pulled the pouch from her pocket and extracted a pill.

"No, Jessica, don't!" Right jumped up.

Jessica laughed cruelly. "Don't worry, Right." She swallowed the pill. "You were right about that much. I am a freak." She washed the pill down with a glass of water that hadn't yet found its way to the wall. "See, I'm quite all right."

Cocky damned bitch. She knew damn good and well that anyone he told would laugh at him or have him committed.

"Should you take those if you're not wounded?" Right's voice held as much curiosity as it did concern.

"Who says I'm not wounded?" She just shrugged. "It won't hurt me, and I need the pickup." She smiled as the strength returned to her body. "Sometimes, I think its all just some horrid dream. I keep hoping I'll wake up. I don't mean to take it out on you, Right. You just have the misfortune of being closest. Sometimes I think I'm going mad."

"Sometimes I'm sure of it," Right said with a supportive smile. "I understand the pressure you're under, Jessy. I understand it because I'm under it, too."

Jessica stood up suddenly and moved from behind her desk. She stood in front of his chair and looked down on him, sizing him up in a way that made him squirm.

She smiled. He wasn't at all bad-looking. She clapped her hands together in delight at her idea. Then she looked him right in the eyes, and without so much as a blink announced, "Let's have sex."

Right returned a look of pure shock. "You've got to be kidding!"

"What? You don't find me attractive?" She sounded hurt.

"I'd have to be dead not to find you attractive." Right pressed his hands together to stop the shaking.

"What's the problem, then?" Jessica leaned down and kissed him gently on the lips.

"Isn't this sort of sudden, Jessy? Shouldn't we..."

"Shouldn't we what, Right?" She knelt on the floor in front of him, and ran her hands up the inside of his thighs. "Wait for the moment to pass? Because that could happen,

Right. The moment could pass, and wouldn't that be a pity? To think that you might never know the things that I might have done for you, Right. Things that you have never even dreamt of." She started to undo his pants. If he was going to resist, he'd already missed his cue. Her hands touched his stomach as she untucked his shirt, and any apprehension he'd had slipped away.

By the time they finished, Jessica Kirk owned him mind, body, and soul.

Right watched her, enjoying watching her dress almost as much as he'd enjoyed undressing her. He was smiling stupidly. He knew he was, and he didn't care.

Jessica finished dressing, sat at her desk, and started playing with her keyboard looking at file after file. She seemed to notice for the first time that he was still lying in the middle of her office floor naked. She raised her eyebrows as if she had no idea how he'd arrived there.

"Come on, Right. There's work to be done." She seemed to have found the file she wanted. "Get dressed and get in touch with Jago. Now that RJ has her army, we're going to have to have more manpower."

Right dressed hurriedly. He was angry, and he didn't look at her until he was pulling on his boots. She was looking over some chart. Business as usual. His breath caught in his chest at the thought. He finished pulling on his boots, and stood up. She still didn't look at him. He looked down at her, and the full impact of her use of him hit. He felt cold all over.

"You bitch." He cleared his throat to remove the choked sound from his voice. "You cold, calculating cunt."

"Is that any way to talk to a superior officer?" She didn't even look up. She just smiled smugly and continued looking at her screen.

He had never admitted, even to himself, that he had any feelings other than fear and respect, and at one time friendship, in regard to Jessica Kirk. But she was, among other things, at least half Argy, and she would have known how he was feeling even if he hadn't. She would have known that physical contact would have made those feelings impossible for him to ignore.

"Damn you, Jessy. I love you. You knew that. I don't want to think that this is all there will ever be,"

She was silent.

"It don't mean shit to you, do I?"

"Actually, I like you a lot, Right." She shrugged. "Serve me well, and who knows?"

He knew what she meant. "I'm not going to be a pawn in your game forever, Jessy," he promised. He turned on his heel and left.

Jessica turned her computer off. She hadn't really been looking at it any way. "I don't need you forever, Right. I only need you long enough to kill RJ."

# Chapter Eighteen

The hardest part had been convincing Mickey that it was in RJ's best interest to have him next door to her instead of the midget.

He had done it with a knife on the wall inside his closet with the closet door closed. It had taken him an hour, and had filled his nose with stale plaster dust. But it had been worth it.

He wiped the sweat from his brow as he peered through the hole. He had been doing this for most of the four weeks since they'd returned to Alsterase. At first he felt dirty and guilty afterwards, but with constant repetition it had acquired the wholesome feeling of routine.

These days, all he felt afterwards was alone.

The whole time he was contorted in his closet, digging and sucking in plaster dust, he told himself how wrong it was. How sick. But he hadn't stopped. Not once. Now it all seemed normal. As normal as if he were the man with the woman, and right at this moment, at least in his mind, he was.

Long after it was over, he still watched. It had become important for him to experience the whole of the ritual. From the earliest beginnings of foreplay right up to the moment that they fell asleep in each other's arms. He told himself that this was in case they said something that would prove she was a freak, but the truth was that, for some reason, it made him feel less perverted.

She lay beside Whitey, her arm around his waist, her head resting on his chest. His arms were wrapped tightly around her.

"I love you," she told him, and he held her still closer.

"I love you, too." He contorted himself so that he could kiss the top of her head. "You're wonderful."

"I know." She laughed.

"You're also a smug bitch." Whitey laughed gently.

"I know that, too." She moved onto her elbow and looked down at him. "You love me anyway," she stated.

"Hell, woman, I love you *because* of it." He pulled her down on him again, and they held each other tightly.

This was the RJ that no one else ever saw. The RJ that only Whitey knew. Well...Whitey and Alexi.

She looked at the clock on the table and grimaced. "Guess we'd better get up and get ready to go hear David's speech." She got up and started to dress without much enthusiasm.

"Ah, come on, RJ!" Whitey begged in an exasperated voice. "This is the fifth speech he's given since we got back. Every time the man gets a fart turned crossways, he gives another damn speech."

RJ laughed. "We still need to be there." She threw him a shirt.

Whitey mumbled something under his breath and got up. "Lately he thinks he's God, or some damn thing. I sure as hell don't like the way he talks to you."

"That's just David," RJ said, shrugging it off. "He's always talked that way to me."

"No, he hasn't," Whitey disagreed while looking for and finally finding his boots. "His voice never used to lack respect. But it goes deeper than that. I can feel it, and I know that means you can, too. He really thinks he knows it all now. It's like he doesn't care what you've said or done. At this point he just wants to disagree with you so that he can see how many people will agree with him instead."

RJ laughed. "You worry too much about what people think of me. I don't give a shit as long as they obey orders." She wrapped her chain around her waist. "Let's go and get it over with."

Whitey nodded and started to follow her out the door. Suddenly he stopped and scooped something off the floor.

"You're getting a little careless, aren't you?"

She turned and looked at what he held. "Damn." She took the kit from him. "It must have fallen out of my pocket." She opened it to make sure nothing had fallen out. Then she smiled at Whitey. "All good little freaks must carry their kits with them at all times." She didn't want there to be, but there was a bitter tone in her voice.

"Don't call yourself that," Whitey said quietly. "Don't be ashamed of what you are."

She kissed his cheek and, hand-in-hand, they walked from the room, closing the door behind them.

They were gone. Alexi pushed away from the hole in the wall and zipped his fly with a smile on his face. He stood up so quickly that he hit his head on the clothes rack. He stumbled out of the closet and went to the dresser. He fumbled through the drawers looking for the projectile weapon which he no longer used, and which he had saved for this very purpose. He found it under a pile of clothing, extracted it, and checked the load. He wiped the sweat from his upper lip with a trembling finger.

"Steady on, Alexi old boy." He forced a smile. "Now's the time you've been waiting for." Gun in hand, he started out of the room.

Hate had become obsession.

Obsession had turned into love.

Love had driven him completely insane.

Alexi joined them late. He stood beside RJ and she moved. *Soon, she won't feel that way*, Alexi thought with a smile.

David was in full swing. "...Soon I will bring our message of freedom to the whole world. Every view screen will come alive with my message..."

"The whole world," RJ frowned at David's words. They had never planned to broadcast the message planet-wide. Only to Zone 2-A. To go worldwide now would pull troops from all over the globe. They weren't ready for that. She shrugged it off and chalked it up to poetic license.

Soon the speech ended, and the crowd started to disperse. Alexi moved till he had a clean shot at RJ. He carefully filtered crap through his brain so that neither she nor her big friend would feel his intent. Alexi swallowed hard. It was now or never.

"RJ!" he screamed loudly enough that he got everyone's attention. "I know what you are, RJ!" He raised the weapon, and started to pull the trigger. There was a noise behind him; an all-too-familiar noise. His finger on the trigger went limp. He felt the warmth spreading down his back. RJ turned to stare in disbelief as the gun fell from his fingers. Then he was falling, legs, arms and back losing all feeling as the paralysis crept over him. His face hit the road. David reached his side first. He rolled him onto his back, and Alexi saw RJ standing over him. He didn't really see the others.

"Why, Alexi? Why?" David cried in a tormented voice.

Alexi knew he was dying, and in that instant he regained at least part of his sanity. He didn't have time for David. He had to tell her. He had to tell her now.

"I'm sorry, RJ," he said in a voice choked with tears he didn't have time to shed. "I knew it wouldn't hurt you. I would never do anything to hurt you. I'm sorry for everything. I love you, RJ. I only wanted you to love me back, and I didn't know how to make you do that. I never knew."

Having made peace with himself, Alexi died on the cold, hard streets of Alsterase, the city of malcontents. He died in the shadow of the prophet and the warlord. A man whom he had used and taken for granted, but who had loved him like a brother, and a woman whom he had loved with all his heart, who had only contempt for him. He died as he had lived, in ambivalence.

Whitey and some others pushed back the crowd. Poley walked from the crowd, blowing smoke from the barrel of the projectile weapon he carried.

"Are you all right?" he asked RJ, and she nodded.

"Yes, thank you, Poley." She hugged the metal man. He hadn't saved her life, but he had kept her secret. She couldn't be sure that any of them would follow her if they knew what she was. To her amazement and delight, the metal man hugged her back. "Getting a little sentimental, aren't we, Tin Pants?"

"I find..." his voice dragged, and at that moment sounded every bit as mechanical as it was, "...I feel an affection for you," he stammered out. "I'm programmed for affection, you know." He said it defensively.

RJ laughed and hugged him again.

"You are messing up my suit," he informed her.

She kissed him on the cheek, then let him go.

"Did I do a good job watching Alexi?"

Now he was fishing for praise. RJ straightened his collar. "You did an excellent job." She looked to where David knelt over Alexi's body. "I had better go talk to David. You try to get rid of this crowd." The robot nodded, and was gone.

RJ approached David. She put a hand on his shoulder. Behind them, they could hear the crowd. They were understandably upset. A member of the inner circle had tried to kill RJ. Murmurs could be picked out as to what they should do with this traitor's body.

"He's the first friend I've lost in this thing, and he didn't die in battle." David didn't try to hold his tears back any more. "Why did he try to kill you? Why? It doesn't make sense."

"I'm sorry, David," RJ said, consolingly. David was not consoled. He stood up and turned an angry face to her.

"Didn't you hear what he said, RJ? Can't you feel something for him?" he said angrily.

RJ wasn't particularly in the mood. "I never liked him, David. You know that. For God's sake, his last living act was to try to shoot me in the back! Excuse me if I'm having a little bit of trouble mourning his passing. I can feel sorry that you lost a friend, but I can't grieve for Alexi, and I won't pretend to. He was a snake and a worm, and I won't miss him in the slightest. One day, David, you will have to decide just where your loyalties lie."

But David wasn't listening. "If you had just been nice to him. If you could have just tried to get along with him. Treated him like a human being!" David screamed, and then accused, "You killed him."

RJ was cool. Her voice low and calm, which made what she said almost worse. "No, David. *You* killed him."

David started to scream at her again.

"No, David. Think about it."

He thought about it, and his face fell.

"As I said, David. I am sorry for your loss." She turned and walked away in the direction of the Golden Arches, leaving David alone with the corpse in the middle of the screaming mob.

He couldn't stay here anymore. He needed to get away from Alexi. He would try not to think about what the people would do to the body. It was just a shell after all. He looked one more time at the body of his fallen comrade. "I'm sorry, Alexi." He ran for the hotel and slowed only when he reached the lobby. RJ was right. He had killed Alexi. RJ had warned him. Warned him from the first of Alexi's treacherous nature. But he hadn't listened.

He saw Dex, the fat man who ran the hotel poised mouth open, ready to speak.

"Don't worry, Dex. We're not bringing him home," David said angrily.

"I was just going to say how sorry I am. He was the only one of you slobs with an ounce of manners to his credit. Guess he must have flipped his cookies. Really no wonder, living with a bunch of wackos."

"Thanks, Dex," David said sincerely, and started up the stairs. He started to go to his room, then thought better of it. He wasn't quite ready to let go of Alexi. He decided to go to Alexi's room. Perhaps there he would find a clue to what had just taken place.

David walked into the room. It had a military orderliness about it, much like RJ's. It seemed that Reliance tidiness had stayed with them even when Reliance loyalty had not.

Now that was odd. All the clothes were out of the closet, and lying on the bed. The closet door was open. He must have been cleaning his closet. Mechanically, David picked up the clothes and started to put them away. The smell hit him just as he reached the closet door, and he grimaced. He looked in and saw a hole in the wall with a five-gallon bucket in front of it for a seat. He didn't want to know this about his friend, but some imp of perversity made him look anyway. He saw RJ's bed, frowned, straightened, and threw the clothes to the floor.

No wonder Alexi had taken to staying in his room all night. He had his very own masturbatorium complete with a built-in peep show. No doubt Whitey and RJ put on quite a show. "Oh, Alexi," David sighed. He walked quickly away from the closet and sat down on the bed, sickened. David had to work quickly. He might not be the only one who would decide to come here tonight. He didn't want Alexi remembered as a pervert as well as a would-be assassin. He also didn't want RJ to know that her private moments hadn't been quite so private after all.

By the time David was finished cleaning up the mess on the floor, patching the hole, and putting Alexi's clothes away, he believed every bad word RJ had ever had to say about Alexi. Finished, he closed the closet door and glared at it for a long time. "God damn you, Alexi!" David finally left Alexi's room, shutting the door firmly behind him. He felt drained. Alexi was dead, killed trying to assassinate RJ. Because, in some sick and perverted way, had he loved her. None of it made any sense.

Alexi must have been quietly going mad for some time, and David had been too wrapped up in all that he was doing to notice. Alexi had needed help. There had probably been a million little signs, but no one had noticed. Or, if they had, they didn't care. David had wondered why Alexi hadn't wanted to tag along with him on his nightly quest for fresh meat, but he had said nothing to Alexi. Hadn't even asked if there was a problem. He liked being on his own again, so he had said nothing. Selfish! He was a selfish bastard, more concerned with having a good time than trying to help a friend. Thinking about it, he realized now that he had known Alexi was in trouble for a long time, but he hadn't cared enough to put himself out.

Well, he had done it. Now he felt like dirt.

He opened the door to his room and found Sandra standing in the middle of it. She was clad—barely—in an extremely short black silk robe that hung open with the tie trailing the ground. Now, David had seen his share of women, and he tended to be a little jaded, but Sandra was a very healthy girl. He swallowed hard.

"Can I help you, Sandy?" he asked, forcing coolness into his voice.

"I thought maybe *I* could help *you*," she said huskily. "I thought you might like some...company."

David crossed the room in two steps and swept her into his arms.

Sandra was famous, or infamous, for participating in sex for the fun of it, or for what she could get out of her partner. If she wanted to move up a rank in the military, she screwed a Major. If she wanted a better living compartment, she slept with the building manager. If she wanted out of prison, she slept with the guard, and when that wasn't enough, she slept with the warden. When she needed transportation, she slept with the man who drove the delivery van.

She had never really cared. Oh, most of the time, it had been pleasant, and sometimes it had been satisfying. A lot of the time, she had done it because she needed to feel wanted, or needed.

But Sandra loved David, and that made all the difference in the world. She wasn't screwing David, she was making love to him. Suddenly, the whole sexual ritual had an almost religious feeling.

Afterwards, she lay wrapped around him, thinking about things like kids and house pets for the first time in her life. His offhand "Thank you" wasn't enough.

"I love you, David," she said expectantly.

"Thank you, Sandra," he said again, no doubt because he couldn't think of anything else to say.

Sandra sank back onto the bed. It hadn't meant a damn thing to him. It had changed her world, but he had made love to her the same way she had made love to countless men. With his body, not his heart. To him, she was just one more girl he'd fucked. For the first time in her life she felt cheap and used.

He touched her arm, and she jerked out of his grasp.

"Ah, come on, Sandy," David said in a pleading tone. "It was wonderful. You were terrific." He stroked her arm, and kissed her cheek. This time, she didn't jerk away. "Wasn't it good, baby?"

"Yes," she admitted grudgingly.

"Then don't blow it by being pissed off now." He turned her chin with his hand and kissed her. She kissed him back without hesitation. "Ahh! That's better." It usually was the second time.

The inner circle journeyed to Topaz's Fort, where they prepared for the broadcast.

"I don't see why we don't broadcast to the entire world. We have the capability," David said. He was nervous and excited, but not so much so that he couldn't argue this point with RJ one more time.

"I am not going to go through all this again," RJ said hotly.

"Well, try one more time, because it still doesn't make any sense to me!" David screamed back, just as hot. He was tired of being pushed aside as if any point he made were invalid.

"We don't have time for this, David. Just get ready."

Poley watched this exchange and frowned. Something wasn't quite right about David.

Right burst into Jessica's office and flipped on her viewing screen. "Right! What the..." she didn't need to finish her question; her answer was staring out of the screen at her.

"...we have troops, and they are armed and trained. We have led many successful attacks against the Reliance, and..."

"David Grant," Jessica hissed.

"He's on every viewing screen across the zone," Right informed her.

"Then get him off!" Jessica ordered tersely.

"We're trying. We're doing everything we can, Jessy."

"...the Reliance is not infallible. It is not unbeatable," David Grant droned on. "I was imprisoned by the Reliance for unlawful assembly. My only crime was to want something better for my people. For this, I was taken to a logging prison to die. But I didn't. I broke out of prison without help. From those humble beginnings, I have carved out a new order. The New Alliance. I have built an army. A strong army, an army capable of toppling the Reliance..."

"*He!*" Jessica laughed, but not too happily. "Is RJ now trying to get us to believe that David Grant is capable of doing any more than tying his own shoes? Who the hell is she trying to kid?" Jessica launched herself from her chair. "I've got to try to shut him up."

"We've already tried, Jessy."

"Yes! But you are incompetent fools!" She stomped out of the office.

Topaz stood next to RJ and watched as David gave his speech. He frowned. David's head was getting so big it was in danger of bursting at any moment.

"I'm not asking you to take up arms and go after the Reliance yourselves. I'm saying that now would be a good time for your eyesight and hearing to become impaired. What you don't see or hear could make the difference between life and death for a member of the rebellion. Whether we succeed or fail may not be determined by the skill of our well-trained troops, or the brilliance of our General, but by the discretion of a few hard-working citizens." The sign Topaz made told him he was running out of time. "The Reliance tells us that we are free. I if this is freedom, we must break these chains of freedom and learn to be true to ourselves again."

Transmission was closed. Topaz nodded. They had closed the transmission themselves. The Reliance hadn't been able to scramble them before they could deliver their message, and they didn't give them enough time to trace its source. RJ stood silently as she watched everyone congratulating each other.

"You'd better reel him in, RJ," Topaz said from behind her.

"What does that mean?" she asked, turning to face him.

"I think you know what I mean," he smiled.

"It was a good speech..."

"Yes, if you think that David Grant is a god. He's trying to convince the world that he is single-handedly taking down the Reliance. We all know it's our hard work, and your brains and skill which is pulling the whole thing off."

"I don't want any credit," RJ said, her brow furrowing in confusion.

"Nor do I." Topaz nodded his head, indicating that he wanted her to follow him, so she did. "I've worked most of my very long life on all of this. The raids on the prisons and the transmission tonight would have been impossible without all my preparation. For all that, I can truthfully say that I want no credit. But I don't want David Grant taking credit for it, either." They started walking down a long, dimly lit hall. "I've been around a long time, and I've seen it happen a million times—oh, yes, at least that. You take some little shit nobody, give him a little power, and before you know it, he thinks he invented God. Some people can handle power. You, for example, do a very good job. So, for that matter—to blow my own horn—do I. But you and I didn't grow up on the underneath side of a shovel, and the power itself is not as important to us as what we can do with it. David used to be that way, but now...Well, he's getting out of hand, that's all."

"He...he hasn't actually *done* anything."

"Your problem, RJ, is that you're allowing your feelings for David to cloud your judgment concerning him. You're just fine dealing with everything else, but when it comes to your friends, you're blind. You won't believe anything bad about them. You refuse to see that they just might have a character flaw. For instance that huge boyfriend of yours…"

"There's nothing wrong with Whitey," RJ said defensively.

"The man did stick a hatchet in his wife's head. Did you ever ask him why?"

"I suppose he didn't like her," RJ said with a shrug. "What's your point?"

"The point is that just because you like someone doesn't mean you shouldn't question their motives," Topaz said with a smile. RJ's brow furrowed with concentration, and Topaz's smile broadened. This was a physical trait that she had, no doubt, inherited from her father. "In short, there is nothing wrong with thinking that David is acting like a pompous little ass, because he is."

"What would you like me to do about it?"

"I want you to talk to him. Knock him down a peg or two before he gets completely out of control," Topaz said, stopping in his stride and turning to face RJ. "Do something before he does something."

"With all due respect, Topaz, what 'something?' He lives for the rebellion; he's not going to do anything to jeopardize it. I don't really think that having an inflated opinion of one self makes one a candidate for disciplinary action." RJ kicked at a pebble on the floor. "But, if it will make you feel better, I'll try to have a talk with him. Come on, let's get back to the others."

They started back towards the main control room. Suddenly, Topaz stopped. He wet his dry lips with his tongue. "RJ, there's something I've been wanting to tell you…" She turned to look at him, and he lost his nerve.

"I'm listening," RJ said after a pause that was all together too long.

Topaz immediately went to the wall and started to run his hand methodically over it. "Now I know it's here somewhere."

RJ smiled indulgently and leaned against the other wall. She crossed her arms over her chest and watched him. "What are you looking for?" RJ asked, shaking her head. "And, more important, what were you about to say?"

He continued to study the wall closely, but started to speak. "Do you believe in Fate?" he asked, then didn't give her a chance to answer. "Some people believe that everything that happens in life is just...well, coincidence. But I don't see how it could be. Do you?" Again, he didn't let her answer. "I mean, when something as random as meeting a beautiful, dark-haired girl in a bar one night winds up changing the whole world, maybe even the universe...I begin to wonder if we have any real control over our lives at all." He fell silent, still checking the wall.

RJ thought about what he had said, and could find nothing in her life that would prove his theory wrong. What were the odds against her being on one side of this thing, and J-6 on the other? What were the odds on a man running blind from prison and running smack into the only person who could help him in his plans against the Reliance? She had kicked Whitey Baldor in the balls because he was the biggest guy in the bar. She'd wanted to make an impression on Alsterase quickly, and it worked. But that big jerk had fallen in love with her somewhere along the way, and risked everything to be with her.

"Well, girl?" Topaz asked, expectantly.

"Some things are more realistically explained that way than any other," she said with a crooked grin. "Now, tell me where all of this is going?"

Topaz was wondering whether or not to tell her when Poley suddenly appeared. He decided that now was not the time. It was only his vanity that had prompted him, anyway.

"Ah, Poley! Came looking for me, didn't you, Tin Pants?"

"I knew where you were. I came to be with you," Poley said.

Topaz turned from his wall searching long enough to look at Poley and raise his eyebrows in mild surprise.

RJ knew what had caught Topaz' ear. "He says he has affection for me. He told me that a couple of weeks ago."

"Well, I'll be damned!" Topaz looked from one to the other, and shook his head. Then he returned to his wall-searching.

"It's not really strange if you think about it. Poley has the ability to learn. He was programmed with our father's basic personality traits, but he is capable of developing his own." RJ put an arm around the robot.

Topaz listened and smiled. It was obvious that RJ also had affection for Poley. It was quite natural that she should, really. She had been raised by herself, far away from other people, much less children. Stewart would have been a busy man, with not much time to devote to a child. Poley would have been the one to take care of her needs as well as be her companion. Poley would have been new in those days, and growing in his own way. So, for all practical purposes, they had been raised as brother and sister.

They had grown up without aging, and perhaps the bond between them was made stronger by the fact that when everyone else was gone, they would still have each other.

And Topaz would always have them. He smiled and then he found a crack in the wall. "God damn it! Would you look at that! The bloody place is going to hell in a hand basket! I must fix this immediately!" And with that, he was off and running down the hall.

RJ looked carefully at the tiny crack and shook her head. Whatever he had to say, it couldn't have been very important.

Poley looked at the crack, and then at RJ. "It's not structural."

# Chapter Nineteen

Jessica stared at her console. She didn't like what she was reading. First, there had been the raids on the caravans, then the
assassination of a key government official, then there were more
raids, including the big one on an installation. Then the prison
breaks, followed by David Grant's transmission to the entire
zone despite the Reliance's best efforts to scramble it. Now
there was unrest among the work units. In some places, unrest
had grown into out-and-out rebellion. They were able to put
down these isolated incidents, but it was costing them a lot of
manpower and a lot of production. Law and order were decay-
ing everywhere, and she was powerless to do anything about it.

And if all that weren't enough, Right was on his knees at
her feet, begging and drooling yet again.

"Please, Jessy. I'll do anything," he pleaded. "Anything at
all."

"I've told you, Right," she sighed. "I'm depressed."

"I got you twenty brand-new rocket launchers and a Z-47
laser cannon. I got them right from Earth Central supply. Not,
I might add, without considerable risk." He started to undo
her shirt. "It's been so long, Jessy."

"Three days is not that long, Right," Jessica said firmly.
"Don't whine, Right. You know I hate it when you whine.
And kindly stop drooling on my slacks." She sighed. "If I let
you, will you go away and leave me alone?"

He nodded eagerly.

"All right. But I'm telling you right now, I don't want it,
and I'm not going to do anything."

"I don't care. Just take your pants off."

She complied and sat back down, picked up a chart and
started going over it.

"Aw, come on, Jessy."

"I told you not to whine," she said, then worked on ignoring him.

He didn't care. He wanted her anyway. He dropped his own pants and moved to enter her. She let him do it, but she just sat there on the edge of her chair, her chart in one hand.

"God damn you, you bitch!" he gasped out. "I should have never fucked you in the first place. I don't know why I even want you."

Then Jessica's control snapped. The chart was allowed to drop to the floor, and she wrapped herself around him. The next thing he knew, she had him on the desk.

"Ah! This is better, Jessy!"

"Shut up, you bastard," she gasped, "and just do it!"

"I love you, Jessy," he whispered against her throat.

"Then you're a bigger fool than I thought you were," but she kissed him as she said it.

A few minutes later, the door opened. "Senator Kirk..." The young lieutenant stopped in his tracks, his face beet red. "Ah, I'm sorry..." He started to leave.

"Don't go, we're almost done," Jessica said, and she was.

"You cold cunt," Right hissed. He got up quickly and pulled his pants on.

"I'm sorry," the lieutenant said again.

"You will be," Right mumbled.

Jessica took her time dressing. Finally, she sat down and started to straighten her desk. "So, what is it, lieutenant?"

"Right, get a wet towel, and clean my desk off."

"At once, Senator," Right grated out.

"Professor Parker is here to see you, Senator."

"Well, send him in!" She rubbed her hands together as he left, and Right started to clean her desk.

"This could be good news."

Right just mumbled something totally incoherent, and went to dispose of the towel.

Parker entered the room.

"I hope you have good news for me."

"I do. The GSH has been born, and all is progressing as you wished."

"Splendid!"

"Do you still want me to deal with its brain in the manner you described?" he asked.

"He would be of little use to me if you didn't." Her tone was dismissive, and Parker didn't wait to be asked to leave.

"Damn you, Jessy..." Right started.

"I'm sorry," she moved to him, and hugged him warmly. "I'm not depressed now, and I'll lock the door this time."


"You could have saved those people, RJ!" David screamed accusingly. "We had a troop within spitting distance!"

"It's not time to activate troops. It's time to lay back and be quiet." RJ answered his anger with pure calm, which only made him all the madder.

"So, hundreds of defenseless civilians died because they listened to us!" David ranted.

"I don't remember you telling anyone that they should throw themselves on Reliance troops," Topaz said dispassionately.

"I told people that they needed to rise up. They listened, and now they're dead," David countered.

"I refuse to be held accountable for the random actions of work units. I certainly refuse to risk troops because of them." RJ was starting to have a little trouble remaining cool. David was getting more and more antagonistic with each passing day. "Troops don't function well in the cold. They have to wear more clothing, they need more food, and their reaction time is cut in half. Why don't you look at this from a positive point of view? As long as the Reliance is busy trying to neutralize civilian uprisings, they can't be looking for us. It does our position a world of good."

"People are dying out there!" David insisted in a horrified tone.

"Don't tell me about people dying. I've seen more of that than you can imagine. The name of the game is war, David. As I said before, the points are counted in cadavers. So far we're winning."

"I refuse to count dead people like points in a game!" David screamed.

"Then maybe you should get the hell out." It was Mickey who said it, but they all thought it.

"Who asked your opinion, little man?" David spat back.

"He has as much at stake as you do, and therefore has as much right to his opinion," RJ said. She had finally reached the boiling point. "Your problem is that you think you can be my conscience as well as your own. We can't afford the luxury of my having a conscience, too. I can only think about the big picture. The greater good."

David nodded his head submissively. "So, what do I tell the people?"

"Tell them that the people of Kingsford died with dignity and honor. Say that they died helping to free us all," RJ said.

"Shouldn't I apologize?"

"No!" Topaz couldn't believe he had learned so little from the tapes he'd viewed. "To apologize is to admit fault. We didn't do anything wrong. Even if we had, it would be political suicide to admit it. No one wants a leader who makes mistakes."

David looked at RJ. She nodded in agreement.

"All right," David agreed.


David stepped into his spot. Sandra gave him his cue. "Fellow citizens, once again I break through the bonds of Reliance security to speak to you..."

"What's wrong?" Whitey whispered in RJ's ear.

She shrugged. "I can't really put it into words. I feel something from David. Something I don't like." Even as she finished speaking, the words left David's mouth.

"It was never my intent to send anyone to their death. Some of you have misunderstood my last message. Those people in Kingsford died in a futile attempt to stop the Reliance alone. I sincerely apologize if my ill spoken words lead to their tragic end..."

"Cut transmission," RJ ordered. She looked at Topaz, who had already done it.

Topaz looked at RJ and shook his head. Even he hadn't expected anything like this.

Jessica had just finished watching David Grant's little show. She smiled broadly. "So, RJ has to deal with incompetent fools, too." She laughed and went to work

"What the hell did you do?" David demanded at RJ.

RJ turned to face him, her features a mask of anger.

"You sentimental fool," she hissed. "There is a reason for everything I do. Why do you think I had you make that first speech? I knew it would create civilian uprisings. Any extra troops she could get would be used up on that, and our men could be that much safer in their positions. You have risked everything for your own precious brand of morality."

David realized with horror what she was saying. "You used me. You used them. How can you live with that?"

"Get off your high horse, David. A few civilians got killed. So what? They did their part for the cause. Because of you, we are going to lose *troops*. Trained, armed troops. Troops that could have helped us conquer the Reliance and get this war over with a hell of a lot sooner. In the end, you have just caused a hell of a lot more death than I ever shall." She was finished with him; there was work to be done.

"Marge, send a message to all units. Tell them to expect double patrols."

"At once," the computer droned.

David looked around the room. No one, including Sandra, whom he had more or less assumed he had wrapped around his little finger, was going to side with him. He didn't understand it. He was right, and RJ was wrong, and surely everyone could see that.

"Don't you think you're being a little melodramatic, RJ?" David asked sarcastically.

RJ looked at him then, and saw the monster she had created. What had happened to David? What had become of the boy who had crashed into her in the woods, whose only desire was to free the people from the fist of the Reliance? Now he wanted more. Now he wanted the power. How had he changed so quickly? What was this thing that stood before her? Could it be exorcised, and David Grant found among the ashes? She was close to tears, but fought for control. She started to scream at him, then tossed up her hands and turned to walk away.

"I didn't do things your way, so I'm automatically wrong. That's it, isn't it, RJ? Who died and made you God?!" David yelled after her.

"Funny, that's what I wanted to ask you." She didn't even turn around; she just kept walking.

"Hey, pissweed," Whitey approached with fire in his eyes. "She isn't the cast-iron bitch you've got her made out to be. You are way the fuck out of line."

"While you were just second in line," David said flippantly.

David didn't see it coming, but he felt it, and even as he lay sprawled on the floor, the world spinning all around him, he knew that Whitey had hit him. His vision was blurred, but he saw Whitey leaving—no doubt to find RJ.

Maybe RJ was right. Maybe he did only see a little piece of the picture. After all, it should have been obvious to anyone that Whitey was going to hit him, when he said the second-in-line thing.

Sandra forgot her anger and rushed to David's aid. She helped him up and brushed him off before his head could clear, and before anyone else had a chance to hit him. She laid him down on a bed, and he felt a wet rag touch his jaw. She had her finger in his mouth.

"I don't think you'll need stitches," Sandra said, conversationally. "He knocked a couple of your molars loose, but I don't think your jaw is broken."

David's vision began to clear. She took the towel away, and he saw her washing it out in the sink. There was a lot of blood. Whitey Baldor had hit him; he was lucky he only had a couple of loose teeth. Sandra looked a little worried, but definitely not hysterical. She remained calm and did what needed to be done.

Sandra could take care of herself.

Sandra didn't need any man's protection.

She was definitely *not* the girl for him.

In the weeks that followed they lost two troops and part of a third. David was duly chastised. He knew these deaths were his fault and could only keep the guilt from pounding on his door by rationalizing that he had done it for good reasons. That he hadn't realized what the impact of his speech would be because he hadn't been fully informed.

In short he blamed RJ.

David stared at the ceiling and rubbed his swollen lip. No, it wasn't still swollen from Whitey's blow.

He had been meaning to dump Sandra ever since his revelation, but he hadn't wanted to hurt her, and he hadn't had the nerve. It could have been a cleaner split, no doubt about that. To put it bluntly, she had come home and found him in bed with another woman. She'd hit him in the mouth and beaten the woman half to death before RJ could get there to break them up.

He felt like the biggest jerk in the world. He really liked Sandra. She was a great gal, but he could never have any real feelings for her. She was just...well...too open. There was no mystery with Sandra. You knew what she wanted because she told you, and as long as you listened, she was easy to please.

David got up off the bed and moved to look out the window. On the street below he could just make out two familiar shapes. RJ and Sandra. RJ would make sure she was OK. RJ always made sure everyone was OK. She always ended up cleaning up his messes. He shook his head. Maybe he should have tried harder with Sandra. But he knew in his heart that he had been right to end it with her no matter how badly he had botched it. There was no future with Sandra; she was no better than RJ.

RJ stood with her back to a wall and mostly just listened.

"Thanks for not saying 'I told you so'," Sandra sniffled and dried a tear from her cheek. "I can't believe the bastard." She shook her head and the tears she was trying not to shed ran down her face. "Damn it!" she said in frustration. She didn't want to be crying, but she couldn't help it. She was so angry and so hurt. "You...you can't imagine how bad I feel..." Sandra laughed at her own stupidity. "Well, I guess you can."

"For several reasons," RJ said with a grin. "You will live, Sandra."

"Right now, I don't feel like I want to." This time, the crying was uncontrollable. RJ moved to give her a shoulder to cry on, and Sandra didn't hesitate. "I hate him!" she cried.

"Well, that should make getting over him a lot easier," RJ said with a chuckle.

"I'd rather be shot," Sandra cried.

"I'll admit that it doesn't hurt as badly, but it messes up your clothes."

Sandra laughed and sniffled. "You're crazy, RJ, but I'm glad you're here."

"There'll be other men, Sandra. Knowing you, there will probably be lots of them."

Sandra started playing the field again immediately. She had a motto: If it was breathing and humanoid, it was fair game. Levits found her favor often, but she wouldn't let him get too close. He wanted a permanent relationship; she wanted nothing remotely resembling that ever again.

RJ watched Levits watching Sandra. Sandra was with some guy at the bar. She'd take him home. She knew it, he knew it, everyone in the bar knew it. Including Levits.

"She'll come 'round," RJ said gently.

"Yeah, I'm part of her rotation now," Levits grated out.

"Give her some time," RJ reassured him.

"I'm not sure any of us have a hell of a lot of time," Levits said. He looked at Sandra and then down at his drink. The drink was attainable, so he drank it.

# Chapter Twenty

Spring brought warmer weather, and with it trouble for the Reliance. Weekly messages from the Rebels brought the work units into a frenzy. It took all of Zone 2-A's manpower just to quiet the civilian uprisings. In the commotion, RJ's prisoner army had no problem at all completing its tasks. They blew up alcohol plants, raided caravans, destroyed Reliance bases and strongholds. They used stolen goods to supply their army. They used the surplus to feed half-starved work units. A kind—and very politically sound—practice.

As the Reliance military force in zone 2-A dwindled, the Rebel army grew by leaps and bounds. It was only a matter of time till the armies of the New Alliance would march across their borders, spilling into the zones of their continental neighbors. The disruption would spread like a cancer over the face of Earth, and then there would be only one place left to take it.

That was the reason for this meeting.

As the World Commissioner cleared his throat, the sweat rolled down Jago's fat cheeks, and he shot an angry look at Governor General Right and Senator Kirk. Right pulled on his collar as if it were shrinking, but Jessica just smiled with confidence and acknowledged Jago's attention with a casual nod of her head.

Then the World Commissioner began to speak. He spent the next hour running down every crime the New Alliance had committed. He ended his speech with, "Jago, things have gone from bad to worse. Things have been allowed to get so out of control that we have drawn the attention of the Council of Twelve. It would appear to me, and indeed the majority of the other leaders assembled here, that you have ignored—indeed, turned your back upon—what has quickly become a very serious problem."

For the most part, Jago's older brother was a cool customer. The only visible sign that he was upset at all was a slight trembling of the left side of his lower lip. It was so slight that no one in the room noticed it. No one but Jago, because he had been looking for it, expecting it, and he knew what it meant.

"Have you anything to say, Sector Leader Jago?"

"With all due respect, World Commissioner. The problem is contained in Senator Kirk's Zone. I have left it in her hands, and given her the assistance of Governor General Right..."

"Enough, Jago. Before me, I see not one, but several requests for more arms, more supplies, and more manpower. Now, the blame is no more yours than theirs or anyone else's. We are dealing with something the Reliance has not had to deal with in centuries, namely an uprising of the civilian work units. We are dealing with something we are entirely unprepared to deal with, something our soldiers have never been trained to fight—an enemy from within.

"Our enemies are very cunning. This RJ hides herself and her face, and gives their cause an air of mystery, makes herself almost godlike to the people. Meanwhile, David Grant speaks directly to the rebel in each and every work unit, and it is beyond our capabilities to shut him up without closing down the entire viewscreen system. If we do that, we'll have riots on our hands for sure. The viewscreen are the work units' only sanctioned form of entertainment. We've been using them to feed the people a steady line of propaganda and subliminal messages for generations. Without them, things will get worse, not better.

"David Grant is the real threat. I have watched him, and...Well, I personally don't believe his story about being a work unit. His speeches are those of a well-trained politician. He knows exactly what to say, and when and how to say it..."

Jessica shut him out after that. The smile left her face. She had actually believed she would get some help from this

council, but if they were stupid enough to think that David
Grant was any more than a minor annoyance...She was going
to have to take care of RJ herself.

They had only put two of them at the rear gate, and these days
that alone was enough to make them jumpy.

"You hear that?" the man asked his partner.

"Yeah," the woman answered and readied her gun. "Sound
the alarm."

"Isn't that just a little premature?" he asked with a nervous laugh.

Just then, the tiny group broke through the brush and
charged. The woman fired, and one of the men went down.
The man sounded the alarm, and the other Rebels fled into
the brush. After sounding the alarm, the male guard ran over
to where his partner was kneeling by the man's body. He looked
down at the man's face in disbelief. He removed his own helmet and visor to make sure he was seeing what he thought he
was seeing.

"Hurry, go tell the captain I've killed David Grant," she
said excitedly.

Before he had time to react, Reliance personnel stormed
out of the base and Rebels ran from the woods to meet them.
When the smoke of battle cleared an hour later, he found his
companion dead and the Rebel's body gone.

"You're sure the body you saw was that of David Grant?"
the Captain asked for the tenth time.

"Yes," he said through gritted teeth. Then added, "Janice
died a hero." He wiped the tear from his eye, and hoped it
was unseen. "She put two bullets in his chest. He was quite
dead."

The Rebels retreated to their camp. David lay still on the
ground, his shirt covered in blood.

A figure clad in a Reliance uniform made its way through
the crowd.

"Enough is enough." RJ took off the helmet and visor and shook out her platinum-blonde hair.

David opened one eye then the other. "It hurt, RJ," he whined, "you promised it wouldn't hurt." He sat up, rubbing his ribs. "The vest almost didn't stop the bullets. I still don't see why you couldn't have used blanks."

"Bitch, bitch, bitch!" RJ tossed the helmet on the ground and took an apple from the bowl that Sandra offered her. "Blanks wouldn't have knocked you down."

"Blanks wouldn't have cracked all my ribs," David said in an injured voice. "And why did you have to use real blood?" He threw off the shirt, trying not to think too hard about where she had acquired the blood.

"When they investigate, they have to find real blood so they can be sure you're dead. I don't like to leave anything to chance, David." She smiled smugly, "that's why I always win...even when I'm losing."

The army sucked rocks.

She had been getting nowhere fast. Same stupid job with no chance of promotion. No special privileges. One day was not a hell of a lot different from the one before. She might as well have been a filthy work unit.

To make matters worse, you now had to worry about some fanatic Rebel bounding over the wall and blowing your brains out just because you were doing your job.

Kirsty didn't plan to die that way or *any* way if she could help it. She wanted the easy life and money. Lots of money. Fine wine and silk robes. There had been a time, not too long ago, when she had believed that the military would give her all that and more. A time when she had believed every word of propaganda the Reliance fed her. But six years in puke-green cotton uniforms and too many glasses of weak beer had dampened her spirit and opened her eyes.

She'd done everything possible to reach a position of high standing. She'd tried sleeping her way up the ranks. Hell, she'd even tried working hard. Every attempt at getting ahead had failed miserably. She was tired of waiting for the things she wanted.

So she went AWOL.

She knew where she was going, and why. She was going to Alsterase, the city of the damned. She'd heard stories of it from spies who had worked there, and it sounded marvelous. All she had dreamed of could be purchased there for as little as her 'services' for a night.

She had no doubt that she would become the most sought after whore in Alsterase. She'd dyed her hair, but that didn't change what she was. She smiled; finally she was going to have it all.

She could see the city just ahead of her now. She was home free. She had made it all the way here without being harassed by either the Reliance or the Rebels, and she felt quite lucky.

The barricade was so well hidden she almost didn't see it. She screeched to a halt, two well-armed men stepped out of hiding, and she knew she had crowed too soon. Considering the fact that she was AWOL and driving a stolen vehicle, she had believed that she'd rather see Rebels than Reliance. She now realized that at least with the Reliance she knew what to expect. Obviously the Rebels had taken over Alsterase, and it was just as obvious that the reason why the Reliance didn't know this was that no one left Alsterase alive.

"Halt!" one man ordered unnecessarily.

"I'm halted," Kirsty said shakily.

"Get out of the vehicle, slowly."

"No problem." Kirsty opened her door carefully, keeping her hands in sight at all times, and slowly got out of the vehicle.

One man rushed forward. He pushed her against the car roughly and started to search her. "She's clean," he told his partner.

Kirsty mentally patted herself on the back for leaving her weapon in the vehicle.

"What do you want here?" the man demanded. The second man started searching her vehicle. Kirsty held her breath.

"I...I was a farm worker...I couldn't take it any more. I tried to get a group together to fight the Reliance. To help the Rebellion. They caught me, and I had to run." This she knew was very close to their dead hero's story. Kirsty was no man's fool; she turned on the tears. "I can't believe you guys are going to treat me the same way. I didn't even hope to find you. I was just looking for a place to hide."

"Look here!" The man searching the car held up a laser sidearm.

"It's not mine!" Kirsty gasped. "I stole this car when I ran."

"What do you think?" the one asked the other, obviously skeptical. Before the second had a chance to answer, she increased the intensity of her tears by half, and started to sob loudly.

"I'm not wanted anywhere! Why don't you go ahead and kill me? Get it over with!" she cried hysterically.

"Now, now, what's all this?" A third man had arrived. She heard the authority in his voice. She dried her eyes and looked at the newcomer. She damn near fell over with shock.

David Grant was alive.

David Grant was alive and well and living in Alsterase.

She really *was* going to get everything she had ever wanted, and she wasn't going to have to stay in some backwater slum to get it.

They were sitting around in RJ and Whitey's room playing bottle caps. The entire game consisted of trying to throw bottle caps into a cup.

"That's it." Whitey reached over and took all RJ's bottle caps away from her. "You can't play any more."

"Why not?" RJ asked with mock sorrow.

"Because you never miss," Levits said as his shot hit the cup, bounced off the rim and landed on the floor.

"Poley can't play either," Mickey said from his perch atop the coffee table.

"Oh, I see," Poley said with a pout. "If you're good at the game, you can't play." He stomped over and lay down beside RJ on the bed.

RJ stroked his dark hair lovingly.

"Let him play," she ordered.

"I don't want to play," Poley pouted. Poley was becoming more and more humanized. Because of this, he was starting to resent being treated differently.

"You can play, Poley," Mickey said. "Just kidding."

"No." Poley was adamant.

"Quit being such a baby," Sandra said in disbelief. "Come and play with us, Poley."

"Ah, leave him alone," Whitey smiled. "Now that RJ and Poley have quit, I'm winning!"

Just then David walked in with a girl and upset Whitey's shot. Sandra won the game and started cheering for herself, doing a happy little dance all around the room as she did so.

They had to be the strangest group Kirsty had ever seen. But it was the woman lying in the middle of the bed that captured all Kirsty's attention. The woman just lay there and sort of oozed charisma out over the room. She was stunningly beautiful, and a half-breed like herself. Her clothing, like that of most of the others, was scant. Only a leather loincloth and a black tank top. Then there was the chain. It was wrapped around her waist and was decorated with coins. It had a feeling all its own, as if it were as alive and vital as the woman who wore it.

Kirsty didn't have to ask; she knew. This was RJ, the reigning Queen of the New Alliance.

"She is not one of us," Poley announced.

RJ nodded. She got up from the bed and adjusted her scant clothing. She nodded her head. "Sandra."

Before Kirsty knew what was happening, the redheaded woman planted her against the wall and searched her, thoroughly.

"For God's sake!" David protested.

"She's clean," Sandra announced.

Kirsty started to cry again just for good measure. David Grant seemed impressed by this dramatic show of fear, and she was going to play it for all it was worth.

RJ wasn't impressed. She circled Kirsty, looking her over as if she were a bug she wanted to crush. Then Kirsty felt the pressure on her mind. A pressure she had only felt on two other occasions. She was able to keep RJ out...just barely.

"Where did you get her?" RJ demanded.

"She just came in. She's running from the Reliance. I don't think..."

"That's right, you don't," RJ said hotly. "She could be a spy or worse."

Poley got off the bed and adjusted his clothing as was his habit. "Is she a hybrid?" Poley asked.

"Yes, and well shielded," RJ answered.

Kirsty was liking this less and less. RJ knew what she was. She didn't know what to do now. She had the feeling that if she did the wrong thing she would end up dead. Just when her whole life was about to come together, too. She threw her arms around David's neck, and started to cry even louder. "What are they talking about? I'm so tired...What are they saying about me?"

"She can't be unaware of what she is," Sandra accused. The way she clung to David was enough to make Sandra hate her on sight.

"She's dyed her hair," Levits agreed. Of course, Levits would have agreed with Sandra if she had suggested that they all dive out the window buck naked.

"What's that got to do with anything?" David asked harshly.

"If she isn't aware of what she is, there would be no reason to try and hide it." RJ scratched her chin. This was a real problem. Usually, she could count on her empathic abilities to give her some insight when she was checking out new people. But this girl had that same ability, and she was purposely using it to keep RJ out.

The problem was that she couldn't hold that against her, because she herself was well shielded, and would have done the same thing. She was sure the girl not only knew what she was, but had more than likely been a Reliance soldier. Her size would have kept her from going very high up in the ranks; she was only about five-four and petite, but they would have utilized her in some other way. The Reliance didn't believe in wasting a hybrid's talents.

"What was your rank?" RJ rapped out.

"I don't know what you mean. I...I was a class-two farm worker. I helped in the kitchens, processing sugar beets." Kirsty moved her head off David's shoulder and dried her eyes. Much to her dismay, RJ caught her gaze and held it.

"You're full of shit," RJ said, matter-of-factly, and lay back down on the bed.

"I'm telling the truth." Kirsty looked with big, innocent eyes at David. "Why would I lie?"

There were a lot of reasons that RJ could think of, but only about half of them were treacherous. In the girl's position, RJ herself would probably have lied. But this was not a reason to trust her. Something about the girl troubled RJ. Made her uncomfortable. If she were truly sincere, she could be a real asset. If she wasn't...she could be big trouble. The safest thing to do would be to kill her, but RJ knew she would never slip that one by David—or the others, for that matter. It did seem an awful waste if the girl were sincere. RJ thought for a moment. She scratched her chin again, and got comfortable on the bed.

"I don't believe your story for a minute, and I don't trust you. Still, killing you outright seems a little premature. Sooo..." She took a long breath. "You will stay out of restricted areas. You will not leave the city. You will not carry, or even pick up, a weapon. The same goes for a communicator of any shape or form. Failure to comply will lead to your immediate termination. Do you understand?" RJ looked at her nails, but still saw Kirsty nod her head. "I said, do you understand?"

"Yes sir!" Kirsty said loudly.

"That was a rather military response to authority," Sandra whispered to Levits who nodded his head in agreement.

"RJ," David shook his head in disbelief. "Aren't you carrying all this a bit..."

"Actually, David," she addressed him with the same disbelieving tone he had used on her, "I'm being rather lenient. As you know, this is a restricted area, as is any area containing more than two members of the inner circle. I trust you will remember that in the future and not bring strangers into our midst." Her voice clearly showed her displeasure.

"RJ..."

"She has exactly five seconds to leave this room."

"Fine!" David left with her, slamming the door behind him.

"Don't like it," Mickey said.

"You just said a mouthful, my friend." RJ got up and started to pace back and forth. After several moments, she stopped.

"Sandra, Levits, make a run of the city. Make sure everyone knows this girl's restrictions, and that they have orders to kill her if she breaks them."

"Poley, Mickey, get over to the island, make a composite drawing and see what Marge can come up with on her."

They each indicated that they heard and understood, and then just stood there. "Go! Now!" They practically ran into each other getting out the door.

"What do you want me to do?" Whitey asked.

RJ looked at him and smiled slyly. "Well, I'm very tense."

Jessica had been dancing on air for weeks. David Grant was dead, and now she and RJ were closer to being even.

RJ had killed her lover, and now Jessica's army had killed RJ's lover.

The death of the people's "leader" had stopped the weekly transmissions, and it had left them disheartened, sucking all the wind out of their sails. Their raids met with defeat after defeat. This had all worked together to make Jessica a very happy little dictator. Till today. Till she looked at the information concerning the Reliance's latest 'victory' and noticed a pattern.

"That bitch!" Jessica screamed and slung something large and glass against the far wall. Right ducked just in time.

"What's wrong, Jessy?" Right asked in confusion.

"She's losing on purpose!" Jessica ranted. She stood up and started pacing back and forth behind her desk.

"That's nonsense, Jessica. You're being paranoid," Right laughed at her suspicions. "Really, Jessy. Listen to yourself."

"This morning..." She walked over and turned the computer screen so that Right could see it. "This morning, they tried to destroy an alcohol plant. We lost seventy-three men, but we were able to drive them back."

Right started to interject, but Jessica held up her hand. "We were able to drive them back only after they had blown up two of the three stills on site. We found the bodies of thirty Rebels. So, you tell me who lost." She punched some buttons on her keyboard and new data filled the screen. Right read it quickly, his eyebrows raised slightly. "They're all the same." She started punching buttons and screens of data scrolled in front of him too fast for a mere mortal to read. "They appear to have lost every single one of these battles, but in every case they either accomplished their objective or did so much damage that they may as well have been victorious. Then they got away."

"But why..."

"Isn't that obvious, Right? If it looks like we're winning, the World Commissioner will send the extra troops back where they belong. She's trying to make us overconfident." Jessica sat down and shook her head. "I tell you, Right. At times, I feel that I will never beat her."

Just then, her call button lit up. She pushed the button.
"Yes?"

"Parker and another to see you, Senator."

Jessica smiled broadly. She looked at Right. "And sometimes I know I will."

She pressed the button in front of her. "Send them in. Send them in at once."

Jessica walked around and around the mammoth of a man looking him over admiringly. "Is he...is he as I said he should be?"

"Yes, I think you will be very pleased." Parker didn't like this. He didn't like any of it.

"His only loyalty is to me?"

"That is correct." Parker liked it less and less. He shouldn't have done it.

"Kill Parker," Jessica ordered the GSH. The monster didn't hesitate, he immediately threw a punch into Parker's throat that killed him instantly but made very little mess.

"Very good." Jessica clapped happily, and sat down at her desk. "Very nice. Right, have this mess cleared away, will you?"

"What excuse will you give for killing Parker?" Right asked in stunned disbelief.

"Well, you see, I learned that he was working with the Rebels," she pushed a button and phony files from Parker's lab filled the screen. Files showing that he had diverted research funds into personal accounts, where the money had then apparently vanished. She must have been working on this for weeks. She had planned to kill Parker all along. "When I called him on it he tried to grab my weapon and I had to kill him. I'll file the report after lunch. Now please call someone to clear this mess away. Better yet, carry it out when you leave."

Right didn't like being asked to do menial tasks. "Have a cleaner..."

"I asked *you* to do it, Right," Jessica hissed, looking with meaning at the GSH.

Right grabbed the body by the feet and started to drag it out of the room. He grumbled as he went out the door. He started to tell Jessica what he thought of this whole thing, but thought better of it. The GSH made him strangely uncomfortable. Right knew it was stupid, but he felt that the thing was evil.

Jessica waited until the door was closed and Right was gone before she spoke to her new toy again. "I'm going to call you Zark. Do you like that name?"

"Anything you choose will be fine." He smiled at her, and suddenly it hit her. This thing loved her. Parker had taken the easy way out, and just made the thing love her. He moved towards her.

"You are everything to me. I have waited so long to be with you."

"Ah, Zark...I think we should," she backed away, "talk about this..."

"I wouldn't hurt you," he promised.

"Hurt me?" she whispered the words as a smile curled across her face. She locked the door.

She had worn the GSH out. It was obvious from the look on his face that he hadn't planned on that.

She laughed at him. "Parker didn't know that about me, Zark. And no one else must. Do you understand?"

"Of course." He was very young, and didn't have much to talk about. Fortunately Jessica didn't need him to be able to hold up his end of a conversation.

She laughed out loud. The GSH cocked his head and gave her a curious look. She smiled broadly. "I have finally found a man who is a match for me. Correction. I have built a man who is a match for me. You and I will do great things together. We'll begin by killing RJ."

Kirsty had kept David at bay for weeks. She told him horror stories about being gang-raped by a troop of Elites who had been passing through the small farming town where she'd been raised.

They were all fabrications, of course, but they kept David sleeping on the floor while she slept on his bed. She would cry, and he would hold her, and promise not to pressure her into anything she didn't want to do.

RJ had never really understood David. Kirsty did. David wanted a weak and helpless woman, and Kirsty didn't mind being waited on hand and foot. As a Reliance soldier, she had been expected to do anything asked of her, no matter what the task.

Now, all she had to do was say the magic words "I can't," or recite the incantation "I don't know how," or call upon her god: "Oh, David!"

She liked this lifestyle. She liked it a lot. The dumber she acted, the more David liked her. The more dependent she became on him, the more he catered to her. Everyone else had always expected her to make an effort, to use her body, her brain, or her talent. It was strange to see a man who seemed to gain his manhood by choosing a partner that he would have to take care of.

Kirsty had no doubt that he had chosen her. David loved her, and the more she put him off, the more he desired her as well.

Oh, Kirsty knew how to play the game. She also knew when it was time to put her ass on the table.

David shook his head, and smiled. "There they go again." He indicated the common wall that separated their room from RJ's.

"They seem to do that a lot," Kirsty said, shyly turning her face away.

"Yes, they do," David answered, trying to keep the frustration from his voice.

Kirsty sneaked a quick peek at the fly of David's pants. Yes, he had an erection again. He did most of the time these days. She sat down on the bed, tracing the pattern on the blanket with her finger. "I'm sorry if I'm hurting you, David."

"What do you mean?"

"You know, because I haven't wanted to...well, you know."

"It's OK, Kirsty," he lied as he gritted his teeth. "I don't mind, really. Whenever you're ready..."

"I'm ready now, David," she said huskily.

David didn't waste any time getting to the bed.

"I love you, David," she breathed as he took her in his arms.

"Oh, Kirsty, I love you with all my heart and soul."

The sad part was that he was sincere. But, what goes around, comes around. While it meant the world to him, it didn't mean a damn thing to her.

Kirsty didn't know where they had all gone. All she knew was that they weren't here.

Even the ever-persistent, ever-watching Poley was missing.

Obisco was the nearest town with a base. She "acquired" a car, used one of the Rebels' stolen Elite uniforms and ID, and had no trouble at all getting in. Once in, her next hurdle was to get the General in charge to take her seriously. Now she was waiting in a room alone, waiting for some big shot to show up.

Nothing had prepared Right for what he had seen only two days before. He had thought he was satisfying her, that they had something together, but after he caught her with Zark...Well, he knew he had been kidding himself. She was done with him. He didn't even understand why she was taking him with her today instead of Zark the wonder toy.

For that matter, he didn't understand why she didn't just send him, and then she could stay in Capitol with the Genetically Superior Stud.

Right was sure it was just another dead end, another farm unit looking to upgrade her lot in life. But lately, Jessica had been seeing to each reported sighting herself.

Why, Right didn't even dare to guess.

"She's through the door there," a man indicated. Jessica and Right nodded and moved towards it.

Kirsty was counting her money. Giving herself titles, and then throwing them out for better ones. She was counting on going through a lot of red tape. She was counting on doing a little time for going AWOL, but as soon as they realized that she was telling the truth, she'd get nothing but money and promotion.

There was one thing that she hadn't counted on.

The door opened, and RJ walked in.

Kirsty's face went white. She bolted from the chair and looked for a door, a window, any means of escape.

"Why are you acting like this?" Jessica asked, as she closed the door securely.

"Because you're going to kill me," Kirsty realized it was futile to try to escape. She sat back down in the chair heavily.

Jessica smiled then. "Who do you think I am?"

"Come on, RJ. Kill me and get it over with," Kirsty almost pleaded.

Jessica laughed in delight. "My God, Right! She really has seen RJ!"

"You've spent too much time in the sun, Jessy," Right said.

Kirsty took a closer look. This was not RJ. This woman was smaller, and her arm didn't jerk.

"Let me explain..." and Jessica did, leaving out just enough so that they knew very little more than they had before. "So, tell me all about RJ. Tell me where to find her."

"She's in Alsterase..."

Jessica shook her head in disbelief. "Reverse logic," she hissed.

"There's more. David Grant is not dead. It was all staged."

"That can be fixed very easily," Jessica hissed. "Tell me more. Tell it all to me."

"First, I want..."

"Whatever you ask for, you will have, and more if it brings me RJ's head on a platter," Jessica promised. "Have you seen a man called Poley?"

"Yes. He follows me everywhere. They're all gone tonight, and that's the only reason I was able to sneak out."

"My revenge will be complete!" Jessica said in a whisper. "Go on, tell me more."

When Jessica had heard all that Kirsty had to tell her, it took her only seconds to find the weak link in the chain.

"Here is what you will do..." Jessica gave her instructions that even an idiot could follow. Kirsty wasn't an idiot, and she had the proper motivation. She wouldn't have any trouble.

It was late when they returned from the island. When David got to his room, he couldn't find Kirsty. He left and went looking for her without any luck. He was worried, and he wanted to alert the troops to go out and look for her. But with all the restrictions on her...well, he just couldn't risk it.

He tossed and turned in bed for a couple of hours, and then went out looking for her again. He came back to the room, and she was still gone. Now he was really worried. Maybe something terrible had happened to her. He had just decided to go wake up RJ when Kirsty came dragging in.

"Where the hell have you been?" he demanded in an angry whisper.

Kirsty was startled. She hadn't expected him to even be awake, much less dressed and ready for action.

"I'm sorry, David. I...it's so silly..."

"Where the hell were you?" David hissed.

"Don't be angry," Kirsty said, on the brink of tears. "I went down to the beach. I lay down in the sand, and I...I fell asleep. When I woke up it was dark. I'm sorry." She turned on the tears.

David strode to her and held her in his arms. "I'm sorry, baby. I was just so worried. Please don't ever scare me like that again."

"I'm sorry, I won't let it happen again." Kirsty promised with a sob. "It was so scary waking up on that big ol' beach all alone."

"It's OK, baby. You're safe now."

It didn't occur to him that there was no sand anywhere on her or her clothes. He didn't even notice the bags under her eyes from lack of sleep. He loved her, and he was just glad to have her safely home.

# Chapter Twenty-one

Kirsty watched the activity in the streets with great interest. Rubble was being shifted and stacked. The barricades were being strengthened, and their numbers doubled. Kirsty wondered why.

So did Whitey.

He walked up behind RJ, who was supervising the building of yet another barricade. He put his hand on her shoulder, and for a minute he thought she was going to jump out of her skin. She calmed as soon as she saw it was him, and she even managed a smile, but it was obvious that she was troubled.

"What are you so worried about?" Whitey asked, rubbing her shoulders.

"I don't know, baby." She looked off into the distance at nothing. "I've got a bad feeling. Like someone twisting a knife in my gut. I've had this feeling a couple of times before, and I've been in this game too long not to trust my instincts." She looked at the newly constructed wall of rubble. "Of course, I *have* been wrong a couple of times, but, hey, you can never have too many barricades."

David walked into the room and threw his jacket down on the bed. "God damn RJ!" he yelled, throwing himself after the jacket.

"What's wrong?" Kirsty asked, turning away from the window.

"We've got a unit under fire, and RJ won't send in the necessary manpower to save them. She says it's too big a risk. So she's just going to keep moving rocks around the city, barricading us off from her paranoia, while hundreds of people die."

"It's a good thing that we have you." Kirsty moved to sit on the bed. "I don't trust RJ. I mean, she doesn't seem to give a damn about people in general, and everyone knows it. Do you know what the people call you?"

"No. What?" He smiled. Just being close to her made him feel better.

"They call you RJ's conscience. Face it. Without you, she doesn't have one." She lay down next to him, and started to rub his chest. "It doesn't seem fair. You give all the speeches and do all the work. You bring all the people together, and then RJ makes you pretend to be dead, and she gets all the glory."

For a second, David thought about that. It wasn't something he hadn't thought before. Then he shook his head. He laughed and moved to kiss her forehead. "It's all just part of the plan, Kirsty. Soon I'll be right back in front of the viewscreen. When the time is right. If you think about it, it's really just the opposite. RJ does all the real work, and I get all the credit."

The confrontation took place a week later. It had been building up for some time, but came about—as most confrontations do—because of an act of stupidity.

The Golden Arches was packed to capacity. The inner circle, including Topaz but minus David, sat at "their" table. They weren't discussing anything more important than who should buy the next round of drinks, but, when David walked up with Kirsty, all talk ceased. RJ didn't look up from her drink.

"What did I tell you about that girl, David?" RJ kept her voice calm only with great effort.

"Aw, come on, RJ. You aren't working on anything. What could it hurt..."

RJ didn't let David finish. "Do I have to spell it out for you, David?" RJ turned to face him. "I don't want her around us. She poses a threat..."

"What a bunch of shit! Any one of you..."

This time, it was Sandra who interrupted him. "You may choose to let love blind you, David. But don't expect the rest of us to." She gave Kirsty a look of hatred, although her motive for distrust was slightly different than RJ's.

"I'd rather be blinded by love than by jealousy," David spat back.

"What's that supposed to mean?" Sandra demanded.

"You say you don't trust Kirsty. But we all know that the truth is that you just can't stand the fact that I love someone who isn't you," David accused.

"You bastard!" Levits shocked everyone by jumping to his feet, ready for a fight.

RJ put a hand on his chest and he stayed where he was.

"You're way out of line, David," RJ warned.

"I think you're the one who's out of line, RJ," David stated. "Where do you get off making all the rules? I'm supposed to be an equal partner in this thing. I say Kirsty stays."

RJ rose to her feet. She looked straight at David. "If I ordered her dead, how long do you think she would last?" RJ could no longer hide her anger. Not when she could feel the depth and extent of his.

David had never been so mad in his life. He didn't know what to say. So he did the first thing that jumped into his mind. He doubled up his fist, and he hit her.

She had expected anything but that. It actually knocked her off balance, and she had to catch herself. Physically, he hadn't hurt her at all. Emotionally, she was devastated by all the hate she felt coming from him. Hate that was all for her. She stared at David for a long, silent moment, wondering if he had really hit her. He was rubbing his fist, and there was a pained expression on his face, so it had to be true. She saw Whitey stand up.

"I can handle this," she whispered.

Whitey nodded and sat down.

RJ looked at David, and he cringed from her gaze in horror. Not because she looked like she wanted to kill him. That
he expected. He watched as the hurt in her eyes changed to
contempt, and knew that the bond that had tied them together
and somehow made them different from everyone else had
been utterly and completely severed. Before he had time to
think any more about what he had done, RJ picked him up by
the collar and threw him halfway across the bar. She covered
the floor in a matter of moments. She stood at his feet and
looked down at him.

"One of us has changed, David. One of us has forgotten
the dream. I don't think it's me. You have made your choice."
She started to walk away.

"What do you mean?" David asked struggling to his feet.
Now his back hurt almost as much as his hand.

She didn't even turn around. "You are no longer part of
the inner circle," she said it as easily as she breathed, and walked
out of the bar before he could answer her.

David stood up. He looked at the remaining members,
where they sat at their table. "She can't do that," he informed them, as if he had the power to make them believe
just by his will.

"No. She can't," Levits said with a snarl.

"But *we* can," Topaz said, shaking his head in disbelief. "I
taught you so much about power, but you didn't learn any of
the important parts. Like when to stop. I vote to approve RJ's
decision."

"I vote we kill the bastard!" Whitey got up and stomped
out of the bar.

"I'm going to count that as a yes," Topaz said with a smile.

"I second Whitey's suggestion." Levits looked at Sandra,
who seemed to be off in her own little world.

"You gave too many speeches, David. Now you think
you're bigshot. But we all know you be dead without RJ,"
Mickey said. He looked down at his drink. "When you hit RJ
you hit us all. You chose your whore over us."

David looked hopefully at Sandra. Surely Sandra would come to his defense.

Sandra hadn't dreamed it would ever get this far. She still loved David. She believed that he was an asset to their cause. But he had just embarrassed her in front of all her friends, and there was only one way to save face. She smiled broadly and lifted her chin proudly to face him.

"Now, you finally know how it feels, you bastard," she hissed. "I find your behavior to be disloyal in the extreme. My vote is to expel him."

"It doesn't mean anything!" David said hotly. "You can't get rid of me!"

"David," Topaz said, trying to be a calming influence. "Can't you see what has happened? This girl may pose no threat to us at all. Probably she doesn't. But she's not human. Surely, by now you know that. She's lying about what she is, and that puts her under suspicion. Ask yourself why she's lying when everyone knows that RJ herself is a hybrid."

David didn't believe for a minute that Kirsty was a hybrid. She was nothing at all like RJ. Besides, she had sworn to him that she wasn't. She wouldn't lie to him. She couldn't. If she was a hybrid, she didn't know it. They were just RJ's puppets, and whatever she said they believed.

"You're all crazy!" David screamed. "You've let RJ's paranoia get to you." He took Kirsty's hand and pulled her out of the bar.

Whitey had no trouble finding RJ. He made straight for the dock. He found her standing on the edge, looking out over the bay.

"You OK?" he asked, long before he reached her. He knew it wasn't a good idea to sneak up on RJ when she was mad.

"He can't hurt me," RJ said simply.

"You know what I mean." Whitey moved forward and took her hand. "Are you OK?"

"Not really..." She cleared her throat. "I guess I didn't want to see how bad it really was. Didn't want to admit that he had turned into such an asshole." She took a coin from her pocket, looked at it for a moment, and then tossed it as far as she could into the bay.

# Chapter Twenty-two

Word of the conflict in GA had reached Alsterase in a matter of hours. Being unable to think of anything constructive, and at the same time not detrimental to their cause, RJ chose to ignore it. But as usual, David did not.

It had been three weeks since they had spoken. When they met in the halls, neither of them so much as waved. Neither RJ nor David was ready for a truce. But now he was going to talk to her whether she liked it or not.

He found RJ and the others in RJ and Whitey's room. They completely ignored him.

"Fine. A city full of innocent people is being leveled, and you sit here playing bottle caps and swilling beer," David said sarcastically. He took another step closer, and the bottle cap hit him in the face.

"God damn it, David!" Sandra screamed, "you screwed up my shot!"

"That shot must have been way off to begin with for it to have landed in his face," Whitey laughed.

"I get to shoot again," Sandra declared.

"Sandy, you were nowhere close to the cup," Levits said with a laugh. "There is no way that you could have hit it."

"She not have another turn," Mickey said, crossing his arms.

"You little fuck, you wouldn't care if she went again if you weren't winning," Levits pointed out.

"You wouldn't be so ready to let her go again if you were winning," Mickey accused.

"I didn't say I wanted her to go again," Levits said, "all I said was you wouldn't care if you weren't winning."

"It's all immaterial anyway, because Poley didn't go yet," Whitey said, "and we all know Poley will win."

David walked out of the line of fire and decided to ignore them. RJ lay on the bed going over some sort of map. "Can we talk?"

"I've just gone over this map for the twelfth time. Not to mention graphs and charts, etc., etc. We can't go into GA. They are too well implanted, and we don't have the manpower." RJ was quick and to the point.

"Surely we could..."

"To put it in simple terms, David. It looks like a trap. I *make* traps; I don't fall into them."

There was no emotion in her voice. The matter was closed. RJ's attention was once again focused on the map.

David turned on his heel and stomped out. He went back to his own room, where Kirsty greeted him with a hug.

"How did it go?" she asked.

"It didn't." He flopped down on the bed and put his hands behind his head. "RJ never changes. Everything has to add up, or she wants no part of it. She never sees it as human lives...Ah, hell, I don't know any more. Maybe she's right."

"No, she's not right," Kirsty declared with fire in her voice. "Can't you see it, David? They're just work units. Work units like you and me. We're expendable. Notice that, except for you and Mickey, the entire inner circle is made up of ex-military personnel. Mickey would do anything RJ told him to, and you...Well, they got rid of you, didn't they?"

David looked at her as if she had just shown him something new and ugly.

"RJ doesn't worry about the lives of untrained civilians. Every time she has made a decision like this, it has been based on how many trained lives would be lost in return for how many untrained lives, and she weighs it ten to one."

David thought about it, and decided Kirsty was right. "But what can I do? I don't have any real power." David shrugged helplessly. "The only power I had was what power RJ let me have. Without RJ I have nothing."

Kirsty suppressed a grin.

"If only you had your own army." Kirsty placed her next words carefully. "An army of work units. People like us who would listen to you instead of RJ..."

"Kirsty, you're a genius!" He got up and ran over to hug her. He lifted her off the ground and spun her around. Kirsty smiled smugly. It was all over now but the crying.

RJ heard the ruckus coming from outside before anyone else. She rose from the bed and went to the window. She saw David standing atop the old vehicle and saw the group assembling.

"What's he up to?" Sandra asked looking over RJ's shoulder.

"Starting a rebellion against the rebellion. Come on, we've got to stop him if we can."

"RJ means well, and it's true that she has led us to many victories. But now she wants us to lay low and be quiet while the Reliance systematically lays waste to an entire city. To GA, a town that is only a few hours' drive away. RJ says the risk is too great. She says that too many trained men will die to save the untrained. In other words, too many soldiers will die to save a bunch of work units. Well, like a lot of you, I was once a work unit. I think the lives of all men are equally important—that no man is more worthy of being saved than another.

"RJ's thoughts are clear and logical. She is right. If we go, a lot of us will die. But if we don't go, if we stand idly by and do nothing to help our brothers, then we are morally wrong! RJ has made up her mind, and that of the inner circle. But we are free men with free choice. If only half of you will go with me, we can run the Reliance out of GA. It's time that we had another real victory!"

"What the hell are you doing?" RJ asked as she made her way through the crowd.

"I'm going to save GA, whether you like it or not," David said as she reached him.

"At whose expense, David?" she quipped. "Will you save it with the lives of men who would foolishly follow you into a trap? Because that's what it is...a trap! If only half of you go, then only half of you will die, accomplishing nothing."

"Are you God, RJ, that you can see the future? She knows no more than you or I. Who will come with me to save the work units of GA? Or is it only ex-military personnel that are worth saving? Is this our brave new world?"

The split was predictable. The ex-military wouldn't follow David to the toilet, but the former work units—nearly half the population of Alsterase—couldn't follow him fast enough. David herded his people into troop carriers and freight haulers.

Kirsty insisted on going.

"You know nothing about fighting, Kirsty. You'll be safer in Alsterase."

"I don't think so, David. You know how RJ feels about me. How they all do. They'll just look for a reason to kill me." She took his hand and started to cry. "Please, David. I'm afraid."

"OK, Kirsty, but we'll leave you up the road. Well away from the fighting."

Kirsty smiled broadly as he walked away to go check on supplies.

RJ approached David. "You won't listen to reason?"

"Will you?"

RJ's cool snapped, but her voice never rose. "I never thought this day would come. I never thought, in my wildest dreams, that you could betray me like this. Betray the New Alliance like this. How could I see that you would use the power that I helped you obtain to turn so many against me. No one could have convinced me that it would come to this. That you would jeopardize everything that we have worked for in an attempt to prove to the world that you are more righteous than I. I should have left you in the woods. You will bring defeat upon us all."

Her words stung. He didn't feel like he was betraying anyone, he was only doing what he thought was right. "If you
really believe that, then why don't you try to stop me?" David
asked.

"Toward what end? Open warfare in the streets of
Alsterase? Don't you realize what you've done? We were a
people united by a common cause. You have purposely di-
vided us. You have taken one people and made us two. You
have made us enemies of each other." She shook her head
sadly. "Topaz is right. Power does corrupt." She walked
away, shoulders slumped, head held low. She pulled a coin
from her chain, and chucked it into the air to let it fall where it
would.

David saw it fall and picked it up. "I'll bring this back to
you when I've won, RJ," he called after her. When she didn't
respond he put it in his pocket and continued to himself, "Then
all will be right again. You'll see."

RJ couldn't sleep. Of course, she didn't really need to sleep
every day, so it was no real problem. She stood at the window
and looked out at the city. Her heart was broken, and she was
worried. She hadn't counted on this. She hated not knowing.
She hated it when things didn't go as calculated. It left her at
a loss. How did you deal with something that you weren't
prepared for?

How bad was it going to be? Should they leave Alsterase?
Were they in danger here? If they were, leaving could be the
worst thing to do. After all, at least they had cover here, and a
plan for defense. On the open road they would be sitting ducks.

"Want me to help you worry?" Whitey asked from the bed.

RJ joined him on the bed, laying her head on his chest and
wrapping her arms around him.

He held her tightly. "It's bad, isn't it?"

"I don't know. Could be. I'm thinking of evacuating to
the Island, at least till things cool off."

"I still can't believe he did that," Whitey shook his head.

"I can't believe that I didn't see it coming. The way he's been acting..."

Whitey laughed. "Honey, no one, not even you, can figure out every angle. Not when human beings are involved."

"I'm scared, Whitey," she whispered.

Whitey was shocked. He couldn't imagine RJ being afraid of anything.

"Of what?"

"Everything. Life was so simple when no one was counting on me. When I didn't care about anyone and no one cared about me. Now...well...if I fail..." She swallowed hard. "I love you, Whitey."

"I love you, too. Everything will be fine; you'll see." He held her tightly.

The primary attack was silent, and consisted of one person, if you could call Zark a person. He kept to the shadows as he walked down the street, and no one saw him. He made straight for the hotel and entered it without a hitch.

Dex looked up from where he'd been almost asleep behind the desk. "What ya..."

The laser was silent, but no less effective. The fat man slumped in his chair, breaking his favorite rule.

The GSH made his way up the stairs heading purposefully towards the fourth floor. When he reached it, he moved along silently towards RJ's room. But even a GSH can't be held accountable for a squeaky floorboard or a human's over-sensitive hearing.

Sandra wasn't quite asleep. She had just left Levits, Mickey and Poley back at the Golden Arches not quite thirty minutes ago. She heard someone in the hall outside, and was willing to bet it wasn't 'the boys.' When they came in, they made enough noise to wake the dead. She got up quietly, slipped into her robe, and picked up her laser. She went to the door and opened it a crack. She saw the stranger, weapon in hand, poised outside RJ's door, and she didn't hesitate. She stepped quickly into the hall and fired. She scored a direct hit, but the stranger didn't even stagger. She knew instantly what she was up against. She hit the floor and rolled so that his first shot missed, then she jumped up and ran for her room. She knew it was a wasted effort, but if she could just keep it busy.

"Freak! RJ! It's a Freak!" The bolt ripped through her temple and flung her into a wall. Fate was kind to Sandra. She fought to the very end and died instantly.

RJ heard the blaster fire and Sandra's warning. She pushed Whitey onto the floor and jumped up, grabbing her chain in one hand and her laser in the other. She never got a chance to use either. The door exploded in splinters, and a titanium-steel projectile ripped through the doorway and across her face and forehead. She fell limp to the floor. Whitey fumbled for the rocket launcher they kept under their mattress. He got it and raised it to fire. The first bolt caught Whitey in the gut. Whitey continued to raise the launcher to a firing position, but before he could fire, a second bolt caught him in the chest. As he lost control of his body, and the weapon fell from his hands, he saw the GSH pull a laser knife.

"No!" Whitey mumbled through a mouth full of blood.

"I suppose it would be kinder to kill you so that you didn't have to watch this." Then he grinned and cut RJ so that her mechanical heart fell out of her chest, and her life's blood poured onto the floor. He left the heart hanging there. Then he grabbed RJ's chain from the floor. He waved at Whitey. "It belongs to my woman, now! Have a good time dying, you two."

Zark went in search of the robot, but it wasn't in its room, and he was running out of time. Soon the troops would come flooding in, and he still had one more thing to get before he could return to Capitol and Jessica.

Zark ran down the stairs. In the lobby, he discharged a fire grenade. That would take care of anything he might have missed.

Levits saw the fire first. "My God! The hotels on fire!"

In a matter of seconds, the entire clientele of the bar was in the street.

"I hear choppers," Poley informed Levits.

Levits didn't want to be in control. He didn't want to..."Poley, Mickey, go sound the alarm. You and you,"—he pointed at two slightly familiar faces—"come with me. The rest of you, go to your units." They all went in separate directions. By the time Levits and the two men with him hit the hotel, the lobby was completely in flames, and there was no way of getting through. "The back door!" Levits yelled, and the others followed. The back door had been nailed shut for security, so they broke in a window. Guns were drawn. "You two, evacuate the lower levels. I'll get the fourth floor."

"Hey, Levits!"

He turned to face the man. "What?" he asked, shortly.

"Good luck, man," he said, and saluted. It was the first time in a long time anyone had shown him that kind of respect.

"You, too." Levits took off at a dead run. He took the steps three at a time, fighting back the fear and uncertainty with every step. The last time he'd been in charge of anything, everything had gone so dreadfully wrong. He had done everything wrong. *Please, God, let it be different this time.*

The first thing he saw when he reached the fourth floor was Sandra's lifeless body. He ran to her and rolled her over. She was obviously dead. He held her close. "Oh, Sandy!" He didn't even try to stop his tears. For a moment, he was just going to hold her and let the flames consume him. Then he saw RJ's door, or the space where the door used to be. He left Sandra and ran for the room. More horror greeted him there. Dead! They were both dead! He started to leave and return to die with Sandra.

"Levits..." The voice was so low, he almost didn't hear.

He ran back to Whitey's side. "Thank God, Whitey! I thought you were dead, too..."

"...will be soon," Whitey choked and blood oozed from his mouth. "Save RJ."

Levits refused to even look at her mangled body. "I can't, Whitey...Maybe you..."

Whitey was sinking fast. "Listen to me, Levits. RJ is a GSH. You can save her! She's got Pronuses...in her jacket..." The light went out of his eyes, and Levits closed them.

"I understand, Whitey. I'll save her." Levits approached the mangled body and felt for a pulse. "Well, I'll be damned!" He looked at the metal heart that lay on her belly. Swallowing hard, he took it in hand and shoved it into the opening in her chest.

It only took him a second to find the jacket and a second more to find the pills in her kit. He put three directly into her mouth from the tube, hoisted her into his arms, and headed for the roof. He loaded her in the chopper, and got in himself. In the distance, he could hear the roar of aircraft coming in. In a few minutes, the air would be full of them. The city that had given shelter to their rebellion would be gone, like Sandy and Whitey. He started the chopper and took off.

"Don't die, RJ." He gritted his teeth. "We have to make them pay, RJ. You and me, we gotta make them pay for all they have taken from us."

He had barely cleared the building when there was a loud explosion, and suddenly the whole building was in flames. This time he had done everything right, and he had still failed. Maybe that was just the way life was. For Whitey and Sandra and all the others who would die tonight, the fighting would be over. But for the survivors, the fighting was just beginning. For him and RJ it could never end.

Not now.

Zark's luck was exceptional that night. He was about to give up his search for the metal man when he looked up and saw him running straight for him.

Poley stopped dead and grabbed Mickey, who would have kept going.

Mickey saw the GSH.

"Go sound the alarm; I'll keep him busy," Poley said. "Run!"

"We should both run," Mickey said, pulling on the robot's hand.

"We can't outrun it, Mickey. Now go! Run!"

Reluctantly, Mickey took off as fast as his short little legs would carry him. He glanced back over his shoulder just in time to see the monster cut Poley's head off with a laser knife, and put it into a bag. The sparks flew, but even the realization that Poley was a robot didn't ease Mickey's feeling of loss. He couldn't let Poley down. He ran faster than he ever had before. He finally reached and sounded the alarm, and Alsterase awoke.

Topaz met Levits at the pad. "I saw the choppers on the radar. I tried to sound the general alarm, it must be on the...Oh my God!"

"She's bad." Levits lifted her out of the chopper. "Well, come on, man, don't just stand there." Levits started for the medical unit. He laid her down on one of the surgical tables.

Topaz looked at the cut on her face and forehead and the gash in her chest. He saw the veins in her neck thumping and knew she was barely alive. "My God!" he said again.

"Whitey said she's a GSH, and she must be, because I gave her three Pronuses, and they didn't kill her. Her heart's mechanical, too. What the hell is she, Topaz?"

"She's everything that Stewart knew. Everything that he wanted to be." Topaz was far away, and he wasn't doing anything.

"Don't just stand there, man..."

"Quite right. What have you done besides the Pronuses?"

"Her heart was out of her chest. I shoved it back in. I..." Suddenly he turned white, ran into the hall, and threw up. Funny, doing it hadn't made him sick, but looking down at the dried blood on his hands did. Thinking about Sandra and Whitey didn't help. When he was done puking, he sat on the floor and started to cry.

Topaz scrubbed and put on gloves. In five-hundred-some years he had learned just about everything, and what he didn't know, Marge did. Together, they went to work on RJ.

The battle lasted four hours before the Reliance admitted defeat and retreated. As soon as the last Reliance plane was out of sight, the survivors started their exodus for the island. When the Reliance returned with reinforcements, they would find nothing.

It was unlikely that they would think of the island. Topaz had worked hard to make it look abandoned and unapproachable. If they did, though, they would find some nasty surprises waiting for them. With sixteen laser cannons, all controlled by Marge, it would be nearly impossible for anything to get close enough to do any actual damage.

Mickey had insisted that they take Poley's body with them. He sat on the boat by the lifeless body of his fallen metal friend and wondered how many more of his friends were dead. He hadn't seen any of them. Not Sandra, Levits, Whitey or RJ. He could hear the others talking.

"David Grant did this."

"That girlfriend of his did this."

"Has anyone seen RJ?"

"No. She must be dead. If she weren't, someone would have seen her."

"I can't believe that Poley was a robot."

"You suppose RJ's a robot?"

"Whitey Baldor wasn't sleeping with a robot."

"Hard to believe Poley was just a robot."

That did it. Something in Mickey snapped. "Poley wasn't *just a robot*. He was my friend. He gave up his life so that I could sound the alarm. He loved life, and he loved his sister. If that don't make him human...Right now, I would gladly give any of you to have him back."

GA had been a disaster. Everything that RJ had predicted came to pass. The whole city was a trap. As soon as they arrived, Reliance troops crawled out of nowhere to surround them.

In the battle that followed David lost all but twenty-three men, and his left arm was broken. It hung, limp and painful, at his side. At the first opportunity, he led his shattered command straight for the rendezvous point where he'd left Kirsty, the vehicles and three guards. Their only chance for survival was a quick retreat.

When he saw the smoke, his tired legs found the strength to run. The sight of the burning vehicles and dead guards made little impression on him as he searched frantically for Kirsty. Calling, crying, searching. Ten minutes later the last of his small command struggled in and collapsed.

"You fool. You bloody fool!" a battered and weary man said from where he sat propped up against a tree resting what was left of his right leg on the ground in front of him. "She burned you, man. She burned us all. She used you, and fools that we are, we followed you."

"She couldn't..." David slumped to the ground. Could it be true? How could it be? He loved Kirsty. Kirsty loved him. *Then where is she? Where the hell is she? How did the Reliance know we were coming?* He buried his face in his hands. What the hell had he done?

"By now, Alsterase will be a black hole on the map."

"We didn't listen to RJ. Now she's dead..."

"NO!" David refused to believe this lie.

"Then where's your girlfriend, Grant?" the first man asked. "She burned us, and you can bet your sweet ass she burned RJ, too."

David stood up. "We'll have to go back. Help them..."

Several men laughed. "Help them do what?" one of the younger men asked bitterly. "Pick up the bodies?"

"We managed to live in spite of your 'leadership,' Grant," the first man commented. "I think I speak for us all when I say

we're better off without you. Face it, Grant, the war is over.
They won, and you helped them. We all helped them."
     They left him there. Not one of them asked him to go
along. For a long time he just sat there looking at his broken
arm. He really should do something about it, but he couldn't
be bothered. The longer he sat there, the more convinced he
became of Kirsty's betrayal. She had never really loved him.
She had used his love for her to pull him away from RJ. RJ had
loved him, and what had he done to her? The answer to that
question was back in Alsterase. He had to get back there. He
got up and started walking.

Zark walked into Jessica's office. She looked up and saw no
smile. For a moment, she thought he had failed. In fact, it was
Right, who was sitting on the corner of Jessica's desk, who
first saw the smug smile light up the GSHs face.
     "Well?" Jessica asked impatiently.
     The GSH walked over to Jessica's desk and dumped the
contents of the cloth sack. RJ's chain rattled out, quickly followed by Poley's head. Jessica jumped up, clapping her hands
in delight, and ran to embrace Zark.
     "Is she really gone?"
     "I cut her heart out and then set the building on fire. She's
dead, Jessy," Zark said proudly.
     Jessica moved back to the desk and picked up the chain.
"Hard to believe that she would put such store in this thing.
Hard to believe that someone as intelligent and powerful as RJ
would become so attached to something like this. Or this, for
that matter." She rolled the head around on her desk. Soon
tiring of her new toys, she picked them up and set them on a
shelf with her other trophies. She turned then to address Right.
     "She and I were so much alike..."
     "When she heard the girl scream she pushed her lover to
the floor. She spent the last few seconds of her life trying to
save him. If she hadn't, she might have beaten me. You and
she were nothing alike."

Zark looked at Right, and the man bit his tongue to keep from laughing. The petty rivalry between them ended at that moment. They both knew they were in the same boat. Neither of them meant spit to Jessica Kirk. They were just toys, and toys are disposable. Maybe she had loved Jack Bristol, and maybe she hadn't, but she certainly loved no one but herself now. Now that RJ was dead, all that passion would leave her, too. She could return to a being of pure logic.

Worst of all, she no longer needed them. They would be kept like house pets—used for her amusement. They had helped her achieve her goal, and in doing so had made themselves unnecessary.

David walked through the day and into the night. Fever and guilt racked his brain. The arm, now swollen and blue, didn't hurt anymore. He didn't know why, he was just glad the pain was gone. In his mind scenes and words kept playing and replaying. Sick and tormented, he didn't even realize that he was walking in the wrong direction.

In his mind, he saw Alsterase in flames. He saw RJ lying in a pool of her own blood. He heard RJ saying, "I never thought in my wildest dreams that you would betray me, betray me, betray me, betray..."

"NO!" David screamed, and slumped to his knees on the ground. "Oh God! What have I done?" he cried. He lay down and looked up at the star-studded sky, which could just be seen through the trees.

The voices cried out at him from the night, and would not be quieted.

"Power corrupts."

"Help them do what? Pick up bodies?"

"If only you had your own army, David..."

"We were fools to follow you."

"You don't look at the big picture, David."

"She's not cast-iron..."

"Is she a hybrid?"

"Yes, and well shielded."

"Now you finally know how it feels, you bastard."

"Down with the Reliance..."

"Please turn the lights out." David now realized that he had never seen Kirsty unclothed with the lights on. No doubt because she wanted to hide the fact that her coloring, like RJ's, wasn't a tan.

"It was fear that allowed the Reliance to rear its ugly head."

"Ax murderer."

"Thank you, boy." An old man dropped a coin into his hand. A coin, bent coins on a chain. RJ's chain gleaming in the sun. A hand reached out for him, a man out of breath and out of hope.

"I'm not your enemy." He took the offered hand and found it warm and strong. He found himself being lifted up. He'd look up and see RJ's familiar grin and all would be right with the world. But when he looked up, all he saw was a grinning skeleton wearing a chain, with patches of platinum blonde hair straggling down from the few bits of scalp remaining.

David woke screaming and jerked upright. He was burning with fever despite the coolness of the night air. His shivering made the arm throb and ache again. He ignored it all, scrambled to his feet and ran as he hadn't run since the day, long ago, that he had broken out of prison.

He had to get back to Alsterase. RJ had to be all right. He would make it all up to her.

If he hadn't killed her.

Kirsty paced back and forth along the deserted stretch of road. She was, admittedly, early. It would have been nice if, just this once, the Reliance had been early as well. She knew she had nothing to worry about, but she still felt exposed sitting out here in the middle of nowhere. She gripped her bag of precious money and papers in one hand, her laser in the other. Nothing but darkness around her, so what was she worried about? She was a hybrid, a trained killer. She had nothing to fear. Yet she couldn't quiet the uneasiness of her gut.

"Brave heart, Kirsty," she said out loud to herself. "You are going to be one rich, blue-eyed Governor." She tried to laugh, but it got caught in her throat and she almost choked. How many people had died today because of her? People she'd known...*David*. So what? David was a sap. He fell for it all—hook, line and sinker...*Because he loved me. Because he trusted me in spite of what his friends told him. He stuck his neck out for me. He was willing to give up everything for me, and I made a fool of him. Then I killed them all. David, RJ, and all the others.* A cold chill went down her spine as she realized just what she'd become. She was evil.

She'd set David up right from the start. She'd played on his emotions and his naïveté. Her every move had been calculated and cold. At the time she originally chose her course, she told herself that it wouldn't bother her. But now that there was no going back, she was appalled by her callousness, cruelty, and capacity for treachery. The only evil in the night was herself. She felt unclean, as if a black cloak of wickedness were swallowing up her soul.

There had been several points at which she'd made choices. Good or bad, righteous or wicked, Reliance or Rebellion. She now realized that she'd made the wrong choices, but it was too late to do anything about it.

She'd thought she would be able to go through life without a single backward glance, but now she wasn't sure that she'd be able to live with all she'd done.

David ran on. Running on nothing but willpower and adrenaline. For the second time in his life, he was running for all he was worth, without direction. And once again it was fate and another human body that stopped him. As he fell, he saw a flying sliver of silver. He'd been in combat long enough to know what it was. He grabbed wildly and caught it. When he turned to face the person he'd run into, pain and night, fever and guilt couldn't hide Kirsty's face. She was every bit as shocked as he was. Without hesitation, he aimed the weapon at her head.

"I know it's not good enough, David. But I'm sorry." She held open palms out to him. "They made me do it, David. I was afraid."

"RJ was right about you," David hissed, "and now, she's probably dead."

"I'm sorry, David..." Kirsty cried. This time, her tears were real.

"RJ saved my life more times that I care to count. She told me things that I never knew. She carried me on her back for hours, and she never asked for anything in return because she was my friend. But you fixed that, Kirsty. I was a fool who got caught up in my own importance, and you knew just how to play on that." His finger started to close on the trigger.

"Please, David, I...There's enough money here for us both to live well. Think about it..."

"I don't want to think about it, Kirsty. If I think about it, I might *enjoy* killing you." He fired and the bolt hit her between the eyes. She fell, dead, but David didn't feel any better. Just then, he doubted that he would ever feel better.

Headlights appeared down the road. David ducked back into the woods and ran. He didn't look back.

It had been three days since the attack. RJ was alive, but still unconscious, and there was nothing to indicate that she would be coming out of the coma any time soon.

Her fingers didn't twitch; even her right arm was still. Her eyes stayed closed and didn't seem to be moving. No mutterings left her lips. She was unnaturally still and silent. While her vital signs improved daily, no one was reassured, they may have saved the body, but that didn't mean they had saved RJ.

The weather outside was a good reflection of the spirits inside—cold, wet and dark. The rebels had plenty of food and water, and the accommodations were better than any they'd had in Alsterase. There was ample booze and plenty of movies, but try as they might they couldn't erase the memories of that night. It was all too fresh and too horrible.

The smoke from the smoldering embers of what was left of Alsterase added to the gloom of the skies. The only light came from the reflection of the flames on the clouds and was anything but comforting.

The cries of the wounded could be heard throughout the fort despite the best efforts of the medics in charge. The medics did all they could, but many of the injured needed doctors. There were no doctors here. Doctors were rich; they had everything they could want, so they didn't rebel. Topaz was the only one who knew all of the medical techniques, and that was only because he could access the information from Marge. Their equipment was limited, and there was just so much that one man could do, even when that one man was Topaz. Some had been so bad that Topaz loaded them with painkillers and let them go gently into the night.

Every day brought more death, but even horror eventually ends. Today for the first time everyone seemed stable. Maybe the rest would make it.

Topaz looked in on RJ. Levits was with her. He wouldn't leave. He hadn't slept properly, and he barely ate. He just sat there talking to her, begging her to live.

When he'd finished crying that first night, he'd gathered himself together and helped organize the air and sea evacuation of Alsterase. When everyone still alive was out, he sat down in RJ's room, and he hadn't left for anything but a call of nature since.

Topaz didn't pretend to know why, but for some reason the fall of Alsterase seemed to have tied Levits to RJ. As if he expected to live only as long as she did, and Topaz thought that was probably true.

"Topaz, RJ's not just a GSH, is she?" Levits asked.

Topaz was a little startled, as he'd been in the room for nearly ten minutes before Levits acknowledged his presence.

"No. Stewart was a geneticist, a cybernetics genius, and a tinkerer. RJ is Stewart's child. And I don't just mean because he created her. He took an Argy woman's egg and impregnated it with his own sperm. He genetically engineered the fetus, and implanted that heart when the time was right. That heart is far stronger than anything he could have structured genetically. He left her emotions intact; let her be her own woman. RJ is in a class all her own."

"He should have been dead, Topaz," Levits said in a far-away tone. "There was a hole in him you could have put both fists into. He willed himself to live long enough to save her. It's hard to believe he's dead. Hard to believe any of them are dead. Sandy..." His voice caught in his throat. "She was everything I ever wanted in a woman—beautiful, bright, cunning, and always ready with a joke. She could always make me laugh. I love...*loved* Sandra. I guess everyone knew that. I had my time with her, just like half the men in Alsterase did." He smiled. "She made me feel special, though. For the time that we were together, she made me feel like I was the only one. I could have made her love me, too, if it weren't for David. She loved him, and he scorned her. Now he's killed her. If there is a God in heaven, then let that bastard be dead, too." He was crying again. He had been crying off and on for three days. It didn't annoy Topaz; Levits had a right to his tears.

Mickey walked in quietly, closing the door behind him. "How is she?" he asked.

"There's no change," Topaz answered.

Thank God for Mickey. Since he was the only member of the inner circle who was not dead, too busy, or otherwise incapacitated, the burden of running the whole show had fallen on his shoulders. In the wake of the disaster, he had made sure that all the day-to-day business was taken care of. Simple things that no one else thought about. He assigned sleeping quarters, made sure the meals were prepared and eaten, and the bodies quietly cremated. He tried to raise morale by having Marge show a variety of light and amusing movies, and edited the public reports on RJ's condition. Tragedy had changed them all, and it had brought

Mickey's leadership abilities to the surface. It had forced
him to become all that he could be, and he had come through
with flying colors. Everyone had always thought of him as
RJ's pet, believing she kept him around out of compassion.
No one would make the mistake of taking him for granted
in the future.

Mickey walked over to the bed and stepped up on the stool
placed there for his use. "The scars still look bad," he said.

That was another strange thing that Topaz had noticed.
Mickey always spoke in full sentences these days.

"I expect they will heal in time," Topaz said.

"What's that?" Mickey asked excitedly.

"What?" Topaz leaned forward and looked where Mickey
was pointing.

RJ's arm was jerking again.

Levits dried his face and looked.

Her eyes flew open, and she sat straight up.

RJ was back!

She rubbed at her Pronuses-dry eyes, trying to regain her
vision. When she reached to push her hair back, she found it
a good six inches longer. She took a deep, cleansing breath
and winced. Her chest hurt, her vision was fuzzy, and her
brain felt heavy and dull. After a few moments, her vision
cleared, and she saw Topaz, Mickey and Levits. Levits looked
as if he had been crying. She couldn't be sure of the scattered
images that filled her head.

"Whitey?...Sandy?" Her voice barely worked.

"Not just now..." Topaz started.

"Oh, God! No!" She started to cry, and found herself in
Levits arms. "Poley?"

"The GSH took Poley's head," Mickey said sadly.

"I'm going to Capitol and kill that bitch." She pushed
away from Levits and jumped out of bed. Her knees gave
way, and Levits had to catch her.

"RJ, that thing cut your heart out of your chest. You're not
going to be able to do anything for awhile," Topaz said gently.

"God damn it!" she cried. "She built that damn thing to kill me; I know she did. Instead, it just killed everyone I care about." The tears fell, and this time it was she who clung to Levits. A few moments later she wiped her eyes and ran her hands over her scars. A lost look crept over her face. "Where's my chain?"

Till then, Levits hadn't thought about it. Now he realized that he hadn't seen it in her room. He realized how naked and vulnerable she looked without it. "I don't know, RJ. I didn't see it, but I was in a hurry because of the fire."

"It took it, just like it took my brother's head," she said with conviction. The significance of Levits' remark hit her suddenly. "You saved me?"

He shrugged.

"Well, at least I was right about you." She couldn't stop her tears, so she buried her face in the shoulder Levits offered. "David!" She spat "No, I did this myself...You tried to warn me, Topaz."

"It's not your fault, RJ. No one blames you. Don't blame yourself. Just get well so we can go kill the bastards," Levits whispered.

"I want him," she cried. "I need him. God, why didn't he stay still? It *hurts*..." Her voice was drowned in choking sobs.

Topaz motioned to Mickey, and he followed him out of the room.

"Well, she's alive," Topaz said, trying to sound happy about it. He *was* happy, but...

"She's going to hurt for a long time." Mickey looked back at the door. "They're both basket cases. What are we going to do? The minute she feels half-assed better, she's going to go off and try to kill everyone. Levits will only encourage her. I don't want to lose them, too."

"We'll just have to make sure that they don't do anything stupid." Suddenly, Topaz became very interested in the floor. He dropped to all fours and began a frenzied search, muttering to himself.

Mickey didn't even blink. He just walked away shaking his head. He had work to do.

David hurt, too. He had finally given in to the fever and lay down by a stream to rest. When he woke up, he set his arm as well as he could using broken branches and strips torn from his shirt for a splint. It took the last of his strength, and as he lay back, panting, he passed out again.

The next time he woke up, dawn was just breaking. His fever seemed to be gone. He felt as if he'd slept a long time, but had no idea exactly how long. It could have been hours, from the smell of his clothes. Hell, it could have been days. Physically, he felt better.

God only knew the extent of the damage he'd done. He didn't even know where he was. Kirsty was dead, his arm was broken, and his sole accomplishment was to have led a group of brave men and women to their deaths. He had to know the worst. He had to get back to Alsterase. The first thing was to stop walking in circles. *A road, any road, and then directions.*

RJ was up and out of her room, but she was far from healed. She was walking the wall, as was often the case since she'd emerged. The wall enclosed what had been the yard of the prison. From this position, armed guards of centuries past watched the prisoners taking their exercise. RJ used the wall to look at Alsterase.

Seven days after the holocaust, the fires had finally died. The rain probably helped, but more than likely there just wasn't anything left to burn. Alsterase was nothing but a charred ruin.

She walked in a short, white robe, seemingly oblivious to the chill in the air. Her hair now reached the middle of her back. She didn't bother to cut it. Hell, she didn't even bother to comb it. Once a day someone talked her into bathing, and Levits combed her hair. She didn't even notice.

She wasn't going to make it. She'd lost too much. At first she tried. Sometimes she even thought she'd be OK. Then she had to go to bed, alone.

*Without Whitey, living just isn't worth the effort.*

She pulled her robe tighter, but the chill she tried to block didn't come from outside. *Home's all burned up, freak.* She gave up trying to get her shit together and just wallowed in her depression. Unlike the ancient guard, her patrol only succeeded in keeping people out.

As David neared Alsterase, he was greeted by the foul stench of burned and rotted flesh, and he knew before he saw the burned husk of the city that his worst fears had been realized. The stench and the flies increased as he walked deeper and deeper into the ruins.

He tried not to look too closely at the bodies, for fear he might see someone he'd recognize. The hotel was burned to the ground, as was the Golden Arches. The stench was much worse in this part of town. The realization that these stinking piles of flesh were comprised of his comrades' remains made his stomach lose its hold on the river snails he'd eaten for lunch. When he could, he ran the rest of the way to the docks, deliberately blinding himself to the carnage.

Most of the boats had been destroyed. It was dusk when he found a sound boat with a nearly full tank of alcohol. He checked for the hundredth time to be sure he wasn't being followed, and headed for the island.

Mickey was shuffling quarters again. Those wounded who were well enough were going to their new quarters, and those still in bad shape were moved so that they could see the viewscreen to ease their boredom.

Morale was higher now that RJ could be seen walking around. It helped that there had been no more deaths. The noise caused by all this organized confusion was nearly deafening, so the sudden silence fairly screamed. Mickey turned and searched out the cause.

Tattered clothing, a ragged beard that didn't cover the cut on his cheek, and his arm in a sling, it was undoubtedly David Grant. If nothing else, there was simply no one else who could have gotten through the security system alive. Mickey felt the waves of hatred and watched as the muttering started and seemed to propel the crowd toward David with murderous intent.

"Enough!" Mickey screamed, and they were abruptly silent. He continued quietly. "There has been enough killing for now. No one man can be blamed for what happened. The Reliance did it. David was just a patsy." Mickey looked at David, and was surprised to see the same lost, blank look on his face that RJ wore these days.

"Come on," he said, and David followed him. Mickey led him to the showers. "I'll get you a clean suit of clothing."

"Mickey...is RJ OK?" David asked, almost afraid to find out.

"No! She's not OK," Mickey hissed. "She's barely alive. Many weren't so lucky. Few got out of this like you did, with barely a scratch." He started to leave.

"Mickey, I..."

"I'll send someone to put a proper cast on your arm." He was gone.

The 'someone' who put the cast on David's arm took great delight in re-breaking the bone so it could be properly set. Still, it felt better after it was all over. Better than it had since it was broken. David went in search of Mickey, but found Topaz instead. Topaz wasn't surprised to see David, so David assumed he must have already spoken to Mickey.

"You look well," Topaz said as if it were a crime.

"I want to see RJ," David said.

"She won't want to see you."

"Why don't you let RJ be the judge of that," David said hotly. He stopped abruptly and got himself under control. "I'm sorry, Topaz. You have every right to hate me."

"I don't hate you, David. Admittedly, you're not my favorite person right now, but I don't hate you. You're doing a good enough job of that all by yourself. Come on, I'll take you to RJ. She's walking the wall again. She usually does these days." Topaz led the way.

"She's up then!" David said in pleased relief.

"If that's what you want to call it," Topaz replied sadly.

Levits saw them from the doorway where he waited for RJ. Before Topaz could stop him, he was on David. "You bastard!" Levits had David by the throat against the wall. "How dare you be alive!"

Topaz pulled Levits off David with an effort and held him. "Calm down, Levits."

Levits struggled in Topaz' arms.

"Don't make me hurt you, Levits."

Finally Levits slumped, his rage spent.

"It's all your fault, you bastard," Levits hissed. "But maybe it is better that you hear it from her. After all, you've hurt her the most."

"Go on," Topaz told David.

David walked out onto the wall. RJ stood at the end of the walk, her back to him. Her hair hung to the middle of her back and blew in the salt breeze. Had it been that long? It had been so long since he'd really looked at her. In the white robe she looked even darker that usual. He wanted to run up and hug her, but knew that wasn't possible anymore.

"I'm not ready to go yet, Levits," she said without turning around.

"It's me, RJ," David said in a low voice.

RJ didn't turn around, but he saw her shoulders stiffen. "You!" She said it as if it were a curse. After a silence that seemed to last forever, she ordered, "Go away, traitor."

"I'm sorry," David said.

Again there was a long silence. Then, to his dismay, she started to laugh. It was an awful sound. "You're sorry," she laughed. "Did you hear that world? David Grant is sorry. Sorry! Oh, now that's rich! You help Jessica destroy me, and you're sorry!" She still wouldn't face him. "Have you seen my lover or my brother? What about Sandra?" Her voice sounded calm, but David felt the rage.

"Not yet," he answered shakily.

"Well, there's a very good reason for that. You see, they're all dead!"

"Oh, my God!"

"Well over half the population of Alsterase is dead. The city is in ruins. Jessica Kirk is happy. She has my chain and my brother's head." As she spoke, she finally turned to face him, and David stepped back in horror. "So, you don't like what they did to my face."

David looked at the ugly red scar that ran down the side of RJ's face, then looked away.

"No, David. Look." She opened her robe, and David saw the ten-inch scar which now marred her once perfect body. She pulled her robe back around her. "A GSH came in the middle of the night. Thanks to your misguided loyalty he knew just where to find us. He killed Sandra, shot Whitey, then he shot me in the head, pulled my heart out of my chest and left me for dead. Levits saved me—Levits and Whitey. You see, Whitey lived just long enough to tell Levits what I am. Maybe it's finally time for you to know what RJ stands for."

"I don't want to know anymore," David whispered, his throat tight.

"Well, I'm going to tell you anyway. I'll start by telling you my full name. R-J-12...Get it, David? It's a series number. I'm a GSH!" she screamed.

David's eyes bulged.

"I'm an unprogrammed, unlimited GSH. A human couldn't have lived. Hell, I shouldn't have. They sent a GSH to kill another GSH, but he wasn't completely successful. He didn't kill my body, just my soul. 'R' is for reject, 'J' for jerking, as in my arm movements. Twelve is my number in the series. Jessica Kirk is one of that twelve. She and I are the last two alive, supposedly. I used to hate being a freak. I used to be ashamed. I thought it made me less human. No more. I have learned a lesson. In fact, I've learned several. The first is that when people love you, they love you no matter who or what you are, or what you do, and the opposite is true for those who hate you. The second is that no matter how superior you are, there is always someone better who is waiting to prove it just as soon as you let your guard down. The third is never to trust anyone completely, because you can never be sure of the people *they* trust. The fourth—never give anyone power that you can use yourself; at least you won't use it *against* yourself. The fifth and most important is that it doesn't matter if your heart is made out of titanium steal alloy, because it can still be broken. Life was so much easier when I cared for no one, and no one cared for me."

She turned her back on him and looked back towards Alsterase. "When I had no roots and my only desire was to eat, drink and sleep when necessary, I didn't really care whether we won or not. But in those days, I didn't know the casualties as individuals. This time, I did."

"RJ, I don't know what to say...."

"That's because words are meaningless at this point." She looked out at the ocean. "There was a time, David, when I loved you. Not just as a friend, but as a woman loves a man. But you wanted no part of me. Then Sandra loved you, and you treated her like shit. You gave your love and your loyalty to this woman who betrayed us all. Just go away, David. I finally don't love you anymore."

"Well, I *do* love you, RJ. I don't know if I can ever make it up to you. All I can say is that I was an idiot. You were right, and I was wrong...."

"That doesn't bring him back. It doesn't bring any of them back. I doesn't take away my scars, fill my empty bed or my empty heart." She laughed bitterly. "Look at you. The word

man. Words won't fix this, David. *Nothing* can fix this. I wish
you were dead, but I don't have the desire to kill you. I wish I
were dead, but I'm not." Her voice broke in sobs. "Go away!
Just go away!"

Mickey put David in a room as far away from everyone else as
possible. The bed was warm, and he was tired, but he couldn't
sleep. He understood Levits' anger at the fact that he was
alive when so many were dead. It was all his fault, and yet
he'd lived. He wished he hadn't. He couldn't get RJ's face or
her words out of his mind. She looked utterly defeated. No
light shone from her eyes; instead they were sunk back into
her head and dark circles bruised them. She'd lost weight, and
she looked weak and unkempt. She just didn't care anymore.
The fighting spirit that had driven them all was gone. She was
broken, helpless, fragile and afraid.

   He sat up slowly, filled with shock and horror. What had
RJ said? *Be careful what you wish for, you just might get it.* If RJ
had been like this in the beginning, he probably would have
returned her love.

   Driven to his feet by his thoughts, he started pacing. "Oh,
God!" he groaned. He'd got his wish all right; now he didn't
want it. He wanted a strong, aggressive and confident RJ. He
wanted the RJ who would kill a man with one hand while she
drank a beer with the other. This cringing, broken creature
wasn't RJ.

   "God forgive me, Sandra." If he had stayed with her and
returned her love, none of this would have happened. Sandra
had needed him, but as a partner, not a protector. That hadn't
been enough for him. Now he realized what a treasure he'd
thrown away. *Too late. All too late.*

   He slumped down on the bed, crushed with guilt. Little
Kirsty, crying, cringing Kirsty, had toppled mighty RJ with
his help. That was biting the hand that fed you with a vengeance. No wonder everyone hated and distrusted him. He
hated himself.

But RJ hated him, and that he couldn't handle.
He had to find a way to gain her forgiveness.

He didn't attempt to talk to anyone in the next two weeks. He
caught a glimpse of RJ every once in awhile. She never looked
any better. Sometimes he watched her walk the wall, aching
to help her. But he knew that he was the last person on Earth
she wanted to see. He stayed away.

For the first time he was able to sit close enough to over-
hear a conversation in the mess hall.

"I think she's gone mad."

"Look at her eyes. There's nothing there."

"I don't think she's ever even going to dress."

"They say she won't even comb her hair; Levits does it for
her."

"They're having trouble getting her to eat."

"What's going to happen to us now?"

That was a good question. Units called in daily from all
across the Zone, but the orders never changed. *Stay put and
keep a low profile.*

The New Alliance, which had started with two people with
the same dream and had grown into a force to be reckoned with,
was crumbling. Dying, even as RJ was dying. Not for lack of
troops, weapons or supplies. Because of RJ's foresight, the losses
in this attack—though large—were far from crippling. No, it
was dying because the nerve center was dying.

David got up and went to watch RJ as she walked the wall.
He heard Topaz and Levits coming and ducked into a doorway to avoid a confrontation.

"She's not getting any better," Levits said to Topaz. "She's
stopped healing. She needs to eat. I can hardly get her to eat
enough to sustain herself. She told me the other day that she
wants to die. I don't know what to do."

Topaz shook his head and stopped walking.

"Instead of becoming less depressed, she becomes more
so," Levits sighed. "Can't you fix Poley?"

"I wish I could, but..." Topaz shrugged. "Stewart was a bit of a realist. He put the robot's brain and personality chips in the head. Without it there is no Poley, just a simple headless service robot. I hardly think that's going to cheer her up."

"I wish I knew what to do. It's as if that bastard jerked her self-confidence out with her heart, and I don't know how to shove that back in," Levits said.

David didn't wait to hear any more. He now knew where his redemption lay. He now knew what he had to do.

He made his way to the main computer room.

"Marge?"

"Yes, David Grant?"

David sighed with relief. Obviously, no one had thought to reprogram Marge. He still had clearance. "I need you to get me into Capitol."

"Difficult, but not impossible," the computer droned.

# Chapter Twenty-three

David left in the night. No one was likely to miss him, and if they did, they'd just be glad he was gone.

Getting to Capitol was the hard part; it took him a week. But getting in was hardly any problem at all, with Marge's help. He let his beard grow and, with the cast gone, dressed in an Elite uniform, and carrying the proper papers, it was a walk in the park.

Of course, one screw up and he was dead meat, but he didn't plan to screw up.

Jessica and Right returned to Capitol from their meeting with the hated Jago, and went straight to her office.

"Do we have to go straight back to work, Jessy?" Right asked, taking her hand.

"We've been gone for three days," she smiled at him. "Don't worry, Right. The beast has been taken care of, and we'll have lots of time on our hands."

She walked into her office, and instantly flew into a rage. "Where are they?"

Before Right could ask what, Jessica was at her desk. She punched her intercom button.

"Lieutenant! Send Zark in here on the double!"

"What's wrong?" Right asked.

"Look," she pointed to a blank spot on her shelf.

Right looked and nodded. "I wouldn't worry, Jessy," Right reassured her, "he probably just took your trophies because he was angry about being left behind. Remember that, unlike me, he is programmed not to displease you." Right flopped down in a chair.

Zark entered the room and moved towards Jessica as if she were a magnet, and he were steel. She held up her hand, stopping him cold.

"What's wrong?"

"You know what's wrong, Zark, and I don't think it's funny. Where are they?"

Zark's eyes followed her out flung arm to the empty spot on her shelf.

"I didn't take them," he said.

"Zark..."

"You know I didn't, Jessy," he said.

Jessica whirled on Right. He noticed the silence and looked up to find both Jessica and Zark giving him suspicious looks.

"Don't look at me," he said in disbelief. "I was with you."

"You could have had someone do it," Zark accused.

"Why?" Right asked.

"Jealousy," Zark suggested.

"As I said, Freak, I was with her."

"Enough!" Jessica screamed. "You two morons may not have done it, but someone did. I want a room-to-room search. I want them found, and I want whoever is responsible killed."

Zark and Right walked from Jessica's office. "Who do you think did it?" Right asked.

"Besides you and I, I don't know anyone who has a motive." Zark looked at Right and smiled. "Whoever it is, they have a stupid sense of humor."

"Maybe it's the Rebels. Those things would have meaning for them."

"Not likely. Capitol is top clearance. To get into Jessy's office on top of that..."

"You're right. But then, who could have taken them?" Right was thoughtful.

"Face it, Jessica is not too well loved among her staff. Any one of them has access to her office, and they all know that those were her prizes. What better way to get back at her?"

"But if they were smart, they would incinerate them." Right was thoughtful, then he smiled. "But the chain wouldn't burn."

They made immediately for the incinerator. Nothing. Nor did a room-to-room search turn up the missing items.

Jessica took the news better than either of them had expected, but she became consumed with paranoia, and a forlorn look entered her eyes.

She felt like she was walking a tightrope without a net.

It took David even longer to get back to the island.

Mickey was the first to greet him. "So, I see you're back," he said dully, and looked behind David. "Did you bring the Reliance to finish us off?"

David ignored his hateful words. "So, where is the platinum blonde goddess this fine day?"

Mickey clearly resented David's cheerfulness.

"Walking the wall, looking at her burned city and praying for death," Mickey said hatefully back, and stomped off.

"Thanks, Mickey," David was off.

Levits stopped him at the door. "Leave her alone, David. Haven't you done enough?"

"I fucked up, all right, Levits? I fucked up, and nothing I can do is going to change that. But, in this bag, I have something that I think is going to pour the self-confidence back into RJ. Are you going to stop me from trying? Look at her, Levits, could anything I do really hurt her at this point? Give me a chance to redeem myself. Haven't you ever fucked up? Haven't you ever done something you regretted? I have to live with what I did, Levits..."

Levits stopped listening and stared at the ground by his feet. Yes, he had done something that he regretted. He'd fucked up, and he knew the hell of living with that kind of mistake. What David had done wasn't really all that different. He looked up, David was waiting for his answer.

"Good luck," he said, and offered his hand.

David took it, and Levits moved so that David could pass. "It's going to work, Levits. You'll see. It's got to work." David approached RJ. She didn't turn to face him.

"What do you want, David?"

"Forgiveness in whatever form you can give it. I bring a peace offering." He set his backpack gently at her feet.

"I want nothing from you, David..."

"They don't belong to me, RJ. They belong to you."

Curiosity got the better of her. She picked up the bag, and opened it carefully. Her shock was so great that she almost dropped the bag. "Oh, dear God!" she breathed. She looked at David and smiled through her tears.

David felt his heart lighten, and breathed again.

RJ gently took Poley's head in one hand, and grasping her chain in the other, stood, laughed, and let go with a whoop that echoed in every hall and vibrated in every stone. Holding her precious items high, she started to dance and sing so joyfully that the lack of a tune didn't bother David in the least.

Levits ran out to see what all the commotion was about. One look, and he broke into tears.

"Come on, Levits! Join me! Dance with me! Shout!"

He didn't dream of declining, even though he felt like an idiot doing it.

"Come on, David," she offered. "Join us."

"Delighted," David said.

Topaz ran out, closely followed by Mickey. "What in heaven's name..." Then he saw. "Well, I'll be damned."

"Come on, Topaz! Come on Mickey! Join us!"

Neither of them hesitated. They danced and shouted together until they danced much of the hate and hurt out of their systems. Finally, they fell silent, exchanging looks that acknowledged their re-acceptance of the challenge. Once again they were determined. Once again they were one. RJ handed Poley's head to Topaz.

"Put my brother back together."

"Consider it done," Topaz said with a smile.

RJ wrapped the chain around her waist and started for the door.

"All right! Let's go kick some Reliance ass!"

# Chapter Twenty-four

Satis lay sleeping. All eight hundred little Reliance soldiers all snug in their eight hundred little Reliance-issue beds. The bank was all closed up. Only six guards were on duty, and two of them were asleep. However, the two guards at the main gate were awake and alert.

But Rebels, especially those trained by sergeants who had been trained by RJ, didn't use gates.

Using insulated bolt cutters, they cut the fence in several different places, and each unit climbed through and headed for their separate objectives.

At each of the four bunkhouses charges were set even as the guards on duty at the bank were silenced.

As a troop stormed the front gate, they lobbed an explosive charge at the door of the bank. The barracks went up almost simultaneously.

The door of the vault wasn't much more of a challenge. Two charges and fifteen minutes later, part of the Rebel force drove off in stolen Reliance trucks loaded with all of Zone 2-A's hoarded precious metals.

Fifty minutes and eight hundred Reliance soldiers later, the rest of the Rebels were leaving the smoldering remains of Satis.

The Reliance was caught off guard. They thought they had killed the beast, and that had left them ripe for plucking.

Meanwhile, in another time zone, Jessica sat snugly in her office sipping a glass of expensive wine and wondering which man she should sleep with that tonight. They each had their qualities. "To Zark, or not to Zark, that is the question. Whether it is nobler to lay both men at once, or..." She let it die in laughter.

She had no idea where either man was right now, but all she had to do was snap her fingers, and they would come running. God! She loved power.

There were rumors that she was being considered for a Sector Leader position, maybe even Jago's. She'd like that.

Raising her glass, she toasted, "To RJ, whose death has brought me great satisfaction." But, as she drank the wine, it had a bitter taste, and her eyes strayed involuntarily to the empty spot on her shelf.

RJ paced back and forth in front of the group. They were a small group—only forty men. But they were the best Alsterase had, and they were hungry for vengeance and blood.

They watched their undisputed leader and waited reverently for her to speak. It was thirty-five degrees, but that hadn't stopped RJ from wearing simple black pants and a tank top. As she paced before them, her Elite boots and her newly polished chain shining, they knew her for what she was, and they accepted her. Hell, they all but worshipped her.

"I don't have any pretty words. You know what they did to us. Now is the time to make them pay. Let's go." She turned and stepped into a loaded troop carrier. Several members of the inner circle were riding in this vehicle, as it was to be the first in; RJ, Levits, David and...

"Are you sure it's a good idea to drive right up to the front gates?"

"Just drive, Poley." She smiled at him. Except for the fact that Topaz was unable to reproduce and replace the damaged synthetic epidermis, he was as good as new. It was obvious what Poley was now.

"Whatever you say, but if you ask me..."

"She didn't." Levits hung on the seat behind RJ. "He's awfully talkative since he got his head back. I think Topaz connected something wrong."

"Ouch!" Poley grimaced and rubbed his neck. A look almost like pain filled his mechanical eyes.

"Don't talk about it!" RJ said hotly. "You know how it distresses him."

"Do you think..." David stopped himself.

She smiled at him. "Mickey can handle it. The men listen to him."

David nodded. If she said it, then it was so.

"RJ, if this sister of your looks just like you..." Levits found himself cut off.

"Differences between RJ and J-6 are numerous. RJ's right arm jerks, she now has a scar on her face..."

"Which is almost gone," Levits reassured her.

"...she is dressed grubbily and is wearing a chain. The chances of our people mistaking RJ for J-6 are one in a..."

"We don't need numbers, Tin Pants," RJ said lovingly. She looked through the windshield. She saw Capitol looming before them—sixty stories of steel and glass, a blight on the planet. She smiled. "Soon, my brother, we shall avenge our father."

"And everyone else." If it were possible, Poley looked just as maniacal as his sister.

RJ glanced at her watch and looked up at Capitol just in time to see every light in the building-city go out. "Right on time. Thank you, Topaz," she said.

"Thank you, *Marge*," Poley corrected.

"Poley, speed up down the ramp and crash the gates," RJ ordered as she kicked off her door and sent it flying through the air.

"RJ! What the hell?" Levits demanded.

"We're going to lay waste to Capitol. Going to lay it low. This time, I want to go in with my guns blazing." She put a hole in the roof with her left fist. Using that arm for balance, she leaned out the door, rocket launcher in hand. "There will be a hot time in the old town tonight!"

"We've got to keep her from watching so many old movies," Levits said dryly as he put on his night-vision goggles. These goggles were standard-issue for this mission. Odds were that the occupants of Capitol would be blind in the blackout, since, according to Marge night vision-goggles were not standard-issue in Capitol. In fact, considering that it was a military post it was dangerously inadequately prepared.

Jessica was halfway through the bottle when the lights went out. She tried the intercom, but there was no response. Ditto on the door. "Oh, great! Another total power failure! Heads will roll if it isn't restored at once."

RJ fired the rocket, and the gates of Capitol exploded in flames. Poley drove through and skidded to a stop in the first floor of the motor pool, which comprised the first two underground floors of the building. RJ jumped from the vehicle into the middle of the room, as if daring someone to shoot her. In the dark, frightened men and women milled in confusion and fear, fleeing from the headlights.

Most of Capitol was asleep. Without power there were no alarms or sirens, no way of warning the residents that they were under attack.

RJ, David, Levits, and Poley left Mickey and the troops to mop up the motor pool. They had bigger fish to fry.

Poley went straight to the elevator and covered the control panel with his palm. After a few moments of clicking and whirring, the panel activated. The others joined him in the elevator.

"Top, Poley," RJ ordered. A few seconds later, the elevator slid to a stop at the roof. "Be careful," RJ kissed Levits on the cheek, slapped him on the back, and watched him walk out the door.

"Just *you* be careful," he flung back at her.

She nodded.

"I expect to be airlifting you out of here in twenty minutes."

"Wouldn't miss it," RJ promised.

The doors of the elevator closed. "Fifty, Poley," she

ordered. As the elevator started back down, she whispered, "I'm coming, Jessica."

Jessica finished her glass of wine. The longer she sat in the dark, the madder she got. "Incompetent fools. There isn't that much that can go wrong." She considered breaking her door open, but thought better of it. She didn't want to have to explain how she got out that way. She needed to learn patience. Some said this was a virtue. Controlling her anger, she carefully poured another glass of wine. She'd have plenty of time to kill the person responsible for this after the lights came on.

Levits was a subtle character. His job was to disable the choppers, just as Mickey's was to destroy the land transport. RJ didn't want there to be any chance of either escape or pursuit. Capitol was a military city. Everyone in it was over sixteen and in the army. There were no innocents here, so RJ wanted no survivors. Levits was inclined to agree. The problem was that there were more guards here than expected. So, rather than trying to take them all out first, he was sneaking around, quietly disabling the choppers. He managed to fix ten of them before he was spotted.

"What the hell are you doing there?" someone asked.

Levits turned and fired then made a dash for one of the airworthy choppers. Shots rang out around him, but the guards' confusion was so great that he made it without a scratch. He piled into a chopper and took it up. Glancing down, he saw the men scrambling for the choppers, and he smiled. "Why not?" He aimed the laser cannon and fired. None of the few airworthy choppers made it into the air. As he started to pick off the guards and choppers, he became aware of discomfort.

"Oh, my God!" He scrambled madly, feverishly unstrapping his belts, and dug a handful of timed charges out of his pocket. White and shaking, he threw them from the chopper onto the roof and broke out in a cold sweat. "Damn! Careless of me."

As he strapped back in and resumed picking off the grounded choppers, he wondered briefly how many he'd thrown out. A check of his pockets assured him that they were all gone.

Mickey and his troops ran through the lower levels of Capitol, seeding them with timed charges, and killing everything that moved. They were having a good time. In fact, they were having so much fun that Mickey had a great deal of trouble getting them to leave when it was time. Their job was done, and they hadn't lost a man. Mickey just hoped RJ was doing as well.

David watched the time but remained silent. He said none of the things that were on his mind. Like, why didn't they just leave Jessica and her GSH to blow up with the rest of Capitol?

"Where is that damned freak!" RJ cursed.

"We could get Jessica..."

"He's more of a threat than Jessica," RJ hissed at Poley. "You know that as well as I do. I don't want him coming up behind us while we're trying to kill her."

Poley nodded. Then he cocked his head to listen. "I hear him. He's coming our way."

Zark heard something. He wasn't sure what, but it was unusual, and seemed to be coming from the roof. He went to investigate. After all, little things like power-locked doors, stalled elevators and no lights weren't likely to stop him.

He rounded a corner, and there stood Jessica. He laughed. "What are you dressed up for?"

She just grinned, and walked over to embrace him. He opened his arms to engulf her, and felt something against his chest. He looked into the eyes of the impossible as the titanium projectile ripped through his heart and exploded. His lifeless body fell to the floor with a thud.

Poley ran out of hiding and started to cut off Zark's head with a laser knife. "Poley!" RJ protested.

"Since our sister likes trophies, I thought I'd bring her one," Poley said with a savage grin.

RJ took her chain from David and started to wrap it around herself.

"How could you be so sure that he would think you were Jessica?" David asked, curiously.

"Simple. He knew he'd killed me. It wouldn't have crossed his mind that I could be anyone but Jessica."

Poley walked over to them carrying Zark's bloody head by the hair. "So, let's go kill J-6," he said, happily.

"You're enjoying this too much, Tin Pants," RJ said.

Jessica was just finishing her wine. Suddenly, the door crashed in, and a head came rolling across her desk into her lap. She thought at first that Zark had located the android's head. Breaking the door would be just his style. Then the sticky liquid soaked through her pants, and the stench hit her nostrils. She looked down, and Zark seemed to grin hideously back at her. She threw the head down and jumped up just as RJ entered the room followed by Poley and David.

"So, we meet at last." Jessica failed horribly at sounding cool.

"I am disappointed in you. You sound surprised. If I had sent someone to kill you, I wouldn't have been surprised to find that he had failed." RJ raised the same weapon she'd used on Zark, and pulled the trigger.

Click. Nothing.

Reacting instantly, Jessica leapt over the desk and ran for the door. Poley tripped her, and she sprawled for an instant before regaining her feet and running. She wasn't ashamed to run. RJ had killed Zark, and now RJ would kill her if she didn't get away. Something struck Jessica in the back, and she spun around hitting the wall. Then she saw the chain coming. It hit her in the head, and she watched with one eye as the other was ripped from her skull. She didn't stop; she regained her footing and ran a little faster, ignoring the pain.

RJ started after her, but Poley grabbed her arm. "No time, RJ. Come on." She struggled briefly, but Poley insisted, "There isn't time!"

Jessica realized that they weren't chasing her, and she knew she only had a second to get that thing out of her back. The two inch, knife-shaped projectile was lodged in her shoulder. The charge hadn't gone off yet, but it could at any moment. Still running, she reached back, pulled it out and threw it down the hall. Before it hit the floor, it exploded, sealing off that end of the hallway. She knew she wasn't in the clear yet. There had to be a reason that RJ hadn't tracked her down. No way would she have relied on that projectile to do the job. They must have seeded the building with explosives. She knew she didn't have long to get out of Capitol, and that's why she was surprised when she found herself heading for Right's room.

She found Right asleep with no idea of what was going on. "Come on, Right! Get up! We're under attack!"

"We're what?" Right asked sleepily. Then seeing the carnage wreaked on her face. "Oh my God, Jessy!"

"RJ's alive, Right. She just tried to kill me, and she's planted a bomb somewhere here in Capitol."

David, Poley and RJ checked their pockets for the tenth time, making sure that they had disposed of all their timed charges, and cursed the elevator for being so slow, but what could they expect, since it was basically working on "Poley Power?" Levits was waiting for them surrounded by the smoldering ash of burning choppers and charred bodies.

"Been enjoying yourself?" RJ asked, getting in the chopper.

"Hey, I had to have something to do! I was getting bored waiting for you guys." With a sigh of relief, he took off with his precious cargo. "I was beginning to get worried."

"Soon, now," Poley said.

"10, 9, 8..." David started the count. He stopped, staring in horror at the object rolling around under RJ's seat. "What the hell...Oh, my God!" He ducked down, grabbed the charge and tossed it out the door on 3...Less than three seconds later Capitol went up as a smaller explosion rocked the chopper. They looked back to see the bottom levels of Capitol blown to pieces, and the rest toppled to the ground, breaking up as it fell. Dust and rubble flew into the air as high as the building had been.

Levits was fighting for control. "Sorry, guys. The explosion must have blown off part of the tail section. We're going to have to land."

Levits landed the wounded chopper with little difficulty, and they all got out to look back at the dust cloud that had once been Capitol.

RJ frowned. Vengeance had not quenched the bitterness in her soul. "Now it can never end."

"What's that, RJ?" Levits asked, looking up from his assessment of the damage to the chopper.

She didn't repeat herself. "The Reliance won't be able to dismiss us so easily now. They can't."

"This thing isn't going to fly." Levits kicked the offending chopper. "So what's our next move?"

"We get help from the Reliance's other enemy."

"You don't mean..." David started to laugh, then he saw the look on her face. "But how do we get them to help us?"

"We are logical allies," Poley informed him as he took his own look at the chopper.

"The hardest part will be getting there," RJ said thoughtfully.

"Well, I have no idea what you're all talking about," Levits interjected, "but I was talking about getting home."

"Shh," RJ ordered, "listen." A few seconds later, they all heard it.

"You don't suppose..."

A lone chopper raced overhead, drowning out the rest of his sentence.

"Bet on it." RJ watched till it was out of sight.

# Author's Bio

*(Written by someone else, because Selina NEVER says ANYTHING in 25-50 words!).*

Selina Rosen lives in rural Arkansas with her partner, her parrot, Ricky, assorted fowl—both inside and out—several milk goats, an undetermined number of barn cats and two dogs. Besides writing and taking care of the farm, she's a gardener, carpenter, rock mason, electrician (NOT a plumber), Torah scholar, and sword fighter. In her spare time she creates water gardens and builds furniture.

Selina's short stories have appeared in several anthologies including *Sword and Sorceress 16* and *Such A Pretty Face*. One of her short stories has been translated into German and published in Germany. Her published novels include *Queen of Denial, The Host, Fright Eater, Gang Approval,* and a novella entitled *The Boatman*. She has four new novels scheduled to premier—one per year in May. She is currently working on *Chains of Destruction* and a second Drewcilia Quah novel, set in the *Queen of Denial* universe.

Her web site is:

http://www.cherryh.com/www/srosen/srosen.htm

Queen of Denial
1-892065-06-1 $12.00

# From the introduction to Queen of Denial by Lynn Abbey

She turned the page and started reading Chapter Two: change of scene, change of character, enough profanity to earn a medal in the merchant marine, and what to my linear ears sounded like a ice chest filled with beer cans caroming across the bridge of a space ship during liftoff. The skeptical, nit-picky part of me wanted to object: an ice chest in space? beer cans in space? But the story moved too fast; it was indeed *Queen of Denial* and I was caught in a tractor beam of humor.

Natural dialog is a bitch to write; ask any script-writer, and if you're writing a novel, you've got to fill in all the camera stuff, too. Usually, what the reader "hears" is the writer's voice telling a story about the characters. More rarely, the reader "hears" the writer as a character who paraphrases all the dialog and summarizes the camera stuff; done well, we call this "style". Very rarely, the reader is treated to pure character, a total immersion into the mind behind a fictional set of eyeballs. Raymond Chandler did this as well as it's been done, but he was writing in the first person; Selina does it in the third.

And it's funny. Painfully, delightfully, barking seals and whooping cranes funny.

Funny is worse than natural dialog. In "real life" spoken humor relies on timing and nuance while physical humor happens at a speed that cannot be captured with an alphabet. And a lot of what seems funny when written down, dies a lingering death when read aloud. (This I know for a fact.) To write a story that is as funny when read aloud as it is when read silently, and poignant, too, is an act of genius–or dementia, possibly both.

I can't begin to describe the many creative processes that have to be going on to create this sort of synergy. I don't think they can be described. A writer either can do it, or she can't; Selina Rosen can, and she did it with her first novel. If I didn't know her, like her, and respect her, I'd probably have to kill her.

## Praise for Selina Rosen's *Queen of Denial*

"A rarity of rarities: a book that makes you laugh out loud. Selina Rosen's debut is very much worth noting...SF's answer to Terry Pratchett."—C. J. Cherryh

"Should appeal to anyone who loves a riotous, wickedly funny read."—Jane Fancher

"A rip-snorting space adventure the likes of which we don't see often enough these days!"—Lawrence Watt-Evans

"*Queen of Denial* is a freewheeling, fun and frantic space opera. It takes the usual conventions of pulp action Science Fiction and stands them on their head by featuring a female lead character as tough as any man in the book, and twice as smart. The story moves at a take-no-prisoners pace, keeping you turning the pages fast as possible. And, in the end, arrives at a most satisfactory conclusion. It's a wild ride and quite an accomplishment for a first-time novelist."—Robert Weinberg, author of *The Termination Novel*

"*Queen* is funny and pointed. Ms. Rosen takes a Star-Trek-like plot, introducing the social ills of a world that could be our own, and attacks them with ruthless humor. Drewcila Qwah isn't your everyday heroine, with a foul mouth and almost every other bad habit known to civilization, but she's likeable and honest. The language may not be to everyone's taste, but it's no more than a working spacer's dialect. As Drewcila might say, get the %&#^* out of here if you don't like it. It's not applied gratuitously, and you'll get used to it. The style is as rough and ready as the heroine, but *Queen* is a fast read with a satisfying conclusion."—Jody Lynn Nye

"Down-home science fiction? Redneck interstellar adventure?

A full-throttle journey through the rural spaceways? Hey, it can happen and happen convincingly when the writer is damned authentic and has lived the tone she's writing about. That's Selina Rosen to a T. *Queen of Denial* cooks-not just with high energy and in-your-face attitude, but with the metaphorical flavors of grits, red beans and rice, and sweet potato pie.

If there's such a thing as blue-collar sf, this is it. No spiffy interstellar SUVs here-Rosen's characters horse the futuristic equivalent of dented vintage Ford S-10s around the stars. With plenty of action, violence, foolin' around, and a generous tongue planted just a touch firmly in cheek, *Queen of Denial* takes some old and honored tropes of science fiction, and turns them into the kind of bawdy full-bodied entertainment Western literature's furnished since long before Shakespeare.

When MIR morphs into a cut-rate orbital truck stop for space jockeys who can't afford the International Space Station, Selina Rosen's debut novel is the sort of book that'll feature prominently in the spinner rack right between the displays of alien fuzzy dice and zero-gee mud flaps."—Ed Bryant

"Selena Rosen turns Space Opera inside-out to give us a brand new genre: Space Vaudeville!"—Mark Simmons

"*Queen of Denial* is a rollicking, high-spirited romp through space that grabs you by the shirt with the very first page and never lets go. The pace is breakneck, the humor bawdy, and the heroine one of the most original I've seen in years. The love triangle alone kept me in stitches. This book is a must for anyone who enjoys top-notch spacefaring adventure!
—K. D. Wentworth

"*Queen* is a fun novel, an old-fashioned space opera that moves at breakneck speed from the first page to the last."—*The Tulsa World Herald*, June 13, 1999

# Come check out our web site for details on these Meisha Merlin authors!

Kevin J. Anderson

Robert Asprin

Robin Wayne Bailey

Edo van Belkom

Janet Berliner

Storm Constantine

Diane Duane

Sylvia Engdahl

Jim Grimsley

George Guthridge

Keith Hartman

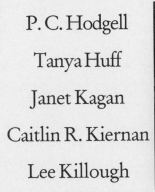

Beth Hilgartner

P. C. Hodgell

Tanya Huff

Janet Kagan

Caitlin R. Kiernan

Lee Killough

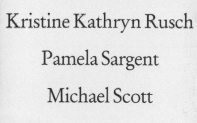

George R. R. Martin

Lee Martindale

Jack McDevitt

Sharon Lee & Steve Miller

James A. Moore

Adam Niswander

Andre Norton

Jody Lynn Nye

Selina Rosen

Kristine Kathryn Rusch

Pamela Sargent

Michael Scott

William Mark Simmons

S. P. Somtow

Allen Steele

Mark Tiedeman

Freda Warrington

# http://www.MeishaMerlin.com